OTHER WOMEN

Emma Flint was born and grew up in Newcastle upon Tyne. She graduated from the University of St Andrews with an MA in English Language and Literature, and later completed a novel-writing course at the Faber Academy. She lives and works in south-west England.

Since childhood, she has been drawn to true-crime stories, developing an encyclopaedic knowledge of real-life murder cases from the early twentieth century. Her first novel, *Little Deaths*, was longlisted for the Women's Prize for Fiction, for the Desmond Elliott Prize, for the Crime Writers' Association Gold Dagger Award, and for *The Guardian*'s Not the Booker Prize. *Other Women* is her second novel.

ALSO BY EMMA FLINT

Little Deaths

'Exquisite and my book of the year. Utterly brilliant'
Will Dean, author of *Dark Pines*

'Set in the early 1920s, this clever mix of romance, thriller and courtroom drama proves love and heartbreak never ages, whatever the era'
Woman & Home

'Utterly, utterly brilliant. *Other Women* is compelling, thought-provoking, harrowing and incredibly urgent'
Caroline Lea, author of *The Glass Woman*

'Based on a shocking real-life murder in the 1920s, *Other Women* focuses on Beatrice, almost invisible until she falls in love with a colleague, and Kate, seen as a devoted wife and mother, until their lives converge'
Red

'Bloody brilliant'
Dinah Jefferies

'*Other Women* takes another tale of a true crime and reimagines it into a novel – this time, the murder of Emily Beilby Kaye by her married lover, Herbert Patrick Mahon'
Alison Flood, *The Observer*

'Staggeringly brilliant, harrowing, haunting and entirely beautiful. *Other Women* takes a thrilling yet compassionate look at the making of a murder, at loneliness and love, at fixation and the sting of shame. A wonderful novel'
Chris Whitaker, author of *We Begin at the End*

'The tension is superb and I honestly couldn't put it down'
Prima

'Poignant and elegant, brutal and beautiful, *Other Women* is a masterclass in modern storytelling'
Helen Cullen, author of *The Truth Must Dazzle Gradually*

'A glittering black diamond of a book. Beautiful and devastating literary true crime. Emma Flint takes a real murder from the 1920s and gives voice to the women involved. Bubbling anger beneath exquisite prose'

Anna Mazzola, author of *The Clockwork Girl*

'It is brilliant. I was swept up in a turmoil of emotion as I read. This is a book that starts as a love story and turns into something much darker indeed'

Harriet Tyce, author of *The Lies You Told*

'The disturbing narrative unspools with a veneer of unsettling normalcy, which make the reveals which Flint masterfully serves up all the more gripping and profound when we reach them'

Philippa East, author of *I'll Never Tell*

'Passion, betrayal, and obsessive love combine to create the stunning tour de force that is *Other Women* . . . Chilling and heart-stopping, this is an instant classic'

Eleni Kyriacou, author of *She Came to Stay*

'A book about fantasy and the lengths that people will go to protect what they love, whether that's another adult, a child, or the dream of another kind of life' *Take a Break*

'Heartbreaking. I wanted it to go on and on, even as I raced to the end. Excellent, absorbing and totally gripping'

Melanie Golding, author of *The Replacement*

'This haunting tale of love and obsession will stay with you'

Heat

OTHER WOMEN

EMMA FLINT

PICADOR

First published 2023 by Picador

This edition first published 2024 by Picador
an imprint of Pan Macmillan
The Smithson, 6 Briset Street, London EC1M 5NR
EU representative: Macmillan Publishers Ireland Ltd, 1st Floor,
The Liffey Trust Centre, 117–126 Sheriff Street Upper,
Dublin 1, D01 YC43
Associated companies throughout the world
www.panmacmillan.com

ISBN 978-1-5098-2656-8

The publisher gratefully acknowledges the publishers for permission to
reproduce 'The Love Song of J. Alfred Prufrock' from *Collected
Poems 1909–1962* by T. S. Eliot (Faber & Faber Ltd.)

1 3 5 7 9 8 6 4 2

A CIP catalogue record for this book is available from the British Library.

Printed and bound by CPI Group (UK) Ltd, Croydon, CR0 4YY

For a long time, the working title for this book was Darling Girls.
This book is dedicated to my own darling girls:
Matilda, Isabel, Zosie and Lula.

And to my beloved grandma, Mary Cuthbert (1928–2023).

And would it have been worth it, after all,
Would it have been worth while,
After the sunsets and the dooryards and the sprinkled
    streets,
After the novels, after the teacups, after the skirts that trail
    along the floor—
And this, and so much more?—
It is impossible to say just what I mean!
But as if a magic lantern threw the nerves in patterns on
    a screen:
Would it have been worth while
If one, settling a pillow or throwing off a shawl,
And turning toward the window, should say:
        'That is not it at all,
        That is not what I meant, at all.'

'The Love Song of J. Alfred Prufrock'
T. S. Eliot, 1915

It's not catastrophes, murders, deaths, diseases, that age and
kill us; it's the way people look and laugh, and run up the
steps of omnibuses.

Jacob's Room
Virginia Woolf, 1922

Even now, over a year after Bea's first sight of the city, London still seemed all movement. Every morning was crammed with jostling elbows and sharp umbrellas, with the rise and fall of voices and the shouts of newspaper sellers. And yet somehow they all flowed in their proper directions, dancing and twisting in and around so that everyone ended up in the right place and no one collided or tripped or went under.

The men were stiff and upright in their greatcoats and their civvy suits – and almost five years after the Armistice, every one of them seemed still to be broken. There were empty sleeves and eye patches that one must not stare at or draw attention to; there were crutches and bandages and dreadful ridges of thick pink skin; and sometimes there was simply an absence in a face where a man had left a part of himself – the brightest and most vital part – in a muddy foreign field.

The women were different. They flowed and rippled and the young ones leapt like salmon for the gaps in the crowd – up onto the platforms of omnibuses, into dark shop interiors. They were neat and slender – sleek hair, dainty ankles, flickering glances and quicksilver laughter.

In between them were islands of older women. The darting silver girls were for noticing, for flirting with and tipping hats to, while the older women were wives and mothers and widows. They had made sacrifices. They had earned the deference of *Madam*.

And besides them, there was a third type of woman: less visible and less noticed, and neither one thing nor another. These women were Misses without youth, middle-aged without wedding rings. They held fast to the banks of the river, avoiding the current, clustering together in the cool green shade.

Bea was one of these other women.

1

Bea, August 1923

The rest of them were in a fever of excitement waiting for him to arrive. Bea watched the girls whispering and giggling behind their hands. Even Mr Morley was uncharacteristically restless, darting in and out of his office like a figure on a cuckoo clock.

Only Mr Montgomery stayed on the other side of his partition as usual, silent save for the creak of his chair and the occasional thump of the drawer that stuck.

Mr Morley had made the announcement two weeks before, stepping into the middle of the room and clearing his throat. 'Ladies, Mr Montgomery, one moment of your time, if I may' – and then, when he had their attention – 'I am pleased to say that we have a new employee.'

A little self-conscious cough. 'As I have said before, stationery is a growing concern – a very *lively* market – and our first salesman will be starting with us next month.'

Caroline sat up a little straighter. Her hand went to her hair. Jessie, sitting opposite her, raised an eyebrow at this, then lowered her eyes and smiled to herself.

Mr Morley went on, 'He will be travelling about the country a great deal, but he will also be coming into this office now and then.'

Miss Shepherd was brisk. 'His name, Mr Morley?'

'His name is Ryan. Some of you will already know his wife: Mrs Ryan works in our Sunbury office as typist to Mr Simpson. So you see, he is already something of a known commodity.'

Mr Morley smiled at his little joke. 'I'm sure you will all make him welcome.'

When Miss Shepherd had gone into Mr Morley's office with her shorthand notebook and closed the door behind her, Caroline leaned forward.

'How are you going to make Mr Ryan welcome then, Jessie?'

'*Caroline!*'

She sat back, laughing. 'I wonder what he looks like.'

Jessie folded her arms. 'What does it matter to you? Have you forgotten about Eddie?'

'I'm only saying. Just because I have Eddie doesn't mean I can't notice other men.' Her expression softened. 'Ryan's an Irish name – I bet he's dark. With green eyes.'

There was silence for a moment. Bea read over the letter she was typing.

Then Jessie said, 'Do you think we'll see a lot of him?'

'Shouldn't think so, worse luck. He'll mostly be visiting customers, won't he? All over.'

'I wonder if he has a car. For all that travelling.'

'On what Morley pays?'

A muffled giggle.

'Shh, they'll hear you!'

Their voices had lowered, softened into whispers, and then Bea had only been able to hear the odd word.

When.

Meetings.

Wife.

Don't.

Now Bea watched them all from behind her typewriter. She watched Miss Shepherd straighten the files on her desk for the third time, and glance at the clock again. They had expected him by half-past nine.

But it was after the quarter-hour when the door opened and a sweep of air entered, followed by the tall outline of a man. He smelled cold and faintly of tobacco, the smell like a window opening on the room's warm female fug.

Before Bea could get a clear look at him, Caroline was on her feet between them – one smooth movement like a stretching cat, and leaning against Jessie's desk so that he couldn't easily pass. She extended her hand.

'Caroline Norris. How d'you do?'

Bea saw the movement of his shoulder in the gap between the girls as he reached to shake Caroline's hand and then Jessie's. He murmured something that she couldn't quite hear.

Caroline said, 'What's the weather like outside, Mr Ryan?' – as if she hadn't come in herself less than an hour before, as if she was somehow incapable of looking out of the window.

Bea shook her head and replaced her fingers on the keys. The *effort* this all seemed to take: the angling of the body, the slanted looks, the careful smiles.

Mr Montgomery emerged then, and the girls found suddenly that they were on their way to fetch a new ink ribbon from the stationery cupboard and to place a typed letter on Miss Shepherd's desk. As they moved out of the way, Bea saw him plainly for the first time. She saw dark eyes, a fresh complexion – and she saw too that he was looking at her, frowning as though he couldn't quite place her.

As their eyes met, he smiled at her, a wide red smile that transformed his face. She felt that smile as a shock that ran hot through her whole body, that made her flush and drop her gaze.

She stared hard at the letter in her machine, then heard Mr Morley's voice and glanced up automatically. Mr Ryan was still looking straight at her, his face serious. But before she could look away, his face softened; his mouth broadened again, just a little.

As they moved into Mr Morley's office, Morley talking

about a forthcoming meeting at Abbott's and how many orders for carbon paper they might expect, Bea began typing again, the movement of her fingers fast and automatic. The clattering was loud and rhythmic and almost soothing – but all the time she was thinking of that smile at the corners of his mouth, of the deepened creases around his eyes.

Mr Ryan left just before eleven, and shortly afterwards Albert brought in the coffee. Invariably he forgot something or dropped something – usually the sugar or the teaspoons; once, memorably, the cups – and inevitably, Miss Shepherd would reprimand him and he would apologize, stuttering, red to his hairline, while the girls giggled behind their hands.

This was the moment when Bea might slip out to the lavatory: past the other offices, around the corner to the right and up the short flight of stairs to the frosted glass door. Here were a few moments of blessed silence amid yellow gloom and strong-smelling pink soap – before the voices came, and then the footsteps on the stairs, and then the girls themselves. Each time they came in a prattle of dresses and boys and magazines and hairstyles, all jumbled in their high excited voices – and despite her seniority Bea would somehow grow smaller and paler in the face of such optimism, such certainty.

Usually Caroline and Jessie would stand together at the small spotted mirror and preen and fluff and turn their heads from side to side, while Bea reached between them to wash her hands and then attempted to tidy her hair with damp fingers, before returning to her desk and to her cooling cup of coffee.

But today was remarkable in another way: the girls spoke to her properly for the first time.

When Bea came out of the cubicle, Jessie caught her eye in the mirror, then cleared her throat. 'We were just talking about

Mr Ryan. Good news, isn't it?' She blushed. 'That the firm is growing, I mean.'

Bea washed her hands then reached for the rather dirty towel that hung beside the basin. 'Very. Let's hope it means more sales.'

She spoke briskly – abruptly, even – wanting only to get back to the relative solitude of her desk.

Caroline leaned past her to look into the mirror, smoothed down her hair. 'It'll be nice to have another man about the place. Someone young.'

Then she glanced sideways and said, 'I like your blouse, Miss Cade.'

'Oh!' Caught by surprise, Bea blushed. Plucked self-consciously at the collar. 'Oh – thank you.'

Caroline ran a finger over each carefully shaped eyebrow and looked into her own eyes as she spoke again. 'It looks a little like a Poiret model I saw in *Vogue* last month. I daresay it isn't?'

'Goodness, no.' Bea looked down at herself. 'No, I think I got it from Derry & Toms.'

'Thought so.' Caroline straightened up. 'It looks expensive, but when you know about these things, you can tell.'

Bea glanced at her. 'Your frock is lovely. Terribly smart.'

The other girl looked down at her own immaculate grey dress and gave a small smile. 'I made it myself.'

'You didn't? How clever of you.'

'It's not so difficult once you have the pattern. It's all in the cutting.' She smiled. 'I always find it better – so much more *satisfying* – to make something unique, rather than just buying something that anyone might be wearing.' She moved aside to let Jessie use the mirror, then leaned against the wall and began to examine her nails.

Not for the first time, Bea noticed the small square diamond on her left hand. 'What a beautiful ring.'

Caroline held out her hand to be admired, turning it so that the stone glinted in the dirty yellow light.

'Edward and I have been engaged for almost two years. We're saving for the wedding.'

It was a very ordinary conversation – nothing particularly interesting or startling in it at all – and then Caroline turned back to the mirror and said out of nowhere, 'Are you walking out with anyone, Miss Cade?'

Bea looked at the other girl's reflection: at the smooth oval face, the gleaming cap of fair hair, the dress and the ring, and then at the narrowed eyes watching hers, and the pursed little mouth.

She shook her head, and there was a moment – just the space of a sigh – where Caroline watched her and said nothing. And then from behind them, Jessie coughed and said brightly, 'Well, you never know.'

She smiled at Bea in the mirror. 'I mean, you're . . .' A small, kind smile. 'You never know, do you?'

Then she cleared her throat and said, 'Do you have far to come in the mornings, Miss Cade? Do you live with your family?'

Bea spoke without thinking. 'I don't have any. Family, that is.'

They both turned to her, startled. 'What, no family at all?'

'I have a sister, but we're . . . she doesn't live in London. We don't see much of one another. My parents are both dead – and my brother was killed at Cambrai.'

Strange that she could mention George so calmly now. That she could sound so dispassionate.

The girls were staring at her – faces white in the dim light, eyes wide.

'How dreadful.'

Their pity felt clammy and cold.

Poor Miss Cade. It must be terrible to be so alone.

Bea focused on her hair in the mirror. 'No, I live in a ladies' club. In Bloomsbury.'

There was a little tick of surprise, and then Caroline said, 'Goodness. How very modern.'

Jessie said, 'What's it like?' – and she grinned: a natural open smile. 'I'll bet it's terrific fun – all midnight feasts and borrowing each other's clothes, and secrets and feuds.'

Caroline's gaze flickered. 'I think Miss Cade might be a little old for midnight feasts and games, Jess.'

Did they think she was entirely unconscious of how they saw her? That she was somehow unaware she must be almost the same age as their mothers? And yet, unlike their mothers, she was without a home of her own, without a husband or the comfort of children.

Bea straightened her blouse. Felt the crisp cotton against her skin. She had spent almost a week's wages last month on a summer coat in peacock blue. Unlike their mothers, she had choices.

Nor would she be grouped together with women like Miss Shepherd: Miss Shepherd who had a career, who earned her own money, but whose clothes were old-fashioned and merely functional, who wore her hair pinned up in the same style as her mother – perhaps even her grandmother – had worn it. Everything about Miss Shepherd was faded: her fussy fawn blouses, her tired skin, her thin colourless lips.

Bea blinked at her reflection.

Then she turned to smile at Jessie. 'It is rather fun, actually.'

The other women in the club had been ghosts at first. It seemed as if they vanished just as Bea entered the bathroom, leaving bare wet footprints on the linoleum, steam from a bath fogging the mirror, the smell of their talcum powder softening the air, long coarse hairs clogging the drain or reaching down the wall.

These unseen women had been a source of endless fascin-
ation and speculation. Hidden away in her room after dinner,
pretending to write letters or to darn stockings, Bea would
listen to their conversations in the corridor outside and notice
that her needle or her pen had fallen still. She came to realize
that a woman of thirty-seven, used to being careful with her
clothes, didn't make much mending anyway. She had no one
to write to other than her sister and a couple of girls she had
been at school with – and their letters were so brief and so
infrequent that she struggled to fill more than a single sheet of
paper in reply.

She had grown tired of these feigned distractions – and then,
simply curious – and so she began to leave her door open in the
evenings, to nod and smile on the staircase and in the dining
room, and gradually the women dissolved from a jumble of
dresses and scent and heels and high laughter, and became distinct and separate.

There was Lilian, red-haired and kohl-eyed, who trailed
scarves and the scent of rich perfume, and who wanted to be
a dancer like Isadora Duncan. There was an Irish girl with
black hair and eyebrows and a pure white lock that lay across
her forehead like lightning, and two or three girls from good
families who had turned their backs on what their parents
wanted for them, and who were instead playing at being
bohemian.

These girls were different from any that Bea had met at
home: they were the kind of colourful, bold girls she had half
expected to find in London. But she had also found women
like her: older women who had come to London alone, just
as she had. Women like Alice, who blushed often and wore
old-fashioned drooping hats over a great cloud of silvery fair
hair. She taught French and Latin in a girls' school in Kensing-
ton, and was taking sculpture classes on Saturday mornings.
And her friend Ellen, a head taller than her, who worked in a

newspaper office and had the room across the hallway – and who was unsmiling and clever, and surprisingly kind.

These were the sort of women that Bea had read about in novels and had hoped to meet: interesting women, who talked about art and politics and ideas. They argued over everything: the characters in the books they were reading, the relevance of the royal family, Ellen's insistence that everyone should have the vote.

Bea had observed in a general way that the men in London were bolder than those at home: they stared at girls more brazenly, their eyes raking up and down – and she noticed that very few of them stared at her. Men raised their hats and offered up their seats because they noticed her skirts, not because they admired her face.

She looked at the girls who were noticed and at the women who were not, and realized: *One is invisible, when one is neither young nor pretty.*

This felt like an extraordinary and significant discovery – but when she mentioned it to Ellen and Alice, she found that they had both come to similar conclusions already.

'It's *ridiculous*.' Ellen was loud in her indignation. 'As though one is somehow *less*, just because one is older. As though we weren't *all* getting older, every day!'

'But it's natural,' said Alice. 'Don't you think so? I mean, men naturally look at younger girls, prettier girls. Why shouldn't they? A pretty girl is nice to look at.'

'Not all of them, surely. And who decides what is pleasant to look at anyway? Who tells us this? I believe it's the same people who think up those awful names they give women like us. Bluestocking. *Spinster*, for Heaven's sake!' Ellen shook her head. 'And all the while, unmarried men are slapped on the back and called lucky devils!' She opened her hands wide. 'Why should it be this way? Who makes these rules?'

Ellen faced the world head-on, interrogating it when it

made no sense to her. And simply through being exposed to these kinds of conversations and noticing her own opinion of them, Bea felt that she was somehow growing into herself.

As the months passed, she had grown used to the intimacies of cold cream and curlers, to women roaming the corridor in their dressing gowns, and had begun to form her own routines. And it seemed that each day she discovered something new about her own tastes. She learned that she liked the smell of garlic, that she preferred novels to poetry, Fry's Turkish Delight to Cadbury's Dairy Milk, that blue suited her better than green. She learned that she could attend church and revel in the stillness and the quiet beauty, and feel no guilt that her belief in a just and merciful God had died with George.

For the first time, her life was absolutely her own – and she might live it exactly as she pleased.

On Lil Tearney's birthday there was a memorable evening of dancing along the top corridor while Ellen wound the gramophone. And Bea quite forgot herself – forgot her large feet and wide shoulders and how awkward she appeared in the mirror and *what people might think*, and she laughed with the rest of them.

Watching Lil spinning and spinning and holding out her arms and letting her red hair stream out behind her, she thought: *Whoever felt such vigour, such bursting excitement, as this?*

2

Kate, May 1924

I am his wife.

I am only his wife.

This is all I know how to say.

To the policemen who come to the house, who take me to the police station, who ask me questions, I say over and over, 'I don't understand. I am only his wife.'

And they both look at me – the fat one with the moustache and the thin one with the coarse ginger hair – they look at me as though I am a child they are disappointed in.

A policewoman is sent to sit with me, and the men leave us together. The woman has skin like white dough, dense and soft, and a purple birthmark that creeps down her neck and hides in her blouse. She fetches me a cup of tea and asks if I want to visit the facilities. This is the only thing she says, in her hard London voice.

As I am washing my hands, I steal a glance in the mirror and I see the policewoman's face inside it. She is flushed with excitement.

'I'm all right,' I say to the woman in the mirror, speaking over the noise of the running water. 'I shall be quite all right. This is just a misunderstanding, that's all. I'm his wife. I know him.'

The policewoman leans against the wall and folds her arms as I dry my hands on the damp towel. She doesn't look at me again after that.

I am taken back into the cold grey room where I finish the weak cold tea, and after a while the men come back and the questions start again.

Over and over and over, and I clench my fists and stare at the crack in the floor that is shaped like a wishbone, and I blink and blink.

The thin one asks about dates, times.

I shake my head.

Then the fat red one asks about *her* and I say, 'I don't understand. Why are you asking these things?'

They wait. And when I can bear the waiting no longer, I say, 'I knew about Miss Cade. I knew all about it.'

One of them coughs. I look up at them in turn. 'There was nothing in it. It was all quite . . . There was nothing in it at all.'

The fat one looks at me for a moment then leans over and says something in his colleague's ear. I watch the thin one stand, watch him open the door. I watch him go out into the corridor. It looks easy, just to stand and leave like that.

The fat one is reading his notes. Tapping his pencil. As I watch, he licks a thick finger, turns a page. The finger goes to his temple and pushes the skin up and back so that it wrinkles.

The door opens. The thin one comes back in and shakes his head.

The fat one says, 'For Christ's sake,' and a little dot of white spit lands on the table.

He picks up his pencil, turns to a clean sheet of paper, draws three or four lines. Along and then down, making rows of squares. He numbers each square, slowly, his little womanish mouth half open, while the thin one and I look on.

'Right,' he says. 'Right.'

He touches the point of the pencil on one of the squares. Number twelve. 'Do you know where your husband was on this date? The twelfth of April.'

I say nothing.

The pencil moves. 'What about the thirteenth? And the two days following?'

'And on this date?'

'And this?'

I close my eyes. I do not want to think about those days.

I can feel them staring, then they push their chairs back with a shriek. I open my eyes and see them shuffle, bend their heads, mutter together.

I look at my hands. One nail is broken and ragged, the skin beneath pink and blind.

The questions begin again.

'I can't remember. It was nearly three weeks ago. How do you expect me to remember?'

I try to keep my tone even and polite, but they look at me with raised eyebrows and now I am aware of the heat in my face and the wetness under my arms.

I ask them again, 'How do you expect me to remember?'

I want to ask them to please leave me alone. Instead I say, 'My husband was nowhere. He was with me.' I look at them in turn. 'We were together the whole of that time.'

Surely now I will be able to go home.

But then they say it.

'Why did you do it, Mrs Ryan?' they say.

And 'What did you suspect?'

Then one of them says, 'Now then, Mrs Ryan. Please try to be calm. Getting upset like this won't help.'

I try to tell him I am calm, but somehow I am on my feet and they are looking up at me in alarm.

And then I am on the floor with my arms around my head. I can hear a low moaning noise, like an animal. It reminds me of something but I can't remember what, and I tug at my hair, trying to remember – then there are hands on my shoulders, and another man is there beside me. He has a kind face and white whiskers. I tell him I am trying to remember about the animal, and he nods and pats my arm, and I realize – how extraordinary! – that someone has rolled up my sleeve and my skin is bare. As I look at my poor naked arm, the kind-faced man pulls back his hand and I see a glint. Like a knife. I clutch at him and I whisper *they are killing me* and he pats me again and smiles and I am falling and falling, and as I fall I remember about the animal and I remember that the noise was like a cow I once heard whose calf had been taken from her. She lowed in distress all night and kept us awake. We were in the Lake District and the bed was lumpy and it was before Judith was born.

I try to tell them about the cow, but their faces are receding, and the light is becoming brighter and more blurred, and I stare and stare and then everything is white.

At last they let me go.

Until tomorrow, they say, as though tomorrow were a treat I might look forward to.

They ask if there is someone they can send for, to take me home.

I open my mouth and say without thinking, 'My . . .' Then I remember and choke on the word.

I clamp my lips shut. They exchange a glance.

I get to my feet, and the thin one raises his eyebrows. The fat one nods and steps towards me.

'We'll drive you,' he says. And then I see how it will be: a black car will turn into the road, curtains will twitch at every window as I climb out and fumble for my key. There will be stares and whispers and, later, every time I step outside, there will be the shapes of women on doorsteps, shoulders angled together, heads tucked in. They will be there every morning when Judith leaves for school.

Judith.

I sit down again, hard, and cover my face with my hands. I feel them looking at one another, then the floor creaks and a voice says my name. I take my hands down and the thin one is there, holding out a crumpled greying handkerchief. He says, 'We'll drive you home.'

I shake my head, pull my own handkerchief from my sleeve. The eau de cologne I dabbed on this morning clears my head a little.

'I can manage, thank you. I'll be quite all right.'

They don't like that, I can tell. All the way down the corridor, past smells of bleach and damp and something stale and almost-human, they keep talking, keep insisting I can't be allowed to leave alone. Then the fat one opens a door, and there is the foyer we were in this morning.

This morning is a long way away. They knocked on the door just after eight o'clock and told me to come with them. I asked what it was about, but they just told me again to come with them.

I asked if it was to do with Tom, and they said nothing. I told them that Tom was away, that he was working.

I asked if something had happened to him, if there had been an accident, and they wouldn't say. But there were secrets in the way they wouldn't say. In the way they wouldn't meet my eyes and in the urgent way they spoke.

I turn to the thin one now. 'I don't know where we are. I don't know which omnibus . . . When you drove me here this morning, I . . . I don't know where we are.'

He looks at the fat one, and then at me. 'We're in Kennington. South London. Not far from . . . not far from Waterloo.'

He hesitates and then he says again, softer, 'Let us take you home, Mrs Ryan. You're in no state to get the 'bus or the train.'

I've never been to Kennington, I think, as I am folded neatly into the back of a motor car. I am sure of it. None of this – these streets, these buildings – none of it looks familiar at all. The engine starts and I want nothing more than to slump back on the seat and close my eyes. I want to sleep for days. Instead I keep my head high and my neck long and I show them nothing.

All the way through Clapham and Battersea, they are still talking, still asking questions. And I realize that they think I have more to tell them. They think I will talk to them now, away from that dreadful room. When I realize that – when I realize they will not let me be – then I lean my head back and close my eyes and wait for their voices to fade away.

I manage to persuade them to stop on the Lower Richmond Road and dart out of the car before they change their minds. The fat one leans out to close the door and says, 'Nine o'clock tomorrow morning, Mrs Ryan. Don't forget.' I look at him and he touches his finger to the brim of his hat. The door closes. The car glides away. And at last I am alone.

I look at my watch. The little diamond watch that Tom bought me for Christmas.

It's almost quarter-past four. Judith will be at home. She will be in the kitchen doing her homework or drawing, drinking milk from the green cup with the painted rose, Mrs Irvine's grey cat snoring at her feet. The room gets the sun in the afternoons so it will be warm, and Judith will be humming under her breath.

Everything in her world is just as it should be.

I make myself walk around the corner, into our road, towards the house.

I will tell Judith I was unwell and Mr Simpson let me leave early. A headache.

Except – won't I have to tell her, eventually? Tom won't be home tonight. Perhaps he won't be home for a long time. Not until they accept that they have this all wrong.

Perhaps she will find out anyway, from someone else?

The thought slides inside quickly, and it is so strong and

so bitter-tasting that it makes me bend and gasp. I reach out for something to steady myself and my hand meets a wooden fence. I feel a sharp splinter of wood break my skin, and I don't care because all at once it has occurred to me – *Oh God, it will be in the newspapers.*

My head is hot and for a moment everything is dark, but the pain in my hand is there to hold on to. I look down at the dot of wood in my palm and pinch it between my nails and tug. It slides out smooth and whole and I lick the bloody spot, and the blood is tangy and alive.

One thing at a time.

Daddy is away.

Daddy is helping the police.

There was an accident, and someone has been hurt.

Daddy is going to be a witness. In court. Do you know what that means, sweetheart? A witness is a person who has seen something important.

Daddy is a witness and he will tell the police what he saw. He will be in court in front of a judge. A real one. With a red robe and a grey wig. Won't that be exciting?

Then will he come home, Mummy?

Yes, love. Then he'll come home.

Before his birthday? Will he be home before his birthday?

Oh yes. Ages before.

I'm going to hem him another handkerchief for his birthday. Like the one I gave him for Christmas. But this time I'm going to stitch the T in red instead of green.

What a good idea. And we'll make a cake for him. Would you like that? A chocolate cake.

Somehow it is half-past seven and I have watched Judith eat her supper and tried to smile as she chattered about school and about the new girl in her class.

'She has ever such a lot of curly hair, Mummy. And one of her eyes looks a different way to the other. I asked her if she could see in two places at once, but Elsie Brigham said I was stupid.'

I have hung up Judith's clothes as she changed into her nightdress, I have brushed her shining hair, one hundred long smooth strokes, and I have plaited it neatly in two gleaming pigtails. I have watched my fingers working just as though this was any other day, watched myself tie the elastic at the bottom, watched myself tuck Judith into bed and bend to kiss her freckled cheek. And I watched myself close my eyes for a moment and breathe in the sweet smell of my daughter – the childish smell of soap and milk and innocence.

And now I am alone again and the door is closed and my hand is reaching up to the highest kitchen cupboard. I take down the bottle wrapped in an old rag. Uncork it.

I pour and raise the glass to my lips.

I hear a door slam, somewhere in the street, and I think of Arthur Dean.

We all have our secrets, Tom.

I can feel the roughness of the rug beneath my stockinged feet, and the uneven wood of the table beneath my hands, but nothing seems quite real. Not the fiery medicinal taste in my mouth. Not the pink and gold sky I am staring at, nor the sound of a car horn on the Kew Road, nor the sickness in my stomach.

Nor the guilt at the bottom of it all.

3

Bea, August 1923

The rain in the north was soft and fell lightly, forming a silver mist that sat on the horizon above fields and ancient stones. It smelled green and cold and fresh. Then there was London rain – and after almost a year in the city, Bea could have told them apart in the dark.

London rain was hard and grey. It made leaves mulch. It lay dark and boggy on the grass in the parks. It spread a smoky stink in the streets. It made skin sweat in crowded shops and Underground trains. It made wood rot, paper pulp, and it streaked stones with dirty rivulets and stains.

It was a Thursday morning in August, four days after Mr Ryan's visit to the office, and it was raining. The heavy yellow sky had cracked open in the night and the rain woke Bea early. She lay in bed, listening to the pattering on the window, to the dripping gutter, to the distant sound of the church bells, now muffled by mist and by damp.

She dozed on, curled on her side with one arm flung over her head, breathing in clean cotton and the sweetish biscuity smell of her skin.

But then the church clock sounded the half-hour, and so she must get up and stretch – one last long luxurious creaking release – and fill the basin from the jug she had left ready the night before.

First came the shock of cold water, trying not to let the sponge drip down her neck or onto her stomach; then the roughness of the towel and the fragrant cloud of talc; the smoothing of cream into skin, the smearing of Vaseline onto dry lips. After that came her clothes: the softness of cotton, the scratch of wool, the slither of crepe.

Sometimes Bea wondered what it would be like to smell of perfume and lipstick grease, her breath to smell of wine and French cigarettes, her room to smell of roses: these were smells she associated with a kind of *womanliness* she could not quite define, but felt sure she would recognize when she encountered it. Instead, she suspected she smelled mostly of soap – a shining, scrubbed and virtuous smell – and, faintly, of neglect. Her clothes were clean but often gave off a very slightly stale odour, as though they had been put away damp.

With the weight of her coat over her arm, she went downstairs – and that was dark smooth wood under her fingers, the clicking of her heels as she crossed the hall, past the high counter where Mrs McIvor sat all day, frowning above a wealth of black satin, barking directions at the maids. And then on into the dining room, where she nodded at the few women she knew, and sat at her usual table in the window.

Hetty slammed down the breakfast tray, and that was cheap white china, chipped and tea-stained, a dull knife dipping into oily margarine, smeary fingerprints on her napkin. And Bea looked out at Guilford Street, at the men and women hurrying to work, and poured her own coffee from the jug and stirred in milk and sugar just as she liked it.

This was how each day began. This was her place in the world.

Today she sipped her coffee and stared out at the rain, and at the brittle brown leaves on the tree in front of the house opposite. Three boys came into view then, boys in grey shorts and matching caps, who dawdled and scuffed, shoving one another into the mud at the side of the road. They were boys with all the usual falling-down socks and tattered satchels and undone shoelaces, and Bea could almost smell their small-boy sweat and the musty sweetness of their unwashed hair, the warm worn leather of their satchels; could almost see the dirt under their nails and the dust on their shorts. She watched the boys round the corner and disappear into London, and had a sudden urge to follow them.

Somewhere in the distance a clock struck eight. She swallowed a mouthful of scalding coffee, then dabbed her lips with her napkin.

She must not be late.

She must not be late. At first this was mere background to her thoughts, like the harsh rubber noise of car horns and the cries of errand boys; like the smells of exhaust fumes and horse manure layered one on top of the other, and the shining pitch being smeared thick on the road like black butter, while the omnibus crept and jolted along Holborn.

A little background thought then, but it grew more persistent until she was murmuring it aloud, through clenched teeth and with her fingers twisted tightly together.

I must not be late.

She could not afford to lose this job. For months, the newspapers had published figures about the number of men who had returned home after four years of service and sacrifice, and who had been unable to find work. Older women, Bea had realized when she first arrived in London, had little hope of finding anything at all.

She had gone to several interviews – and after two or three weeks, it seemed to her that she began to notice the same tired faces in the halls and waiting rooms. They were mostly ladies who seemed to be in straitened circumstances, dressed in faded, outdated clothes and smelling of mothballs and lavender, sliding slowly into genteel poverty as the world around them changed. Bea had sat among them, pitying them, watching them rub the spaces where their rings had been, watching them wonder why their late husbands hadn't been more careful, why there was no longer enough left in the bank to last them a lifetime.

There was one lady she had noticed several times: a thin yellowish face, dark eyes, grey hair pinned neatly under a shapeless hat. Each time Bea saw her, she was wearing the same brown suit, the same worn-down shoes. She watched her blink nervously under the electric light and avoid the eyes of those around her; watched her flinch when she was called through. And watching her, Bea had felt a kind of despair, and a clear determination that she would never end up like these women, wholly reliant on being noticed and chosen by someone else.

So she had taken the first job she could get – bookkeeping, at a domestic staffing agency in the West End. It had been obvious from the start that the firm was in trouble.

Mrs Le Mesurier who ran the agency had been frank about it. 'Hardly anyone can afford servants these days, Miss Cade. We have the War to thank for that, of course, along with so much else' – and after ten months, Bea had seen the advertisement for the job at Morley's and had jumped ship.

Morley's was a step up in every way – more money, more responsibility – and she was lucky: Mr Morley still preferred to employ female typists.

She had only been there five weeks – and she must not be late.

The omnibus jerked forward – three, four times – and came to a halt again. Bea looked at her wristwatch. She took a breath, gathered her things and stepped down onto the pavement.

*

Miss Shepherd was first in the office every morning – the girls had speculated more than once in Bea's hearing about whether she actually slept there – but Bea tried to make sure she was always the second to arrive, before Mr Montgomery, and certainly before Mr Morley himself.

Today Miss Shepherd was at her desk, going through the early post. She glanced automatically at the clock, then nodded at Bea. 'Good morning, Miss Cade.'

Then she rose, patting her hair and smoothing down her skirt – as though the mere act of greeting Bea had disturbed her – and went out to prepare Mr Morley's tea tray.

Bea was left to herself – left to sit at her desk and straighten the blotter, the ruler, the box of pencils. Every morning she remained completely still for a moment or two, just relishing the silence and the dry papery smell of the room. It smelled like a place where work was carried out unobtrusively and efficiently. There was no looseness in this room, no hint of emotion: no one had ever sweated in here, or bled, or wept.

Mr Montgomery came in at two minutes to the hour as always, wrestling with his mackintosh and umbrella, his copy of *The Times*, and his little grease-stained packet of sandwiches. He nodded to the room without raising his eyes and retreated behind the partition to his desk. Bea listened for the little sigh he gave as he sat, for the pause as he reached for a pinch of snuff from the tarnished brass box beside his inkwell, and then for his loud, satisfied sneeze.

Now she must roll a new sheet of paper into her typewriter, check the ribbon and take up the first of the letters Miss Shepherd had left ready for her. Just as she laid her fingers on the keys, Caroline and Jessie arrived, all pink cheeks and chatter and loud laughter fading to their 'Oh, good morning, Miss Shepherd. Miss Cade' – her own name something of an afterthought, as always – and then their whispers and hushed giggles as they noted Miss Shepherd's frown and the red flush at the hollow of her neck where her cameo brooch sat.

Beyond that, the morning went on just as usual. The rattle of typewriter keys began in earnest, loud and insistent, the noise rising against a backdrop of polite requests to borrow an India rubber or to adjust the blind. The telephone rang occasionally; orders for writing paper, carbon paper and typing paper arrived by the second post; invoices were sent out.

And then just after lunch, the telephone rang again. When Bea answered, she heard, 'Mr Morley, please.'

'I'm afraid he's in a meeting.'

'Oh, I . . .'

'Can I take a message?'

They spoke at the same time and he laughed. 'Sorry, you first.'

'Can I give Mr Morley a message?'

'Would you? Tell him, please, that the meeting at Callaghan's went very well this morning. I think we can expect an order from them by the end of the month.'

Now she could hear a northern accent: thick flat vowels, careful sibilant consonants. Exaggerated *d*s, thick *t*s like they were caught in his throat. *O*s like deep echoes.

She knew who it was, of course – who else would it be? But something in her, something small and stubborn, something that wanted him to know she had not really noticed him, made her ask, 'And your name?'

'Oh, how stupid of me.' Somehow Bea could tell he was smiling. She saw again those wide dark eyes fixed on her own.

'It's Ryan. Thomas Ryan.'

She kept her tone business-like. 'I'll give Mr Morley the message.'

'Thank you, Miss . . . I'm sorry, I don't know your name.'

'It's Cade.'

'Miss Cade.' He said her name slowly, and now she was in his mouth, warm and low.

'You're not . . . are you new as well? I think I spoke to another lady when I telephoned last week.'

'Miss Shepherd? She's at the dentist this afternoon.'

'Oh dear. Poor Miss Shepherd.' She could hear that he was smiling again, and it was all perfectly polite and conventional, and then, 'Although she sounded like a bit of a dragon. I bet she's giving the dentist as good as she gets' – and Bea was so astonished, she laughed out loud.

Mr Ryan laughed with her. 'I shouldn't say things like that! I'll get into terrible trouble one of these days.'

Caroline would know what to say, Bea thought. Or Jessie. They'd be able to think of something witty, something—

'And now I really ought to go. I think there's someone waiting to use the telephone.'

Heat flooded her skin. 'Oh, of course – I'm sorry.'

'Not at all. The fault is entirely mine. Good afternoon, Miss Cade.'

She imagined him lifting his hat to her, imagined a smile tugging at the corners of that red mouth.

When he had ended the call, she sat for a moment holding the earpiece against her hot cheek. Then she heard a muffled giggle, and looked up despite herself. Caroline's gaze slid away quickly and Bea stared hard at the wall above her head.

They were ridiculous, these girls.

4

Bea, September 1923

Mr Ryan rang again, and then again. Somehow he always managed to telephone when Miss Shepherd was away from her desk.

He gave Bea complicated messages for Mr Morley.

He mocked himself: 'I simply cannot read my own terrible handwriting, Miss Cade!' 'I've managed to arrange two appointments for the seventeenth – Lord, what a fool I am!'

He asked after her health, agreed that this was the warmest September in years. He wished her a pleasant weekend, then asked if she'd enjoyed herself on the river, at the exhibition. How was the concert? Once, he mentioned a performance of chamber music he had attended, and she tried to remember if she had noticed what his hands looked like. She imagined long artistic fingers.

The more they talked, the more his speech quickened, became musical. Since arriving in London, Bea had kept her voice to a low murmur when talking to strangers. She had been asked to repeat herself several times, and was unpleasantly conscious of her accent against the voices around her, all hard edges and strange vowels, sounding as though the speakers were rolling boiled sweets around their mouths.

But now, for the first time, it was easy to let her accent come through a little. It was something else they had in common.

He came to the office again, and again Caroline was on her feet before the door had closed behind him. But this time she hung back a little and let Jessie talk – almost as though they'd agreed it between them. Bea watched them, imagining the conversation – 'I have Eddie, you take him' – like children dividing up a bag of toffees.

She bent to her typing again, but then Jessie laughed suddenly and Bea looked up, startled – and now he met her eyes. His mouth was moving as he replied to Jessie, but he was looking at *her*, and as she met his gaze – astonished, hot, swallowing – he looked away quickly, like a small boy caught with his hand in the biscuit tin.

He focused on Jessie again and he tipped his head attentively, he nodded gravely, listening while she described a dress she had seen in a shop window on the way to work – *I'm really not sure if it will suit, I have to be so careful with my colouring* – tossing her red curls, waiting for him to fill the space with a compliment; and he did, he was suitably, properly gallant, but all the time there was a smile around his eyes.

Is he laughing at her? Am I the only one who sees it?

Then Miss Shepherd came in and frowned at them, and the girls melted away. He followed Miss Shepherd into Mr Morley's office – meekly, like an errant schoolboy. Bea glanced over at the door as it closed behind them and thought: *It's like a secret between us.*

Bea had been at Morley's for over two months when she first mentioned it in a letter to her sister. Perhaps it had taken that long for it all – the increased responsibility, the step up in salary – to feel real and definite.

Jane's reply to her news surprised Bea: she suggested they might meet. They had only seen each other twice since Bea had arrived in London more than a year earlier.

They met in a tearoom on St Martin's Lane. Jane's train came into Charing Cross, so it was convenient for her.

As Bea came round the corner, a movement in the street caught her eye, and she turned in time to see a bag of green apples slide from a shopping basket. They hit the pavement one after another, and two of them burst apart and lay glistening in the gutter. The others rolled away and were snatched up by a pair of ragged girls who ran off down an alley.

The woman carrying the basket hadn't noticed her loss. She stood at the side of the road, waiting to cross, staring down at her hands.

As Bea came nearer, she saw clearly the dirty nails, the callouses, the raw red patches between her fingers. The woman had tired eyes and a bruise on her cheekbone, and brass blonde hair fading to grey, like smoke, and a brown hat jammed on anyhow, so that the curls were flattened and lay hopelessly against the neck. She was rubbing her wedding ring, turning it so that the gold gleamed. Her eyes were wet as she gazed at it, as the ring turned and turned.

There was a gap in the traffic. The woman stepped into the road.

Bea walked by and pushed open the door to the tearoom.

Her sister was the first person she noticed. Jane looked up and straight at her. She lifted one hand in a meaningless wave as Bea navigated the tables and the waitresses.

Then she half stood, elegant in lavender, leaned forward to kiss her, and Bea was woven into a memory of childhood. Beneath the powder and the perfume, she could smell her: the sour-sweet smell that had always brought ripe blackberries to mind. In the blink of an eye she was back in the narrow bed with the missing bedpost, jammed between her sister and the cold wall, her knees curled into Jane's for warmth and her nose pressed into her neck, breathing her in, listening to her snores. Another blink, and she was sitting on a hard chair in a crowded tearoom, and opposite her was the sister she scarcely knew.

There were menus on the table between them, and Jane frowned at hers and tutted.

'Eightpence for a cup of tea? I don't know how you manage in London, with prices like these.'

She sounded just like their mother.

Bea watched her bent head, and took in the grey hairs at her temples and the lines on her forehead.

Jane ate as though she wasn't hungry. She cut her food into small precise squares, then popped each one in her mouth quickly, so that only a flash of her small precise teeth was visible. She chewed rapidly, her eyes on her plate, without apparent enjoyment. Bea watched her until she couldn't eat any more and laid her cutlery down tidily.

Jane swallowed the morsel she was moving around her mouth, and looked at her sister's half-full plate. 'Trying to slim, Bea?'

Her gaze slid over Bea and back to her own plate. She speared a cube of veal and ham pie and brought it up to her mouth. 'Really, I don't know why you bother.'

Her mouth was a small pink pucker, the golden pastry crust tucked inside. Her red tongue, folding and folding.

Bea looked down at her hands, crumpled into fists on her lap. Forced a smile. 'How are the children?'

Jane's face loosened and became softer. She pushed the food into the corner of her mouth, nodded. Chewed faster and swallowed.

'Hardly children any more. James is almost twenty, and Helen is eighteen.'

She paused, gave Bea a sharp look. Bea didn't know what that meant: she knew perfectly well how old they were. She sent postal orders every birthday and every Christmas.

Jane chattered on about James's new position – clerk in a bank – and about his lodgings in the City, and then about

Helen's fiancé. 'Of course, making a good marriage is so important for a young girl. It colours *everything*.'

Bea said, 'I expect the house will seem very empty when Helen has gone' – and she meant nothing by it, it was just a commonplace remark to fill the silence and move the conversation on.

But Jane put her fork down and looked away and said, 'I've been thinking about that. I can't help it.'

She looked at Bea and her voice was hollow. 'You do everything for your children – everything – and suddenly they're gone, and you wonder . . . well, it makes one wonder what it's all about.'

She picked up her glass, drank some water. Swallowed hard.

Bea watched her and then, without thinking about it, put out her hand to touch her sister's. 'Jane, I'm—'

But Jane slid her hand away, reached out to add hot water to the teapot, said abruptly, 'What about you?'

Bea retreated, tucking her hands back onto her lap. 'Me?'

'You seem to be doing awfully well these days. A job in the City, a smart address in Bloomsbury.' She poured the tea. 'I've been reading about you in the newspapers – you career girls, bachelor girls, whatever you call yourselves.'

She went on, 'It's quite the thing, isn't it? I expect you're out all the time: theatres, parties, concerts. I must seem terribly dull to you.'

'Of course not. I don't—'

'Stuck out in Kent, rattling around in that big house, giving dinners for Charles's partners, helping Helen plan the wedding.'

'It sounds—'

'What you don't seem to understand is how important these things are to Charles's position. The dinners, my work with the Conservative Ladies' Association – they all matter. Even Helen's wedding matters.' She took a sip of tea, looked Bea in the eye. 'I may not have a *career*' – and it was spat out, like an obscenity – 'but I do have responsibilities all the same.'

Bea looked away. Nothing had changed between them after all.

Back at Guilford Street, Bea climbed the stairs – wearily, heavily – and closed the door behind her. She lay on her bed, still in her coat, heedless of her shoes.

Perhaps she should have tried to make Jane understand how it was for her, and for women like her. Where Jane saw smart career girls, Bea saw women with frizzed modern hairstyles that they'd seen in advertisements and that didn't suit them; women with lines around their eyes that no amount of cream or powder would cover. And women who, despite the well-cut clothes, had red rough hands and nails cut to the quick.

It's our hands that really give us away, Jane. That point to us as women who don't have houses or husbands; as women who have to earn our own living.

Did Jane have everything she wanted? Bea supposed she must.

She sighed. Stretched. Looked about her.

What would she ask for, if she could have anything?

A quiet room; books; friendships. The means to support herself.

It was a small list, and yet it seemed sometimes to be far too long or too short. Jane clearly thought it lacking.

What ought I to have done, Jane? Stayed at home, in that empty house, with only the ghost of our poor brother for comfort?

And not only George, for she had been surrounded by the dead. Mother, Father – even the memorial at the crossroads carved with the names of boys she had known for most of her life, since before any of them could toddle. She had lived with ghosts and memories for too long – what she needed was life: light, noise, the sound of strangers getting on with their day.

Bea rose and went over to the window. She rested her forehead against the cool glass and stared out at the expanse of sky, at the rooftops stretching towards the distant horizon, at the jumble of narrow houses, church spires, grander buildings that might have been offices, banks, schools. Dusk was approaching and the streetlamps were beginning to glow. London was spread out before her like a treasure map garlanded with fairy lights.

Her bedroom at home had overlooked a row of identical backyards and the lane beyond. Everything was packed so tight, there was no space to breathe. Everything merged and melted so that it was sometimes hard to tell where your neighbours ended and you began: the children running in and out of each other's houses with the same dirty faces and scabbed knees; the women indistinguishable at the washing lines, all headscarves and aprons and eyes screwed up against the sunlight.

Voices, smells of dinner, even secrets, floated from house to house so that your bit of brisket tasted of their tripe and onions; so that your dreams contained next door's midnight arguments about the barmaid at the Brandling; so that everything you did and felt and wanted was next door's dinner-table gossip.

Everything had been so small, she realized.

And then, with a sense of wonder: my *life* was so small.

When Mr Ryan telephoned the following week, he didn't mention his visit to the office, but his voice softened when he recognized hers. 'Is that Miss Cade?'

He telephoned more often. His questions crept closer, then slipped inside. What had she thought of the play – was she generally an admirer of Mr Coward? Did she prefer comedy or something darker? Was she over her cold? Had she ever smoked a Turkish cigarette? Did she know Brighton at all?

'I walked past an oyster seller the other day,' he said. 'And I wondered if you'd ever tried one. Did you know they taste like the sea?'

She thought about his wife. Even then, she was thinking about his wife.

The two women had never spoken on the telephone, and Mrs Ryan had never visited the London office. Bea imagined a slender figure, thin arms and wrists circled with gold, shining black hair.

The girls talked about him more than ever: 'He's like one of those film stars.'

'He's better than that – Mr Ryan's *real*.'

You don't know him, Bea wanted to say. You don't know that he played football on Saturday and turned his ankle; that his birthday is on the twenty-third of June; that he can't stomach the taste of gin.

You don't know him at all.

Bea found that she needed to say his name out loud. She resolved to mention him to Ellen and Alice. Just in passing.

But she was unable to find them in the dining room or the drawing room – in fact, both were quite empty. The staircase and the first-floor landing were also deserted – only one of the maids was there, sweeping the carpet.

'Where is everyone, Hetty?'

But the girl only shrugged. 'Don't know, miss.' And she sniffed and went on sweeping, entirely uncurious.

Bea went on to the second floor. There was no one in the corridor, and when she tapped on Ellen's door, there was no reply. She tapped again. 'Ellen? It's me.'

And then a door opened along the corridor and Ellen's head emerged.

'We're in here.'

She followed Ellen into the bedroom – Nancy Shawcross's bedroom, she realized. 'What is it? What's happening?' But there was a loud shushing, and the door was closed firmly behind her.

Bea had time to notice that the room was crowded – four girls sitting on the bed, and several more cross-legged on the floor – before Nancy said, 'We don't want Mrs McIvor to hear. It's Lilian Tearney.'

'What about her?'

'Apparently she's been going about with a man.' Nancy's words tumbled out too quickly, pushing over one another in their eagerness to be heard. 'An American. He promised to marry her, but he's gone home now. And he's left her' – she paused for effect, her face flushed – 'with an unwanted bargain.'

'An unwanted . . . ?'

Nancy flicked her gaze down to her stomach. Her eyes gleamed with a queer excitement.

'Oh *no*. Oh Lord. Where is she?'

Alice nodded towards the door. 'In her room. She won't let anyone in, but we heard her crying.'

'Poor Lil.'

'Poor Lil, my eye.' This was from a tall figure leaning against the wall. Theo Ingram was wrapped in a silk dressing gown, cigarette holder in one hand and face shining with cold cream. The other hand cupped her elbow, one knee was raised to expose her white thigh, and her foot tapped the wall behind her.

She said, 'Lilian's a damned fool to get caught like this.'

Bea stared at her, then turned back to the others. 'What will she do?'

Ellen said, 'We were just talking about that. Annie says there isn't much she can do.'

Bea looked over at Annie Barton, a no-nonsense, hearty sort of girl who was training to be a nurse. Annie shrugged. 'There's all sorts of stuff she might get hold of. Pills, powders – things that will cost her.'

'Will they help?'

She shrugged again. 'It depends what you mean by "help". I've heard about girls who've taken something and managed to bring on an early labour – which generally means that the baby's too small to live. But I should think most of them end up in hospital – and if the doctor suspects they've done it deliberately, he has a duty to call the police.' She shook her head. 'I don't know what might happen to her after that.'

There was an awful silence. Then Annie said, 'That's not the worst of it.'

Theo tipped back her head and blew out a long plume of smoke. 'Come on then, darling. Tell us the worst.' Her cat's eyes glinted. 'We can all see you want to.'

Annie glared at her but continued, 'I read about one woman who took something and ended up with a prolapsed uterus. That means . . . well, it requires an operation. And it may mean she can't have any more children.'

Someone gave a shocked intake of breath.

Annie went on, 'The trouble is, you can't tell what you're taking. A pill might result in the baby's death. Or, if the baby does survive, it won't be . . . I've heard about all sorts of . . . deformities.'

'Dear God.' That was Alice, who looked so white Bea thought she might faint.

'God doesn't come into it though, does He? Just a man who was only after one thing. And apparently he got it.' Theo looked at them all, then picked a tobacco flake off her lip.

When they went back to their own rooms later that night, Ellen paused at her door. 'Bea? What did you want?'

'What?'

'Weren't you coming to find me earlier? You knocked on my door.'

'Oh.' The news about Lil had almost driven Mr Ryan from her mind. 'No – it's fine. It . . . it doesn't matter.'

'Are you sure?'

'Quite sure. It wasn't important. Goodnight, dear.'

Bea went into her own room, shut the door behind her and closed the curtains.

She must keep Mr Ryan to herself. Lil had been pulled apart that evening and found terribly wanting – her secret laid out naked, and dissected and judged. Bea wanted to protect her own secret, such as it was. It was so faint – just one look, really, half a smile – so gossamer-fragile, that any kind of cruelty would tear it apart.

5

Kate, May 1924

It is a beautiful May morning, and I am pressed hot inside this crowd of waiting women, damp and swollen and squeezed like a cotton sheet at the laundry. I can feel the heat shining in my face, prickling under my arms, oozing between my toes. I can feel the fear in my belly, in my throat, in the way I cannot think what to do with my hands.

I wonder if Tom can see the sun. I wonder if his hands are shaking and sweating, as mine are. If he was also unable to eat breakfast.

I have imagined what it must be like for him. I have thought about it over and over, picking at it, worrying at the knot of it. I have imagined grey cells, grey uniforms, weak grey light and the grey faces of men.

There are men here in the crowd too, but it is mostly the women I see and hear and smell: a press of flower-like dresses and high calling voices, an animal heat and excitement.

For days, the newspapers have been full of stories about the lure of this case for women. That is the word they use: *lure*. I have tried not to read them but I have not been able to avoid the headlines or the photographs. They have written about how women in satin and furs came to the cottage in motor cars mere hours after the first newspapers reached the streets. They were followed by shop girls on bicycles and kitchen maids on foot, squinting into the sun and grinning foolishly at the photographers. There have been outings to the cottage – charabancs and picnics and best hats. There have been reports of bribes to the policemen on duty to be allowed to look through the windows, to pick primroses in the garden, to collect pebbles from the path. To see, to touch, to smell.

I expected crowds today, of course, but I thought perhaps the cottage would still be the bigger draw. This is only the Magistrates' Court. Only a formality, Tom's solicitor says. It suits him to say this, I think. Mr Edgerton is a little, stooped man, everything about him tarnished and muted with age. Brown teeth, grey hair, thick yellow nails. I can imagine him dealing with boundary disputes, with wills and legacies and charity bequests.

He says the real drama will be saved for the trial. But this is the beginning of it all, and no one can say yet where it will end – and the not-knowing makes me so afraid I have to clench my jaw to keep my teeth from chattering.

The crowd is vast and impatient. On one side of the street are the newspapermen: rolled-up shirtsleeves and braces, jackets thrown carelessly over one shoulder, a certain way of talking around cigarettes. On the other side are the women. What shocks me is the holiday feeling among them: the neat bright hats, the pink cheeks, the mingled smells of perspiration, powder, cheap scent. I am wearing a grey business-like suit, clutching a plain functional handbag and a piece of paper stuck with flowers made of coloured card.

The group of reporters includes some with cameras: their twinkling silver lenses like enormous eyes, watching. One of them sets himself up in front of us and calls out to us to smile.

'Look alive, ladies! Play your cards right and you could end up on the front page!' – and they giggle and blush and position themselves.

I cannot be in this photograph. There may be women who could stand square in front of these men and look into these lenses, who could hold their heads up and speak out about their husbands – I am not one of them.

I slip behind a girl in a large straw hat and duck my head. The cameras flash once, then again and again: dazzling bursts of light that leave me dazed.

Someone – one of the men – calls out, 'Popular boy, ain't he, this Ryan?' and I see a few smiles. The woman next to me cackles. I see her bright eyes and something wet and white in the corners of her mouth, and the cameras flash again as I turn away.

Mr Edgerton said I would have a place reserved inside, on one of the front benches where Tom would be able to see me. But when I tried to tell the uniformed policeman at the door, he didn't listen, and I could not bring myself to say it again in case anyone heard me. Then he told me to *get in the queue with everyone else, please, madam* – and he refused to look at me or to see that I am not like these women.

So here I am, where I do not belong, and I am waiting with everyone else. I can feel the tension in the crowd and their cat-like readiness to spring.

And then it happens. The bolt scrapes back and the cameras flash, all at once, like a shudder. The women surge forward as one, before the door has fully opened, and the newspapermen hold their press passes high, calling out their entitlement to enter. I am carried with them all, pushed and squeezed and buffeted – and suddenly I am frantic with worry that we will not all fit, that I will not be there when he looks for me.

I am swept inside clutching my bag and the precious piece of paper, already creased from my damp hands. I am shoved, kicked, elbowed, pinched. A woman next to me loses her footing, stumbles, and her hat falls: a moment later I feel the give of it under my foot. Someone takes hold of my collar, trying to pull me back, hissing: 'A guinea I paid for my place in that queue. A *guinea*!'

For a second, I imagine turning to slap her. Raking my fingernails down her face, leaving deep and bloody lines.

Instead I pull free, refusing through sheer stubbornness to relinquish my place, and at last we come to an open doorway where the current of pushing bodies slows.

The newspapermen are diverted in one direction, while the rest of us taper into narrow streams and trickles. We reach a bank of benches and I make room for myself at the end of the last row.

I lay the paper face down on my lap and try to smooth out the sorry creases, the impressions my fingers have made. I fold my coat and set it on top. I press the backs of my hands against my hot cheeks and neck.

And all around me, women shuffle, fuss, sink into the hard wooden seats. Feet scrape, then are still. Chatter dwindles and dies.

We wait.

The room grows hotter. It is lined with wooden panelling and sliced by brass rails into quarters and eighths, into tiny boxes.

Women begin to fan themselves with papers. A low murmur rises as they realize that nothing is happening.

Then a distant clock strikes nine, another door slams open and men spill into the room. Men in dark sober suits and black robes, with pink faces and wigs of grey wool that make my scalp itch as I look at them. I recognize Mr Edgerton, stroking his faded moustache, taking a seat at a table in front.

Then another murmur swells, and this one goes on rising and rising as Tom appears in the midst of us all.

He is wearing a blue suit. A white shirt. They are the same clothes he put on last Thursday morning. A hundred years ago.

The woman behind me mutters, 'Handsome brute, isn't he?' and her companion sighs and says, 'Like a caged animal,' and there is a hitch in her voice.

He stands erect between two blank-faced men in dark uniforms, each with four silver buttons down the front. He is very pale and perfectly composed, but I feel sure that if I were sitting close enough, I would be able to see the little pulse in his temple that looks like the soft top of a baby's head, beating and beating.

I am watching him so intently that when one of the men in black calls out, 'Court now in session. Silence, please, ladies and gentlemen,' I flinch, and have to hide it with a cough.

Tom sits. He runs a hand over his hair. Stares at the brass rail in front of him. He looks at no one.

Other men stand and sit. They make statements, ask questions. I cannot tell these men apart: they are all pink and black and grey. I cannot understand what they are saying. I cannot tell which of them is for Tom and which of them wants him found guilty.

More questions. Murmuring. I stare at Tom, and when there is a pause in the questioning, he raises his head like a dog scenting a chase. He says, 'Not guilty' – and there is a sigh in the courtroom that follows his words. This is the first time I have heard his voice since that last morning. And he sounds both clear and familiar, formal and distant. He is calm – so calm! – and his calm is my undoing, for it is here that I realize he has accepted this is happening. He has accepted that he must stay calm, that he must be accused and defended, that he must play out the entire performance before we can go out into the street and get on with the rest of our lives.

I feel five points of red pain dig into my palms, and I look down to see my hands curled small and tight.

Mr Edgerton rises, bows to the judge and says, 'We will reserve our defence, my Lord.'

Another man stands. There are more questions, more statements.

Then the judge nods and says, 'Very well. The prisoner will be committed for trial.' Just as Mr Edgerton said he would.

Someone calls out, 'All rise!' and we stand like obedient schoolchildren while the judge gets to his feet, gathers his robes about him, and exits.

After all that, it is over in thirty-three minutes and we are all left blinking in surprise.

A low hum of conversation breaks out and settles on the room. Tom is led below and Mr Edgerton begins to gather his papers, leans over to speak to a younger man sitting next to him.

I stand and step out into the aisle, staggering a little. My legs are shaking. I am still clutching the piece of paper.

I look at Mr Edgerton again. He has his books and files in his arms now – he is looking about him, checking he has everything, preparing to leave. As I join the flow of women making their way towards the door, he moves into the aisle, and suddenly speaking to him seems like the most important thing in the world. I squeeze between two women, and one of them turns and glares at me. 'We're all trying to get out, love. Wait your turn.'

I call out to Mr Edgerton, and for one dreadful moment, I think he will not hear me and I will have to leave having done nothing to help Tom, nothing at all – then I call again, and at last he turns.

I hold up the piece of paper as though this will mean something to him. He nods at me and steps aside, out of the crowd, to wait for me. Now the women are looking at me properly and pausing to let me by: there is an avenue of women, brightly coloured and staring, and I pass down it, my eyes fixed on the man at the end.

When I reach him, he puts his hand on my shoulder. There is a ringing in my head and I cannot make out his words. I hold out the paper and he looks down at it.

'Please give this to my husband.' My mouth is dry. 'It's from his daughter. Please see that he gets it.'

He reaches out to take it from me, and for an instant it is suspended between us: a square of coloured card with flowers cut from a magazine and pasted on the front, and words printed above in shaky letters.

Come Home soon Daddy
I love You

6

Bea, September 1923

Bea found herself thinking of him at odd moments.

When she went into town to buy wool for a jumper or face powder or hairpins, she found instead that she was lingering in the haberdashery and the perfume departments, picking out lengths of lace to trim her nightgowns with, weighing up soap scented with roses against that smelling of violets. She had lately discovered the lingerie department, and had come to understand the pleasure of wearing things that shimmered and rippled when she was alone in her room, and which, when she was clothed, made her move more slowly, made her newly aware of her hips and her breasts and her waist.

She found, too, that she was spending more time in the ladieswear department: looking at clothes she couldn't afford, rubbing the material between her fingers, even trying them on. And when she buttoned a blouse or held up a dress against her body, the first thought that came into her mind was not *Is this comfortable?* or *Do I like this colour?* but rather *Will I be admired if I wear this?* – and then, in a rush of heat and shock: *Will he admire me in this?*

The more she wondered about Mr Ryan's tastes, the more he was present in her thoughts. At first he was a delicious idea to be taken out in quiet moments and savoured – when brushing her hair or choosing what to wear in the mornings; while rising from her desk or typing a letter or crossing the room to speak to Miss Shepherd. These moments seemed to come more often, and then more often still, until he was the first thing she thought of on waking, until she had to concentrate hard not to trace the letters of his name on her shorthand pad. Until he was in all of her thoughts wherever she was.

She realized that she was waiting for him to come back: skin prickling, senses worked to a pitch. She wondered if this was how it was to be an animal: alert to every footstep in the corridor, to each man of the right age who passed her in the street.

And then one afternoon she was alone in the office, bent over a page of figures, concentrating so hard that she didn't hear the door open, didn't hear anything until she heard, 'Miss Cade?'

That voice.

Her pen stilled. She laid her hands flat on the desk. Saw an ink blot on her wrist and tugged at her cuff. Tucked her hands in her lap.

He was standing in front of her, close enough that she could touch him. And now she made herself look up.

Her first thought, shockingly: *There you are. At last: there you are.*

How smooth and white his teeth were against his brown outdoor skin. He was as fresh and open as an apple.

'I'm Thomas Ryan.'

She pressed her damp hands against her skirt – *don't clutch at it, don't wipe them!* – and he said, 'We've spoken on the telephone.'

'Yes. Yes, I know.'

Her words were as thick and clumsy as stale sponge cake and they stuck in her mouth as red flared into her face and prickled all the way down her neck and below her blouse. She was hot and damp, her collar tight at her throat.

She hadn't realized that she had given him her hand, but there it was in his two, almost as big as his own. And Lord, there was another ink blot on her forefinger and she could have

cried, when he spoke again and she looked up. Straight into his
dark eyes, crinkled at the corners and tip-tilting with delight.

And all she could think, over and over: *There you are.* Finally.
There you are.

'It's a pleasure to meet you, Miss Cade.'

There was a beat of unbearable silence. 'How can . . .' She
cleared her throat. 'How can I help you, Mr Ryan?'

'Do you have Mr Morley's diary?'

'Yes. Yes, of course.' Her voice was almost steady, but when
she stood and turned to reach up to the shelf for it, she was
suddenly horribly aware of her awkward posture, of the width
of her hips, of her skirt pulling and tightening over her behind.

She picked up the diary, laid it flat on the desk and bent
over it to hide her face.

'Did you want to make an appointment?'

He said nothing, and she looked up and saw he was smiling
again. Her own mouth began to widen in response, just as he
said, 'Well, yes – but for this month, perhaps.'

Glancing down at the page, she saw she had opened it to
March. For a moment she considered throwing the diary at him
and leaving someone else to sort the whole sorry mess. Then
she stole another look at him and saw that he was smiling at
the mistake, and not at her. Breath left her in a puff of relief.

'Did you have a particular day in mind?'

Suddenly he was all business. 'Mr Morley wants to see me
after my meeting in Carlisle on the . . .' He consulted his own
pocket diary. 'On the twenty-fifth.'

She felt his head come up, felt his gaze resting on her again,
but remained bent over the diary. 'Shall we say Tuesday the
twenty-sixth, then?'

'Oh, I have a holiday on the twenty-sixth.' Something soft
in his voice made her raise her eyes and he went on, smiling,
'It's my daughter's birthday.'

'Your *daughter*?' It was out before she could catch it – harsh, shocked, telling.

'Yes.' He was grinning broadly now, all pride and love and possession. 'Our Judith.'

Our hung between them, hinting at a life she could only guess at. Such a little word, all soaked through with meaning.

She heard herself say – flatly, politely – 'How nice. How old will she be?'

'Eleven.'

There was a pause, and she was trying to think of something appropriate to say, when suddenly he stepped closer and lowered his voice.

'I'm having the most terrible trouble thinking of a present for her. What did you want when you were eleven, Miss Cade?' – and the soft, delightful intimacy of it quite took her breath away.

He was gazing at her – almost pleadingly, it seemed. 'What were you like as a girl?'

She could feel his breath on her skin. Her fingers flew to her throat and she pressed the tender, pliant hollow, seeking something for her hand to do, feeling her pulse fluttering inside.

'I was . . . oh, I was a quiet child, I suppose. Solitary.'

He smiled, a small private smile this time, quite unlike any other she had seen him give. 'I can see that you would be.' She barely had time to take that in, when he went on, 'And what would you have liked for your birthday?'

The answer came to her, quick as blinking, and she spoke before she could think of something more interesting to say.

'Books. I always wanted books.'

There was genuine delight on his face now. 'Oh, capital! Judith loves to read. Perhaps you could suggest something? I was always devouring adventure stories as a boy – *The Coral Island, The Dragon and the Raven* – anything by Mr Henty, really. I have no idea what girls like.'

She looked at him, at his open, eager expression, and imagined him as a child. He looked as though he'd never heard a harsh word, never been hurt.

'I loved *Alice Through the Looking Glass* – but I expect she's read that. And *A Little Princess*. She might like *Little Women* – although perhaps that's too grown-up for her. I liked E. Nesbit very much. *Five Children and It* or *The Phoenix and the Carpet*, you know.'

She added, 'But my favourite . . . I think *The Secret Garden* was my favourite.'

He smiled at that. 'Secrets are always magical, aren't they?'

He wrote down the titles and authors in the back of his diary with a small silver pencil. Then he did something quite extraordinary: he reached again for her hand, the rough red hand that was resting lightly on the desk, took it between both of his own, ignoring the ink stains and the callouses and the bitten skin around her left thumbnail, and he pressed it gently.

'You've saved me, Miss Cade. And I am eternally in your debt.'

She was conscious of nothing but the warmth of her skin where he was touching her; of a damp hot prickling at her hairline; of the brightness of his eyes.

He let her go, bowed slightly, and it wasn't until he was almost at the door, nearly colliding with Caroline and Jessie as they returned from lunch – staring, fluttering, barely noticing her at all – that she remembered, and called out, 'Mr Ryan?'

All across the room, not caring who might hear her, or see her blushes.

He turned and took a step towards her. 'Yes?'

'Your appointment? Next week?'

Now he laughed openly – a safe public laugh that took in the whole room – and came back to her desk. 'What an absolute dunce I am! Where would I be without you, Miss Cade?'

She let his words slither down under her blouse like a gold

chain, to be taken out and wondered at later, and smiled, forced herself to be cool and efficient.

'Shall we say the twenty-seventh then? At eleven o'clock?'

He checked his diary. Made a note. 'Thank you again.' And then smoothly, without missing a beat: 'Will you be here on the twenty-seventh?'

'I . . . yes. Yes, of course.'

'Then I can tell you which books I bought for Judith, and how she liked them.'

7

Bea, September 1923

Jane would have said at once, *But he's Married* – like that was all there was to him. She would not have understood that the fact of his marriage was generally absent. That he never carried it with him, the way some men and all women do. That it was like dandelion clocks and the way clouds must feel: insubstantial and easily made to vanish with a single breath.

On the twenty-seventh, it seemed perfectly natural when he came out of Mr Morley's office to ask if his little girl had enjoyed her birthday and which books he had chosen for her. As he began to answer, Caroline stood and came towards them – but Bea kept talking, kept asking questions without leaving any room for interruption – and gradually Caroline and the office faded into the background.

She led him into a conversation about which writers he admired, and found that he appreciated the French writers – Zola, Balzac, Hugo – even that he had read one or two in the original French. It was fitting somehow that he spoke French. He was different – entirely different – from any man she had ever met.

During his meeting with Mr Morley, Bea had been unable to keep her eyes from darting between Morley's door and her wristwatch, so she knew their meeting had finished at seventeen minutes past twelve. It was a shock, therefore, to see Mr Morley come out himself as they were still talking, to hear him say to Miss Shepherd that she might go to lunch now as he would be at the bank until after two, and to glance at her watch and realize that it was almost one o'clock.

While Mr Morley was speaking, Mr Ryan murmured a soft goodbye, and she watched him slip away with a mixture of regret and relief that he understood her position in the firm and respected it.

But when she came out of the building to take her own lunch hour, there was a touch on her arm and he was standing by the railings, looking for all the world like an eager office boy waiting for his sweetheart. She flushed as he removed his hat and made an elaborate bow.

'I should like to take you to lunch, Miss Cade. To thank you for your help with Judith's present.'

He bowed again, and for a moment she wished she had taken the time to powder her nose and comb her hair. But then he took her arm and she forgot herself and was aware only of him: his hip brushing hers, his elbow, the length of his stride.

He took her to a restaurant behind the station. She had often noticed the red-curtained windows and the white pillars on either side of the door, but had never been inside. They sat together at a table by the wall, and she watched him scan the menu, frowning, then smile up at the waitress. She opened her mouth to ask for the sole, but he was there before her, ordering two cutlets.

'Oh, I . . .'

He took her menu, handed them both back and smiled at her. 'The cutlets are excellent here.'

Then he looked around the room and she followed his gaze: took in the arrangement of white-draped tables, the rose-coloured carpet, the newly varnished woodwork. There were four or five couples dotted throughout the room – and for the first time, Bea felt part of a couple herself. Mr Ryan had chosen her lunch; he had concerned himself with her comfort. She noticed this and she noticed the rightness of it. A little shift, a little click – like a lock sliding neatly into place.

She turned back to Mr Ryan and saw that he was watching her. He smiled and then she was quite unable to meet his bright gaze. They talked a little about the books they were both reading, and he mentioned that he liked detective novels and was halfway through *The Secret Adversary*. She lifted her head and, quite without thinking, exclaimed, 'Oh, I *so* enjoyed that!' – but her voice was too loud and she felt that shameful heat leap into her face again, and was entirely grateful when the waitress interrupted them to set down their plates.

The meat glistened with fat and the potatoes were barely warm, but she was glad of something to do with her hands, glad his attention was on the slicing and sawing and chewing.

Then she saw that there were two salt cellars on the table and no pepper, and that he had used one and taken up the other. He raised it above his plate as he turned to look towards the window, distracted by the sound of a car horn. As it hung in mid-air, she wondered how to tell him without making him appear foolish – and then he tilted his wrist and salted his food for a second time and all she could do was watch as he replaced it on the table, almost but not quite covering a brownish stain on the cloth.

As they ate, Bea listened to the woman at the next table talking to her husband – 'It's quite impossible, Richard, you must see that. I really don't think we have any other choice, although Heaven knows who will do the . . .' She glanced at them and saw the woman pouring milk into her coffee, stirring in sugar, talking on and on as the spoon clinked, her hands trembling. Her husband gazed at his own cup, not speaking, not moving, his eyes dull and distant.

On the far side of them, a man sat alone at a table in the corner: an ex-soldier from his upright bearing and the empty sleeve pinned to one arm. He was cutting a chop using the side of his fork, and the uneven scrape of metal on china set her teeth on edge. Bea itched to help him, and realized that she was waiting – for the next noise, or for his fork to fail and fall.

Instead, she turned her attention to her own food. She cut her meat into tiny pieces, pushed them around her plate. She made herself swallow a slice of carrot and felt it stick in her throat.

When he had finished, they talked again, this time about the books they had read as children: his favourites, her favourites, the ages they had been when they'd discovered *Mother Goose* and *Treasure Island*. That led to their childhoods, and to his kindness when she told him about the loss of her parents and – faltering a little – of George. In turn, he talked about his mother's death and how close they had been. He understood how it felt to move through life acutely aware that part of oneself was missing.

He did not talk about his wife and Bea did not ask about her – although she was conscious of her all the time, sitting silently at the table with them, her hands twisting as she listened, her face in shadow.

Bea turned deliberately away from her, and asked, 'Where did you work before coming to Morley's, Mr Ryan?'

He looked down for a moment and then back up and directly into her eyes. 'Things have been rather difficult since the War. Well, they have for most of us, I expect. Jobs. The general upheaval. All of that.' He gave a sad little smile. 'I do not wish to seem self-indulgent, but there are things in my life that are . . . that are still difficult.'

He held her gaze, and once more she had to look away. She wanted to say something – something consoling, something to let him know that she had heard him and that he had her sympathy. She needed to show him that he was not alone.

But the moment passed, and now he was looking down at

the tablecloth, almost absently, and when she cleared her throat to speak, he started, and then signalled for the bill.

When they came out of the restaurant, he took her hand and pressed it gently between his two.

'Goodbye, Miss Cade. Thank you again for your help.'

The pressure of his hand lessened then, and he began to withdraw. Without thinking, wanting only to keep him there, she said, 'Where are you . . . are you meeting a customer this afternoon?'

But he only said, 'No – I'm going home now. My wife needs me.'

There it was at last – one little word, as quick and as hard as a slap – and he had said it as easily and directly as though it was the most casual word in the world. It was as though he said it all the time and never considered the impact it might have.

She could not think of a single thing to say in response – and he merely tipped his hat and walked away, leaving her watching him, and watching too the figure that was now taking shape more clearly in her mind. Somewhere on the outskirts of London, there was a station where he would alight, and a road down which he would walk, then a path up to a door – and behind that door were rooms full of objects she had never seen. Objects chosen by his wife, arranged by her, dusted and polished and touched by her, and taken for granted every single day.

And in one of those rooms, his wife would be waiting for him – and soon he would open the door and go directly to her. His lips would brush hers. His hand would stroke her skin or her hair.

Bea could not see her face, not yet – but she was there.

8

Kate, May 1924

The next week is restless and nightmarish. When I manage to sink into sleep, I am always met by the same dream – damp, glistening stones; a far-off dripping sound; something swinging in the shadows above me, making the stones light and dark, light and dark.

I wake rigid and stiff, my fist in my mouth to stop the scream that is rising there – and that is sleep gone for another day.

There are reporters outside the house every morning, but I ignore the shouts and the questions about my husband. I go to work as usual. I answer the telephone and type up letters and make Mr Simpson's coffee from behind a bright and brittle front.

On the second day, I come back from lunch to find Mr Simpson reading a newspaper at his desk. He starts when I come in, reddens, pushes the paper into a drawer. I pretend not to notice; I busy myself hanging up my coat and sliding my feet out of my shoes beneath the desk.

He clears his throat. Removes his spectacles and polishes them. Replaces them and clears his throat again. When I look over at him, the light reflects on the lenses, making it impossible to see his expression.

'Mrs Ryan, I want to say how deeply sorry I am . . .'

'Thank you, but there's really no need.' I look at his spectacles and make myself sound smooth and brisk enough that his voice slides away. 'Do you have that letter from Reynolds', Mr Simpson? The one about the late payment?'

I cannot dwell on this. If I let myself think about it, I will crack wide open, and who is to say when or how I might be whole again.

I must show that I can do my job as well as ever. I must go on as usual, making breakfast and supper, washing up, darning stockings, polishing shoes.

What else can I do?

A lengthy telegram arrives from Mr Edgerton – no expense is spared, and somehow the money must be found to pay him.

The trial will be at the Sussex Assizes, in Lewes. The next session opens on the seventh of July, and Mr Edgerton thinks ours will be among the first cases to be heard.

He hopes I am bearing up. He says that his client would like to see me. His client would like me to send money for cigarettes and chocolate.

I lay the telegram down and sit heavily.

Lord only knows how I am to travel to Lewes every day, or – if there is no train that will get me there on time each morning – how I am to meet the cost of lodgings.

And what am I to do about Judith? I could leave out a cold supper each morning and Mrs Irvine would look in on her and make sure she cleans her teeth and goes to bed on time – but there will be no one to kiss her goodnight or comfort her or answer her questions about her father.

And whatever I do, whether I stay in Lewes or travel down each day, I will need to take time off work. That will mean a conversation with Mr Simpson, perhaps even with Mr Morley. I don't let myself think about what I will do if they won't give me the time off, or if they decide they have shown enough patience with my situation already, and that this is the final straw.

So much worry. So much expense. Tom will have thought of none of this, of course. Nor will Mr Edgerton, nor any of those men in their black robes and grey wigs.

I am suddenly exhausted. I want to crawl back into bed and wake up when Tom is home and everything is just as before.

I make myself sit up straight.

It's only eight weeks until the trial, Katie. Just eight weeks of waiting to get through.

Perhaps nine or ten before this is completely over.

It will all be over in ten weeks. At the most.

When I go into work the next morning, before I can think too much about it, I tell Mr Simpson I would like to take my fortnight's holiday early this year. He nods and makes a note of it, without once meeting my eyes.

At the end of that fortnight, I will come back to work and we will go on just as before.

When Mr Simpson is out seeing a customer, I draw out a calendar with a ruler and coloured pencils. I will tick off the days, one by one, all the way until the last day, which I decorate with curlicued corners and blue forget-me-nots.

At teatime I show Judith the calendar. Her lips move silently, counting days. She looks up at me and her eyes are brimming.

'You said he'd be home for his birthday.'

'I . . .'

'You *said.*'

'Well, I'll be here, love. We can celebrate Daddy's birthday for him. Then we'll have a proper tea party when he's home.'

Her head is bowed and I reach out to touch her arm but she jerks away and runs into the hallway. I hear a clatter of shoes, a sob, the slam of her bedroom door.

When I open the door, she is lying face down on the bed, legs tight together, fists clenched. Her head is turned to the side, her eyes screwed shut, lips pressed thin.

'Judith?' I take a step closer. 'What's wrong?'

Nothing.

I close the door and approach the bed slowly. Step over her shoes and sit carefully, all the while watching her.

Nothing.

'Judith?'

She buries her face further into the blanket.

I reach out and wrap my hand around hers, which immediately curls into a ball. It sits within my own like a stone, all furious knuckles.

'Judith. Tell me what's wrong. It isn't just Daddy's birthday, is it?'

The stone shifts. Grows smaller. Tighter.

'Is it about Daddy? Has someone said—'

Her head snaps back and her eyes open suddenly, show huge and wet. 'You *knew*!'

She pulls her hand free, wriggles away from me. Her face is flushed and damp curls cling to her forehead.

'You *knew* and you didn't tell me!'

'What do you—'

'Where's Daddy?'

It hurts to look at her face so I slide my gaze away, let it rest on the row of dolls on the shelf. One sits further forward than the others, her head slumped, her legs sticking over the edge.

'*Where is he?*'

'He's . . .' I clear my throat. I don't know what to say to her. 'He's in trouble, love.'

Judith stares and the flush deepens. Then her rigid expression collapses and suddenly she is weeping. I reach to take her in my arms, and for a moment she lets herself be held, lets herself soften and melt — and then she pushes away and up against her pillow, and buries her face in her arms.

I look at the soft childish hands, the neat square nails, the scar on her left wrist from falling in the park. Only five weeks ago.

I stroke her hair. She jerks her shoulder to push me away.

'Did someone say something at school?'

She sniffs and lets her hands fall. 'They . . . Emmy Saunders said she heard her father say that Daddy was in prison.'

'Oh God. I'm sorry, love. I'm so sorry you had to hear that.'

'Is he in prison?' She is staring at me, eyes wide and accusing. 'Why is he in prison?'

I think of all the things I might tell her. I think about the police station. The courtroom. I think of Tom standing pale and tall behind the brass rail, and the way his mouth moved as he said, 'Not guilty.'

'It's . . . it's complicated.' I pat her arm, pointlessly, helplessly. 'He'll be home soon.'

And when I hear myself say this aloud, the knot in my stomach loosens, just a little. My voice is stronger when I say it again. 'He'll be home soon. The police have made a mistake.'

'What kind of mistake?' And then, 'Why don't you tell them it's a mistake? Why aren't you helping him?'

'I . . . They won't . . .'

'Why won't you help him come home? Why haven't you told them they've got it wrong?'

'I have, love. I've told them that. They don't believe me.'

'Then you have to try harder, Mummy. You have to help him. Who will help him, if you don't? You *must*.'

The reporters are still there. I have come to overlook them, have almost grown used to them, the way one might get used to a cracked window pane or a laddered stocking. But then, one afternoon when I come home from work, one of them, a long-faced older man with a rather sly look, comes right up to the gate and says my name.

He says 'Mrs Ryan' – and it is not even a question, it is said with authority as though it is leading to something – and like a fool, I turn around. He bares his teeth then, and I realize I am trapped. I put my head down and walk quickly up the path, but he says it again, louder, and again – and then the others join in and there is a chorus of them, shouting and furious and demanding answers.

I slam the door behind me and lean against the wall, and I am panting as though I have been running. I close my eyes and wait for my heart to slow, wait to feel normal enough that I will be able to walk upstairs and face Judith.

'Mrs Ryan?'

For one terrible moment it is as though they have managed to creep under the door or through the letterbox like mustard gas – but then I open my eyes and Mrs Irvine is standing directly in front of me.

'Are you all right?'

She's not a bad woman, Mrs Irvine. She has always been kind to Judith and me, and for a moment, the temptation to unburden myself to her flares like pain. I have to remind myself that she would not understand. That no one understands.

I speak quickly. 'It's a mistake. It's all a dreadful mistake. Mr Ryan is with . . . he's helping the police sort it out. He'll be home soon.'

She is still looking at me and I cannot read her expression and I open my mouth to say something else, something smooth and reassuring – when there is a knock on the door.

I clench my fists. *Oh God.*

I don't know if I say the words aloud, but Mrs Irvine just steps past me and opens the door. I move to the side, where they can't see me.

'Yes?'

'Mrs Ryan?'

'No.'

I can hear the smile in his voice as he says, 'I beg your pardon, madam. Jack Oldroyd, *Daily Post*. I meant to say, may I speak to Mrs Ryan?'

I stare at Mrs Irvine, willing her to please not look at me, but she doesn't move and the expression on her face does not change.

'You may not.'

He huffs out a little laugh. 'Madam, I'm here in the public interest, and I think you—'

'Public interest? What public interest? You're disturbing me in my own home.'

He changes direction as swiftly as a ferret after a new scent. 'Do accept my apologies, madam – I hadn't realized this was your house. Are you Mr Ryan's landlady? May I have your name, for my readers?'

'Certainly.' She smiles and I think I am going to be sick. 'It's Mrs Sling-Your-Hook.'

There is a pause and now his voice is rougher. I hear greed underneath it, like slime on the stones at the bottom of a river.

'I just want to talk to Mrs Ryan. Ten minutes, that's all.' And a little lower: 'There's a few shillings in it for you if you help me.'

There is a little pause then, and he pushes inside it. 'There's a lot of interest in his case, madam. Handsome chap like that. Family man. A lot of our readers are very sympathetic to his situation.'

I think about it. Just for a moment. Would it help Tom? Could I bear it?

Then Mrs Irvine is there, like a ship with the wind in her sails. 'Mrs Ryan doesn't need your interest or your sympathy.

And I don't either. There's no story here, young man. Now go away, or I'll send for the police.'

She slams the door and lets out a long breath.

'I don't know what to say, Mrs Irvine.' I am trembling. 'Thank you.'

She shakes her head. And then she looks straight at me and says, 'I've never had any trouble with my lodgers before. Never.'

'Mrs Irvine, I'm—'

'If it wasn't for your little girl . . .' She sniffs. 'Let's just say I'm considering my position.' She brushes past me and begins to make her way down the passage towards her kitchen.

She says over her shoulder, 'Don't talk to them again. I don't want them here.' And then, like it is nothing, 'Don't give them anything and they'll soon get bored and go away.'

But like flies who have smelled spoiled meat, there are more of them the next day. Still more the day after that. A crowd by the end of the week.

9

Bea, October 1923

On the days when she knew he had appointments in London and might therefore drop into the office, Bea was quite unable to concentrate. Her gaze moved in quick direct lines from the paper in her typewriter to the door, skittering over the blotter, the paste-pot, the box of pencils, then back to the letter she was typing.

Directly in front of her was Jessie's back, which always reminded her of rows of desks in a schoolroom. Opposite Jessie, Caroline faced them both: every time Bea glanced up, it seemed that she met Caroline's cool grey scrutiny.

Mr Ryan had mentioned a new suit – 'Blue serge. Quite the thing, my tailor tells me' – and she found herself noticing every glimpse of material that might answer that description.

And then one day the door opened and he was there again. It was just like before – but now everything was different.

He came forward, seemingly not even aware of Caroline or Jessie.

'Miss Cade.'

She gripped the table. Swallowed. Sat straighter.

He kept coming forward until he was right at her desk, and he was smiling. 'I'm here to see Mr Morley.' He glanced down at his watch, and then back at her. 'I'm a little late, I'm afraid.'

She was smiling back, and it wasn't until hours later, washing her hands in the ladies' and thinking of him, that she became conscious of her smile in a way that was entirely new and strange. Her hands slick and lathered, the smell of carbolic all around, and herself still and shocked as she looked at her frozen smile in the mirror and saw all the things he must have seen: round eyes like gooseberries, pale lashes, too many yellowing teeth between thin lips.

She closed her eyes then, and willed his face to come back to her. To cancel out her own.

But that was later, and now, with him before her, there was only the heat blooming on her skin, the ache in her cheeks from smiling. And the look of him: his mouth, his dark eyes and those laughing creases around them – all fixed on her.

When she brought him and Mr Morley tea, she noticed other things: the shine of his hair and the rakes left by his comb, the stiff gleaming white of his collar, and the smell of something spicy and sweet and strange as he leaned back in his chair.

She noticed too that there was a freckle on the back of his neck – just *there*, at the softest part.

She raised her hand, was about to reach out and touch it, to trace the outline with the tip of her finger, to see if there was any discernible difference between it and the skin on which it was marooned – then Mr Morley cleared his throat.

'That will be all, Miss Cade' – and she caught herself, and left the room with the image of that smooth and vulnerable neck uppermost in her mind.

Ten days later, he came again. Again, Bea was the one to bring tea, on her feet before Miss Shepherd had finished the request. This time, he took the tray from her and thanked her in a low voice as Mr Morley kept talking. She raised her gaze to his; she could not help it. He ducked his chin and looked at her with those dark eyes and let his mouth hang upon a smile. She did not have time to look away before a blush licked her skin. His smile widened and his voice was soft as he said her name.

How nice to see you again, Miss Cade.

When she sat at her desk again, stared unseeing at the paper in her typewriter and put her fingers automatically to the keys, she realized she was still trembling.

Five days after that, he came again. The time halved: she noticed it.

He came in and walked directly up to her desk. She kept typing as he came nearer, her head bowed, her fingers tapping out nonsense and unable to stop.

Miss Shepherd is sure to notice it in the wastepaper basket but I cannot I cannot I cannot

Then he was standing in front of her, his hands on the desk, within touching distance. He was there, and she must say something.

'Can I help you, Mr Ryan?' Her voice was almost steady. She straightened her spine. It was not possible to meet his eyes, so instead she stared at his eyebrows.

'Good morning, Miss Cade. Can you give me a list of the orders placed by Robertson's in the last quarter?'

It was no use, no use at all. To focus on his eyebrows was like staring at the frame of a window when a whole city was laid out sparkling beyond. She looked into those dark eyes, and felt the now familiar heat spread across her skin.

'I . . . I beg your pardon?'

Stupid. *Stupid.* Her head felt light and she groped blindly for the edge of the desk to steady herself.

'The Robertson account? I'm looking for an order history.'

'Yes. Yes, of course.'

She fumbled through the files on her desk, paper slipping under her damp fingers.

She heard giggling and did not look up – but then she felt him turn away from her, towards the girls, and there was another giggle, and another.

She laid the Robertson file on the edge of her desk – a

careful distance away – and began to type again: slowly now and with purpose. She tried not to listen to the girls, or to hear his laughter.

But it was impossible. Caroline's rather shrill voice, his low steady one, Jessie's bright laugh – it was like an intricate dance of bowing, stepping back, coming together again, and Bea was quite unable to shut it out.

She stared at the paper in front of her until the letters blurred into black shapes that moved up and down to the rhythm of their voices. Mocking her. When she could no longer bear it, she looked up again, just as he said something to the girls in a quiet confiding tone. He leaned towards them, inviting them in. Caroline smiled and tossed her hair, then caught Bea's eye. And her smile did not falter, but rather hardened. Her lip curled – just a little – and she narrowed her eyes.

Poor Miss Cade.

And yet it was Bea whom he had taken to lunch. It was Bea he had chosen. It was her, it had been her from the beginning – not these ridiculous girls.

And so Bea merely smiled back at Caroline – widely, openly – then replaced her fingers on the keys, and began to type again.

One Saturday morning, the telephone rang. When Bea answered, there was a pause – and then his voice came over the line. Soft. Intimate. Just as though he was in the office beside her.

'Miss Cade.'

A quick intake of breath. She turned her body sideways so that the others shouldn't see her face.

'Yes.' She was almost whispering. 'Yes, Mr Ryan.'

'I'm glad it was you who answered.'

'I . . . Did you want Mr Morley?'

'No. I want to ask you something.'

'Yes?'

'Would you have tea with me today?'

'Yes. Of course. Yes.' It was a long time after she had put down the receiver that she remembered it was Ellen's birthday. They had planned to go to a matinee with Alice.

She would send them a note. Say she had been asked to stay behind after lunch. Ellen would understand.

She had never been to this teashop before. It was a teashop because they were there for tea, but it had a French name that made her feel clumsy.

There were eight or nine couples dotted throughout the room, using the striped wallpaper as a backdrop against which to arrange themselves, whispering behind ferns in brass pots.

Mr Ryan pulled out her chair, and the weight of something brushed her waist as he pushed it in again. It could have been the chair arm or it could have been the soft touch of his hand, and all through the business of menus and ordering and waiting for the waitress to leave, she wondered.

She looked around her – at the poorly executed sketches of London street scenes arranged on the walls, at the man with the toothbrush moustache at the next table, and at his brittle, bored companion. She concentrated on looking at these things because she wanted to look at him so badly it made her mouth dry. And when she did dare to look up, he was watching her already.

'I'm so very glad you agreed to come out with me today.' He leaned forward, just a little. 'I hope we are going to be very good friends.'

She blushed and, hating herself for blushing, asked him about the football match she knew he had played in the previous weekend.

As he talked, she watched his mouth slide from words to his easy generous smile, watched his fingers straighten the silverware and then rub at a mark on a saucer – and every time she glanced up, his eyes were on her, quite as though he cared what she was thinking.

The meal was indifferent: the bread dry, the tea stewed, the cakes made with margarine instead of butter. She crumbled a slice of sponge and left her plate untidy and did not protest when the waitress cleared before she had finished.

None of this – the food, the waitress, the sleepy pianist by the window – none of it mattered. What mattered was he and she alone without interruption and the building of this closeness between them. Everything was steady and sure and his gaze remained on her – until the end of the meal, until the entrance of a thin elegant woman in fox furs with a little dog in a jewelled collar. Then his gaze shifted away from Bea for the first time. For the first time his fingers faltered, his speech slowed.

Bea looked over to see the woman being seated – two waiters; tablecloth discarded as not clean enough; the snowy fall of the replacement cloth; a bowl of water for the dog.

She watched him watching her, as everyone in the room was watching her, and groped for something to say, something to bring him back to her.

'How are you finding it at Morley's, Mr Ryan? Satisfactory, I hope?'

He turned back to her, smiled. 'Much more than satisfactory. It's marvellous to have a job that means I'm able to get out and about, and meet so many people. It suits me very well indeed.'

'I don't think I've ever heard of a husband and wife working for the same firm before.' She tried to laugh. 'Isn't it a little . . . I should think most people would find it rather unusual.'

He laughed with her. 'I suppose it is.'

She couldn't help what came next – didn't want to hear at

all, but was quite unable to stop herself. 'You and your wife must be very close. I mean, you must get on terribly well to . . . you know, to live *and* work together.'

He looked down and bit his lip, and she waited. Then he said hesitantly, 'My wife is . . .' He shook his head. The woman with the dog was quite forgotten now.

She held her breath until his gaze came back up and his eyes looked straight into hers. 'I will be frank with you, Miss Cade. Things are . . . I have not had an easy time of it, these last few years.'

She realized that her hand was moving towards his, and before there was time to feel self-conscious, it was lying on his, and pressing gently.

'I am so sorry, Mr Ryan.'

He said nothing, just turned his hand under hers, revealing the pale vulnerable underside, and he closed his fingers around hers and tightened them. And that was an answer.

They sat like that for a moment, skin against skin, warm and steady despite the thud of her heart, despite the pulse running through her entire body.

But just like before, Bea was conscious of a third figure at the table – his wife: slender, faceless, watching.

He stroked her hand with his fingers – and it was so delicate and so gentle that her back arched, just a little, like a cat. He said, 'You must call me Tom. I am Tom to my friends.'

And she smiled and felt herself open like a flower in the heat of his smile, and she said only, 'Beatrice.'

'What a beautiful name.' His gaze danced over her face and her skin burned where it touched her. 'It suits you very well, you know.'

And then he said, 'Do you know the story of Dante?'

He talked about an Italian poet who had fallen in love with a girl named Beatrice. He pronounced it *Bea-ah-tree-chay*: this must be the Italian way.

He said, 'It was love at first sight – a love so powerful and so true that it inspired some of the most wonderful poetry in existence.'

He said, 'His love for her was so strong and so all-encompassing that it lasted for the rest of his life: even after his marriage, even after her death.'

Bea asked, 'So they were not married to one another?'

'Oh no – they both married other people. But their love was quite beyond that. It was something altogether purer.'

In the shadows, his wife blinked, and all the while Bea's hand lay in his and their faces were turned to one another.

Then the waitress came again, and they sprang apart although they were doing nothing wrong – both smiled awkwardly, but they were the same smiles and the same embarrassment, so somehow the awkwardness was there and yet not there.

The girl sniffed and asked if they wanted more tea, and he was already shaking his head.

'Just the bill, thank you,' and he gave the waitress *that* smile, so that her surliness melted and she nodded and blushed and blinked.

When she had gone and they were alone again, she and *Tom*, he ducked his head shyly and said, 'Miss Cade? Beatrice . . . ?'

And her name was so delightful in his voice, so sweet and full of promise that she almost missed the next part.

'Would you like to . . . my wife doesn't care for the cinema, and I'd very much like to see the new Edwin Greenwood picture. Would you like to see it with me? Perhaps one evening next week?'

And she was smiling and nodding before he had finished speaking. *Yes. Oh yes.*

As they took their seats, sinking down and falling back into the deep plush red, the lights dimmed and the music started up.

Tom took out his cigarette case and she leaned in to him and whispered, 'May I have one?'

She hoped that he would light hers himself – his lips on the paper leaving a faint warmth, a trace of moisture and his mouth – or even that he would light it from his, so that for a moment they might share the same heat. But he merely held out his case in the ordinary way, waited for her to take one and then struck a match. It flared and sucked in all the light and he was suddenly invisible. Just another body in the dark.

She bent and inhaled, then leaned back and watched as the screen flickered into life. The main feature, *Heartstrings*, was a film she had wanted to see for some time, and at first she tried to concentrate on the movement of the figures and the music. But little by little she began to be aware instead of the twin blue streams of smoke, and of him beside her. The soft hitch of his breathing. The rustle of fabric as he adjusted his position. The smell of his hair oil.

She let herself glance at him quickly, absorbing the memory of his profile, then closed her eyes and tasted the way that the light from the screen outlined his neat features: the straight nose, the curve of his mouth, the sweep of his eyelashes.

Then she heard his warm breath in her ear, and his whisper. 'Beatrice? Are you all right?'

Her eyes flew open and she turned her head and somehow their noses collided – and whatever she had imagined, it was never like this. Even through the sharp wet pain, she was laughing and he was staring at her and then, as she wiped the tears, she saw him smile. His smile was a wonderful gift that widened and let her in, until they were laughing together, laughing so hard that her stomach hurt. A man in front turned and shushed them – and somehow this stranger's frown, his cross beetling eyebrows, made the whole thing even funnier and she could not stop laughing even when Tom took her arm and reached for her coat. They picked their way through jutting knees and disapproving tuts towards the exit.

Then they were outside, and by the time she was conscious of the cold, the laughter had died to smiling ripples, to memories of something uncontrollable. She looked at Tom and his nose twitched, and it almost set her off again, but he stepped forward and she realized that his eyes were serious. His mouth – well, his mouth was always smiling, but she had never realized how soft it was, how soft and red, and how soft and sick her stomach felt. Then his mouth was on hers and there was no room for thought, just the taste of his lips, the rasp of his skin, his arms around her.

She was dimly aware that he had steered them away from the road, that they were in a doorway and she was pressed against something damp and rough and her hair was caught and pulling, but his body was firm and hot against hers, and his mouth was moving against hers. He was sighing and murmuring her name and it was so sweet and so wild on his lips that she opened hers in return. There was only heat and softness and the warm smell of him – and then his tongue was inside her mouth and she was trembling. She had to clutch at him and her stomach was turning over and over as though she was a child again on the shuggy boats on Tynemouth Longsands.

He pulled her closer and moved his hands under her coat and down her back. There were layers of cotton and silk between her skin and his, but she felt naked. Her whole being: tingling and heated, yielding and melting. This must be what love felt like.

This must be love.

10

Kate, May 1924

Every morning I wake with my skin and hair wet from the same nightmare. I make myself get up, pour out my washing water, lay out my clothes. And then I hold back my hair and I bend over the bowl, take a breath, push my face under. I make myself stay down there until the pictures behind my eyes are quite gone, and only then do I straighten up – gasping, red, raw.

I make breakfast for Judith, I comb and plait her hair, I button her coat and hold her to me. Then I brace myself, open the door – just a little, just enough for my body to fit in the gap. I ignore the rush and the shouts and the waving notebooks. I look beyond them to watch her walk down the front path, past all those eyes and elbows. Some of them glance at her but no one speaks to her directly. I wonder what I would do if they did.

I watch her from the hallway, half hidden from the outside, feel the protective weight of the door against my right shoulder, the solidity of the wall tight against my left hip. I watch her open the gate and turn into the road and although I tell myself every day that I will wait until she is out of sight this time, this is when I turn and jump back inside like a hunted animal into a hole.

Today, when I have closed the door, I press my back against it. I will have to leave for work shortly; I will also have to walk past all those eyes and voices and hands. But not quite yet.

I almost feel like I could fall asleep right here. I shut my eyes for a moment – and three sharp raps thud against my back and I cry out.

It is like that first reporter all over again. This time I back away down the hall and a lock of my hair slides from a pin and falls over my face. I wind it around my fingers, tight, unable to look away as Mrs Irvine pushes past me to open the door; as light floods into the hall, together with a babble of those hard voices, desperate to get inside.

And then, closer, I hear a low voice with a faint burr in it say, 'Good morning, madam. I'm here to see Mrs Ryan. Detective Chief Inspector Wild.'

The door opens wider and the safe small hallway is falling away and the morning is rushing in and there is a man: tall and dark against the light, with no face at all.

Then he comes forward and removes his hat and I see that he is really quite ordinary: sparse greying hair, a long mournful face. He has a neat grey moustache and beneath it, a narrow pale mouth.

I find my voice. 'I'm Mrs Ryan.'

'Good morning, Mrs Ryan. Might I have a word?'

His voice is soft, so soft that I almost have to lean in to hear him, but his eyes are sharp and watchful. He reminds me of a dog we had when I was a child: as he got old, he seemed to grow gentler, more placid. He would let us tease him and prod him and pull his fur – then there would come a moment where he would turn and growl and snap. Wild is like that dog. He is hiding his bite.

I hold out my hand and he shakes it, and it seems absurd that we are so polite, so civilized, in such a situation. This man has arrested my husband, has locked my husband up, would see my husband found guilty – and here I am leading the way to the staircase and trying to remember if I have washed up the breakfast things.

Mrs Irvine has paused in the hallway. 'Oh,' she says, and we both look at her. 'Oh, but do use my front room, Mrs Ryan. Save you both the trouble of going upstairs.'

I imagine her in the back parlour, a glass pressed to the wall, sweating with curiosity. 'You're very kind, Mrs Irvine, but I shouldn't dream of it. And besides, Mr Wild may need to look through Mr Ryan's things.'

I glance down at him, and see that he is watching me. There are creases around his eyes that make me think perhaps he is also aware of Mrs Irvine's motives, and that he is laughing at her. This should make me like him more, but I turn away and begin to climb again.

When I open the door, I notice a dirty cup and saucer; that the rug is not quite straight; that my hair is still hanging over my face. My hands twitch, but I walk directly to my usual chair in front of the fireplace. I sit and press my palms together, fold my fingers over.

Wild has a slight limp and favours his right leg. He stands in front of me, and for a moment, a little part of me, a little greenish-yellow dot of spite, wants to keep him standing. I hope his leg aches.

But I must think of Tom. 'Do sit down, Mr Wild.'

When he begins, it is not what I expect. He wants me to talk about myself.

'Tell me what you suspected, Mrs Ryan.'

I look at him. I wait.

'What did you think when you found the cloakroom ticket?'

I don't know how to begin.

The lines around his eyes soften. He must be used to people who do not talk.

He looks over at the mantlepiece. At the vase of dry and curling lilac stems. At our wedding photograph in its silver frame.

It was a warm morning, a lifetime ago. I look at Tom in his good suit, and at the girl beside him, barely out of the schoolroom, pink and shining and self-conscious in a column of silk and lace.

'How long have you been married, Mrs Ryan?'

I look at him, but there doesn't seem to be anything more to his question. 'Thirteen years.' I clear my throat. 'Thirteen years in August.'

The slipping silk under my fingers as I smoothed it; the tickle of lace at my throat; the smell of the orange blossoms Tom had bought me from the market, the stems still bloody-brown from the stallholder's fingers. He was standing in for his pal, Tom told me, for the man who sold bits of pigs from the stall across the way.

And Tom himself in a tight collar, the sheen of sweat and the stink of beer still on him from the night before, my brother standing by, holding his elbow to steady him.

Wild says, 'You must have been very young.'

I give him a tiny shrug. 'I'd known him before. He was . . . Tom knew my brother. They were at school together.'

'And you have one child?'

At once, I think of Billy, the way I always do when someone asks about my children.

I swallow. 'A daughter. She's eleven.' I won't have him thinking that's why we married.

He nods. 'I've got three myself.'

'Three?'

'Children. Two boys and a girl. They're hard work.'

No. I will not do this. I will not let him sneak his fingers inside my tight, careful edges and prise them open.

Suddenly, without any warning or change in tone, he says, 'Tell me why you went through your husband's pockets. What were you looking for?'

He leans forward a little. His eyes are narrowed. I almost expect to see his ears prick up and his nose twitch.

'What made you look in his pockets, Mrs Ryan?'

What do I tell him? How do I make him understand how it

was: Tom coming and going without warning, his manner odd and distracted? How do I make him understand what it's like to be married to a man like Tom?

I am always aware of other women: the glances, the whispers, the smoothing of hair and the biting of lips. I see their eyes pass over me and rest on him: often they do not even notice me, and if they do, I am not a threat. As far as they are concerned, I am merely an awkward fact.

It is not Tom's fault – it is simply how things are. And because of that, temptation has often fallen in his way.

But while he has succumbed – sometimes – he has always come back to me.

I know him. I understand him. And I have been a part of his life for so long that it is not possible to untangle us. We stood up together in church and made promises that wove us together. We have made two children between us. These things are for ever.

Until now. Until two months ago, when there was a knock on the door and I opened it, and there she was: standing in front of me, asking for Tom, blushing and afraid.

It was her fear that made me realize she was different. Her white face, her trembling mouth, and the way that Tom left with her and didn't come home for hours.

It's just Miss Cade. From work. It's just work.

But even after he came back and we went to bed, I could feel him lying awake beside me, staring into the dark.

How do I explain all of this to Wild?

Miss Cade wasn't like the soft pink girls who fluttered about him: flirting, giggling, hoping for attention. She was pale and drawn and she looked exhausted. Her nose and forehead were shiny; her hat was crammed on anyhow. Her voice shook when she said his name and there was an ugly flush on her neck. And whatever she said to him, it was enough to give us both

a sleepless night and to make him hug Judith tightly to him
before she left for school the next morning.

For days he was odd, distant. I would look up from my book
or sewing to find him staring at me. But every time I asked him
what was wrong, he simply shook his head or left the room.

I thought that things with Miss Cade were more serious.

I thought perhaps he had fallen in love.

I look at Wild now. He clears his throat. 'Your husband did it,
Mrs Ryan. What they're accusing him of. He is guilty.'

I shake my head. 'No.'

'I'm sorry. I know this is hard for you, Mrs Ryan. I know
you don't want to hear this . . .'

I put my hands over my eyes and he falls silent. Then he
speaks again, more softly.

'If you know any more about any of this, Mrs Ryan, it's best
you tell me now and get it over with. Then we won't need to
come back.'

I hear the threat lurking beneath those words, and the
thought of him coming back with others overwhelms me.
The thought of men coming into this house, with their uniforms and their helmets, their heavy boots on the stairs, going
through all our things, mine and Judith's. Their great dirty
hands on our clothes, smearing greasy fingerprints on my scent
bottles and on Judith's books, her dolls, her clothes. The idea
of Judith's bewildered tears, her questions – *Why are they here?*
Why can't you make them stop? – is what finally breaks me.

'Get out. Just get out get out bloody well *get out*!'

He raises his hands, he gets to his feet, and he leaves.

My mouth is open and dry and my heart is pounding, and
whether it is with fear or fury, I cannot tell.

11

Bea, October 1923

Tom came back a week later.

For Bea, it was a week of rising early to curl her hair, of dashing to the ladies' washroom every hour to check that her nose wasn't shiny. There were no more appointments in the diary, and she could hardly ask Mr Morley when he was expected.

She was reprimanded by Miss Shepherd for daydreaming – and for the first time in her life, she did not care.

She watched Caroline and Jessie giggle together, heads bowed over magazines and dress patterns and secrets. Jessie wore a new blouse and began to wear her hair differently.

Bea looked over at them, bent over something on Caroline's desk, and she saw only his profile and his mouth, felt only his arms around her.

She watched them; she thought of him – and beneath wool and tweed and satin, she trembled.

It was a Tuesday when he returned: an ordinary dull afternoon of the kind that dragged. It was after three and she had given up on him coming that day and was wondering if she should buy some chocolates on the way home, or seek out Ellen or Alice and plan an outing for the weekend. Something to make her feel that the day hadn't been entirely wasted.

Then he – *Tom* – was there. He said good afternoon to the room, then looked around, winked at Jessie – and at last his eyes rested on her, and his gaze soaked warm and pink all through her until she had to look away.

Mr Morley came out of his office and Tom moved towards him. They met by her desk and shook hands. Bea tried to focus on what she was typing, on anything but the sound of his voice and the memory of his mouth on hers.

Tom turned so that he had his back to her. This was a little easier: that grey jacket, those narrow shoulders, could almost belong to anyone. He clasped his hands behind his back while Mr Morley spoke. She looked at those square close-clipped nails, at the white scar on the second finger of his right hand. She remembered how those fingers had pressed into her skin as he held her close. How insistent they had been. How bruising.

Then, as she watched, one of those slim hands opened and a little folded paper fell onto her desk and landed softly, in the space of a single shallow breath.

Without thinking, without looking up, she slid it into her sleeve and stared hard at the typewriter keys, until she heard Mr Morley's door close and could retreat to the ladies'.

Come for a drink later. I'll wait for you at the entrance to Great Winchester at half-past five.

No names. If the note was found later in the wastepaper basket, or dropped carelessly in the stairwell, there was nothing to link it to either of them.

And so it went on: two weeks, three.

They had never talked about what was happening between them, and she was afraid of all the things she didn't know.

Did he have this kind of closeness with other women? Had he once had this with his wife?

Despite herself, despite Lil Tearney and Theo Ingram, she

had thought again of talking to Ellen and Alice about him. But she did not know how to begin the conversation with them.

She had come to realize that they each had a clear role in their friendship: hers was to respond to Ellen's bold questions, to Ellen's brilliance, to the way that Ellen twisted every conversation until it was wrung out into an argument. And Alice's part was to soothe them afterwards, to make them laugh or to bring them back to the practicalities of where they would have lunch or how to get clothes dry in the winter.

Bea couldn't make Tom fit, no matter how much she wanted to.

We are an *us*, she wanted to say.

But beyond that, what else would she say to them?

When she was with him he was splendid: solid, whole, the maleness of him apparent in the way he walked and held a glass or a cigarette; the way he always knew what to order or how to charm shop girls and flower-sellers.

But away from him, he was a series of images in her mind, like a line of photographs. A single dark eye, long-lashed, knowing; a distant figure, striding ahead in the park; the smooth curve of his cheek; a certain way of smiling or pronouncing a word.

'Dear girl. Dearest darling silliest *darlingest* girl.' He was foolish with her in a way she could not describe to anyone: a teasing, familiar way that was born out of his confidence that she would follow his lead.

Surely this was what made the intimacy between them different. This must be something quite apart from the silly flirtations he had with other girls; different, even, from the duty he had to his wife.

She would never be able to make Ellen or Alice understand. She had been invisible her whole life, and now she was seen – and not only seen, which after all is one-sided, but *understood*.

It would be impossible ever to explain this, and she began to keep her distance from the others. She treasured the knowledge of him, and now she came to treasure the secret fact of him, and how that secret beat close and hot in her blood.

One evening they were to meet under the clock in the station. She was a little early and stepped back until she could see the clock face. She waited impatiently as the minute hand ticked around. As it crept towards the half-hour, she couldn't help it – she began to scan every face beneath every hat brim as her stomach rolled and tightened.

She willed herself to stand up straight, to keep her shoulders back, her mouth closed and full, her face expressionless. But she heard the 5.42 to Ipswich announced, and then the 5.49 to Peterborough. She looked up and watched the minute hand inch towards the eight, and then towards the nine.

How long should she wait? Should she . . . There he was. In the midst of currents of rushing commuters, the crackle of loudspeaker announcements and the deep bellow of engines, he smiled as he walked towards her. Now they were the only two points that mattered, drawn together by a thread pulled tight. She could not hold back: she came forward, all the way into his arms. Felt the familiar bulk of him beneath his overcoat, the straight lines and sharp creases, the ripple of muscle at his back. He bent towards her and for a moment she smelled the heat of him and the perspiration and the spicy sweetness of his hair oil, felt his mouth on hers, and the press of his hands on her skin, then she leaned back to look up at him.

She said, smiling, 'I was beginning to wonder if you were coming.'

He frowned. 'Why?'

'Well, you're a little late.'

'Late?' He looked up at the clock. 'It's only just quarter to.'

'But we said half-past.'

He smiled at her. 'We said quarter to six, silly.'

She opened her mouth to reply and he kissed her again, hard, dizzying, and pulled her into him. His hot breath on her ear. 'I'd hardly forget this, would I?'

She had checked her reflection before she left the office. She was brushed, smoothed, powdered, perfumed. Her nails were filed and buffed, her eyebrows shaped. Her hair gleamed and fell fashionably to her jaw. Despite all this, when she looked at herself in the mirror, she saw the things Tom must see: the lines at the corners of her eyes and mouth; an old scar at her hairline; a blemish on her chin that powder could not hide.

But when he kissed her, everything else fell away. The rest was nothing: there was only his mouth, his hand on her neck, the warmth and the assurance of him.

She looked up at him and said, 'Not here, darling, not with so many people around,' but what she wanted to tell him, with her arms tight around him and her skin hot and her eyes surely bright, was that she wished they were alone. She wished for the smallest, meanest room, if it would give them privacy and time to be together, silent and close.

But in the here and now, she took Tom's arm and they began to walk. Along Liverpool Street, down Blomfield Street, against the flow of flannel and gabardine and tired faces hurrying for trains and trams. They turned left and then right, her arm still in his, their bodies pressed close and their steps slow and in time.

And then they were round into the gentle curve of Finsbury Circus where the pavements were almost empty and they could slow their pace further. It had rained that afternoon and the air was soft and green.

Tom stopped to light a cigarette and she said suddenly, 'I wish we could go away together. Just to be alone for a few days.'

He exhaled a plume of smoke. 'Where to?'

'Somewhere by the sea. France, perhaps. Oh, I know – the Riviera.'

She had seen a picture in the *Post* of the blue sea, the stretch of sand so white you could imagine the bright heat that had bleached it.

'Imagine it, darling. A boarding house, somewhere no one knows us. A room of our own. We'd eat those long sticks of bread for breakfast, with fresh butter and jam. Sitting by the open window, looking out over the beach and the promenade.'

Tom laughed. 'And what would we do all day?' His voice had the sing-song rhythm of make-believe. She smiled at him.

'We'd bathe in the sea. Read. Walk. Eat wonderful food. Drink wine.'

He laughed again. 'Such decadence!'

She looked up at him and felt the glow that came from making him happy. 'Or we could go to Egypt. See the wonders of the ancient world. We might dig up gold and jewels and never have to go into an office again!'

But even as he smiled down at her, that inward distracted expression came over his face – and there was his wife again, watching from the shadows, reminding him of responsibility and duty and the last train home.

Bea felt a sudden swell of anger. Couldn't she let them have this? Couldn't she give them one little moment of imagined happiness?

It must have been then that she began to hate his wife.

She held off as long as she could, but in the end the wife was a scar that she had to pick and probe.

It was an unseasonably warm Saturday, and they were walking in the park on a sun-drenched expanse of grass, amid shining copper trees, the white Regency buildings rising around them. Like wedding cake, she thought, and nestled closer.

Tom patted her hand and she thought of how they must look together; their arms linked, their steps matched. She thought of all the times she had walked in this park, on this very path, on her own or with Ellen or Alice or Annie – and now she watched the women walking in pairs or alone, as she had once walked. She watched their small steps, their quiet conversation: they were sparrows among the peacocking couples.

She glanced sideways at Tom, at the half-smile playing about his lips, at his gleaming hair, at his upright posture.

But there alongside them was a third figure: slender, graceful, her shining black hair snaking about her shoulders as she also turned her head to look at Tom.

Bea tried to focus on him – on the weight of his arm against hers and on the press of his hip – but the idea of *her* swelled in her mind until the thought was too heavy to hold and she had to let it go.

'Tom. You said once . . .'

He waited.

'You said that things had been difficult for you.' She swallowed. 'You said – hinted – that there were difficulties . . . in your marriage.'

She felt him flinch, but he said nothing.

'Your wife.' She took a breath. Made herself go on. 'What is your wife like?'

And now he stopped. When she gathered the courage to look at him, he was staring off into the distance.

'You're very different, Beatrice.'

And he lit a cigarette and walked on as though the subject was closed.

She caught him up and slipped her arm through his again. 'Why did you get married?'

He sighed then, but he didn't stop walking.

He's going to tell me that he married her for love. That he still loves her.

She held her breath.

I can't bear it. I can't bear to hear that from him.

For twenty paces he said nothing at all, just stared ahead at the line of trees and let the silence grow between them.

Then he stopped again. Dropped her arm and ran his fingers through his hair.

'We were very young.' He bit his lip and looked out over the river. 'And I married her . . . I married her because she needed me. She still needs me. She has . . .' He looked at her and shook his head. 'She has none of your independence. Your spirit.'

'I'm . . .'

'You're rather a solitary figure, aren't you?' He reached out and traced the line of her jaw, so delicately that she shivered. 'Do you know who you remind me of?'

He went on without waiting for her answer. 'You put me in mind of Jane Eyre.'

His hand still against her face, he said, 'It's a strange comparison, I know, but your courage reminds me of hers. You're very brave, darling. Not many women would manage such a lonely life. Not like you have.'

He let his hand fall but his eyes were still on her, still holding her. 'I admire you so much, Beatrice. I feel so . . .' He shook his head. 'I have never felt this way before.'

She tasted the impact of his words just as he bent to kiss her. It was like a first kiss all over again, tentative and trembling – but weighted now with this new expression of feeling.

Then he led her into the light, across the grass, towards the bandstand, where the band was playing a waltz and a crowd had gathered. He turned to her again, a smile playing at the corners of his mouth. He let go of her, bowed and held out his hand.

If he had been any other man, she would not have been able to step forward, not in front of all these people. But this was Tom. And so she looked into his eyes and reached for him again. He took her in his arms and they began to dance, slowly at first, and then faster and faster until they were spinning, until she was dizzy, until the only still point was his face. If he let her go, she would fall.

He smiled at her fear and flung his head back, his face turned up to the sun. He spun faster still as the music leapt and swelled above their heads, as he moved her and swung her around and around. She looked at him, gilded and magnificent – all she had to do was hold tight and let him lead.

And as they danced, thoughts of his wife moved further and further away. She grew more and more distant until Bea was able to persuade herself that she was quite gone.

But she was not gone, not entirely. Bea found herself thinking of Tom's wife more frequently. Her curiosity was like a splinter at the centre of her. She worried and worried at it, until eventually she knew she had to see Mrs Ryan for herself.

Mr Morley always told them never to throw anything away. Tom's letter applying for the job, and a copy of Miss Shepherd's reply suggesting a date and time for his interview, would be filed somewhere.

She arranged a half-day's holiday, and went into the office early that morning. It took her almost twenty minutes – and she heard Miss Shepherd arrive downstairs just as she located the correct file – but just in time, she found what she was looking for.

There wasn't time to read the letter, only to scribble down the address on a scrap of paper and tuck it into her sleeve. All through the moments of greeting Miss Shepherd and discussing the weather and the delays on the District Railway, Bea felt her heart pounding and pounding. She had his address next to her skin.

At one-thirty, she put the cover back on her typewriter, said goodbye to the others, and went to the washroom. Combed her hair, tried her hat three times before she got the angle just right. Then she powdered her nose, straightened her blouse, rubbed the toe of each shoe with her handkerchief until they shone.

She got off the train at Richmond, checked the map in the station. Then she turned right and began to walk.

Since coming to London, Bea had spent her half-holidays exploring the West End and the City, but she had never been as far as the surrounding counties. Richmond was unlike anywhere she had ever visited. The houses were red-brick, solid, with large windows and distance and privacy between each one, and neat trimmed gardens or gravelled drives in front.

Everywhere was fresh gleaming paint and gloss-green hedges – very different to the dry and yellowing plane trees on Guilford Street or the ancient oaks and rambling undergrowth in the London parks. She saw a nanny pushing a perambulator, her brown and white uniform crisp and immaculate, and a grocer's boy in a neat cap and tunic carrying a box to the back door of a house, his shoes crunching softly on the raked gravel. Other than that, the streets were empty, everything silent and satisfied.

She turned onto his street, and it was the same as the others – and yet not the same. This was the pavement he walked on every day, that was the door he touched, those were the windows from which he looked out onto the world – and behind those windows were the rooms where he lived his other life.

The office in Sunbury kept the same hours as the City office; both shut at five. Bea had time to kill before Mrs Ryan would be home from work. She walked aimlessly until she saw a signpost pointing to Kew Gardens. Some part of her mind registered the beauty of the autumn colours, the clear cool air, the rippling joyous birdsong. But as she sat among all the red and golden glory, she knew that the smooth and lovely face of the day hid an entire world of ugliness. There was pride and greed. Here lay envy and wrath.

She arrived back in Pagoda Avenue as dusk was falling. There was an empty house opposite his – a house with blank uncurtained windows, brown leaves blown and rotting in the corners of the garden, a faded TO LET sign at the gate. Bea slipped into the driveway and stood in the shadows of the peeling porch.

As she waited, she was trembling. She did not want to see her – this woman who had borne Tom's child and who had trapped Tom into marriage when they were too young to understand what love meant. And yet she ached to see her. She needed to know what kept him with her.

It seemed to Bea that a long time passed before she heard footsteps approaching. The neat click of dainty heels slowing to turn into the driveway opposite. A light high voice humming a tune that Bea did not recognize.

Bea peered out and saw the back of a figure on the doorstep: a neat cloche hat, a beautifully tailored coat, and the slim calves beneath.

As she watched, the door opened and closed. A moment later, a light came on upstairs, and Bea saw bookshelves on one wall, the top of a vase or a jug at the window. Then someone moving about the room: a long-sleeved, rather old-fashioned blouse; dark hair, pinned up. The figure approached the window and for the first time, Bea saw her face. Pale, blurred, absorbed. She couldn't make out the features, but the mouth was moving: she must still be singing – carelessly, unthinkingly happy to be at home, happy to be waiting for her husband.

Bea saw too the rise of her small hand as she reached for the curtains, as she pulled them closed, as she shut out the rest of the world.

This was the image Bea carried home: that small hand, the sweep of her white sleeve, the tiny flash of gold on her finger.

This was the image she saw as she lay in bed, staring into the dark: the whiteness of that hand, resting on Tom's hand. On his face, his hair, on his body.

She clenched her fists against it and closed her eyes – but it came again and again. That flash of gold. That ownership.

12

Bea, November 1923

The following weekend, Bea went to the park with Tom again. It was a blue-bright day: surely one of the last sunny days of the year.

As they walked, Bea was aware that she was thinking of her body differently. For the first time in her life, her body was no longer private. Tom knew how it moved; he knew the feel and the shape of it under his hands. She had become more conscious of the swollen parts and the looseness; of the bumps and scars and flakes of skin; the tickle of ingrown hairs, the bristles and the sweat. And she was more conscious of other women, women who were smooth and lovely, their skin as white and pure as marble, and everything beneath precise and taut and controlled.

Bea's body was uncomfortably present: it pushed her skirts outward, it filled the roomy blouses she wore because the sleek modern dresses she longed for were designed for narrow, boyish girls. Girls like Caroline and Jessie and Mrs Ryan: girls who were barely there.

They walked as far as the lake, and she suggested they take a boat out. Tom rowed them round to the other side of the island, away from the strolling crowds and the curious eyes, then tucked the oars in, letting the boat drift. For a little moment, the sun beat down on their skin as the water rocked them, and the moorhens chirruped from the shallows. Then he leaned forward to kiss her – and this time it was different. He pressed her back and back until they lay together in the bottom of the boat and his hands were at her waistband, pulling her blouse free, fumbling with buttons.

She took his hands in hers and held them while he kissed her. 'Tom, no. Not here. Not . . . I'm not . . .'

He only kissed her harder, pressing her back against the rough wood so that she had to shift her weight. His mouth was at her ear and he murmured, 'I need . . .' – and then somehow he was lying on top of her and her legs were either side of his body. He kissed her face and her mouth and her heartbeat quickened as his tongue touched hers, as he groaned. And his weight shifted in turn so that he was heavy against her, *there*, kissing her so that the pressure grew to an ache and a new kind of urgency, so that she was trembling. He murmured again: 'I've never done anything like this before, but with you . . .' He kissed her again and again. 'With you, it's different, darling.'

But she pushed him away gently and then, when he did not stop, more firmly. She sat up and there was his voice, hoarse and low.

'Beatrice?'

She did not trust herself to speak – merely shook her head. He said her name again, drawing it out as he ran his finger along her arm, up to her jaw, stroking her cheek and then rubbed her mouth with his thumb.

'Beatrice. Darling girl. You make me so . . . you make me want to be with you.'

She stared at him dumbly and he reached for her again – and his hand on her thigh, sliding the hem of her skirt up, brought her back to herself.

'Tom, no –' pushing him away – 'we can't. Please. No,' until eventually he sat back, frowning, running his hands over his hair, replacing his hat.

She said, 'Tom, I'm sorry' – and he shook his head and picked up the oars again.

'No, I'm sorry.' He was beginning to pull, heading back to the bank. 'I should have realized that you . . .' He shook his head again, then let the oars drop and reached out to stroke her face.

'Sometimes I can't help myself. It's like we were meant to be together, you and I.'

She stared into his eyes. His hand, warm on her cheek, was the only thing she could feel. She raised her own hand and placed it over his and held it there. She held it as tightly as if she was drowning.

One afternoon a letter arrived at the office addressed to Mr Morley.

Bea watched Miss Shepherd tear it open with her ivory-handled paper knife before she brought it over.

'This is from the Sunbury office,' she said – and at first, Bea did not see anything in this. 'Would you double-check the calculations, Miss Cade, and draft a response. It needs to go by the four o'clock post.'

There were two sheets of figures and a short covering note advising that the value of orders placed by this firm had decreased by 11 per cent in real terms over the past year – and also that payment was consistently late. The note suggested that the account be closed and a final invoice be sent, and Mr Simpson had written *AGREED* by this, and signed and dated it in his neat print. The note was initialled *K. R.* – and still Bea did not see. She drafted a reply and went back to ask Miss Shepherd to whom the reply should be addressed.

'Well, to Mr Simpson,' she said, barely looking up, as though Bea was lacking in common sense. And when Bea held out the cover note, she only sighed and said, 'Yes, the *note* was written by Mrs Ryan, but the *figures* have clearly been drawn up by Mr Simpson.'

Mrs Ryan.

Bea stared down at the sloping black writing. At the place where the ink had begun to fade on one line and then came through freshly darker on the next, where the pen had been dipped in ink between that line and this – and that sudden certain knowledge of something *she* had done, something commonplace and practical, something Bea could see as clearly as her own hand, made her catch her breath.

'Miss Cade?'

This piece of paper was something *she* had touched. Bea ran her fingers over the corners, over the folds where *her* fingers had surely touched it.

'*Miss Cade!*'

'I beg your pardon, Miss Shepherd. I was—'

'You were wool-gathering, Miss Cade, and you don't have time to daydream. Albert will be here shortly to collect the letters. Do *concentrate*, please.'

Bea sat down at her desk, her heart pounding. She typed automatically, the image of that *K. R.* bold and clear before her, and finished the letter just as Albert came in. Miss Shepherd tutted, signalled to him to wait, then read it through, signed and blotted it, and slid it into the envelope that sat ready.

And it was gone: Bea need not think about any of it again – about that writing, about that pen, that moment where it had been dipped and filled and had started up once more.

There was nothing left of her in the office, save the folded cover note on Bea's desk, and that was easily tucked away and hidden in a drawer – and, at the end of the day when Miss Shepherd was in the lavatory and everyone else had gone, slipped into Bea's handbag, to be taken out in the quiet of her own room that evening: taken out and torn into tiny scraps and scattered on the fire. They were turned to ashes in an instant, and then not a single trace remained of her at all.

*

It was two weeks until Christmas, and Tom hadn't been to the office for almost a month.

When Jessie mentioned it, Caroline replied, 'Mr Ryan is very busy with customers. We always have more orders in the run-up to Christmas. You'll find that out when you've been here a little longer.'

'I bet he's the sort who shops early for Christmas.' Jessie sighed. 'I expect he'll buy Mrs Ryan something *lovely*. Jewellery, maybe' – and Bea tried to stop listening, tried to block them out.

But they went on. 'Or perfume.'

'Mmm. Something terribly *intimate*, anyway.'

Bea met Jane for lunch. Her sister had written to say that she would be up in London for the day.

> *Why don't we meet at the Maison Lyons on Shaftesbury*
> *Avenue, just for a change? I thought we might go somewhere*
> *a bit nicer, as it's Christmas.*

The restaurant was horribly crowded, and it took Bea some time to find Jane, who sat half hidden by a pillar and surrounded by bright parcels. Bea noticed a new coat – fur-trimmed – laid over one of the empty seats.

As she rose to kiss her, Jane said, 'I really don't know how I shall get that lot home on the train.'

'Can't Charles meet you with the car?'

'Goodness, no. I wouldn't dream of asking him. He's terribly busy at the moment.'

The menus arrived, and Jane leaned forward and patted her hand. 'My treat. As it's Christmas.'

Then she said, as she always did, 'I really don't know how you manage in London, with prices like these.'

And this time, Bea said, 'I manage.'

Jane shook her head. 'Well, you must be earning good money.'

When they had ordered, Jane fidgeted with the cutlery, lining up the knife and fork, turning the spoon so that the head pointed left.

Then she looked up and said quickly, 'We wondered – well, I wondered.' Was she blushing? 'I wondered if you'd like to come for Christmas. To us. To spend some time with Charles and the children.'

'*Oh.*' And for a moment, it was everything Bea had imagined.

'It will be quiet, of course: just the four of us. And Helen's fiancé. His parents may drop in for a drink on Christmas Eve. And there'll be—'

'Jane. That's kind of you. But . . . I can't.'

'You can't?'

'I'm sorry.'

'What are . . . do you have other plans? You're surely not going to spend Christmas alone?'

'Oh, no. No, I . . . I mean, yes, I have plans.'

And she blushed, a hot tell-tale blush that rose from her neck and flooded all the way up to her forehead.

Jane's eyes widened. 'Bea, are you . . . have you met someone? A man, I mean?'

Bea dropped her gaze. Was quite unable to stop the smile breaking out. 'I . . . well, yes. Yes, I have.'

When she looked up, Jane was smiling at her. A proud, sisterly smile. 'Oh, Bea, how wonderful. Will you be spending Christmas with his people?'

'He . . . yes. Well, probably.'

She frowned. 'So you don't have any definite plans?'

'He . . .'

'Has he actually invited you for Christmas?'

'He will. I'm sure he will. He's just . . .'

'Just what?'

Oh God, why was she unable to lie to her? It had always been like this: Jane pushing and probing, she twisting in her seat to avoid her questions.

'He's . . . he's not in a position to.'

'He's not in a position to invite you to his *home*?'

'He's . . . no. I don't know. I'm sure he wants to spend it with me. But . . . he may not be able to.'

Her face was burning. She stared down at her cup, at her hands around it. At her bitten nails.

A new tone entered her sister's voice. 'Why not?'

'He . . .' She made herself look up. 'He just can't. Anyway. Tell me what you've bought for—'

'Why can't he invite you for Christmas?' She sounded exactly like the thirteen-year-old Jane who had stormed into their bedroom and demanded to know *where* was the length of ribbon she had bought the day before.

'Bea. Is he . . . he's not married?' Jane had a foolish smile on her face. One that said, *I know this is impossible.* One that said, *Tell me I have this all wrong.*

Bea looked away. 'It's not what you think.'

'Beatrice.' Jane's voice was hushed. Horror-struck. 'How *could* you? Bea, you *must* end this.'

'I'm—'

'You can't see him again. Surely you can see that?' She leaned forward. 'What were you thinking? You must write to him. Today. Tell him you can't . . .'

Bea reached out and clutched her wrist. 'Jane, listen. I love him. And he loves me. His wife is—'

Jane snatched her arm away and actually put her hands to her ears. 'I don't want to hear this. I *cannot* hear this.'

Then she dropped them into her lap and stared at Bea. 'What on earth are you doing? This is so . . . it's so self-indulgent.

You're not a character in a book, Bea – this is a choice you have made. Have you even considered what people will think?' She shook her head. 'I can't understand you. I can't even listen to this. It's . . . it's all wrong.'

She opened her bag with shaking hands, took out a ten-shilling note and dropped it on the table. She did not look at Bea. She pushed her chair back.

'Jane, please. I . . .'

But she had gathered up her coat and her parcels, and she was gone.

What kind of future do you think I have without him, Jane?

It's not just the fact of him, or even the way he makes me feel.

It's me – who I am, and what I have without him.

I am earning good money, but I cannot know how long it will last. And lately I have begun to notice young girls on the street, and on the Underground. Girls with smooth skin and a brisk step. Girls with ambition and hope.

They work hard. They smile more. They brighten up the place.

While women like me – women with no husband and no security, women for whom all of this matters – we are always afraid.

There is an invisible tribe of us: women who each live in one little room. We wash up our own cups and saucers, and we rinse through our own stockings and underwear in the basin in the corner.

And as we grow older, we grow more afraid, until sometimes it feels as though we are merely waiting for the axe to fall. For the pitying glances, the whispers behind hands. For the words 'Could I have a moment, please?' and a brown envelope with a week's wages.

And after that, what then? How easy do you think it is to find work as you get older, as you become less attractive and less efficient?

It is not so difficult to picture doors closing in my face; to imagine pursed lips and head-to-toe glances, or increasingly shabby clothes and growing desperation.

It is not so difficult to see how respectability and dignity could slip through one's fingers.

Can you imagine what that life would look like? Growing accustomed to one cheerless room, to a cold hearth, to penny buns for lunch every day and making the tea leaves stretch to another cup. Having to walk to work on all but the wettest days, because the money saved might mean the difference between a new pair of shoes and a bad winter cold – and falling ill would mean no pay at all, which would mean falling behind on everything.

I don't think you can imagine any of this, Jane. You have your large house and your rich husband, your car and your furs and your allowance – and if anything were to happen to Charles, no doubt he has left you well provided for. You can't imagine what poverty might be like – even how it might feel to fear poverty – but this is what a future without security looks like.

Is that what you want for me?

Is that the future you would choose for your sister, when there is another future already laid out waiting for me, smiling and holding out his hand to me?

Bea was so tired of it all – the fear, the feeling of being odd, of being an outsider, of being not quite *right*. And she was tired of the loneliness, of carrying it around like a thick shawl, trailing it behind her, feeling the weight of it. The shame of it: her skin prickling with the awareness of it and knowing that the worst of it was that others could see it. It clung to her like dirt, like a foul smell she couldn't wash away.

Just once, she wanted something different. She wanted flushed cheeks, frost-sparkling fur, roasting chestnuts. She wanted dancing firelight, the smell of pine needles, the thrill of wrapped parcels. She wanted to do all the things she had dreamed of doing when she had been a child imagining adulthood and freedom: to stay awake all night, talking and laughing and sharing secrets – then to stay in bed all day and make a nest of blankets and pillows, and fill the hot hollow centre with books and chocolates and warm and tender kisses. She wanted always to be warm.

She imagined what Christmas could be: she and Tom. Closing the curtains and shutting out the world, shutting out ideas of light and dark and night and day: eating roast potatoes for breakfast, drinking goblets of golden wine at eleven, dipping mince pies in brandy and cream for lunch.

I am owed, *Jane. I am owed this – and I want to wallow in the delicious forbidden surfeit of it all.*

But Tom had not written or telephoned – and still he did not come.

13

Kate, June 1924

June is salt. The weather grows warmer and I move through the days sluggishly, damp at the temples and at the places where my limbs meet my body, daydreaming about rain and cool water.

When I look in the glass, I see the face of a stranger: grey and drawn. There are new lines, new hollows under my eyes.

Judith sees everything. She sees how helpless I am, and how afraid. She sees the shadows under my eyes; that I cannot eat; that I forget what I am doing halfway through doorways, halfway to reaching for things on shelves.

What she does not see is love. Love for Tom. Love for her. Or perhaps she does see it and doesn't think it's important, weighed against everything else – or she doesn't care. She is young enough to take love for granted.

I try not to think about Tom or the future, or about *what if*. I am too frightened to think anything beyond today: this cup of tea, this loose thread, that meal cooked, this day endured. I have come to picture the days as a kind of rocking motion – do *this* and then *that*, get through today in the office and Judith's endless questions at the tea table, get through the washing-up and the ironing and the mending – and *then* you can lie down in the dark where you don't have to pretend.

I am balancing it all, I think, when a letter comes from Tom.

*

I watch for the post each morning – ever since Judith opened a letter from one of the newspapers offering fifty pounds for my story, and begged me to write to them if it would help her father.

How can I explain to her how I feel about having my name and photograph in the paper? The thought of being stared at and talked about and judged by strangers is like having my skin peeled back and the raw underneath put on display. I can't tell her that might be the final straw for Mrs Irvine, and then we would have to find somewhere new to live, on top of everything else.

I pick the envelope up off the mat and see the return address at the same time as I hear a scream from Judith's bedroom.

I am running up the stairs before I have time to think what might be wrong – then I am at her door, imagining a trapped finger or a wasp sting. What I do not expect is to find Judith curled on her bed, white-faced, her hand pressed against her mouth, tears in her eyes.

'Mummy, I'm dying. Help me. I'm dying' – and she points to the floor so that I see, beside the bed, her discarded drawers and the blood at the crotch.

'Oh love, no. No – it's all right. It's all right.' I feel the slow slide of relief at the same time as I am shocked. She's only eleven years old.

'What is it? What's wrong with me?'

'Nothing. Nothing is wrong, my love.' I take her in my arms, kiss the top of her head, rock her back and forward.

'I'm sorry, love. I should have told you, but I didn't think it would happen so soon. It didn't happen to me till I was nearly fifteen.'

'But what is it?'

I explain it to her – the blood that means she will be able to have a child of her own one day.

I tuck a lock of hair behind her ear. 'It's perfectly natural. It happens to all women.'

'But I don't want a baby! And it *hurts*.' Her indignation is so furious that I have to hide a smile.

'I know. I know it does. And of course you don't want a baby now, but you will one day. When you're older and have a husband and a home of your own. This is your body's way of preparing you for it.'

'But why now? Why does it have to happen *now*?'

'I don't know, love. We don't get to choose when it happens.'

'So now this is . . . what happens now?'

'Well, this happens. Every month. Unless you're expecting a baby.'

'*Every* month?'

'Until you're quite an old lady. Older than me, at any rate.'

'What do I do?'

Her hands flap, and I show her the rags: how to fold them, how to rinse them out.

'Can't you do it?'

Years of dirty nappies. Of stains, dried in: mud, egg, milk. And now this. I bite the inside of my cheek so hard I can taste my own blood.

'You can manage.' I clear my throat, try to make my voice softer. 'You're nearly grown up now. You don't need me.'

But she has already turned away. I have got it wrong again.

And when I bring her up a hot-water bottle and a cup of sugary tea, she pretends to be asleep. Even when I tuck the blankets around her, she keeps her eyes closed. They flicker under her eyelids and give her a sly appearance.

I pick up her bloodstained drawers, go back downstairs. The stains are dried now. Brownish.

If I were a different kind of mother, this would be a day for celebration. My daughter, becoming a woman. But she's still so young.

I push the drawers into the kitchen stove, prod them with the poker until they are deep in the fire. They burn with a sweetish smell and I close the door.

Then I pour another cup of tea, sit at the table, and feel something rustle. I don't remember putting Tom's letter in my pocket, but here it is.

He begins by asking why I haven't sent the money or the clothes he asked for, through Mr Edgerton.

> *I cannot buy cigarettes. I am only able to write this because I borrowed some paper and ink. I cannot even afford newspapers, Katie – I have to rely on Edgerton bringing them to me.*

After all these weeks, he startles me. He has become the name in Mr Edgerton's telegrams, the idea of Tom, and the face in the photographs on the mantlepiece rather than my flesh-and-blood husband. Reading his words, I can hear his voice again. I can see that trick he has of twisting his mouth as he talks. I can feel the rasp of his cheek when he kisses me. All of it comes rushing back – the smell of his hair oil, the scar on his earlobe, the way his left eye droops a little.

He encloses a visiting order, tells me to come soon. Tuesdays and Wednesdays would suit him best, but I must come soon and bring money. He sends his love to Judith, tells me he misses us both. He signs it *Your Loving Husband*.

The prison is a great dark square against the pale sky. It is silent all around – no one stops outside to talk and the traffic creeps past – but inside everything echoes and clangs. For all the cold stone, it is like being inside a cast-iron bath.

I hand over the visiting order but they barely glance at it

before they take my bag and poke through it, raking and rustling and only pausing when they find the envelope.

'What's this?'

They don't wait for an answer; they tear it open, count the
notes inside.

'It's for my husband. He asked me to bring him money – for
newspapers and cigarettes and things.'

'You can't give him money. Not directly. Didn't they tell
you? The money comes to us and we make a record of it, then
he tells us what he needs.'

'I don't understand. He said to—'

'You can't give him money.'

The man's face is as round and cold as the moon. He does
not meet my eyes.

I have no choice. I give him the money and he takes me to
Tom.

The visiting room is like a church hall: draughty and smelling of boiled vegetables and carbolic soap. There are rows of
tables and chairs, a low rumble of voices that goes round the
walls and up to the high ceiling.

Tom is in the middle: when I ask, they point him out and
I walk down the aisles, between the men who look me up
and down, and the crying women and the fidgeting children.
I never even thought to bring Judith. Tom never asked, and
besides, it is a school day. I look at all these other mothers and
I think, *They must not care about their children. These children
will grow up as bad as their fathers.*

Then I realize I am thinking of They and Us, when in fact
Tom is in the same position as them.

He stands up to greet me, kisses my cheek and asks about
Judith before we even sit down.

'She's all right. Doing well at school.'

He leans forward. 'But how is she, Katie? How is she in
herself?'

This is the first time I have been within touching distance of him for almost seven weeks. He is a little thinner, but his eyes are bright and his colour is good. Regular food and sleep. No drink.

I don't know what to say to him. 'She's . . . she's not been finding it easy.'

His eyes search mine. 'Why? What have you told her?'

'Just that it's all a mistake. That the police have made a mistake.' I pull my chair a little closer. 'But she's not stupid – there are reporters outside the house. You're not there. She knows something's wrong.'

'Oh hell.' He clenches and unclenches his fingers. 'Maybe you should tell her . . . Tell her . . .'

I keep my voice low and even. 'It doesn't matter what I tell her. The important thing is that you'll be home soon.'

He nods. 'Yes – tell her that, Kitty.' And more urgently, 'Tell her I'll be home soon.'

Then he asks, 'What are the newspapers saying about me?' and I tell him that I cannot bear to read the papers. That I cannot have them in the house because of Judith.

'Of course not, but surely you read them on the train to work?'

I stare at him. 'Tom, why would I want to read them? Why would I want to know what they're saying?'

'Why would you *not*? Don't you want to know what I'm facing?'

I am on one side of a vast deep valley and he is on the other, and there is a great gulf between us.

'I have had enough of reporters.'

He doesn't ask what I mean by that: he merely frowns and then he says, 'Did you bring my cigarettes?'

'I gave your shirts to Mr Edgerton. And I brought money for cigarettes, like you asked. But they took it from me when they searched me.'

'Oh for God's sake! I'll never see it now.'

'But they told me to give it to them. What could I . . .' Hot tears fall on my hands.

'You should have given it to Edgerton as well. Christ . . . All right. It's all right, Kitty, you weren't to know.'

I grope for my handkerchief, wipe my eyes, reach for his hands and hold on. For the rest of my visit, the conversation between us is strangely normal. I don't know if this is deliberate on Tom's part, or even on mine, but it is comforting. We talk about the small things: my journey that morning, Mrs Irvine, Tom's complaints about the food in here.

And all the time that we are talking, we hold on to one another. We hold on tightly, like children lost in the dark.

14

Bea, December 1923

The days dragged, until by Christmas Eve Bea could bear it no longer.

Both the City and the Sunbury offices were to close at three, but she telephoned Miss Shepherd in the morning to say she had come down with a cold, and would stay in bed rather than risk passing it on just before the holiday.

Later, she took a train to Sunbury. Outside the station, she asked directions of two or three passers-by: a woman with a little girl tugging at her hand (*Mummy, you promised!*), an older man who smiled and wished her a merry Christmas, and then she was outside the office.

There was a cheap cafe opposite: Bea went inside, ordered a pot of tea and sat down at a table in the window. Just on three o'clock, the door of the office opened and two figures emerged. She was too far away to see them clearly, but she could make out that they were a man and a woman.

She threw a handful of coins on the table and rushed to the door. As she came out into the street, the figures parted, the smaller one in the grey coat turning left, and the other calling over his shoulder, 'See you in the new year, Mrs Ryan!'

Bea swallowed. Then she pulled her scarf around her and began to walk after the woman in grey. She entered a shop on the high street and Bea followed her blindly, barely noticing the other customers or the goods on display, aware only of the woman in front of her – the bulk of her coat and the thin ankles and the way she shifted from one foot to the other as she waited. Then it was her turn to be served, and she was leaning forward to speak to the girl. Her voice was low, husky – she had the same way of speaking as Tom, the same way of forming her *t*s and her *o*s. She looked up and pointed to something on a shelf. It was then that Bea glimpsed her quarter-profile – the long nose, the high cheekbones – just for a moment, like something seen through a half-open door. The girl lifted down a skein of blue wool, and they bent over it together. The woman ran her hand over it, then took up a strand and stroked it gently between her thumb and forefinger.

And then she nodded and reached into her bag for her purse, and as she took it out, a handkerchief came with it and fell to the floor. Bea waited for her to notice it, but she was looking at the girl again, and the girl was winding and carding the wool, so Bea bent and tightened her fist around the handkerchief – and as she straightened up, the woman was putting the wool and purse away in her bag and then walking to the door with her head bowed. And Bea was at the counter and the girl was looking at her curiously as she clenched the handkerchief and her nails dug in around it and her fingers squeezed and squeezed and trapped it tight.

She pointed at a card of buttons: small, neat, shining. 'I'll take those,' she said, smiling like a girl in a picture. 'They're just right for my new blouse' – and her voice was quite steady, quite ordinary.

The girl smiled too and put them in a paper bag, and Bea handed over the money and said good afternoon and happy Christmas, and she sounded quite normal. Then she counted to three as she went towards the door, four as she heard the bell jangle above, five-six as she held the door for a lady coming in, seven-eight as she walked into the street and nine-ten-eleven around the corner to a little cobbled mews.

She opened her hand and white cotton unfurled from her

fingers like a flower coming into bloom. There was an ink stain in one corner, where someone had wiped a pen-nib. In the opposite corner there was a little embroidered *K*, the edges worked so they curled upwards.

Bea held it in her palm again and brought her hand to her face, and smelled something faint and floral, something not quite strong enough to be perfume. Toilet water, perhaps, or skin cream. Something that had touched *her* body and been warmed by it.

She crushed it in her hand and then rammed it down hard into her pocket, and the scent was caught and held there. She breathed long and deep, and when she could no longer taste it in the back of her throat, she straightened up and walked slowly back to the main road. Then she saw the woman again – emerging from a toyshop, her head bowed, her arms full of parcels. She turned left and began to walk, and without any kind of conscious thought, almost without any feeling at all, Bea fell in behind her.

They boarded an omnibus together; stood inches apart with a group of schoolgirls between them. She was almost close enough to touch. Her back was still to Bea: now she could see the detail of her hair where it emerged from underneath her little hat. She could see the way it would not lie flat; could imagine how it would feel under her fingers, how it would spring up if she stroked it. How it would smell if she were to bury her face in it, and the sounds that scissors would make if she were to cut through it: the snick of steel blades against the dry coarse mass of it.

At Richmond station, the omnibus emptied and they made their way through the darkening streets, a little distance apart. They passed men dragging Christmas trees, women carrying bags stuffed with wrapped and ribboned parcels and pale plucked geese, with sprouts and brandy snaps and striped sugar sticks. Every window above them glowed golden against the darkening sky: each was a perfect bright square of love and comfort and companionship.

Mrs Ryan was walking more quickly now. She had her key in her hand before they even reached the corner; she was indoors before Bea reached the gate.

And then she was inside, in the warmth – and Bea was left out in the street, looking up.

Their windows were the same as all the others: yellow and welcoming, filled with a tree and bright baubles. Bea stood there for a long time – waiting, listening – but she heard nothing from inside the house and saw no one come into the room at the front. She stood there until her hands and feet were numb, and then she gave up and went back to the station, the tears frozen on her cold cheeks.

Most of the women at the club had gone to families or friends, and only eight remained on Christmas Day itself. Dinner was a desultory, dreary affair, with Mrs McIvor presiding at the head of the table. The cook and the maids had gone home at noon, so they ate cold beef and potatoes. The meat was stringy and dry and left an unpleasant taste in the mouth.

After dinner, they sat in the drawing room and played charades and passed round chocolates. The others giggled at Mrs McIvor, dozing with her mouth open in an armchair, occasionally emitting a loud snore.

Bea watched them, and felt herself entirely apart from them.

She excused herself as soon as she could, went to her room and lit a fire. She sat in the chair and tucked the eiderdown around her while she waited for the room to warm up.

And all the time, she thought: *I want a different kind of Christmas.*

She wanted to give Tom the things he deserved: a shaving kit that shone like silver with sable brushes and a crocodile-skin case; copies of every book he had ever loved, bound in red leather and embossed in gold; handmade suits; silk pyjamas; monogrammed cufflinks.

She thought of him in that warm lighted house with his wife and daughter: three distant figures, close and snug, heads angled together, forming a half-circle that entirely excluded everyone else. And she felt like a child, shrieking *But what about me!* – and knowing that no one would hear.

Eventually she tired herself out from wanting so much, and curled up and slept.

When she woke, the fire had gone out, the room was cold, and she was utterly, entirely alone.

It should have been a relief to return to work.

But she waited every day for Tom to walk into the office, and still he did not come.

She slept badly; she lost her appetite; she snapped at Alice, who tapped on her door one evening and asked if she was unwell.

There was one particularly bad weekend – wet and empty, where everything felt ill-fitting and uncomfortable and hollow. Bea had spent most of Sunday in bed, dozing fitfully, so that by nightfall she was unable to sleep and lay staring into the darkness, thinking of him all the way across London.

It hurt to think of him in a room she had never seen. It hurt to think of him sprawled in an armchair, the texture of which she had never felt, his elbow propped and his face serious as he read.

It hurt to think of the smells she would never know, woven into the fabric of the chair and the wool of the rug under his feet: the particular type of soap he used, the mingling of cooking fat and cigarettes, the faint tint of sherry spilled stickily on a surface and not wiped properly. It was the domestic details she needed, the quiet everyday facts that make up a life: she wanted to know the row of books on the shelf behind him, the weight of his ashtray, the colour of his favourite teacup.

She needed to know the sound of his breath as he slept, the way the fine hair at the nape of his neck felt first thing in the morning, the exact shade of blue that washed his eyelids as he dreamed.

But the only room where they could be together was this tiny room of her imagination. In there, she could hold him, know him, give herself to him with neither fear nor restraint. In there, they were open and honest and love was not a word that had to be avoided.

One wet afternoon towards the middle of the month, after everyone else had left and she was quite alone in the office, she stopped in the middle of the invoice she was typing, put her face in her hands and began to cry. It was an uncontrolled *wet* kind of crying, and after a few moments she realized what a relief it was, and she gave herself over to it.

It was only when the worst of it had subsided and she was wiping her eyes and nose with a rather sodden handkerchief that she heard a polite cough and realized that Mr Montgomery had come out from his cubbyhole and was standing beside her desk.

She was so appalled that she forgot even to pretend that everything was all right. Without looking at him, she apologized for disturbing him, declined the greying handkerchief he held out to her, and fled to the ladies' washroom with her face burning.

But when she had bathed her eyes and repaired the worst of the damage to her face, she came back to the office to find that not only had Mr Montgomery passed up the opportunity to

escape, but he had made two cups of tea, pulled his chair over
to her desk and was plainly waiting for her.

'Miss Cade. I – *hem* – I wondered if I might offer you
some – *hem* – assistance? If there is anything I can do, anything
at all, I am at your disposal.'

And now she looked at him in surprise, for they had never
spoken to one another like this – indeed, they had barely
spoken at all, other than to discuss questions of correspondence
or the balance of the weekly ledger.

'That's very kind of you, really, Mr Montgomery, but I am
quite all right now. I can only apologize again for that most
unfortunate loss of control. I assure you, if I had realized for
one moment that you were—'

'No, no, not at *all*, my dear. I am delighted to have been
able to provide – *hem* – even the smallest comfort to a lady in
your . . . when it was needed.'

He pushed one of the cups over to her and she sipped his
dreadful tea, not wanting to appear ungrateful, wondering how
she might be able to leave gracefully. Then Mr Montgomery
spoke again.

'May I speak to you, Miss Cade?'

She bit her lip – after all, they were speaking, and his formality after her earlier behaviour struck her as rather funny – but
she turned towards him and put down her cup.

He seemed to be gathering himself to say something, and
Bea braced herself for a ticking-off – had she forgotten to send
out the Prendergast invoice, despite his reminders? – and so
she was utterly astonished when he reached out and placed his
hand over hers.

'Since you – *hem* – came to work in our little office, Miss
Cade, and I have had the singular honour of making your
acquaintance, I have come to hold you in the highest esteem.'

She continued to stare at him until he took his hand away.
He cleared his throat. 'It has been a – *hem* – a pleasure to see

you develop and ripen into a mature woman. The kind of woman who would make a worthy wife.'

Her mouth fell open and she felt the dryness of air in her throat. She was quite unable to move or speak.

'And now I find myself in a position to seek a companion. A helpmate. Consolation in my old age, if you will.' He smiled at her. 'Miss Cade, I should be most privileged if you could see your – *hem* – your way to filling that position.'

She stared at him, at his poor suit and his threadbare shirt, his long nose and the fringe of pale hair that framed a smooth head dotted with brown freckles like a breakfast egg.

She could not think of a single thing to say. But far from discouraging him, her silence seemed to urge him on.

'I flatter myself that I have the means to keep a wife in comfort, Miss Cade. I have been careful with my investments. And I have a house on the – *hem* – Hampstead Road, furnished by my late mother, who had most excellent taste. And I—'

Just then, there was a commotion in the street – the blare of a motor-horn, shouts – and he turned his head towards it, like an old dog blindly scenting a rabbit.

She looked at his profile, and at the crepey skin on his neck that reminded her of the ears of the elephants at the zoo.

For a moment, she imagined how it would be: a well-appointed quiet house in a good neighbourhood; half a dozen silent rooms; a ticking clock; twin beds in a bedroom decorated by his mother. She imagined the laundry she would have to do – the yellowing stains under the arms, the tidemarks on the collars, the greying shirts he would expect her to make as new.

It would be safe. There would be no possibility of any other life.

She would be safe.

Then she imagined how he would feel under her fingers – the dry papery texture of him, the jutting bones, the talcum powder trapped floury and sickly in the folds of his skin.

He turned back to her, frowning, lips pursed, waiting for her answer. She swallowed and made herself form words – polite words with no room for any misunderstanding – and she watched his face crumple. She felt a stab of pity as she watched his mouth moving, acknowledging her reply, bidding her goodnight.

When he had left, she imagined his lips touching her cheek. She imagined them pressed closed and dry to hers. And she thought of insects: of the whisper of a moth's wing in the dark.

15

Bea, January 1924

Towards the end of the month, Tom came back to the office.

On the surface it was as though he had never been away. He flirted with Caroline and Jessie; joked with Mr Morley. He didn't look at Bea at all.

She waited and then, suddenly afraid that he would leave, she called him over and asked him to check the figures on an invoice. As he bent over the paper, she slid a note across the desk. She held her breath while he read it, while he considered his answer.

But he raised his head and smiled at her without any hesitation. And that evening, he was in the pub before her. Waiting for her.

'How was your Christmas?' He asked this in a casual, careless way, and she answered in the same tone.

'Marvellous, thanks. I stayed in London, saw friends. Went to one or two parties.'

She kept her eyes lowered as she talked. She did not ask him any questions.

She wanted him to ask her what was wrong. She needed something for her anger to spark against; needed to see him shocked by the fierceness of it.

But as they talked, her gaze crept up and up, almost against her will. His knee – grey twill; his wrist – pale, with a dusting of dark hair; his blue shirt – new; his chin – the dimple as pronounced as ever. Up and up to his own eyes, fixed on her. Their gazes met, caught. And she was trapped.

He took her hand in his. The familiar creases appeared around his eyes as he smiled at her.

'I missed you.' His eyes were serious now.

She said nothing and he only looked, waiting for her response. She could not look away, but managed, with an extraordinary effort, to close her eyes.

She felt him move closer.

'I missed you so much, darling.' And now his breath was on her cheek, in her hair. 'I missed you every single day.'

His lips on her skin.

'My own darling girl.'

On her cheek.

'Don't you know . . .'

On her brow.

'. . . how I feel about you?'

And then, soft against her lips, and she was holding her breath, holding the moment inside. He tasted of whisky and cherries and she took his face between her hands and kissed him hard.

She felt him smile against her mouth – and when they broke apart, she was smiling too, because nothing had changed between them after all.

But Tom's absence had changed something in her. Relief was tinged with fear, with thoughts of what he might have been doing during those long weeks. She imagined him with other women – not just his wife, but endless, faceless women who paraded through her dreams.

She began to watch other women watching him.

One evening she stood on the corner of Chiswell Street and

watched him amble along Finsbury Pavement like a man who had nowhere in particular to be.

She saw several women look at him, turn away briefly, then have to look again. She saw how they were all wide-eyed, flushed, distracted. She saw them swallow and stare.

He was wearing a new overcoat – quality, grey – polished shoes and a soft felt hat. He carried an apple, tossed it into the air, caught it one-handed, took a great wet bite. He glanced in shop windows, stopped to buy a newspaper. He threw a coin to a man in a faded khaki greatcoat sitting cross-legged at the kerbside, head bowed and hopeless. Tom walked on, eating the apple, humming.

His face was fresh and pink with cold, his eyes bright and quick. His smile – to the newspaper vendor, to the shop girl in the window who halted her display of hats to stare back at him – his smile was wide and open and guileless.

The sky was yellow and violet and the clouds hung low and heavy, dipping to the rooftops. A light rain was falling, and occasionally he ran his hand over the material of his overcoat, wiping away the drops of water, reassuring himself.

He was never still. Waiting at the crossing for a gap in the traffic, he tucked the newspaper under his arm, picked a thread off his lapel, raised his hat to a woman who brushed against him. She must have been at least fifty, but she was as susceptible as the rest – as the shop girl, for example, who could not have been more than seventeen. Both blushed. The lips of both women parted as his gaze lingered. Neither seemed able to pick up their day again.

I am as stupid as all of these women. I stand and stare, feeling the cold nipping the tips of my fingers, the rain seeping through my thin shoes and soaking my stockings, and I am unable to move and unable to look away.

The flow of traffic slowed, and he lifted his head. The damp air clung to his skin, to his eyelashes, like dew. The rain kissed

him. It ran down his cheek, under his collar, onto his warm
neck, his chest, his broad back.

Bea bit her lip and imagined the heat of him, under his
clothes, under his collar. She imagined the taste of him, rain-
washed, skin flushed, body warm from his walk.

She imagined his heart beating beneath his clothes, beneath
that glowing skin, and she imagined tracing the shape of his
heart through his chest with her finger.

And there in that busy street, under the sulphurous sky
with the buildings tilting above her, she imagined kissing him.
She imagined licking and biting and tasting those secret damp
places. She put her hand to her own throat and felt her pulse
throb, and she looked at those other women and she knew that
they were all imagining those things too. That, however briefly,
all those women belonged to him.

But he would belong entirely to her.

As a freezing January gave way to a damp February, they
spent their evenings sitting close and warm in cheerful pubs,
stretching out the evening with whisky for him and sherry for
her, letting the fiery sweetness sink down, letting it spread and
burn.

At a certain point in the evening, Tom would catch her eye
and his hand would tighten over hers. They would finish their
drinks and leave the pub together, side by side, close but not
touching.

Then they would walk, fully conscious of one another but
still not touching, not speaking, until the tension became too
much, and they turned to each other, into the nearest doorway,
alleyway, dark corner. They would kiss and the night would
fall away and it would not matter that there was no indoors
and no bed and no privacy. There was nothing but that kiss,
that heat. Nothing but his mouth, his cold hands, her warm

skin beneath those layers of wool and cotton and silk. Nothing but the sound of their moans, the dampness of their mingled breath. Heat and dampness and love. Nothing but that.

Nothing but that – and yet he still left her every night. She felt his leaving before it happened: in his distracted replies, in the sly way he checked his watch when he thought she couldn't see. She learned to recognize a particular line on his forehead that deepened as he worked up to it – and now that she had tasted his absence, she was determined that he should never want to go. That he should never leave before he absolutely must.

Sometimes she would use her body and her mouth to stop him going. At other times she would whisper to him in the dark: tempting, promising, delaying.

She took his cold hands and placed them inside her clothes, letting him feel the heat of her. In turn she felt how uneven his breath was. How desperate.

And then, one night, he said, 'You are always surprising me, Beatrice. You are so unlike any other woman I have met.'

Then his mouth was on hers again and she thrilled to this new awareness of her position in his heart, as they clung together in all their mutual brilliance.

One grey afternoon, he sent her roses. Where had he found roses like these at this time of year – huge and lavish and smelling of paradise?

There were twelve of them, each one as deep and bright as fresh blood.

There was no card, but without the certainty of a message came the space to imagine him in the florist's shop, his dark eyes serious as he contemplated the blooms. She thought of him taking up one stem after another, inhaling scents, stroking petals with a gentle finger, until he had a perfect dozen.

At one time, she would have hurried to show them to Alice or to Ellen. Now she took them straight to her room and put ten of the stems in a vase by her bed. They were the closest thing she had to him – and she wanted them to be the first sight she saw when she opened her eyes each morning.

She took up the last two and pulled them apart: one velvet petal at a time, until she had a lap full of roses and her hands smelled of sweetness and richness and pleasure.

And then, in the middle of the day, she rang for Hetty and asked her to bring up hot water for a bath.

As the bathroom filled with steam, Bea dropped the petals into the water one at a time until the scented clouds rose fragrant and thick, and a carpet of petals covered the surface of the water so that it looked like a garden. She placed the sole of her foot softly on the red-spattered surface, and felt the skin of it break and open for her. And then she stepped inside his gift and lay back in the water and breathed in the scent he had chosen for her. She rubbed the soft petals between her wet fingers, closed her eyes and imagined herself naked and unafraid in such a garden.

She ran her hands over her wet skin and imagined they were his hands. She touched herself the way that he touched her, and all around her the drowned petals spun drunkenly.

The following week he slipped a note onto her desk that had only an address, a date and a time. It was not an area of London Bea knew well, but she knew its reputation. She knew what this meant.

She dressed with shaking hands. She washed with perfumed soap, and she put on new underclothes: French, silk, and so fine she could scarcely feel them against her skin.

She made herself arrive a little after the time he had given, but he wasn't there. She waited in a doorway across the street with her hat pulled low and her collar turned up as dusk approached.

She became aware that she was trembling, that her breath was uneven, and that everything was wet, that she was sweating and her skin was damp, that her eyes were wet and that she was wet between her legs. She took a long breath and pulled at the collar of her dress to let in air. There must be no smells, no stains.

The address he had given her was an old and unkempt building. The peeling paint and mismatched bricks gave it the appearance of a parcel that had come apart and whose contents were in danger of spilling out. The steps had recently been scrubbed, although not with any great care – the dirt had been smeared into grey streaks, and the corners were black with soot. A lamp glowed orange in the basement area, and a dim light flickered on the second floor, but she could see no movement inside.

She peered out of the doorway towards Old Compton Street, expecting Tom to be coming from the Tube, but when she looked back at the house, he was approaching the steps from the other direction, his hands cupped around a cigarette. She watched for a moment as he clicked his lighter, as it caught and he inhaled – and as he leaned against the area railings, she looked at his profile in shadow beneath the brim of his hat, at the curling smoke and the light rain falling silver in the glow of the lamp. She shivered.

At the sound of her footsteps, he turned and smiled and tossed his barely smoked cigarette onto the street. He did not touch her.

Bea looked up at him and thought about what must happen next.

'Darling,' he said, and his voice was warm and rich. She shivered again.

Tom pulled the bell, and a mournful echo rang through the ground floor of the house.

As they waited, Tom turned to her and said, 'I've booked us in a false name. So no need to look surprised when they mention it.' He squeezed her hand. 'It was to protect you – your character. You do understand, Beatrice?'

Before she could reply, Bea heard footsteps and laboured breathing, and the door was opened by an extraordinarily fat woman with bright henna'ed hair. She took in Bea in one quick up-and-down glance, then turned her attention to Tom. The doughy folds of skin stretched into a smile that revealed brown teeth and eyes outlined in kohl.

'Good evening, Mr Waller. What a pleasure. What a pleasure *indeed*. Come in, come in. This way, dear. There we are. Like that, yes, come in.'

She nodded and clasped her hands and bobbed and bowed so that her jet earrings wobbled, and then stepped behind a wooden counter in the dark hallway, into a small recess hung with a heavy velvet curtain. She bent down, revealing a line of white along her scalp, startling against the red of her hair, and came up with a key which she held out to Tom.

He took a note from his wallet, folded it between two fingers and passed it over the counter, and she tucked it somewhere amongst the voluminous folds of her dress.

'Room nine, dearie. Second floor. You'll excuse me not taking you up myself – my legs, you see.'

She reached down again and handed Tom a candle, lit it for him and said, 'The gas don't work upstairs, I'm afraid. Leave the key on the counter when you leave,' and then she bared her brown teeth again and slid behind the heavy curtain. Her footsteps faded and a door closed somewhere deep in the house, and then they were quite alone.

Tom began to climb the narrow staircase, the candle throwing long shadows on the peeling wallpaper. She fixed her eyes on his feet as they climbed: on the scrape of mud that stuck to his shoe, the loose thread escaping from one woollen sock. As he lifted his leg, his trouser rode up, revealing pale skin, wiry dark hair, a red mark where his sock had slipped down.

Then he lifted his candle higher and Bea was left in the shadows with the image of that exposed white limb, that dark hair.

The house smelled musky and somehow animal, as though it had been shut up for a long time. At the top of the stairs was a square landing with five or six doors off it. One stood ajar: she followed him inside and smelled damp. Tom set the candle on the table, then moved behind her and closed the door.

She stared into the candle flame until black and gold was all she could see. All she could hear was her own breath coming harsh and fast, and then Tom came behind her and she felt the warm bulk of him at her back. He slid off her coat and kissed her neck, and she closed her eyes, letting the flame burn inside while he undid the buttons on her dress one by one; achingly slow and patient.

As the fabric gradually parted, the straps of her best slip and the length of her back were revealed to his gaze. He stroked downward to the place where her back dipped and curved, and put his thumbs either side of the base of her spine. Then he leaned forward and said, so softly it was like breathing, 'I have imagined you with dimples there – one' – he pressed one thumb gently – 'and two' – then the other. He moved his hands upwards – at first the thumbs, as yielding as mouths, then spread his fingers and ran his whole wide hands up to her shoulders while she stood and trembled and kept her eyes shut for fear that she might open them and find that she was dreaming.

He turned his hands and stroked the backs of his fingers against her neck, as light as air – then leaned forward again and let her feel his breath, and kissed the point where her hair met skin and was at its softest and finest. His lips lingered, and then his mouth was at her ear.

'You have a mole,' he said. 'Just . . . there. Where I kissed you. A beauty spot. Did you know?'

She tried to speak but he had stolen her voice, and so he merely kissed back down her neck and then up again.

'No?' His soft voice in her ear. His breath on her skin. The heat and the harshness of his whisper.

'Then I am showing your body to you, just as you are showing it to me.'

And he smoothed his hand across her neck, pushing her dress and slip, letting them slide along her skin until they hung loosely, the straps caught at her upper arms. He paused for a moment, and she heard a rustle of fabric behind her. Then he kissed her revealed collarbones, the taut gleaming skin that never saw the sun, and he whispered into her shoulder, 'Do you want to show me, darling girl?'

She leaned her head back and he kissed her exposed throat and licked the spot where her pulse leapt. He said again, 'Do you want to show me everything, Beatrice?' and all she could hear was her name in his breath and all she could feel was his mouth on her skin and the heat of him and how beautiful she was in his eyes and in his voice – and without any kind of conscious decision, she moved her shoulders, and her dress slid down and her slip fell with it, the fabric rippling and sliding and pooling at her feet, and there was nothing between her and him but her underwear. One little scrap of silk.

'Show me everything,' he said, and turned her around to face him. She opened her eyes then, and all she could see was him: his dark eyes, his warm and gleaming skin, long bare legs climbing to the ghost-white tail of his shirt. He slid his hands to her waist, beneath her underwear, letting the silk slide until it hung on her hips, and he knelt then and kissed her stomach, the curve of her waist, and looked up at her.

His lips moved but she could only hear the roaring of her blood as he pushed and she swayed and the single scrap of silk fell. And then she was naked and unashamed and he was worshipping her.

She saw adoration in his eyes and it made her bold and she said yes. Yes.

He rose up and his whole body was against her, taut and solid, and his mouth was on hers and her lips opened under his and she tasted something sharp and sour – but she had no time to feel because she was falling. She groped for the mattress beneath her and lay back, and his mouth was on hers again and his tongue pressed against hers and their hot stale breath mingled as she opened to him, and somehow her legs were around him. Then he was lying between her hips and he was *there*.

Suddenly, awareness of what they were doing rushed in hot like shame. She twisted her head to tell him to wait, *stop*, please – but that hardness was *there*, pushing, pushing, and he was inside and all was heat and pain and pressure filling her and filling her.

She burned and pressed her hands against his chest and breathed against the pain, and he shifted and pulled away and she cried out against the sudden absence of him – and then it came again, and again and again, and the burning became a liquid heat, vital, melting. She rose to meet him, pulling him to her, her hands clutching him as he groaned and threw back his head. There was a pressure, a heaviness, then his weight on her, hot and damp.

And the rest was silence.

16

Kate, July 1924

It is July and Tom stands above us all. He is in a wooden box something like a balcony, wearing a grey suit I have not seen before, and one of the shirts I pressed and gave to Mr Edgerton. I stood in the kitchen, laid out the shirt and smoothed it flat and listened to the familiar hiss and thud of the iron, thinking *I have done this a thousand times, but never like this.*

His eyes are large and watchful in his face, and his skin appears oddly suntanned, as though he has spent time outdoors. I wonder where he got the stuff to make his hair lie flat and gleaming, if he has a friend in there who has lent it to him.

I am in the centre of the public gallery, half hidden among thirty or forty faceless strangers. I clasp my hands together to stop myself from picking at the raw skin around my nails, in case I give myself away. Then I realize it looks as though I am praying for him, so I must stop that too, and lay them flat in my lap and let my palms sweat through my best brown skirt.

A woman in front of me says, 'Don't he carry himself well?'

Her friend nods. 'Got breeding. They say he's educated.' They are wearing bright hats, one blue with a patterned band, the other deep red with a feather. Both look new.

Another woman, this one to my left, reaches forward to lay her hand on the rail. It is a very small hand, ringless, with short neat nails like a child's.

I look over at Tom again – at his clean profile; his mouth

set thin and firm; his high collar. I keep my eyes on him as his dance around the courtroom. He is like the new boy in a schoolyard: back to the wall, wary of fists and feet.

Keep still! If you would only keep still and stand up straight, then they will all go on thinking of you as just like them.

The man to my right digs in his pocket, pulls out a watch — and we are crammed so tight that his elbow is in my stomach, and he tuts as though my stomach is a nuisance. The watch is out, and it tick-ticks. My neighbour stares at it and shakes his head and I brace myself for the elbow again, but then he stops dead. Because a door has opened below and a line of men is entering, flowing into the jury box.

Suits and shirts, dark and fair, pink and pale. I notice a tall man, clean-shaven, with a pronounced chin and a rather sleepy expression, then a well-built man with a broad nose and thinning hair. They look like a queue of people boarding a tram: a group of perfectly ordinary men whom chance has brought together.

Mr Edgerton mentioned in one of his letters that the judge had ruled women might not serve on the jury. 'There are details in this case that the judge considers improper for women to hear about.'

It occurs to me now that this may make things more difficult for Tom. He has always drawn sympathy from women: they might be more likely than men to understand that he is not a monster. That he is not capable of this crime.

I look over at Tom again as the jury take their seats, and now — thank God — he is steadier, chin up, eyes clear. His hands are hidden so that no one can see if they are trembling, and there is a flush bright on each suntanned cheekbone that could pass for a fresh complexion.

I lean forward, far enough that the woman behind me hisses that I am blocking her view. I ignore her and put my hand on the rail in front beside the hand of the other woman, and the coolness soothes me as I watch the men shuffle and sit and ready themselves.

A man in a black robe and a grey woollen wig stands from among the others just like him. He faces the jury and clears his throat.

And so it begins.

'Gentlemen of the jury: the prisoner at the bar, Thomas Patrick Ryan, stands charged with ferociously, wilfully and maliciously killing and murdering Beatrice Cade, at Langley, near Eastbourne, on or about the fifteenth of April 1924.'

I clasp my hands tight. I swallow hard.

None of this seems real.

The voice rises a little, the rolling trace of Sussex a little clearer as he says, 'Your duty is to say whether he be guilty or not, and to hearken to the evidence.'

He sits in a whisper of fabric and there is a collective sigh and a stirring as though a wind has blown in and woken us all.

Then another of these black-robed men stands.

His face is fleshy, his colour healthy, as though he has recently spent time outdoors. He looks rested, calm, satisfied. His mouth turns up at the corners, giving him the look of a man who knows his business and is confident he can discharge it. In other circumstances, his might have been a pleasant face.

This is Moran, the prosecution counsel.

I stare at him because if I look at Tom again, I will break down and I will not be able to control myself.

It is my fault that he is here.

This is all my fault.

I imagine Moran waking this morning in the best bedroom of a local hotel, while I stood on a crowded platform at Clapham Junction. As I perspired in the stuffy train compartment with the window that was jammed shut, he was ringing for hot water, washing with good scented soap. Scraping a shining razor over that soft skin and then taking a clean shirt from the wardrobe that someone else had washed and ironed.

As I was walking up the hill from the station in my tight shoes, he was eating bacon and kidneys in the dining room of that hotel, nodding at the waiter without seeing him, gazing out of the window at the bright morning and thinking about the work that lay ahead of him. I try to imagine him thinking about Tom – and there my imagination stumbles to a halt because I cannot conceive what thoughts might be whirring and dropping into place behind that well-fed, half-smiling face.

I realize I am trembling, and I grip my hands together, careless now of what people might think. I must hold on.

Moran straightens his robe. He bows to the judge, who nods and grunts and dips his pen in the inkwell. He faces the jury. He places his hands behind him, straightens his back.

The court is ready.

Moran begins by asking the jury to dismiss from their minds anything they have heard or read of the case. They gaze back at him as though what he is asking is not only rational but possible.

My brother Fred told me a riddle once: when you ask a man not to think of an elephant, what is the first thing he will think of? I ran it through my head and was puzzled, for the first thing I thought of was an elephant.

The jury look at Tom. I see elephants passing through their minds.

Moran continues: 'Beatrice Cade was thirty-seven years old when she died. She was an athletic fair-haired girl, with half her life ahead of her.'

I think of the woman I met once, for perhaps a moment or two. I remember the tired eyes, the greasy skin, the crumpled hat. That was the woman at the centre of all this. That was the woman who has caused such disruption to all of our lives – and she was so ordinary. She was the kind of woman you fail to notice on the omnibus every single day.

Moran pauses. Waits until he has the full attention of the jury. 'The defence will attempt to argue that Miss Cade died when she fell and hit her head.'

He turns to his opponent – Tom's barrister, Mr Tate. Makes a small bow of acknowledgement. Mr Tate – slight, dark, with unruly eyebrows and a red face – watches him the way that a cat watches, and does not move.

'The defence will claim that the prisoner merely panicked and destroyed her body. But' – and one finger goes up now, bidding us to listen – 'but I put it to you that this was a deliberate act of wilful and premeditated murder.'

I hear a little intake of breath from the woman on my left, and an excited whisper rustles around the room. I pull my arms in, tight, so that my neighbours cannot feel me shudder.

Moran pauses to allow the whisper to rise and then die, and draws himself up to his full height. 'If this is proven, it will be my duty to ask you to return a guilty verdict. I will ask you to find Thomas Ryan guilty of the murder of Beatrice Cade.'

He looks at each man on the jury. He looks at them slowly, one by one.

And now I force myself to face it. He is not only asking them for a guilty verdict – he is asking them to put a noose around my husband's neck.

Moran will hang my husband if he can.

This is the first time I have let myself think these words – but I see again the rope from my nightmares. The newness of it. The neat loop. The weight and the stiffness of it.

And all at once, I cannot get enough air. There is a lump in my throat; I raise a hand to my own neck, touch nothing save my damp skin.

I can only swallow and swallow, and it is like ice rising and falling inside me.

Moran steps forward and turns to the judge. 'My Lord, I call the first witness for the prosecution.'

A door opens, and I hear a familiar lopsided step.

17

Bea, February 1924

After that evening, she was changed. She was changed out-
wardly because she could not eat. She could not sleep. She lay
in bed at night and ran her fingers over the new-formed hollows
in her body, and she imagined that they were his fingers. She
fell into a troubled sleep at four, five in the morning, and then
overslept – and for the first time in her life, she did not care.

He had taught her the softness of her skin. She stroked the
smooth expanse of white below her wrist and felt how vulnerable it was.

He had taught her the length and the arch of her neck. She
learned to hold it long and high, and to close her eyes and to
feel like a flower on a stem. And for the first time in her life,
she was beautiful.

But the real change was inside her. That delightful sense of
sacred intimacy between them meant she was reborn. She felt
raw and new: colours seemed brighter, voices louder.

She left work early one afternoon, unable to concentrate and
pleading a headache. But instead of going home to drink cocoa
in front of the fire and play backgammon with Alice, she
walked in the rain and she thought of him.

*I want to go for a long walk with you, dearest. I want to walk
through this wet cut grass with you, smelling that fresh black mud
and those damp violets and this rain.*

I want you to be here, in this deserted park, so that we may hold each other close while we walk, my hand on the smooth bare skin under your shirt, yours around the curve of my waist, your fingers burning with your need.

The rain began to ease off, and the clouds to clear. She was shivering, feverish, as though he had infected her. She lifted her head and saw the warm lights of a cafe across the road.

Inside was bright and fogged with steam, full of darting waitresses in neat white aprons, couples exchanging shy glances over teacup rims, women with parcels resting tired feet. There was a long marble counter running the length of the room, and a broad red-faced man stood behind it, plump and dark and glistening with sweat.

Bea took a seat in the corner by the window, facing into the gilt-edged mirror that covered one wall. She watched the reflections of the other customers: the conversations, the laughter, the secret glances between one another and at themselves in the glass.

She ordered tea and, after a moment's hesitation, an éclair. Then she placed her chin on her hand and looked at the room in the mirror again – but this time she saw nothing. He was soaked all through her and she was saturated with him.

She took out her diary, tore out a sheet of paper and wrote to him.

I want to come to you now, to tea and a fire and to a quiet private room where we can slowly peel off our wet clothes to reveal cold flushed skin to kiss and kiss and kiss.

I want to fall into bed and into you and hold you and whisper for hours. I want our mouths close and hushed and kissing and sharing everything.

And eventually in silence I want to fall asleep at the same time as you, and wake to kiss the shape of your beautiful mouth.

She raised her head and let herself swim up and up so that fragments of conversation around her came into focus.

'. . . and I told him he'd better buck up his ideas or we'd all be out on our ear, but he said there was no . . .'

'Oh but my dear, haven't you heard? Her husband drinks, apparently. And hasn't worked since I don't know when. So really, there's only one way . . .'

The éclair arrived on a plate with a little lace cloth. It was fat, golden, glorious. She bit into it, and felt the ooze of cream on her tongue, then the crumble of pastry flakes falling behind it.

She took up her pencil again. Let her eyes drop to the paper.

I want you
I need

Her heart beat wildly but she was unable to stop. The pencil flew over the paper and she was sure that her concentration, and the flush on her cheeks, must be drawing attention – yet she could not stop.

I need your desire your tenderness your love.
I need I want I want to make a life with you.

She put down the pencil and pushed the plate away. She did not need food. She needed only his smile. His voice. *Him, him, him* – close and gazing at her so that she could see the exact point where his irises darkened, the precise detail of how his eyelashes curled. He rose bubbling and rich in her until she was drunk with him.

She looked up and out of the window. She believed she could tell, as she sat in the tearoom, after the rain and under this bright bleached new-washed sky, which of the men who walked by would stray, and which of them would not.

It is never who one thinks it will be. She could tell from

the way their eyes held hers, or didn't, and the way their gaze dipped and rose again, like fish bobbing to the silver surface of a river to catch a bite.

She could tell, too, which of the women who walked by had experienced passion, as she had – and which of them were merely breathing, merely going through the motions. The latter trod slowly, eyes dull and burdened and fixed on the ground or on an invisible middle distance of children and the butcher's bill and the train they must catch.

The others looked up; they made eye contact; they smiled or frowned. Some glanced up at the sunlight-washed facade of the shabby building opposite, at the peeling paint and the moss-specked balustrades gilded in fading gold. With their lifted eyes and their minds open to beauty and to the unexpected: these were the ones who let life in.

Bea thought of Jane's pinched voice. Of her certainty as she said, 'Making a good marriage is so important. It colours everything.'

And she saw again the dark figure of his wife. Waiting. Watching.

Bea stared at her, then looked away. What was between Tom and her had nothing to do with marriage. It was far beyond laws and papers and rules. Theirs was a union of souls.

She looked into the mirror again and stared at the faces inside: at mouths opening and closing and at cups being raised and lowered. And she saw him – the way his eyes danced as he talked of his daughter, of days at the races, of taking a boat on the river. She thought of the way he looked at her. His mouth.

Her chest ached. She thought: *If you were here now, if your body was before me and your skin exposed, I would lick you. Devour you.*

I would possess you.

18

Kate, July 1924

Wild enters the witness box and is sworn in. He takes a little notebook out of his inside pocket and lays it on the stand before him.

Moran faces the jury. He waits until they are all looking at him again, and he begins.

'Imagine, gentlemen: Waterloo station, on a perfectly ordinary Thursday evening. The first of May, this year. The concourse was crowded with office workers, travelling from the City back to the suburbs.'

He walks slowly along the length of the jury box. They do not take their eyes off him as he turns and begins to walk back.

'Imagine the engine smoke, the voices of guards and porters calling out platform numbers and train destinations. Imagine, if you will, the bustle, the hurrying footsteps, the guard's whistle shrieking out a warning.'

Those around me lean back in their seats. They fold their arms; they relax. This is a world we all know.

'Now imagine the station itself. The newspaper seller, the tobacconist, the tearoom – and opposite them, the left-luggage office. It is one such as you have all seen a hundred times – a low counter, shelves filled with suitcases and bags and umbrellas.'

His gaze sweeps over the jurors. 'A very ordinary place, filled with the everyday details of dozens of ordinary lives.'

His voice becomes a little lower. Confiding. 'There were two attendants on duty on the day in question. Mr Lawrence is an older man, with more than twenty years' experience under his belt. The other, Mr Jacobs, is barely seventeen.

'That evening, everything was just as usual. They took in luggage. They handed out tickets, located missing items. Perhaps Mr Jacobs glanced at the clock once or twice. Wondered if he might suggest a cup of tea; thought about how long he must wait until the end of his shift. We can forgive him his impatience, I think' – a little smile – 'on the day in question, he was only four months into the job.'

And now Moran turns to the witness box. 'Chief Inspector Wild, your men were posted in Waterloo station for several hours on Thursday, the first of May. Is that correct?'

'Yes, sir.'

I keep my eyes fixed on Moran. I will not look at Wild.

'Would you please tell the court about the events of that day, and how your men came to be there.'

Wild clears his throat. 'We had received a telephone call from a concerned member of the public, informing us that there was a bag in the left-luggage office that contained suspicious materials. The gentleman who telephoned was able to give us the number of the ticket corresponding to the bag.'

I think about that ticket. I cannot help it. I remember the feel of the rough cheap paper, the ink blot in one corner.

'On the twenty-ninth of April, Police Constable Edwards was sent to examine the bag in question. He opened it, which action enabled him to confirm the suspicious nature of the contents. He reported his findings and was ordered to return it to the luggage office.'

A little whisper, like the faintest breeze, starts up. The judge frowns around the courtroom, then turns his attention back to Wild.

'It was agreed that a watch would be put on the station, and that we would question the individual who collected the item.'

He clears his throat again and reads from his notebook.

'PC Edwards and Sergeant Twomey spent the afternoon of the twenty-ninth of April and the morning and afternoon of the thirtieth of April and the first of May in Waterloo station. At six o'clock each evening, they came off shift, and I went to Waterloo myself to relieve them until the left-luggage office closed at nine.'

'Is that usual practice, Chief Inspector?'

He looks up from his notebook now and speaks slowly, as though he is thinking out loud. 'It isn't, no. I was curious. I thought it was possible that the person who had deposited the bag might turn up one evening that week, and I decided to spend a couple of hours there myself each night.'

Back to the notebook. 'I sat in the Wellington Cafe in a seat near the window, from which I had a clear view of the left-luggage office. In the event, I didn't have to wait long; at quarter-past seven on the third evening – that is, on the first of May – a man approached the luggage counter. He was dressed in a brown overcoat and a felt hat. I noticed him particularly because I was waiting for a man alone, carrying no luggage.'

I think about the man in the brown coat approaching the counter, fumbling in his pocket, producing the pale green ticket. I see this as clearly as though I was there.

My heart beats faster, then faster still.

'The man gave a ticket to one of the attendants, who left to fetch the bag. At this time, I remained in the tearoom.'

I picture the man in the brown coat leaning against the counter, lighting a cigarette. I see the pulse in his temple thudding and thudding.

'The attendant returned with the particular Gladstone bag we were looking out for, and handed it to the man in the brown overcoat.'

I raise my hands to my face – but I must not cover it, and so I press my fingers hard against my lips. Now I am looking at Wild. I am willing him to stop this somehow, to change the ending.

'The man took the bag and walked quickly away.'

He would have looked neither left nor right: all his attention would have been focused on the station exit.

Almost there.

Almost.

But Wild says, 'Once I saw him collect the bag in question, I left the tearoom' – and now I see him stand and take the dozen or so steps that would change everything.

I see him stop in front of the man with the bag.

'I asked him, "Does this bag belong to you, sir?"'

I will him to say no. To walk on, to walk out, to come back to his life with us.

But – 'He said, "I believe it does. Yes."'

'I then asked him for his name.'

'What was his response?'

'He asked why he should tell me his name.'

I picture the man in the brown coat looking surprised. Perhaps even a little insulted.

'I said, "I am a police inspector, and I must ask for your name."'

Now I imagine the man in the brown coat attempting a smile, knowing how effective that smile is, how his charm has always helped him out of a tight spot before.

'He said, "Well then, my name is Ryan."'

'And I said, "Mr Ryan, I must ask you to accompany me to Kennington police station."'

Moran looks at the jury as he says, 'And what was the prisoner's response to this, Chief Inspector Wild?'

For the first time, Wild pauses. He raises his hand and strokes his index finger over his little moustache as though it is a pet mouse.

' "Nonsense." ' He clears his throat. 'Ryan said, "This is nonsense." '

I can picture it all: the man in the brown coat lifting his head, the strain on his face apparent: the exhaustion, the sweat on his brow.

And yet I also see his raised eyebrow, and the way he strives to give the impression that he is quite above all this.

Moran pauses, and lets us take this in. And then, 'When you arrived at the police station, Chief Inspector, did you open the bag?'

'I did. I opened it in the presence of the accused.'

'And what did you find inside?'

Wild flips forward in his notebook. 'The bag contained a large knife and a number of items of ladies' underwear. Two pieces of blue silk with light brown lace trim, cut from larger items. A pair of torn bloomers.'

He clears his throat. 'All of them – the knife and all the items of clothing – they were all heavily bloodstained.'

There is a murmuring in the courtroom, as low and definite as the sound of a flock of birds rising up all at once. The faces around me are bright with curiosity and excitement. For a moment, I think I will be sick.

I wonder when she bought that underwear. She chose it, surely, with Tom in mind. She would have imagined herself wearing it for him. Would have imagined herself transformed. All that hope, invested in those stained and squalid scraps.

Blue silk and lace belongs in quiet shops with thick carpets and hushed voices. *Do try this one, madam. Can I wrap these for you, madam?* It belongs in dark bedrooms: between soft sheets, in drawers lined with lavender and clean paper.

It does not belong here, in this bright room, under the eyes of all these men. Just for a moment, I imagine how it would be if it were my underwear being talked about in this cold and

clinical manner, in this public place. I imagine the hot shame
and the indignity of it. And to my astonishment, something
cracks inside me, something small, and a little drop of pity
oozes out.

I must swallow it down. I must concentrate on Moran and
on Wild.

'After producing those items in the presence of the prisoner,
what did you say?'

'I asked him, "How did you come to have these things in
your bag? What are these stains?" And he said, "I may have
carried meat for dogs in this bag. I must have used these rags
to wrap the meat."'

'And what was your response to this, Chief Inspector?'

'I said, "That will not do. I believe these stains are human
blood."'

There is a low intake of breath. A whisper that grows louder
and echoes around the room until it is almost a hiss.

Wild clears his throat. 'The prisoner made no reply to
this. I said, "I shall have to detain you while I make further
inquiries."'

'What did he say to that?'

'He said, "You seem to know all about it." I said, "I cannot
tell you what I know. It is for you to give me an explanation of
the contents of your bag." He remained silent for quarter of an
hour, and then he said, "I wonder if you can realize how terrible
it is for one's body to be active and one's mind to fail to act."
He then sat silently for another half an hour.'

I glance at my husband's drawn face. There are lines at the
corners of his mouth. His jaw is clenched tight and his shoulders are high and stiff.

I find that I cannot imagine those thirty minutes: the
silence, the watching eyes. The weight and the terror of it.

'What did he say then?'

'He said, "I am considering my position." Then he was silent for another quarter of an hour.'

'And then?'

'He said, "I suppose you think you know everything. I will tell you the truth."'

'What did you say to him?'

'I cautioned him and he made a statement, which was written down in my presence by Inspector Merriam.'

'Thank you, Chief Inspector. I think we will hear that statement now.'

19

Kate, July 1924

Moran makes a gesture and the clerk stands, amid a general shuffling and a throat-clearing. He takes up a sheaf of papers, and reads:

'First of May, 1924. Statement of Thomas Patrick Ryan.

I have been cautioned that anything I say will be written down and may be used as evidence.

I first met the woman about nine months ago. Her name was Beatrice Cade. She was a single woman. She told me she was twenty-nine: I thought she was aged about thirty-five.'

Tom is standing straight, his head high. He looks at the jury, then over at the reporters. His face, under that strange suntan, is expressionless. He is gripping the rail in front of him, and the bones of his knuckles gleam through the skin.

'*She was an educated person. A cultured person.*'

Was that what it was between them? Her *cultured* nature?

The clerk is still reading.

'*She lived in a ladies' club in Guilford Street, and she worked at Morley and Morley, Copthall Avenue, London Wall. She was there when I first met her in connection with my duties as sales manager for that company.*'

The clerk clears his throat. '*I became on intimate terms with her about three or four months ago.*'

I knew this was coming, had been prepared for it by Mr Edgerton and by the questions of the two policemen that first morning – but the shock of hearing it said aloud like this makes tears spring to my eyes.

I blink hard. I try to breathe slowly but the warm stale air that seeps into my lungs tastes brown and filthy.

No one notices. No one looks at me.

Tom made this statement on the first of May. Three or four months before that was January or February.

In January we saw Lily Morris at the music hall together. In February we had a few people in for a drink on my birthday: Mrs Irvine and her sister; Reg and Dolly Finch from the bowling club. Everything was just as usual.

'*Miss Cade and I frequently spoke on the telephone and in January or February, I am not sure which, she suggested a day out together. I accepted, as I was anxious to discuss some business in which the firm was concerned. We spent the afternoon together and Miss Cade was extremely affectionate.*

'*She told me she was particularly fond of me and wished to be friendly. Intimacy took place on that occasion; as a result, I realized she was a woman of the world, which knowledge came as rather a shock to me.*'

I hear tutting. A furious push of breath from the man to my right. The newspapermen are bent over their notebooks, hurrying to get it all down, greedy for details.

Intimacy took place on that occasion.

Tom bought me a new nightgown for my birthday. Pale lawn, so fine that my skin glowed pink through it.

'*Intimacy later took place on several occasions at various locations.*'

The women in front of me both shake their heads in their bright new hats. They lean back. Their mouths are open.

That night he watched me undress. Watched me slip the nightgown over my head, watched it slither down my body while I breathed in the newness of it, the shop smell.

He came to me and kissed me, then again, harder. He laid

me down on the bed and ran his hand up my legs, pushing the nightgown above my waist. He lay on me and the warm weight of him, the muscle and the heft of him, made creases of the fine fabric. I felt them red and urgent on my skin.

Intimacy took place on several occasions. At various locations.

I remember that afterwards I was sore. That I washed quickly in cold water. That when I turned back, he was lying with his hands behind his head and a cigarette in his mouth. That he grinned at me, and that the smell of us was drying sticky on him.

'*Afterwards, Miss Cade reproached me on several occasions as being cold. She told me quite plainly that she wished for my affection and was determined to win it if possible. I felt sorry for her and did meet her rather more frequently.*

'*I felt more or less at the mercy of a strong-minded woman whom, although I liked her in many ways, I did not tremendously care for.*'

Tom keeps his chin up and is looking over at the reporters again. Two of them are half smiling as they write. The man beside me shakes his head.

'*In April she became thoroughly unsettled and begged me to give everything up and go abroad with her. She informed me of her great love and affection for me, but I told her plainly that I could not agree to such a course of action. I said I would consider the matter, however, in the hope of gaining some time, and she suggested I should take a holiday and go away with her for a week or two. She said we should take a house where we would be alone together and where she would convince me with her love that I could be perfectly happy with her.*'

He would never have left us. *Never.* She must have been quite mad to think otherwise, even for a moment.

But somehow it is not so easy to dismiss her like this. I keep seeing her as she was that day I met her: tired, pale – and unhappy, I think now. But not mad.

'*I did not want to do this, but she persisted. Ultimately I agreed, feeling it was my best course, if only to gain time to consider the situation. Then a few days later she told me she had given out her engagement at the club where she lived. She had told them she was going to be married and would then live abroad. This information startled me considerably.*'

Why would she say these things? Telling people she was engaged, telling them she was going to move away, that she would live abroad – these are enormous decisions. Definite decisions. Why would she say any of this, knowing that it wasn't true?

'*In the second week of April, Miss Cade went to Eastbourne and found a house in the district. She wrote to me and told me she felt convinced that the spot and the nature of the cottage would be ideal. She wrote, "Tom, you'll never regret it. I can make up fully for all you may have to give up."*'

I look over at Tom. His shoulders are slumped now, and he is shaking his head gently. His posture says, *If only I had not gone along with it all. If only I had been firmer.*

If only.

'*I met Miss Cade at Waterloo station on the Sunday – that is, the thirteenth of April. She was charmed with the house and told me again that she knew she was going to succeed in her object, that she would convince me to come away with her. To my mind, this was now almost an obsession with her.*

'*We travelled to the cottage together; it was just outside Eastbourne. I stayed there with her until Tuesday, the fifteenth of April.*'

I think of Kennington police station; of the fat policeman with the moustache. His fingers around the stub of pencil, his tongue moving as he drew out the calendar. *Where was your husband on the twelfth? And the thirteenth? And the two days following?*

I think of the push and the scrape of his questions, the

way he prodded the numbers on the calendar with his dirty fingernails.

Tom told me that he was travelling for work. That he had meetings arranged in Carlisle and Nottingham and Peterborough. I said, 'What, at the weekend?' and he shrugged and said those were the only dates they could do.

'*On the Tuesday, the fifteenth, we came up to London for the day.*'

He came into the Sunbury office on the Tuesday. He asked if I would have lunch with him; I told him I was too busy. He looked tired but when I asked if he was all right, if his trip had been a success, he merely nodded and said he would have to go away again.

I asked when he would be back, and he flushed and said, 'I won't be questioned about my movements, Kate.'

'*Miss Cade and I returned to Eastbourne that same night. I do not know where she went while we were in London – she left me for several hours and I think did some shopping. I met her again at Waterloo to return to Eastbourne.*'

The clerk's voice goes on, evenly, as though he were reading a train timetable or a news item of no particular interest.

'*During that night, the fifteenth, we quarrelled. We had only just arrived at the cottage when the quarrel commenced. The cause of the quarrel occurred in this way: I had arranged with Miss Cade to do certain things, but my better nature prevailed. I had agreed to go to the passport office to arrange for a passport, but I did not do so. She asked me about it and I informed her that I had not been for the passport and did not intend to do so.*'

I can well imagine it. *I won't be questioned about my movements.*

'*She asked me to write to my wife, stating that we were going abroad, that we were going overland to Paris for a time and then on to South Africa. I refused absolutely to write such a letter and felt that matters between us had now come to a crisis.*'

I look at Tom again. He is standing straight, his chin high, staring at a point above the clerk's head. I dig my nails into the palms of my hands.

'*My refusal on this occasion appeared to anger Miss Cade beyond endurance, and she suddenly picked up a weapon – an axe, a coal axe – and threw it at me. It struck me on the shoulder but did not injure me beyond a bruise. It then glanced off and hit the door of the bedroom, breaking the handle.*'

A woman in front of me reels back as though she herself has been hit. I want to put my hands over my ears to stop this, to stop all of it.

'*I felt appalled at the unwomanly fury Miss Cade showed and suddenly realized how strong she was. She was a very big, strong girl. She appeared to be quite mad with anger.*'

I try to imagine Tom's voice saying these words to a policeman with a pencil and a notebook. I find that I cannot imagine any of it – this passion, this fury, will not be caught tight, will not be trapped in these neat measured sentences.

'*She dashed at me and clutched at my face and neck. In sheer fright I instinctively closed with her, doing my best to fight back and to loosen her hold. We struggled and eventually in the course of the struggle, we fell over a chair, and her head came in violent contact with the coal scuttle. My body was on top when she fell. Her hold relaxed and she lay apparently stunned.*

'*The events of the next few seconds I cannot remember except as a horrible nightmare. I saw blood beginning to ooze from Miss Cade's head where she had struck the coal scuttle. I did my utmost to revive her, but found she was dead.*'

And now there is a sigh in the room, as though they have all been holding their breath, waiting to reach this part of the story. We have come to the heart of it – the accident, the fall, the death. Now we are facing the fact of the body.

I dig my nails deeper, and the pain is white-hot.

'*As the realization of my terrible position flooded my brain, my mind was at breaking point. I cannot remember clearly the next few minutes, but I think I wandered or sat in the garden for some time in a state bordering on madness.'*

And now Tom's head is bowed, and his hand is over his eyes.

'Eventually, however, I came back to the cottage and pulled the body of Miss Cade into the second bedroom, where I placed it gently down, covering it with her coat. I placed underneath her head various items of clothing, both in the manner of a pillow and to soak up the blood which was still flowing from the wound in her head.'

He tucked her in. Like a child.

I cannot help thinking of Judith. The softness and the small-ness of her sleeping body. Her little white hands on the pillow beside her. The gentleness of sleep.

I swallow.

The clerk clears his throat and says, 'Then, in different hand-writing: *This statement has been dictated by me and contains the whole truth as I remember it.* Signed T. P. Ryan.'

Finally it is over. The clerk lays the papers on the table and sits down. His face is red, as though he has been running.

Moran stands, bows to the judge. 'My Lord, I have one fur-ther question to put to Inspector Wild, to clarify some of the points made in the prisoner's statement.'

The judge waves his hand impatiently: Moran turns to the witness box.

'Detective Chief Inspector Wild, at the time of the prisoner's first statement, did you know of any crime committed against Miss Cade? Had you even heard the name of Miss Cade?'

'We knew nothing of Miss Cade, nor of her death. The cloakroom ticket was all we had linking the prisoner to the cottage.'

The cloakroom ticket. Such a little scrap of paper – the kind of thing one sees and touches every single day. And without it, Miss Cade's body might be lying there still undiscovered.

This is my fault.

I could have burned the cloakroom ticket. I could have thrown it on the fire. I could have chosen to forget about it, as I have had to forget so many other things.

Oh God, why did I not burn it!

20

Kate, April 1924

It was the end of April, almost a month after Miss Cade had come to the house. I had endured weeks of unexplained disappearances and restless nights.

I waited until Tom had gone out one evening and I went through everything: his clothes, his books, the drawers of his bedside table. I looked among his underwear and toilet things.

I don't know what I was looking for. Proof of something, I suppose – where he might be, what he might be doing. Something I could confront him with.

I went through his pockets and shook out his pullovers and thrust my hand so hard into the pocket of his raincoat that the lining tore. All the time I was listening for him coming home. Wondering what he would say if he caught me.

At last I sat on the bedroom floor. I was trembling, my face was wet and my heart pounding. And in front of me were my pitiful findings: a few scraps of paper with women's names and addresses – some in his handwriting, some not; two or three receipts; a book of matches from a London nightclub. And a cloakroom ticket from the left-luggage office at Waterloo station.

The names and addresses, the matches, were to be expected. But the cloakroom ticket was another matter.

I imagined a suitcase packed with his clothes. I imagined a suitcase full of *her* clothes.

I imagined him making plans to run away with her.

I picked the ticket up, ran my fingers over the cheap, rough paper, traced the outline of the numbers with my nail. J2413.

I said the numbers aloud, forward and backward. I added 2+4+1+3, then 24+13, as though there might be some logical answer.

Then I heard the front door close. Footsteps in the hallway. I listened and waited, but it was only Mrs Irvine. I let out a long breath and put the ticket in my apron pocket and the other scraps of paper at the bottom of my jewellery box. And all the time I was re-hanging Tom's shirts, rolling up his socks, re-stitching the lining of his coat, I wondered what I ought to do with it.

I could speak to Tom: simply ask him what he had left in the cloakroom. I ruled out that idea immediately: he would say a pal had asked him to leave something there and he hadn't got round to passing on the ticket, or that he'd just found it inside a newspaper or an old book. Once I put him on his guard, I would never find out what he was hiding – and suddenly the thought of not knowing was unbearable. For the same reason I couldn't just put it back. I had to know.

That left me with two choices: take the ticket to Waterloo myself, or ask someone else to do it. I could get the train from Sunbury one evening after work. It wouldn't take long.

But I imagined picking up his suitcase and being confronted with proof he was going to leave me – or worse, picking up *her* suitcase, full of her things. Her personal, intimate things. I imagined having to face all of this in a public place, and I shrank from the thought of it. I couldn't do it.

Then I thought of Arthur Dean.

Mr Dean lived next door to us. He was perhaps in his fifties, with silver hair brushed back from his forehead and a fine thick moustache. He reminded me a little of the photographs of Earl Haig that were in the newspapers during the War. When Judith and I had moved here, three months before Tom came home for the last time, Mr Dean had been the first neighbour we met.

Tom had been away for years: we were both lonely, and we became friends. I got into the habit of popping over in the evenings when Judith was in bed, and we'd have a cup of tea together. There was no harm in it: he was old enough to be my father.

We talked easily – about the weather, the price of coal, the new draper's shop that had opened beside the station. He never asked about my husband or about our past.

And then Tom came home, and my friendship with Mr Dean was at an end.

When I thought of Mr Dean, I was glad he was no friend of Tom's. Perhaps that meant he would tell me the truth.

Before he'd retired, he'd been something in the railway police. Surely that meant I could trust him with this?

The next morning, I took my key and slipped out, quickly, so that Mrs Irvine wouldn't ask where I was going so early. I knocked on his back door and he opened it, still in his shirt-sleeves and holding a cup of tea.

'Why, Mrs Ryan. Are you all right?'

I hadn't been in his house for over a year.

I almost pushed past him. I closed the door behind me.

'Mrs Ryan? What's happened?'

'Nothing. I hope. I'm . . . I'm all right.'

'Is it Judith?'

His kindness was unbearable. It made me short with him. 'Judith is still asleep. I need your help.'

'My help? Well, of course. Whatever I . . . anything I can do, of course.'

I took a breath and when I looked up, he was frowning at

me. 'Is it . . . I don't have much money in the house, but I can . . .'

'Oh, no. *No.* It's not that. Thank you, but . . . no.'

I took the ticket from my pocket and put it on the table between us. Then I sat heavily, without waiting for an invitation.

'It's Tom. It's . . .'

I didn't know how to go on.

Mr Dean looked at me for a moment, then filled the kettle, set it on the stove, sat down opposite me.

'It's all right, Mrs Ryan. Just tell me in your own time.'

I got it out eventually, faltering and avoiding his eyes. I told him that Tom had been away a lot. That he had not always been as loyal to me as he might have been.

'I found this in his pocket. And I'm . . . well, I'm worried.'

My hand rested on the ticket. I didn't want him to take it and make this real.

He reached out and patted my wrist.

'Don't you worry, love. Let me deal with this for you.'

I had to look away again, to hide the tears that sprang from nowhere. I couldn't bear his pity.

Then I handed him the ticket. This is what I cannot stop thinking about: I handed it over willingly.

Mr Dean was back that evening. I was waiting at the window and when I saw him turn in at the gate, I ran downstairs to meet him at the door so that Mrs Irvine wouldn't hear the bell. When I opened it, he looked startled and stepped back. I pulled the door to behind me.

'What was it? What did you find?'

He looked away and his face was white, and I realized that his shock wasn't at my opening the door so quickly. The shock was due to something else.

I asked him again, 'What did you find?'

But he only shook his head and wouldn't meet my eye.

Then he dug in his pocket and gave me back the ticket.

It sat in my hand like something at once familiar and repulsive.

'Mr Dean?'

Nothing.

'Arthur?'

Finally he looked at me.

He said, 'It's not what you think, Mrs Ryan.'

He said, 'Mr Ryan isn't . . . he's not with a woman.'

Then he reached out and folded my fingers around the square of paper. 'Put it back where you found it. And, whatever you do, don't talk to him about it.'

'Put it back? I don't understand.'

'Put it back. Put it back and don't tell him you've found it.' He was already turning to leave. 'Put it back right now and forget about it.'

'How can I just forget about it? Tell me what you found. Please.'

He looked down at my fingers. The ticket lay between them, rough and creased and full of secrets.

'I can't. I . . .' Then he ran his hand over his chin. 'Look, I'll be back. I'll be back at the weekend. All right? Just put it back now, and I'll come over on . . . on Sunday and we'll have a chat.'

But by Sunday, everything had changed. On the Friday morning, there were two policemen in my kitchen.

'When did you charge the prisoner?' Moran's voice startles me.

Wild says, 'When he had finished dictating his statement. Ryan was formally charged at ten-past one in the morning on the second of May. He received the usual caution that anything he said could be used in evidence against him.'

'Did he say anything?'

'He said, "It was not murder, as my statement clearly shows."'

Wild puts down his notebook. Straightens up. Tugs at his jacket.

It was not murder.

It was not murder.

There is a collective sigh; a general fidgeting; a feeling of release.

Everyone looks at the judge. He removes his glasses and puts a finger over each eye – one, two, pressing tight to keep us out. And then they are gone and his eyes open wide and, looking at nothing in particular, he says, 'I think we will stop for luncheon. We will reconvene at . . .' He looks at the clock. '. . . at half-past two.'

He struggles to his feet and grunts and straightens himself, and one of the other men stands too, pulling his robes about him like a bird tucking in its wings at dusk. This one raises his sharp little nose to us all and calls, 'Court adjourned, ladies and gentlemen. Court is adjourned.'

Those around me push to their feet. Ties are adjusted, jackets tugged down, hats set on and straightened. Only the woman to my left remains seated. Her head is bowed, her face obscured by a mass of fair hair, so fair it is almost silver.

The courtroom fills with a low muttering that quickly grows more strident as they try to make themselves heard over one another.

'You ever hear of a married man – a respectable sort, with a family and a good job – doing something like this?'

This isn't really a question, but I hear grunts of agreement.

'Poor bugger. That girl had him cornered.'

A sigh. 'Aye. Don't know what he was doing getting involved with her in the first place.'

'It's them offices in the City. Full of women in short skirts. Short hair. All that nonsense.' A wet cough, full of the memory of tobacco packed tight in a pipe. 'That kind of thing never ends up anywhere good.'

'What a position to be in, though. Can you imagine it? Girl falls and cracks her head and the chap's left looking at a murder charge.'

'Aye, right enough. It would have been . . .'

The women in front of me are standing in the centre of the row, heads bent together under their new hats. One of them looks up and over at the place where my husband was standing; the other at the door he walked through. I watch their heads dip together again, the red brim and the blue almost touching. I hear low laughter.

I get to my feet and begin the long walk to the end of the row. I ache from holding myself still and clenched.

It was not murder. I must focus on this. She wanted him to leave me – they quarrelled – there was a struggle.

It was a terrible thing, but it was not murder.

The jury must see this. They must see that it was an accident.

Apart from the public gallery, the courtroom is almost empty now – just one or two men tidying papers, straightening chairs, the terrible squeak of their shoes on the wooden floor, the pathetic thread of a tie dangling as one of them bends to pick up a pencil.

When I push open the heavy wooden door, I am met by a vast wall of noise. Voices, shouts, a distant ringing telephone, all rise up and up to the vaulted ceiling and echo high above the cold and dirty floor.

There is a line of men, and one or two women, against one wall. As I approach, I realize they are all queuing to use the telephones. There are two instruments, in little booths with glass-panelled doors. All of those queuing are holding notebooks covered in shorthand. Some are reading over their notes, scribbling, correcting, crossing out; but most are talking in groups of two and three. As I walk the length of the queue, their conversation reaches me like ripples from a skipping stone.

'. . . very good impression. Quite the . . .'

'I thought his statement was absolutely . . .'

'Awfully plausible. Seemed to me quite how any one of us might . . .'

I lift my chin and I walk with my head high towards the light and the heat of the afternoon.

After lunch, the judge asks Wild if there is more to Tom's statement.

'A little more, my Lord. I questioned the prisoner further about the events of Tuesday the fifteenth of April, particularly about what he had done after the death of Miss Cade. He then made an addendum to his statement.'

'Do we have that?' The judge looks at Moran, who nods. 'Then let us hear it.'

The same clerk stands and clears his throat self-consciously, then begins to read.

'*I put the body in the second bedroom and covered it up with her coat. I came into London on the evening of the sixteenth of April and went back to Eastbourne the following night, seventeenth of April, fairly late, taking with me a knife I bought in a shop in Victoria Street. I also bought at the same shop a small saw. When I got to the cottage I was still so upset and worried that I could not then carry out my intention to dispose of the body. I did so on the following day, which was Good Friday.*'

Good Friday. Judith was not at school and I was not at work.

We went to Kew Gardens.

We picked daffodils.

'*I cut the body up and put the various parts in Miss Cade's trunk.*'

There were so many daffodils. A golden carpet of them.

'*I left the trunk in the bedroom and locked the door.*'

I must concentrate only on this voice. On this flat and disinterested voice, which reads these words as though they are harmless.

'*I have been down several times since, wondering how I could dispose of the body.*'

We went to the tearoom opposite the gardens and I let Judith choose the cakes. She asked me where her daddy was, when he would be home.

Suddenly I cannot bear this any longer. All I can see is Miss Cade's white and frightened face, and all I can feel is a wave of heat and damp and a pressure behind my eyes – and then I am standing and pushing and pushing along the row. I press against the round hardness of kneecaps, down against the shape of feet. I hear *For God's sake* more than once and I think I hear the word *wife* and it almost stops me – except that I cannot stop.

I see my hand rise, I feel the comfort of wood under my fingertips, and then I am beyond the door and sucking in draughts of cool air. I lean against the wall and tip my head back and I breathe again.

A man comes up to me – another black-gowned figure like the ones inside, but this one is thin and stooped and has a face that looks concerned. He asks if I am quite all right and when I do not answer, he asks if he can do anything to help me. If he can fetch my husband.

And then I stare at him, and I laugh and laugh like a woman who has lost her wits.

LONDON POST, 8 JULY 1924

Bungalow Case Opens In Lewes

A great crowd gathered outside the Assizes Court at Lewes this morning, when the trial against Thomas Patrick Ryan (34) was opened. Ryan is charged with the murder of Beatrice Cade, the London girl secretary, whose age was given as 37.

Directly the doors were opened, there was a rush on the part of the crowd, women struggling with men in the attempt to push their way in. Coats were torn and hats damaged in the melee. Within a few moments over 200 people had squeezed into a space normally accommodating 40 to 50.

Superintendent Wensley, Chief Inspector Wild and Inspector Merriam of Scotland Yard were present.

'IT WAS NOT MURDER': RYAN'S REPLY TO CHARGE

The accused, a tall attractive man with dark eyes and hair, made a good impression. He wore a well-cut grey suit and his hair was carefully brushed. He appeared perfectly composed and bowed to the judge on entering the dock.

He is an athletic man who carries himself erect and walks with a casual swing – indeed, there is something soldierly about him and his features are sharply cut.

Mr C. L. Tate, barrister, appeared for the prisoner.

The clerk read the charge, which is that of 'ferociously, wilfully and maliciously killing and murdering Beatrice Cade on or about 15 April 1924.'

Detective Inspector Wild said, 'I received the prisoner into custody at Kennington police station. I charged and cautioned him, and he said, "It was not murder, as my statement clearly shows."'

The accused man is a native of Liverpool, where he lived until about 1912. He was closely associated with the Sunday school of the St James' Church in that city and was later employed by a confectioner's firm in Leicester, where he is remembered by colleagues as a reserved, quiet fellow.

He played goalkeeper for a church football team and was a member of the Catholic Men's Society.

POPULAR RICHMOND SPORTSMAN

He has a wide circle of friends and is especially popular in Richmond sporting circles, where he has a reputation as a good lawn-tennis player and a runner of more than average merit.

He has acted as an MC at local whist drives and dances, and is a well-known member of the Mid-Surrey Bowls Club, the headquarters of which are at Richmond. Last year he was honourable secretary for the first annual tournament, and had arranged to act in a similar capacity this Whitsun, his name being printed on the bills and tickets.

'He is one of the most likeable fellows imaginable,' a clubmate told the *London Post* yesterday. 'His family were from Ireland originally, and he had an Irishman's ready wit. He came to Richmond a year ago, and soon established himself in local favour. He often brought his wife and daughter to the bowling club.'

21

Bea, March 1924

The day had begun wearily, with a cold room and chilblains, and a pullover with a mark on the sleeve that no amount of sponging would remove.

It was a damp Monday at the end of March, and the dining room was curiously silent. Bea had a headache and an unpleasant, metallic taste in her mouth. She asked for tea instead of coffee, managed half a slice of toast, hoped she wasn't coming down with something. She could think of nothing worse than long days in bed in her cold room with no chance of seeing Tom, with only novels for company, while the house waited, empty, for the others to return from work.

The tea and toast revived her a little, and she went into the hall to put on her hat and gloves at the mirror. As she crossed the hallway, she was overcome by a wave of nausea so sudden and unexpected that she reached out and steadied herself against the wall. Nancy Shawcross noticed and asked if she was all right and she managed to nod, but it came again, and she pushed past the astonished girl and ran upstairs, still clutching hat and handbag, one hand over her mouth, praying she would be there in time, that she would be spared the humiliation of disgracing herself in the corridor. There was a dangerous moment where she could not find her key and had to fumble in her bag, almost weeping with frustration, but then she felt the familiar cold weight beneath her fingertips and opened the door, dropped her things and left them where they fell, and pulled the chamber pot from beneath the bed.

Afterwards, she leaned against the wardrobe, placed her hands on her stomach and breathed deeply. She blew her nose, and then reached for the glass on her bedside table and took a sip of water. Another moment and she was recovered enough to stand. She washed her hands and wiped her mouth, combed her hair, and looked at her pale reflection. She pinched her cheeks and smeared Vaseline into her lips, and found a roll of peppermints in her bag. The taste cleared her head, and she was surprised to realize that she felt quite well, and that according to her watch, she was somehow only eleven minutes late.

She arrived at the office just as the clock was striking the quarter-hour, but other than a ticking-off from Miss Shepherd, the rest of the day passed uneventfully.

However, the next morning, the same thing occurred: the headache, the tiredness, the feeling that she could not stomach coffee or an egg, the nausea, and then the overwhelming urge to vomit. The second night she lay in bed and thought about this strange sickness – the sudden onset, the lack of other symptoms.

And then all at once she was thinking about her mother, dashing into the scullery at breakfast time day after day while she and Jane ate their porridge at the kitchen table and swung their feet. In a rush she was back at her seat by the stove, spoon in hand, the warm milky taste sliding down inside, her ankle aching from where Jane had kicked her twice, and her mother groaning and cursing in the room beyond.

And then the sickness stopped, and her mother's stomach began to swell.

And then there was George.

Her heart began to thud. Her mouth was suddenly dry.

No.

She sat up and reached for the lamp and looked wildly around her.

No. Oh Christ, no.

She stood and rummaged in her bag until she found her diary. Her hands were shaking.

She began to turn the pages back. Last week – too soon. The week before, she had worn her yellow dress twice. No.

The week before that, she had played tennis with Annie . . . She turned back and back, panic building.

No. Please, please, no.

Seven weeks.

Almost two months.

How in God's name had she not realized?

Why had she not thought about this?

And then: Tom.

She fixed on him as the one still point in this storm of fear.

Tom surely knew . . . he must know what to do.

She had never thought there was a need to talk about this, had imagined he was somehow taking care to prevent this.

Oh God. Tom.

He must help her. He must.

She couldn't.

She didn't know.

She needed.

She wrapped her arms around her unfaithful body and began to sob then, quietly, desperately. She was trembling, and sat down, pulling the blankets around herself, still weeping, shivering violently.

Shock. I am in shock.

It was a slow clear thought, and it prompted her to rise and dress, to pull on a dressing gown over her clothes, to wrap herself in a shawl. To make herself shapeless and unwomanly.

On the landing below, there was a gas ring where one could make a hot drink before bed and she went there now, needing the comfort of familiar things. She put the kettle on and found the sugar and leaned against the wall, her body pressing into the solidness of it, into the definite fact of it.

And then the kettle began to boil, and she snatched it off before it could begin to shriek, and she made tea. She stood in the dark hallway shivering in her warmest clothes, feeling naked inside her cocoon of flannel and wool and respectability. She sipped her tea, and felt it reach down, hot and black and sweet, until she found the strength to climb the dark staircase to her room and face this new reality.

She would write him a letter.

She would look in Mr Morley's diary and find out when he might next be in the office, and she would find a way of giving the letter to him then. Even if it was not for a week or so, she would have it ready.

She tried to remember if she was expecting to see him soon. She had seen him for a drink . . . last Wednesday? Tuesday? Her mind seemed quite empty of every fact except one.

It took her hours to compose it, and when she had finally made a fair copy and bundled together her balled-up drafts to be discarded in anonymous dustbins on the way to work, it was after five o'clock. She stood at the window and watched the dying of the night, and she thought of the version of herself who had left her childhood home to come to London, who had explored the city quite alone and full of curiosity and courage. She wondered where that woman, that courage, was now.

She must find her, somehow. It was that woman who would get her through the days until she could see Tom and he would tell her what to do.

She undressed and got back into bed feeling calmer. She had a plan. She had done what she could.

What felt like moments later, her alarm clock rang out, and she woke with the memory of a dream clinging to her like perspiration.

She lay still, wondering why her heart was pounding, why she was trembling. She remembered the outline of a tall figure – a woman, she thought – holding out a set of scales, the brass gleaming dully. She remembered the tolling of a bell and the distant sound of sobbing.

Then she sat up, wondering if the feeling of heaviness in her stomach was her imagination, or if this was how salvation might come. She pulled the chamber pot out from under the bed and crouched over it, hoping. But when she stood and let her nightdress fall again, there was nothing but an inch or two of straw-coloured water.

She dressed slowly and struggled through breakfast, feeling as though she was sleepwalking. Every movement felt like an effort and she longed to go back upstairs, to leave her clothes in a heap on the floor, to slide between cool sheets and close her eyes and pretend that none of this was happening.

But she must not be late. She could not afford to lose this job. Whatever happened, she would surely need money.

So she endured the now-usual sickness, then put on her coat and hat and caught the omnibus to the office and said good morning just as usual.

Tom's name was not in the diary. In an ugly parody of her actions the night before, she leafed through the pages, forwards, backwards. Hoping.

Querying Miss Shepherd brought no answers, only an impatient, 'If there are any appointments, Miss Cade, they will all be in the diary. Surely you know that by now,' and partially concealed giggles from Caroline and Jessie. She was beyond caring about any of them.

She offered to take Mr Morley his tea, racking her brains to find a way of introducing the subject, but he was talking on the telephone and simply nodded as she laid the tray down.

She went back to her desk and placed her fingers on the typewriter keys, let them move automatically, watching the white expanse of paper gradually growing black with ink. She sat, unmoving, through the coffee break, through the lunch hour.

'Just a headache. I only need to sit quietly.'

'No, I'm sure it will pass, thank you all the same.'

All through that long day, she waited for Mr Morley to come out of his office and say casually, 'Mr Ryan will be coming in on Friday. Put it in the diary, would you, Miss Cade?'

There was nothing.

She waited for the familiar shape of him in the doorway. For a telephone call. For any sign he was thinking of her.

Nothing.

When five o'clock struck, the others sat up, tugged the covers over their machines, pulled down sleeves, picked up handbags. She copied them, slowly, mechanically. There was nowhere she had to be. No one who would care if she was somewhere rather than nowhere.

In the ladies' washroom she combed her hair, smoothed her skirt, smiled and hoped her voice sounded normal.

'Have a nice evening, Caroline. I hope your aunt enjoys her birthday.'

'Goodnight, Jessie. No, I won't come out with you just yet, I want to do something about this blister on my heel. Goodnight.'

And the door closed and the echo of their footsteps faded and she was alone with her reflection and the silence and a long evening stretching out ahead. She blinked back tears. Swallowed twice. She would not give into despair. She would *not*.

She snapped her bag closed and walked fast and firm down the stairs and out through the front door into an unseasonably warm evening. And all around her there was love – couples arm in arm, heads together, steps matched. She could see their smiles, and the glow and the closeness that set them apart. She stopped in the shadow of a doorway and wrapped her arms around herself, each hand on the opposite elbow – tight, warm, safe.

She could bear this.

She must bear this.

She began to walk again. She held on tight to her elbows. She swallowed tears again and again. She raised her chin and looked beyond those smiling couples, through all that terrible love.

After a while, she realized she was shivering. The shadows had grown longer, the streets were empty. She needed more of the golden light, a little space, soft air. She walked faster, following the setting sun, but her steps weren't fast enough and a strange panicky suffocation rose in her, rolling high and curling over her head, higher even than the tops of the buildings she was scurrying between. She would never outrun that wave. So she looked up and hailed a cab, heedless of the cost for the first time since she'd arrived in London. The driver sputtered to a halt and she paused, her hand on the door. She heard his voice, distantly, all chewing tobacco and wet gums.

'Where to, miss?'

She looked along the road and saw a dome and a figure holding scales. The image was so like the one that had woken her that morning, that had been in a dark corner of her mind all day, that she could only gape at it like someone who had lost her mind.

She tasted something like iron in her mouth and made herself swallow. She raised her hand to her forehead and closed her eyes. Perhaps she was losing her wits. Maybe shock had driven her out of her mind. Perhaps madness would even be a comfort: someone would have to take care of her. Would have to take care of . . . of it.

She had a fleeting vision of a narrow white bed in a small room with white walls. Empty. Simple. Pure. She imagined the relief of giving up her sanity. Of sinking back.

And then she felt a hand on her arm. She opened her eyes. She realized she was still clutching the door of the cab.

'Miss?' The hand on her arm again. She turned and the driver was watching her. His face was flushed with broken veins, his chin peppered with stubble and his eyes soft.

'You all right, miss? Taken a bit of a turn, have you?'

She took a breath. Took hold of herself. 'Where are we, please?'

'Where are we?' He frowned. 'Ludgate Hill.'

She kept staring at him and he put his head on one side like a friendly dog.

'You ain't from London, then? That down there's the Old Bailey. That's the Criminal Court.'

He nodded along the road and she looked again at the great dome rising against the pale evening sky. At the outline of the figure of Justice looming above the city. And that sense of panic rose again. She pulled open the door of the cab, climbed inside.

'Could you take me to the nearest park?'

He peered in at her. 'The *nearest* park?'

'Regent's Park. Take me to Regent's Park.'

She leaned back against the seat, inhaling the scent of tobacco and the dusty smell of the seat upholstery. For the first time that day, she felt almost calm.

They reached the park and she paid the fare and told him to keep the change. He touched the brim of his cap, then hesitated. 'You mind how you go, miss.'

And then his engine caught and he drove away, leaving her feeling oddly lost.

He had dropped her on the Outer Circle, and she took the

first path she saw leading into the gardens. The golden evening was fading to the violet hour before twilight, and the park was deserted, except for a crowd of boys playing cricket across the way.

She walked slowly towards the Inner Circle and the rose gardens, her pace deliberate and measured, quite as though she had some keen purpose in being alone in a public park at dusk.

I am a decent woman.

I have worked hard, I have always paid my bills on time.

I have always tried to do the right thing.

How in God's name have I come to this?

She thought again of her mother: of her tired face every morning after George had failed to sleep; of George himself: screaming, red, real. She thought of Jane crying because her boots had worn through and her feet were cold, and their mother shaking her head and saying, 'You'll just have to manage. We can't afford the cobbler now there's three of you to feed.'

For a moment she almost sobbed aloud. She pressed her hands against her mouth and breathed hard through her nose, and then she made herself keep walking. She walked through the soft green evening, past the scent of the rose gardens, and remembered a time when Tom had sent her roses. She tried to focus on that time – but those other unquiet thoughts kept creeping in, until her head was crowded with money and calendars and dates and with him and him and him.

She longed to be walking these paths thinking only of supper or of an overdue library book; instead, she was accompanied by this *thing* that filled her dreams and flowed in her blood and made her sick and ashamed and desperate.

She had only one comfort and she clung to it.

This has made a part of him, a part of me.

I am made flesh of his flesh, and now we are joined together for ever.

*

By the time she reached home, she had made up her mind. She couldn't wait to give him the letter. She would mark it private and confidential, and urgent, and she would post it to him. If he was travelling on business, surely his wife would forward an urgent letter on to him.

The following day, she went to the post office in her lunch hour, where the clerk told her the letter would reach Richmond by the evening post.

'And if it has to be forwarded to another town? How long will that take?'

He looked at her as though she was stupid.

'Well, that will depend on where it's being forwarded to.'

'Oh. Yes. Of course.'

'Do you know which town it might be sent on to? Or even which county the recipient might be in?'

'No. I have no idea where he might be. No idea at all.'

The next morning she was in the office early. She sat at her desk, offered to go downstairs and fetch the post when the boy was late, even managed to smile when Jessie joked about the price of stamps. There was nothing from him.

Every few minutes she looked at the clock.

The second post came. Nothing.

A telegram, then?

As the hours ticked by, she thought: *How cruel hope is.*

By mid-afternoon, he had still not contacted her.

He is not coming back.

She felt panic rising and she tried to push it down, tried to ignore it. But her fear would not be ignored, and the shadows kept looming.

He no longer loves me. I will be alone with . . . with this.

A child would mean years of shame. Isolation. It would mean poverty.

She thought of Lil Tearney; of Theo Ingram picking tobacco from her lip.

She imagined a dingy room. A baby screaming. Dirt. Squalor.

She imagined lies, resentment, fear. How would she earn money? How would they eat?

Were there charities who might help? Homes for women who . . . homes for women like her?

They never found out what happened to Lil. She had locked herself in her bedroom for two days, had refused to talk to any of them – and then one evening her room was empty and no one knew where she had gone.

She was not Lil. Tom would not let that happen to her.

Surely he would not let that happen.

Oh God, where is he?

Then: *Perhaps his wife has found out about us.*

Perhaps he has been in an accident and is lying unconscious in a hospital bed.

But wouldn't I know if he was injured or suffering? Wouldn't I feel it?

She went into the ladies' washroom, stared at the red eyes that met hers in the mirror, and wondered what was left. Without Tom, what was she?

I am a fool.

What a fool he has made of me.

She stared at her reflection and thought of an old joke she and George had made about vanishing cream. Perhaps one evening, she would massage cold cream into her face, and the powder would be rubbed away, then the grime and soot of London would dissolve, then her skin itself would fade, and she would simply disappear.

She shivered, then wrapped her arms around herself because she badly needed to be held. She took another breath. And as she walked back towards the office, the heat and dampness of her fear began to melt, little by little, and harden to something cold and obstinate that she had not known was inside her.

Why was he not here? Why was he letting her face this alone?

By the end of the day, that coldness, that hardness, had become a determination to act.

She must do *something*.

And so, when the clock struck five, she stood, pulled the cover over her typewriter, picked up her hat and coat and walked out of the building. She did not powder her nose or comb her hair or check her appearance in the mirror. She jammed her hat down onto her head anyhow, and with her coat over her arm, she went down into the Underground and caught a train west. Just as if this were an ordinary day and she was an ordinary woman going home for supper.

She could still feel that cold hard knot, ready to rise and spread and fill the spaces between hope.

She got off the train and walked down the familiar tree-lined streets, feeling it growing, letting it drive her on.

She walked quickly. Purposefully.

I will not beg.

I will not.

She arrived at the turning to his road. Watched her hand rise to the door and listened to the loud knocking, echoing into the air. She knocked again and again, past reason, to a place of pure need.

And the door opened.

22

Kate, July 1924

I am still sitting outside the courtroom, gathering myself to go back inside or to begin the long walk to the station, I am not sure which, when the door to the courtroom opens a little and one of the black-clad clerks slips out. He looks about him for a moment, then sees me sitting on the bench against the wall, watching him. His face clears and he hurries over.

'Mrs Ryan?'

'Yes?'

'From Mr Tate' – and he hands me a note.

When I read it, I am not sure whether to be sorry or glad: I have been granted an interview with Tom that afternoon.

There is nothing in the note to tell me where to go, but as I look up from the paper, the clerk is already sliding back into the courtroom, so I must wait.

Twenty minutes later, the door opens again, wider this time, to permit the public gallery to empty and the reporters to race to the telephones. I stay on the bench, silent and still in all that rush of colour and heat and noise, not wanting to draw attention to myself by pushing my way inside against the crowd.

I am quite invisible to those around me as I watch them juggle hats and shopping baskets, as I listen to their chatter about which train they hope to catch and whether the chemist will still be open. I hold on to the little piece of paper, folding it between my fingers, wondering what I will say to my husband.

It's just Tom.

I'm going to see Tom. Tom, who I know almost better than I know myself.

Tom, whose wife I have been for thirteen years.

I know all of this, and yet I am afraid, and I am afraid because I do not know the man they have described in the courtroom.

When I look up again, the corridor is empty. I go into the courtroom and see the clerk who gave me the note collecting papers and pencils from the jury benches. As I approach him, he says, 'I'm sorry, madam, you can't . . .' then he recognizes me, and falls silent.

'Can you tell me' – I hold out the note – 'can you tell me where I need to go?'

He nods. 'Yes, of course. It's below the . . . here, let me show you,' and he leads me outside, holds the door for me, then takes me along a corridor and down a flight of steps. I can feel his curiosity itching – *What is he like, your husband-in-the-dock? What is it like to be you?* – but he is blessedly silent. It is colder down here, and the air smells damp and sunless. We come to another door; he knocks and it is opened from the inside.

'All right, Powell? Got a lady here to visit her husband.' He jerks his thumb at me, nods, then disappears back up the dim passage. The door opens wider and I look up to see a man standing there. He wears the same uniform as the guards who stand in the dock with Tom each day, but I have not seen him before. He is enormous: at least a head and a half taller than me, and so wide that he blocks the whole doorway. His shirt-sleeves are rolled up and his forearms are pink and mottled like hams. He steps back to make room for me to enter, and a great bunch of keys jangles at his waist. I hear his breath whistling through his nose.

The room is small and cheerless, with peeling grey paint and a draught coming in from a window high up in the wall. The guard lumbers over to a table in the corner and picks up a ledger.

'Name?'

'Ryan. I'm Tom Ryan's—'

'Oh yes. We've got you here. A Mr . . . Mr Edgware telephoned through earlier.'

'Mr Edgerton is my—'

'Must say, Mrs Ryan' – and my name sounds like an obscene word in his mouth – 'you're very different from the usual class of wives we get in here.' He grins. 'Bit of a cut above, you might say.'

His eyes crawl over me like flies on a dinner plate. I resist the urge to scratch. I stare at a crack in the wall just to the right of his head.

'Mind you, it seems that Mr Ryan thinks he's a cut above the rest of us an' all. Very lah-di-dah, ain't he? Didn't like the *facilities* we provide here at *all*.'

He laughs, and his laugh turns into a hacking cough. When it has subsided, he wipes the back of his meaty hand over his nose and mouth and says, 'Come on then, let's take you down.'

He opens another door in the far wall and leads me slowly along a series of corridors lit by flickering gas lamps, each more dismal than the last. Then he opens a door and we are in another room, not unlike the one we came from. It is very cold, and there is only a battered table and two mismatched wooden chairs.

And there is my husband. His hands rest in his lap and his shoulders are slumped. He looks very different to the neat upright figure of the courtroom.

As I come in, he starts to get to his feet, until another guard, leaning against the wall, barks, 'Sit down, Ryan!' and he sits, cowed.

I have never seen him obey anyone before, in that shrinking, cringing manner.

I take the other chair and the guard who brought me here says, 'Enjoy yourselves, won't you!' and leaves, chuckling. We listen to his slow tread fading, and then Tom says, 'Kitty. I'm so glad to see you,' and I look at him.

I see what I was not able to see in the courtroom: the lines around his mouth and eyes are deeper. That strange artificial stain is clear on his face. Then I look more closely and see that the colour stops at his jaw. His neck and his wrists, where his jacket has ridden up, are pale.

'What is that, Tom?' I nod towards his wrists.

He looks down as though he has quite forgotten. 'Oh – it's tobacco juice.'

'What?'

He looks up at me. 'It makes your skin darker. It's an old lag's trick, apparently – I heard it from the fellow who was in the cell next to mine last month. Thought it might make me look healthier. Make a good impression on the jury and all that. What do you think?'

I think it looks strange and rather ridiculous. I don't want to waste the precious minutes of my visit talking about tobacco juice.

'Tom, I—'

'And what do you reckon to the suit? Seven guineas – not bad at all!'

Seven guineas? *Seven guineas* – when we have only one wage coming in and legal bills mounting up every day?

He is looking down at his jacket, running his hand along his sleeve. 'Mr Tate got a tailor to come in from Eastbourne.' He takes the lapels in his hands, straightens them, brushes them down, then looks at me. 'What do you think? I don't have a mirror – you can't even shave yourself, which I—'

I take a breath. 'Tom. We don't have much time. There are things we need to talk about.'

He sits up straight. His face becomes serious. 'Yes, of course. How do you think it's going? Do you think the reporters seem sympathetic?'

'I . . . well, yes. I suppose.' I have barely looked at them. I have been focused on Wild, on Moran, on Tom's statement.

'I wonder if I ought to look towards them more often. Make eye contact.'

'Tom, I need—'

'And what about the jury? Do you think they seem well disposed towards me?' He runs a hand over his hair. 'I wonder who they might choose as foreman. They say that a foreman can—'

'Tom, *for God's sake!*'

He stops, surprised. 'Good Lord, Katie, what's the—'

'You . . .' I glance at the guard. Lower my voice. 'You were . . . you were *with* another woman.'

I find that my teeth are clenched. That the words are coming fast and hard like blows. 'Do you know what this has been like for me? Having to hear that – in there, with all those people?'

He drops his head. Lets his breath out in a long sigh.

I stare at the thick dark hair I have run my fingers through a thousand times. At the soft whorl of his parting.

I have forgiven him for so much – but I cannot forgive the public nature of this. The appalling shame of it.

Suddenly I itch to hurt him, the way he has hurt me. 'You know I could divorce you for this.'

His chin jerks up. '*What?*'

'On the grounds of adultery. I could do that.'

He stares. 'You can't.' He slides his hands towards mine and the guard barks at him: 'No touching, Ryan!'

He stops and says again, 'You can't do that, Kitty.'

'I can, Tom. They passed a law last year. I read about it.'

'You can't.' He shakes his head. 'I wouldn't let you.'

'All I need is proof you've been with another woman.' I feel laughter pulling at my mouth, cold and bitter as a bridle. I have to bite it away. 'I think I have enough proof, Tom, don't you?'

'You *can't*.' His hands reach out again, hover over mine. Just in time, he remembers, pulls them back only a little so they remain stretched across the table like prayers. 'Think of the scandal.' His eyes are almost black. 'Kitty, think of Judith.'

'*I think of nothing but her!*' It comes out harsh and low and he glances up at the guard. 'All these years, Tom . . . all those other women . . .' I feel my throat swell with tears and shake my head.

He reaches for me again, and this time it is me who pulls my hands back. I look down at the table. There is a heart scored into the surface and *Mary* is carved inside it.

I lift my head and look at him. 'Do you know the newspapers have printed photographs of you? And of *her*. I have tried to avoid them, but they are all over the front pages. There was even a photograph of you and Judith.'

He recoils at that. 'Of *Judith*? Where the hell did they get a picture of Judith?'

'It was the one that photographer took at the fair. Last summer.'

'Did you give it to them?'

'Of course not! How can you even ask me that?' I sit back, stare at him. He says nothing. 'The photographer probably recognized you in the newspaper. Or remembered your name. He told us he kept the negatives, said we could go back any time for more copies. He's likely sold them by now.'

He shakes his head, but still says nothing.

'Anyway, that's not the point. The point is . . .' I am suddenly exhausted. 'The point is all of this – the trial, the reporters, travelling to Sussex each day, keeping up a front for Judith. It's too much. It's just . . . it's too much.'

He takes a long breath. 'I know, Kitty. I know, and I'm sorry. It's not been a bed of roses for me either, these past weeks.'

Now his voice is low and soft. 'You do believe me, don't you? Tell me you do. You do believe that I didn't mean to hurt her?'

My chest aches. 'Of course I believe you. I know you didn't . . . I know you didn't do what they're accusing you of.'

He closes his eyes. 'Oh, thank God. Thank God.' He opens them again and they are bright with tears. 'I was so afraid, Kitty. I've been so afraid that you'd abandon me. You don't know . . .' He swallows. 'You don't know how good it feels to hear you say that.'

I make myself sit straight and tall. 'But you did share a bed with her.'

'I know, darling. I know, and I'm sorry . . .'

'You broke our marriage vows. Again.' I let that sit between us for a moment. And then I say, 'It's not just that. Everyone knows. It's all come out in public. Everyone knows what kind of man you are. What kind of appetites you have. *Everyone.*'

I push harder. I want him to feel the strength of what I feel. 'The shame is killing me, Tom. *Your* shame.'

He stares at me. My anger is new to him: he doesn't seem to know what to do with it.

I look down at my hands on the tabletop: at the rings he put on my fingers that I have never taken off. And the anger cracks. 'Oh God, Tom. What a mess. What a terrible mess.'

'I know.' His hands inch forward. Stop. 'I know.'

'I wish I could rewind the clock and go back to before any of this started.'

He shakes his head. Gives me a small smile. 'Probably not as much as I do.'

He looks into my eyes and I notice the gold flecks around his irises. I had forgotten.

I keep looking into his eyes and I am lost. I just want him home with us, where he belongs – and suddenly the wanting is so strong I have to press my own hands together to stop myself from reaching for him.

One more week, and this will all be over.

23

Bea, April 1924

Bea had thought she knew her.

She knew the slender frame by now: the thin legs, the delicate feet. She knew the narrow shoulders – narrower than Bea's own – and the fine white hands.

She knew her handwriting, the scent she wore, the colours she preferred. She knew the low tone of her voice, the rhythm of her walk, how she held herself when still.

But now Bea saw her face close up for the first time – and all her imaginings fell away in a moment. The expressive dark eyes, the gleaming skin, the expression of assurance: all gone. And in their place was a tired gaunt woman with lines around her mouth.

This was not Tom's wife. This was someone utterly and entirely ordinary.

The woman took a step back from Bea and her eyebrows came together, and she raised a hand to her hair – scraped back untidily, showing the greasy roots. Gold glinted on her third finger.

'Yes?'

Bea looked at her: at the yellowish skin, the long thin neck. At that gleaming ring.

She smelled meat cooking, heard a child calling somewhere in the distance. She pushed her nails into the palms of her hands, deep and secret.

She cleared her throat and tried to speak with authority. 'I'm . . . I'm looking for Mr Ryan.'

The woman stood quite still. She blinked. And then she called over her shoulder to Tom – and, as she did so, she reached up and took hold of the door frame. She gripped it tightly and her eyes raked over Bea. Up and down, until Bea pulled her coat around her. It was not yet visible, but she hid it all the same.

'I'll fetch him. Wait here.'

The door slammed, and Bea was left on the step like an unwanted parcel. Like an unwanted bargain. She thought again of poor Lil Tearney and felt an unaccountable urge to laugh, and swallowed it. She thought she might be sick.

She heard footsteps approaching the door, raised voices behind it.

Then the door was pulled open again and Tom was there.

She stepped forward and he stood, looking at her. His eyes glittered and there were bright spots high on his cheeks. His jaw was clenched.

She had never seen him angry before, she realized. All her rage retreated before his, and fear came rushing back in.

He came outside and closed the door behind him.

'What are you doing here?'

She could not feel his voice on her skin, could not feel any part of him at all – but it was still somehow like facing down a storm, and she stepped back.

'Did you . . . did my letter arrive?'

Something flickered across his face, so briefly she wondered if she had imagined it. He looked away from her and spoke into the distance.

'Yes. It arrived.'

There was a terrible silence and she had to fill it.

'And?'

He whipped his head around and stared at her and he

looked – she was so startled it took her a moment to place it – he looked *outraged*, as though she had committed a dreadful social error and disgraced him.

'You wrote to me at my home, Beatrice. At my *home*. What if my wife had read your letter?'

The skin around his nostrils was white.

She swallowed. 'I had no choice! What else could I have done? I had no other way to get in touch with you.'

He shook his head. 'How do I know . . .' He lowered his voice. 'Are you absolutely sure?'

She blinked at him, not understanding.

'Are you quite sure that you're . . .' He nodded towards her stomach.

'Of course I'm sure! I'd hardly have written or come here if I wasn't.'

He said nothing, only looked away.

'Tom?'

He looked back at her and his jaw tightened. 'How could you have let this happen, Beatrice?'

She was astonished and took a step back as his meaning reached her.

'You were clearly a woman with . . . well, a woman of some experience when we met. You must have had some idea of what would happen.'

She could only stare, too shocked even to cry.

And then: 'What do you *want* from me?'

She had not realized until now what she wanted – but as the realization came to her, she dug down and tried to remember how her own anger had felt. She raised her head and looked directly at him and she made herself say it.

'I want . . . I need you to help me. To help us.'

He flinched at that, and walked away from her. She followed him to the road, where they stood behind a hedge, hidden from the house.

'I can't manage alone. I can't . . . I need a husband. And the baby needs a father. Our baby.'

The word was out for the first time, and it sat between them, red and bloody and shrieking. Neither of them could look at it.

Tom took a long breath. 'Beatrice. You know that I . . . you know I'm already a husband. And a father.'

And when she said nothing, he said, more firmly, 'You know that, Beatrice.'

And underneath, she heard the unspoken words: *Be reasonable, Beatrice.* There were rules for a situation like this, she understood now. When panic and shock arose, there were other things that should follow. Reason. Logic. Duty.

And she ought to be demonstrating that she grasped this. That she respected it. She ought to show that she respected his marriage and his position.

She should be making plans to go away. She should be looking for ways to deal with this problem, to make it vanish quietly and without fuss.

Be a good girl, Beatrice. Do the right thing, Beatrice.

She curled her hands into fists and dug her nails into her skin. Hard. And she said, slowly and clearly, 'I want you' – to make her go away, make her disappear, *get rid of her* – 'to leave them.'

It was as though a pane of glass came down over his face: now when she looked at him, she was unable to see him clearly, to understand what he was thinking. Her gaze skidded over him, as though he was made of mist and fog.

She said, 'The baby needs a name. You must leave them and be with me. With us.'

He said nothing.

'Tom?'

Nothing.

'Please. You must . . . you *must* leave them.'

Then she heard – suddenly, ridiculously – Miss Robinson's

voice. A history lesson about the death of Queen Elizabeth. The scarred wood of her schoolroom desk, the greasy pigtail of the girl in front – Maude? Maggie? – and Miss Robinson reading aloud the words of the dying Queen: 'Is *must* a word to be addressed to princes?'

Tom was looking back at the house now. She stepped closer. 'Tom. Please.'

At that, his eyes snapped back to her, and he stared at her. She still could not guess what he was feeling.

She rushed on. 'Your wife.' She swallowed. 'Your wife and daughter. Your daughter is almost grown up now. They don't . . . they don't need you like I do. Like we do.'

And now her voice had a shrill, desperate edge to it. He heard it too – he glanced back at the house again, and then he forced a smile. 'Wait here for a moment.'

He went back to the house, stepped inside. There was a long unbearable moment before he emerged with his hat and coat.

'Come on. Let's go and have a drink and talk about it.'

They walked in silence, not touching. Tom raised his hat to a couple on the opposite side of the road, then to a woman who stared at them both until they had passed.

The pub was at a junction of three roads. It was a dark little place with smeared windows and a narrow door. It was the kind of place where people came only because they needed a drink and it was there.

Tom settled Bea in the snug and went to the bar. She stared out of the window at the row of houses opposite. On the end of the last house was a fading advertisement for Guinness, over which someone had recently pasted a bright poster. There was a border of shapes in red and black and the words SOUTH AFRICA in tall letters at the top. Below that was an expanse of yellow, eight or nine brown stick-like figures, and a man in the foreground with skin so dark it was almost blue. The whole thing was lurid and sickly against the grey afternoon light, and she turned away from it.

Tom came back with two brandies. It was the first time he'd failed to ask her what she wanted to drink.

He took a gulp of his as he sat down and she sipped hers. It was strangely soothing and she drank again.

Tom had seated her so that she was facing outwards, and he had his back to the room. So that no one coming in would recognize him, she realized.

She waited for him to begin.

When he did, he sounded tired. Flat. 'I don't know what to do. I can't . . .' He shook his head. 'My daughter . . .'

'Tom, *this* is . . .' His pained look made her lower her voice. 'This is your daughter. Or your son.'

He ran his hand over his head in that old familiar gesture. Swallowed the last of his brandy.

And then he took a deep breath and he said, 'It's not. Not yet. It's just . . . it's not a child yet. But Judith . . . Judith needs me.'

'*We need you.*' Without thinking, she reached for him.

He flinched. Pulled back. Glanced around him.

He leaned towards her and spoke in a low voice. 'Can't you . . . won't you think about . . . the alternatives? We can find someone to take care of it. I can't . . .'

He sat back and closed his eyes for a moment, then: 'I can't support two households.' He reached in his pocket for a handkerchief, but instead of lifting it to his nose or his eyes, he kept it clutched in his fingers, rubbing it and twisting it.

'I can't . . .' he said – and then, like a child, 'I don't know what to do.'

Bea looked at his trembling hands, at the shadows beneath his eyes.

He said, 'You need to be sensible, Beatrice.'

He leaned forward. 'Think, darling – only think! If you were to give it up . . . why, things could just go back to the way they were. *We* could go back.'

His expression softened and he looked into her eyes. He stretched out one hand and stroked his fingers gently against hers, then moved his hand away again.

Could they ever go back to how things were – before?

Then she thought of how it felt to grow up in a house where one did not belong. She thought of how this child – their child – would feel, growing up without parents, knowing itself to be unloved and unwanted. And she said, 'No.'

His eyes widened. He opened his mouth to speak but she said, 'We can't go back. How can we go back?'

She pressed on. The certainty was there now, clear and cold as winter rain and she would not let him do this.

'I won't give this child up, Tom. I can't do it. I won't.'

She swallowed. 'You must see that you *have* to leave her. Make her see that . . . We need you.'

He shook his head. 'I don't see . . . I don't . . . What do I tell her?'

She took a breath. She must give him some of her strength. Her conviction. 'Tell her the truth.' Surely it was that simple.

He jerked his chin up. Looked at her in horror.

'I can't.'

'You must.' She made herself say it. 'You *must*, Tom.'

He looked down at his hands, still clutching his handkerchief. Twisting and twisting. Bea saw now that there was a crooked *T* embroidered in green thread in one corner. He ran his nail over the uneven stitches. Tears filled his eyes and he blinked them away.

She pushed her own glass towards him and he drank gratefully.

'For God's sake, Tom! You must do *something*. This . . . this isn't going to go away.'

At last, he nodded. Still staring down at the handkerchief: 'Yes, I can see that.'

She let out a long breath and took the glass out of his hand. She placed her lips where his had been, and drank.

When she put the glass down, he was watching her. She smiled at him. 'I do love you, Tom. We'll be happy, I promise. I'll make you happy.'

'I'll tell her. This week.' And then – slowly, biting his lip, considering the idea – 'After that, we might go away for a little while. Just long enough for her to get used to things.'

She felt a smile tugging at the corners of her mouth. Let it bloom. 'Oh, Tom! Oh, *yes*.'

He was nodding now. 'We might even think about going abroad to live. Afterwards.'

She reached out and laid her hand on his arm and felt the warmth of him and the tautness of the muscle beneath his shirt.

She must remember this moment in the months and years to come – the moment when they had begun to talk about a future together, a real future. This was where the balance had shifted from him and his wife and daughter to his new family. Towards all these bright possibilities.

He cleared his throat and when he spoke again, his voice was stronger. 'We'll go away for a week or so, then come back and fetch our things. Say goodbye properly.'

'It's a wonderful idea, darling. And much the best way for everyone.' Now that it was over, she could be kind. 'And abroad, somewhere no one knows us, we could start again, just the two of us.' She touched her stomach gently. 'The three of us.'

There was a little beat of silence and then she said, 'Where do you think we might live?'

He glanced at her and then turned to look out of the window – and when she followed his gaze, she saw he was staring at the poster on the wall of the house opposite. He looked

at her and raised an eyebrow, then dipped his chin towards the
yellow, the red, the brown.

'*South Africa?*'

He smiled. 'Why not?'

She said, 'It's so far,' and he nodded. 'Exactly. We need to
get right away. From everyone. From all *this*.'

His wrist jerked, and the movement took in the shabby little
pub, the landlord wiping down the bar with a greying cloth,
pretending to listen to a woman standing at the bar with her
elbows set firmly in front of her and her mouth sticky with port
and lemon. It took in the thickening fog beyond the window,
the smell of unwashed bodies, the knowledge that she must go
home alone tonight, even after everything.

She looked again at the poster and the colours were warm
and light against the dinginess of this strange day, which had
begun so badly and ended with everything she wanted.

When she turned back, his eyes were bright. 'It's not the
first time I've thought about this. I've heard it's a great country for men who are willing to work hard.' He leaned forward.
'I know two or three chaps who've gone out there and made
good.'

Then he shook his head. 'It doesn't matter *there* who your
grandfather was or where you went to school.'

She still couldn't imagine it. How was it possible to board a
ship in England and then disembark somewhere so unknown?
She thought of photographs she had seen in books and magazines: of mountains and vast seas, of strange fruits piled in
pyramids. How did one move from this life to that?

She took a breath and made herself smile. 'How long is the
sea voyage, do you know? Would we sail from Southampton?'

'From France.' As he spoke, there was a noise from the bar,
and Tom turned to see the woman leaning towards the landlord, hitting the counter with a soft fist to emphasize her words.

He turned back to Bea. 'We'll take the boat train.'

That at least was more familiar. They could have a week in Paris. Perhaps two. She thought of dressmakers, galleries, of the kind of cafes she had seen in paintings and read about: long mirrors and surly waiters and cheap bottles of good wine. They might find a little hotel with wrought-iron balconies and green shutters, with home-made jam at breakfast, and coffee in bowls. And a landlady with dyed hair and kind eyes who would call her *chérie* and tell her how romantic their story was. How very *French.*

'Perfect.' She squeezed his fingers and waited for him to look at her. 'But first, we'll go away. Just for a little while. Exactly as you said.' She smiled at him again. 'It will give me time to show you how happy I can make you. Let's call it an experiment. One where I can prove how much I love you.'

He nodded.

'So we are agreed then, Tom? We'll leave Morley's and go away? Together?'

'Yes.' He cleared his throat. 'Yes, we'll do that. But' – and now his other hand slid forward to cover hers – 'when you tell them in the office that you're leaving, don't . . . don't tell them about us. Don't mention me.'

'I don't . . . what do you mean?'

He pulled his hand away and ran it through his hair. 'I don't know exactly when I'll have the chance to tell my wife.'

'But . . .'

'I should hate for her to find out from anyone but me. You do understand, darling?'

She needed him to see that she could be kind, and patient, and worthy. She nodded.

'And even after I tell her, after we're gone . . . well, she may still have to work there. It would be dreadful for her to be the subject of gossip. You can see that, can't you?'

After we're gone.

'Of course, darling. We must do what we can to smooth things over. For everyone.'

She could see how terrible it had been for him – how painful was the idea of leaving his child.

But it was done now. The decision was made.

At last he raised her hand to his lips. And now his wife was slipping away, quite unimportant, in the rush of love and triumph.

24

Bea, April 1924

Two days later, Bea stepped off the omnibus and walked down Moorgate for the last time.

Every sensation was as clear and bright as though she was feeling it for the first time: a loose stone under her thin-soled shoe; the smell of pipe smoke from a group of men in shirt-sleeves; the turn onto Copthall Avenue, feeling the seam of her stocking rub against the corn on her toe, thinking through what was about to happen. And then the approach to the office – the stone steps worn smooth and pitted with use, the coolness of the smeared brass rail under her fingers, the dimness of the hallway. All for the last time.

She was filled with air – buoyant, white, dazzling – lifting her so that she barely felt the lack of sleep or food. It filled her and kept out the grey, the drudgery, the dreariness.

Into the office for the last time, waiting for the girls to trickle in behind her, and then forward to Miss Shepherd's desk. She had not thought through what she was going to say, and so it came out in a rush, in a series of bubbles, each one floating from her like a rainbow and popping in a glorious joyful burst *one-two-three*.

I am resigning.
I should like to leave at once. I know I will forfeit my wages but
But I am leaving
I am leaving London.

The bubbles were all burst and the words sat between them, and they could not be taken back. And now the air was out of her and she was standing squarely on the office carpet and her back was aching and her shoes were pinching and all three of them – Miss Shepherd and Caroline and Jessie – they were all looking at her in astonishment.

Miss Shepherd laid down her pen and removed her spectacles. Rubbed the bridge of her nose.

'Miss Cade, I . . . I hardly know what to say.' She shook her head. 'I had thought you were . . . well, I thought you were perfectly content here. I had come to think of you as a possible . . . Might I at least ask why?'

She could not contain it, not at all – one final glorious bubble full of light and colour: 'I am getting married.'

'*Married?*' That was Caroline, and Bea turned and smiled directly at her, wide and blazing and triumphant. Then she stretched out her left hand and both girls stared down at the sapphire and diamond ring on her third finger, and then back up to her flushed and shining face. And then Caroline blinked, twice, and looked away.

Miss Shepherd said, 'You are . . .' She cleared her throat, replaced her spectacles. 'I had never supposed . . .'

No, Bea wanted to say. No one did.

She looked at Miss Shepherd, at her fawn blouse, her tweed suit, her ringless hands.

Now you see how very different I am from you.

She waited until Albert came in with the coffee, until the girls went off together to the lavatory, then followed them.

As she approached the ladies', she heard their voices: low, strained. She pushed open the door and there they were by the sink, frozen, staring at her. She nodded to them, and went into the cubicle and imagined the words they would be mouthing and the way their faces would be stretching around those words.

When she opened the door, they stepped aside to let her use the sink. She washed her hands, arranged her hair with damp fingers, and all the time she was watching them both in the mirror.

It was Jessie who spoke first. 'Do tell us about your fiancé, Miss Cade. We thought . . . well, we didn't know that you . . . that you had someone.'

Bea looked at her in the mirror and smiled. 'I didn't. Not until recently.' She reached for the grimy towel. 'He rather swept me off my feet.' She dried her hands slowly, looking down at her ring and smiled again. 'He's terribly passionate.'

And now she looked at Caroline's reflection. 'You know how it is when a man simply must be with you. He won't let anything get in the way of our getting married as soon as we possibly can.' Caroline watched her and said nothing.

Bea hung up the towel, turned back to her reflection, smoothed down her skirt.

Jessie leaned against the sink and tilted back on her heels. 'Where will you live? Does he have a house in London?'

'Oh, no. We're going to live abroad.'

Now Caroline spoke. '*Abroad?*'

Bea turned to her and smiled. 'We're going to honeymoon in Paris and then decide where to live.' She mustn't mention money, not directly – that would be vulgar. But: 'We shan't need to make a firm decision at once. We plan to travel for a while.'

Jessie put her head on one side. 'How romantic! May I see your ring again?'

Bea held out her hand, fingers splayed, and watched the sapphire gleam under the artificial light.

And as she did so, she thought of the little jeweller's shop near Farringdon that she had visited the day before.

She thought of the man there who had sold her the ring: thought of his stooped figure, his thin hands. He had blinked slowly as he came to understand that she was not there to buy a gift, or to sell something, or to have her watch repaired. These were practical things, things with purpose and sense to them.

A woman buying a ring for herself – and a solitaire for her third finger at that – made no sense to him at all.

The man said nothing of any importance, merely measured Bea's finger and made enquiries about her budget, then brought out tray after tray of glittering promises.

And then at the end, when she had picked out the biggest, darkest sapphire she could afford and nodded – 'That one, I think' – he made one last attempt to resolve it in his mind.

'Will your . . . ah . . . will the gentleman be collecting this?'

Bea shook her head. 'No. Thank you. I'll take it now.'

She had paid him in full and then she had taken the ring out of the little velvet box. Leaving the satin lining empty and wanting, she slid the ring onto her own finger.

As Jessie bent over her hand now, Bea watched Caroline glance down at her own ring and then back. She watched the way her lips pursed and the line that deepened between her eyebrows.

And now she imagined Tom resigning too. She imagined him saying to Mr Morley, saying to the whole office: 'I'm going away with Miss Cade. We're terribly in love. I love her and we're getting married.'

She imagined how he might smile. The way he might leave the office without another word. And she imagined their shocked, stupid faces staring after him.

*

She wrote to Jane.

I know we parted on bad terms. But I have some wonderful news. News I must tell you in person.

When Bea arrived at the Corner House, Jane was already there, looking towards the door, her face tense and expectant. She rose, unsmiling, and bent towards Bea, her lips almost touching her skin. As they sat down, the waitress brought a pot of tea.

'I ordered earlier. We have things to discuss, and I didn't want the girl overhearing.'

Bea was unwinding her scarf, taking off her coat. She waited until Jane was watching, then removed her gloves, slowly, unable to stop her smile breaking out and broadening and broadening.

'I've been thinking about our conversation at Christmas. And about what you . . . *oh!* Oh my goodness. Is that . . . ? Bea?'

Bea held out her left hand so that Jane could admire the ring. She turned her wrist so that the stones sparkled, and Jane stared.

Then she snapped upright. 'I don't understand, Bea. This is the same man? Surely he's still . . . he must still be *married*?' Her voice was hushed.

'He's going to leave her. He's going to tell her this week, then we're going away. He's going to ask for a divorce.'

He would divorce her. He must.

'A *divorce*? Good God, Beatrice, you can't have thought this through! Divorce is for . . . well, it's for *degenerates*. You read about it in the scandal sheets – girls in cheap hotels, all that business.' She was shaking her head. 'No one respectable gets divorced. *No one.*'

Bea took a deep breath. 'We're going abroad. Somewhere

with fewer rules and restrictions. Somewhere divorce doesn't matter like it does here.'

'Abroad? Just the two of you?' Jane's eyes narrowed. 'How long have you known him? *Do* you know him – really?'

Bea pulled the teapot towards her and lifted the lid to stir the leaves. 'I know enough. I know he loves me. He's giving up everything for me.'

She set down the spoon and met Jane's eyes. 'Look, I know what you think. And I understand why you feel this way. Really, I do. But he's awfully good to me. And I can't give him up. I . . . I just can't.'

'Bea, I don't—'

'No – please, listen. I want to explain.' She looked down at her ring. 'I've felt for so long that . . . well, that I didn't really know what I was doing with my life. I've never really been able to plan for the future.' She swallowed. 'I know you won't understand that – you have Charles, and the children – but . . . well, I've been alone for a long time.'

'I suppose you blame me for that.'

'No, of course not. Jane, I—'

'When Mother died, I was all you had. I should have offered you a home then. I should have done *something*.'

'Jane.' Bea put a hand on her sister's. 'Don't.'

'But I . . . I can't . . .'

'It's done now. And everything's worked out – I have Tom. I'm happy. You don't need to worry.' And then, astonished: 'Do you know, I think this is the first time I've ever seen you cry.'

Jane waved this away. 'Ignore me. I just . . .' She took a lace-edged handkerchief from her sleeve and blotted her eyes. Sniffed and said, 'Where will you go, do you know yet?'

Bea could hear the effort it took for her to keep her voice steady. She tried to make her tone light in return.

'We're thinking of South Africa.'

There was a pause and then Jane said, 'But it's so far away.'

'Well, I really think this could be the making of Tom.' She rushed on, 'Anyway, we're going to Paris first.'

'Very romantic.' Jane's tone was dry – but when Bea looked at her, she shook her head. 'Sorry. It's just – well, it's rather clichéd.'

Bea smiled. She felt that she would never stop smiling. 'I don't care. We're going to get married there. In Paris. Can you imagine?'

After all, they must be married soon – and why not Paris?

She looked down at the ring, moved her hand again so that it sparkled, and her smile broadened. 'We have so many plans. We both want to travel. I just feel so . . . well, you know how it is when you're in love. We have such a marvellous future ahead of us.'

Jane laid down her cup and looked at her. 'Are you sure? I mean, absolutely sure? You'll be a long way from home if anything goes wrong.'

'Nothing will go wrong. What could go wrong? Jane, I'll be forty in a couple of years. I'm hardly a silly schoolgirl – I'm old enough and sensible enough to make my own decisions.'

'I know.' Jane sighed. 'I know you are. It's just difficult sometimes to see . . .' She blew her nose. 'When are you planning to leave?'

'Not just yet. This isn't goodbye.' She smiled. 'But soon. Neither of us wants to wait.'

'I know you're not a child any more. But you will remember, won't you, that if anything does go wrong, I'm here. You can write to me, I can wire you money if you need to come home.'

Bea swallowed her irritation. 'I know you mean to be kind. But I'll—'

'And in the meantime . . .' Jane fumbled in her bag, took out her cheque book. 'This is for you' – scribbling – 'in case you need it.' She tore out the page, folded it, held it out. As Bea's fingers closed over it, she said, 'Cash it, and keep the money. Just in case. Promise me.'

'Jane, I . . .'

'Please. Promise me. It would reassure me to know that you have a safety net.'

This time it was Jane who reached out for her hand. She clasped it, and they sat in silence. Like sisters.

It was three days since she had heard from Tom.

Suppose he had changed his mind? Suppose he . . . No. He loved her. And this was *his* plan. He wouldn't go back on his word.

When she reached the club, she went straight to her pigeon-hole, but it was empty. She closed her eyes for a moment and took a long breath. Would she have to go back to Richmond? Must she . . . She heard her name being called, and turned to see Mrs McIvor holding out a telegram.

'This arrived an hour ago.' She peered at Bea over her spectacles. 'I believe I have made myself perfectly clear on the matter of telegrams, Miss Cade. They require effort outside of the staff's normal routine and as such, they can only be accepted in the *most* dire emergencies.'

Bea had torn it open, was scanning the contents.

'I trust this *is* an emergency, Miss Cade?'

'An . . . ? Oh, yes. Yes, quite so.' She stuffed the telegram into her bag and straightened up. 'I'm afraid I must give you notice, Mrs McIvor.'

'Notice, Miss Cade? You surprise me. I was under the impression that you were *quite* satisfied with the terms here.'

'Oh, I am! I have been. Really. But I . . .' Pink with pleasure and unable to contain her smile, Bea held out her left hand.

Mrs McIvor leaned forward, then looked up at Bea. She seemed to require an explanation.

'We're . . . I'm getting married. The telegram was from . . . from my fiancé. Letting me know that everything is fixed up. We're getting married, and then we're going abroad.'

'Well.' Mrs McIvor's tone was decidedly chilly. 'It all seems rather . . . rushed, Miss Cade.'

'Yes. Well, Tom – my fiancé – has a job fixed up. An awfully good one. It's all arranged. It's all happened rather quickly.' She smiled. 'You're one of the first people I've told, Mrs McIvor.'

Something passed over Mrs McIvor's face and her expression lightened. 'How very . . . gratifying. I see that congratulations are in order. I shall prepare your final account, Miss Cade. And in view of the . . . celebratory occasion, and the expenses you will no doubt incur in the near future, I shall only charge you the full month if I am unable to find a replacement for your room.'

'Thank you, Mrs McIvor. That's very kind. I'll be moving out in the next week or so. I'll let you know' – and she ran up the stairs to begin her packing.

An hour later, Bea sat on the floor amid the wreckage of her room. She was surrounded by piles of books, by screwed-up balls of newspaper, her few ornaments, shoes, a hat box – and her bed was covered with coats and dresses and scarves. She blew the hair off her forehead, then took out Tom's telegram again.

FOUND COTTAGE STOP NEAR EASTBOURNE STOP BOOKED FOR TWO WEEKS STOP MEET WATERLOO LEFT LUGGAGE 5.00 SUNDAY STOP

On top of one of the piles was a striped blouse that Alice had always admired. Bea picked it up, shook it out, held it up in front of her. Then she folded it over her arm and looked around the room again. Scent bottles, her hairbrushes and hand mirror, a little row of books on the windowsill. The book at the end was new, unopened.

Bea took the book and the blouse and walked into the

hallway – quickly, before she could change her mind. Ellen's door was open and she could see that the room was empty. She walked along the corridor, and knocked on another door and waited.

When Alice opened it, she looked surprised at first. Then she smiled – openly, guilelessly – and said, 'Bea. How nice to see you.' She opened the door wider and Bea saw Ellen behind her, frowning as though she was trying to place her.

Alice turned a little and said, 'Come in.'

Bea shook her head and held up the blouse in front of her body. 'I can't. I only came to say goodbye.'

'Goodbye?' Ellen came forward so that the two of them filled the doorway.

'I'm leaving. Moving out.'

'But . . . but where are you going? Do you have a new job?'

Bea looked down into Alice's small anxious face and tucked her left hand into the pocket of her skirt. She wouldn't lie to them.

'Not yet. I just came to bring you this' – and she thrust the blouse into the space between them.

'And this' – she held the book out to Ellen. '*Jacob's Room*. It's by a woman author. It's meant to be very clever.'

Alice was holding the blouse crumpled in her hands like a dishrag. She reached out and touched Bea's arm. 'I don't understand. Are you all right?'

And now Ellen said, 'This is awfully sudden, Bea.'

Bea looked down at Alice's little white hand resting on her wrist. She blinked, then coughed to clear her throat. 'Quite all right. I just need a change.'

She blinked again, then patted Alice's hand and stepped back, so that Alice was left clutching at the air.

'Anyway. I just wanted to tell you. I just wanted you to know.' She nodded at the pale, blurred faces in the doorway, and turned away.

Three steps across the hallway, with her head high and the weight of their curiosity pulling at her, and then she was back in her own room with the door closed behind her.

Whatever happened, she would not come back here. She would pack everything up, take it all with her. And when the two weeks were up, when Tom returned to tidy things up in Richmond, she would stay at a hotel and wait for him.

She leaned against the door and looked around her, trying to take it all in, telling herself to fix it in her mind like a painting or a photograph: the leaf detail of the cornice, and the patch by the door that still showed through the cream paint as a sickly green. The huge Victorian wardrobe that she had always hated, as it stole all the light from that corner of the room. The faded wallpaper; the cheap blue rug on the narrow strip of floor, and the darker wood around it where a larger, grander rug had once sat. The fireplace with the yellow tiles; the washstand with jug and cracked bowl; the shelf above with three or four books huddled at one end. The picture postcard on the mantelpiece, left by a previous tenant, showing a river scene with bluebells and two small rowing boats. She had intended to buy a vase of wax flowers to put beside it, she remembered now.

Somehow she'd never found the time.

25

Kate, July 1924

On the morning of the second day, one of the black-clad men –
a little rat-faced clerk – stands and says: 'The prosecution calls
Mrs Charles Bishop.'

At first I think that perhaps this is another woman of Tom's
acquaintance, but as she makes her way to the witness box, I
see that she is wearing full mourning: a smart black hat, a black
dress, black furs despite the heat. She is a fat woman – plump
hands striped with sparkling rings, a broad face with little red
eyes half lost in folds of flesh.

Moran says, 'Your name is Mrs Charles Bishop?'

'Yes.'

Her voice is clearly audible, but she keeps her head bowed,
her shoulders hunched.

'And your relationship to Miss Cade?'

'Beatrice Cade is . . . she was my sister.'

The reporters scribble quickly and a murmur ripples around
the courtroom. I think Mrs Bishop hears it, for a faint blush
colours her cheeks, and she sits a little straighter.

It is not sympathy, not exactly, but something like curiosity. This is as close as they can get to Miss Cade. Mrs Bishop
is their Madame Tussaud's waxwork: they can see her, they can
almost touch her hand, and that hand once touched the dead
woman.

I do not want to be close to Mrs Bishop at all. It is difficult
even to look at her – at the path her tears have made through

her face powder, at the slight tremor in the hand that occasionally lifts a handkerchief to her eyes.

I glance at Tom and see that he is not looking at her either. All his attention is on Moran.

'When did you last see your sister, Mrs Bishop?'

'We had tea together in April. At the beginning of April.'

'Can you tell us the substance of your conversation with Miss Cade on that occasion?'

'She told me that she was engaged to be married.' Her voice trembles and she cannot help looking over at Tom as she says this: just a flicker of her eyes, but it is there.

He keeps his eyes lowered and shakes his head very slightly. The woman beside me shakes her head too.

'Did you give her anything that day?'

'I gave her a cheque for thirty pounds.' Her voice is steadier now.

'And was the cheque cashed?'

'It was.' She looks at Tom again, for longer this time. Her eyes are hard and grey and glistening.

'Were you close to your sister, Mrs Bishop?'

'Oh yes. Very close.' She rushes on, the words spilling out of her. 'We saw each other as often as we could, although our lives were very different – which was only natural as I was married and she was leading a . . . a different kind of life in London.' She holds her handkerchief to her nose for a moment, and then she says, 'I moved down south while she was still a girl. To Kent, where my husband is in business.'

'What kind of girl was your sister? Was she, for example, a fiery person? Did she ever demonstrate a bad temper?'

Mrs Bishop is shaking her head before he has finished speaking. 'Oh, no. Beatrice was a quiet, cheerful girl. She didn't have a temper.' She dabs her nose again and swallows. 'She was not a passionate sort of person at all.'

I hear a little sob from behind me, and I turn to see the

woman with the silver hair who was sitting next to me yesterday. Today her hair is mostly covered by a large old-fashioned hat. I haven't seen a hat like that since I was a child and so I expect her to be old, spinsterish – but when she lifts her head, I see that she is very young, and that the hat frames her face like petals around a flower.

She is staring straight at Tom and as I watch, the woman next to her – taller, sharp-nosed – reaches out and takes her hand in both of her own.

I hear Moran say, 'How did Miss Cade earn her living?' and I turn to face them again.

Mrs Bishop says, 'She worked as a typist at a factory in Newcastle. After our mother died, she moved to London and found a position as a bookkeeper – then in June or July last year she got the job at Morley's.'

And now I can hear the flat northern vowels under the refined accent she has cultivated, no doubt to fit in with her husband's smart friends.

'Mrs Bishop, for the benefit of the jury, can you identify this photograph?' Moran turns to the jury – 'Exhibit 54, gentlemen.'

The photograph is held up by the clerk before being passed into the witness box. We all crane to see. It shows a woman glancing back over her shoulder at the camera. A narrow scarf is tied around her hair, which is pinned up to show her long neck, circled by a string of beads. She is not looking at the photographer, but glancing off to the side, a slight smile playing over her lips. It is a careful photograph. She has tried hard to look mysterious. Coquettish.

She does not look at all like the woman who came to my door that evening.

Someone grunts behind me – 'Mutton dressed as lamb, that one.'

Mrs Bishop holds the photograph in front of her for several

moments. 'That's Beatrice,' she says, and her voice is thick. 'That's my sister.' Her voice cracks on the last word, and I feel the weight of it, despite myself.

With surprising delicacy, given what I have seen of him so far, Moran gives her a little longer to look at it, then signals to the usher to pass the photograph to the jury. She looks after it as it is carried across the room, and then Moran moves on.

'Let the record show that I am now handing Mrs Bishop exhibit 42, a diamond and sapphire ring. Do you recognize this item?'

She takes it from the clerk and looks at it for a long moment. 'Beatrice showed me this ring before she left London. She said it was an engagement ring.'

There is a gasp from behind me at this, and a low hum of conversation breaks out.

Someone calls for order and I bow my head. I had no idea about this. No one has mentioned an engagement ring to me.

Mrs Bishop says, 'She was very proud of it.'

I fold my hands. I rub my own rings, over and over.

'Beatrice told me that the name of the man she was engaged to was Tom. But she . . . she never told me his surname.'

Her eyes are fixed on Moran, and I see that now she is deliberately avoiding looking at Tom.

'What else did you know about Miss Cade's fiancé?'

'She said he had a good post in South Africa. He wanted her to go with him. I understood they were to be married—' Her voice cracks again and she takes a deep breath. 'They were to be married in France on the way to South Africa.'

Now she looks at Tom. Her lips are very thin. She looks at him as though she wants to hurt him.

He is still looking down, and now he shakes his head again.

'Thank you, Mrs Bishop.' Moran clears his throat. 'And now we come to exhibits 61, 62 and 63 – that is, a tortoiseshell brush, comb and mirror.' He waits for the clerk to pass them over. Looks at the court typist hunched over her machine, and raises his voice a fraction. 'Let the record show that these items were found by the police in the cottage during their search on the second of May. Mrs Bishop, can you positively identify these as belonging to your sister?'

Mrs Bishop holds the brush in both her hands. She is very pale. She bows her head and breathes deeply. I wonder if her sister's hair is still tangled in the bristles, if she can smell her sister's perfume. For a moment I almost think she will kiss the handle – but she raises her eyes and says, 'Yes. These things belonged to my sister. She had them since she was a girl.'

'Thank you. And these, this pendant and these glass beads – exhibits 67 and 68 – do you recognize these?'

She takes the gold pendant from the clerk, runs the chain between her fingers. 'Yes,' she says. 'I remember this. I have seen her wearing it. And the beads' – stroking them – 'these were my sister's too. They belonged to my mother and she . . . when she . . .'

Suddenly she turns on Tom. 'That was my *sister*, you *animal*, that was . . .'

I cannot look at him. I keep my gaze on the red wet face and on the respectable fur coat as she is led away amid a hum of voices.

'Well. *What* an exhibition. You'd think she'd know better than to behave like that in a court of law.'

'They clearly weren't even close. Didn't you hear what she said? She moved away years ago.'

'Crocodile tears, then. I hate to speak ill of the dead, but didn't you think . . .' The voices drop to a murmur and I hear, 'Did you notice . . .'

I stop listening and look at the door she went through. I think of the way she bowed her head over the hairbrush, how her voice broke on the word 'sister'.

*

The next witness is Walter Montgomery, from the Copthall Avenue office. I sit back in my seat when his name is called, not wanting him to see me. It is more than a year since Mr Montgomery visited the Sunbury office, but he has a good memory.

I needn't have been concerned: all of his attention is first on Tom – he stares at him, curls his lip, then pointedly turns away – and then on Moran and the judge, to whom he addresses himself.

'Your name is Walter St John Montgomery?'

'It is.'

'And you are senior accountant at the firm of Morley and Morley, of 10 Copthall Avenue, London?'

'I am.'

Moran frowns at his notes. 'How is it that you are here today, rather than Mr Morley? I understand he was actually Miss Cade's employer?'

'Mr Morley is unfortunately unwell. He is in – *hem* – in hospital with heart trouble.'

I am astonished to find myself blinking back tears when I hear this. I had thought I had no room to feel anything towards anyone other than Tom. But now I find that I am sorry for Mr Morley, who was a good man, and who had his share of trouble before all of this. He lost his only son in the War. When I started at Morley's, I told Mr Morley that Tom was away, in the army – and he offered him a job when he came home.

I realize now that it is not likely I will ever see Mr Morley again. Even if he recovers and returns to work, and when Tom . . . if Tom and I get through this, I will not be able to stay at Morley's. We will have to move again, make another fresh start.

That will mean more deceit and more loneliness. It will mean leaving Richmond, perhaps even moving away from the south-east. We will need to walk away from almost every memory that Judith has of her childhood.

Mr Morley was kind to me, kind to us both. I wonder if he knows yet about Tom's background. About all the lies I told.

Every part of me aches with tiredness. I wish I was here out of idle curiosity or morbid interest, like the rest. That I could just walk out now, just go home and forget about all of it.

Mr Montgomery is still talking in his thin, rather high voice.

'Miss Cade was employed by the firm as a shorthand typist and bookkeeper from – *hem* – from July 1923 until April of this year. She gave her notice and left our employment at the beginning of April: it was my – *hem* – understanding that she was engaged to be married.'

His eyebrows rise as he says this last part.

Moran says, 'Can you tell us something of the prisoner's position at the firm?'

Mr Montgomery glances at Tom. Wets his lips.

'Mr Ryan – that is, the prisoner – was employed by Morley's as a salesman and – *hem* – worked directly under Mr Morley. In this position, he sometimes visited our office, where he had the – *hem* – opportunity to become . . . acquainted with Miss Cade.'

'And his wife?'

It is a shock to hear myself referred to like this, in the silence of this room, in earshot of all of these people. I bow my head, try to hide my flushed face, hope that those around me will assume I am affected by the heat.

'The prisoner's wife is employed at our – *hem* – our Sunbury office, under Mr Simpson, the chief clerk.'

'What were Miss Cade's duties at the firm?'

'She did some of the typing for Miss Shepherd, our office manager, and she assisted me with the keeping of our accounts.'

'Was her work satisfactory?'

'Her work was perfectly satisfactory, yes.' Do I imagine the slight emphasis on the second word?

'She never gave any cause for complaint?'

'As far as I am aware, her work gave no cause for complaint, although she was somewhat – *hem* – *flighty* for a woman of her age.'

There is no mistaking the emphasis this time. Nor the little smiles from those around me that follow his remark.

The rest of the morning is mostly taken up with short statements.

Four or five hotel receptionists and chambermaids give evidence about where Tom was during February and March, and with whom, and the reporters take down every word.

They spent evenings in various hotel rooms in London, it seems, and a Saturday afternoon in a hotel near Reading.

Intimacy took place on several occasions. At various locations.

In the afternoon: something quite different.

Two men carry in a bulky object covered by a sheet and place it on a waiting table. The cloth is whisked away and there is a little ripple of surprise; one or two relieved laughs.

A doll's house. There could be no object more out of place here.

Low chatter rises and loops around the room, and we all lean forward to see more clearly.

It is perfectly constructed: a one-storey cottage, set within a garden, with a low wall running around the whole. The walls are white and the roof has been painted to resemble slate. There are two windows on each of the walls and, on the side facing me, a door between the windows with – I lean forward further – a low step and a lintel. Some of the garden is painted green and the rest dabbed grey and white to show pebbles.

It's a pretty house – the kind of very English cottage that

one thinks of when one imagines holidaying in the country or by the sea.

Moran steps forward and addresses the judge.

'Exhibit 183, my Lord.'

And then to the jury: 'This is a model of the cottage at Eastbourne where the prisoner stayed with Miss Cade.'

He looks at the house. 'I think we will have the roof off' – he makes a gesture and the men come forward again and take the roof away.

Now we can peer inside it. Now we can imagine figures passing to and fro, behind this window, through that doorway. And yet, oddly, only one of the rooms is furnished. It is the room onto which the front door opens directly, and it is decorated as a sitting room, with a settee and armchairs, all covered in floral fabrics. There is a table, a patterned rug, flowered wallpaper. There are even postage stamp-sized pictures on the walls and a tiny clock, the size of a fingernail.

While these men argue about purpose and positions, about what could be heard and seen, about what may or may not have been said and done, while those around me whisper and lean forward to listen, I look at the house and I see – just a house.

I imagine opening the front door and stepping into the room. I imagine sitting at that table to write a letter; in this armchair to read a book. Was it warm by the fireplace or did the damp salt air creep in around the windows and under the door? Would the pattern of the rug have bothered me as being too garish, or would I have grown used to it after a day or two?

Then I wonder what *she* thought. Did she find it welcoming, or too cold, too damp, too remote?

For the first time I wonder what it was like to be her. What did she expect when she stepped through that door? What did she feel?

Was she afraid?

And once I have let that thought in, I find I cannot make it leave. The possibility of her fear infects me. I see her as she was that afternoon on the doorstep of my home: her hand clutching at her coat, swallowing over and over and unable to meet my eyes.

26

Bea, April 1924

It was not quite dark when they arrived. The taxi from the station took them right to the door and stopped, and the driver turned around and said, 'That's seven and eightpence.'

Tom was staring out at the low dense shape of the cottage against the purple night. She touched his arm: he started, and fished in his pocket to pay, then opened the door and they made their way up the path.

They stood at the door for a moment, almost as though they were expecting someone to open it. Waves crashed on a distant shore, and Bea thought she tasted salt on her lips. Behind them, the driver started the engine, and she half turned to watch him leave. The headlights flared wide and white, then the car moved off and the light died.

Tom put the key in the lock and pushed the door. It stuck for a moment and he had to use his shoulder to open it. Then he held it for her to enter, and she was inside and for a moment there was only thick darkness and a strong smell of damp and his breath behind her. Then he moved past her and she heard him stumbling forward, and then there was the flare of a match, a gradual brightening and a soft yellow glow – and he came back through a doorway carrying two oil lamps.

She set down her handbag and saw that they were in a small living room. Her overwhelming impression was of clutter and clashing prints. The curtains were a riot of blue and yellow daisies, the wallpaper cream with clusters of wildflowers. There was a threadbare rug patterned red and purple, a little bureau desk against one wall, and a worn table with two mismatched chairs. An ornate clock, stopped at five past twelve. She'd had her trunk sent on ahead, and it sat against the wall, familiar and somehow comforting.

Tom moved restlessly around the room, picking up ornaments, fingering the covers on an armchair. 'It smells rather stale.'

'Didn't you say they were sending in a woman to clean it? Air it out.'

He shrugged. 'Perhaps they forgot.' He looked around him again. 'It's not terribly . . .'

She placed her hand on his arm. 'It's perfect, darling. The important thing is that we're together.'

He smiled at that. 'And alone.'

Without thinking, she removed her gloves and said, 'I meant to check the weather forecast before we left. I don't suppose you had time?'

He didn't answer, and when she looked up, he was staring at her hands. At the ring.

And now that he had noticed it, she was ashamed of it.

'Beatrice?'

'Oh! Oh, it's just a . . . it's silly, really.'

He said nothing, just looked at her.

'It's not . . . I know that you . . .' She bent her head and rubbed her thumb over the dark stone. 'It's difficult. For me. It's difficult to be a single woman, travelling with a man. It's difficult to stay in a house with . . . with you. I didn't want people to . . .'

She looked at him again. 'You do understand, Tom?'

He nodded, but now he was looking at the ring again. 'Is this . . .'

'It's nothing.' She tugged at it. 'It was a silly idea. I'll take it off.'

He watched her and said nothing.

'I see now that it's dishonest.' She was turning it, pulling at it, trying to get it over her knuckle. 'I don't want us to start out together on a lie.'

Finally it came loose and she slipped it into the pocket of her skirt.

'Beatrice, I—'

'No – look, it's gone. Let's forget about it.'

He looked at her for a moment longer, and then he held up the lamp and they examined the room more closely. There was a brick fireplace with a dull brass fender. A tarnished coal scuttle. A shelf with a radio and an uneven row of books. There was a mismatched collection of china figurines, some pastel drawings – mainly seascapes – and three or four candlesticks.

Tom knelt by the fireplace. 'Blast it – there's hardly any coal.'

'I'm sure there'll be more somewhere, darling.'

He didn't answer, and so she picked up the other lamp, went through the far doorway and along the passage until she found herself in the kitchen. The floor was stone flags, the table in the centre bleached white, scratched and scored with the marks of knives. Most of the cupboards and shelves were bare, making the low dank room more dispiriting. There was a strange earthy smell, like vegetables kept too long in a cellar, and a box on the table. She took a step forward, peered inside. A rather hard loaf, milk, eggs, tins, matches. A packet of tea, a pot of jam.

She crouched at the stove, looking for kindling, then heard steps in the passage, saw lamplight flickering.

'It's terribly cold.'

'It'll be all right, as soon as I get the stove going. Could you bring more light over here?'

Instead he went to the window. She watched him hold the lamp so that it shone into the glass and then back again. She could see his reflection, which was not him at all, but a shape made up of shadows and hollow sockets.

She lit the stove then filled the kettle and put it on to boil.

Unpacked the groceries and began to open drawers. Tom turned at the scraping sound.

'What are you looking for?'

'A knife, to cut the bread.'

She bent to tug at the last drawer, heard his footsteps moving away down the passage.

By the time the bread was buttered, the tea was brewing and she had found a jug for the milk, the kitchen was warm and the worst of the smell had faded. It felt almost cosy now: a little yellow dot against the vast empty night around them.

She took off her coat and hat, straightened her dress and looked at her own reflection in the dark window. She pushed a lock of hair back and ran her fingers over her eyebrows.

Then out of nowhere, she thought of Caroline and Jessie and the ladies' lavatory at the office, and smiled.

She walked to the doorway. Listened. Heard nothing.

'Tom?'

Her voice sounded tentative and tiny against all the weight of the strange house. She looked back at the bright kitchen for a moment, and then heard a rustling noise from the furthest room. The door was almost closed: she could only see a tiny sliver of light against the dark hallway.

She stepped forward.

'Tom? Are you in there?'

'Just a moment.'

'Didn't you hear me calling you?'

'Go through to the living room. I'll be there in a moment.'

She reached the doorway and saw him through the gap. His suitcase lay open on the bed, and he was half inside the wardrobe with his back to her. She pushed the door.

At the creak, he whipped round sharply, then saw her and smiled.

'Sorry, darling. You made me jump. Is supper ready?'

*

They ate their picnic in the living room, tucked cosily by the fire. Bea looked at Tom spooning bramble jam onto a slice of bread, pouring tea, prodding the coals. This was their first real taste of domesticity. This was the first meal she had been able to prepare for them. The first time they had sat by their own hearth.

The sheer pleasure of this struck her as funny – the ordinariness of it, and yet the wonderful strangeness – and she smiled at him over the rim of her teacup.

'Do you realize, darling, that no one knows we're here? No one at all?'

He smiled at her then. 'Isn't it marvellous?'

She told herself she must never lose this moment. She must hold on to how perfectly happy she'd been.

After supper she went into the main bedroom first while Tom put out the fire and checked that the doors were locked. He had moved her trunk into the smaller bedroom, and she opened her Gladstone bag, which she had packed with the things she would need for the first few days.

She took out the nightdress she had bought the week before. It lay on the bed like a pool of clear water – a pale green eau de Nil. Even the words were beautiful.

She undressed quickly: she wanted him to find her ready and wrapped like a gift, not fumbling with buttons and hooks. When she slipped the nightdress over her head and let the cool satin slither down her skin, she felt, just for a moment, like someone in a magazine or a film. She felt beautiful.

She found her hairbrush and her sponge bag and took them over to the dressing table. She brushed her hair, smoothed cream into her face and neck, pressed perfume onto her wrists and into the hollows of her throat.

She looked at her pale face in the mirror. At the shadows and the planes where the lamplight caught her. She swallowed.

This would be their first whole night together. There would

be time to watch the moonlight sculpting his brow, his cheek-bones, the curve of his mouth. And tomorrow would be the first morning she would wake in his arms.

She turned down the lamp and slid between the cold sheets. She spread her hair over the pillow and ran her hands along her sides, over her stomach. She felt it flutter, imagined the swoop and dive of life in there.

The creak of the door and the bright flare of his lamp startled her awake. He came into the room and began to undress without speaking. And so she simply lay there, watching as he hung up his jacket and trousers, as he tugged his tie loose, as he moved about the room in his shirttails, folding clothes and opening and closing the wardrobe door. Then he turned his back and unbuttoned his shirt. It fell away from his shoulders, it slid down to reveal the gleam of his skin, the swell and dip of his muscles; the deep straight line of his spine, and the V-shape at the base.

Her mouth was suddenly dry, and she moved restlessly beneath the sheets. He turned to look at her and his eyes were huge and black. He turned down the light and came towards her. She rolled towards him as he lay down, and his mouth opened under hers, and she heard and tasted his ragged breath as he moved above her. His skin was so warm, the places beneath his arms and where his thighs met were damp and hot.

Then he groaned into her mouth and she was aware only of him as she opened for him and again as she moved with him, as she stretched and arched and sighed beneath him. She wrapped her legs around him and her arms went under his and she held him close as he thrust, and she felt him shudder.

He lifted his head and he called out into the night *Oh God Oh God* and as their heartbeats slowed and they lay together still and close, she felt wetness on her face. She tasted salt and reached up, and she realized he was weeping.

27

Kate, July 1924

On the third day, a new witness is called. Another woman, this one in a hat with a low brim. She wears a belted jacket and a white blouse that reveals her throat.

There are lines running from her nose to her mouth and at the corners of her mouth, and her complexion is sallow and pockmarked.

Dowdy. This woman is dowdy.

And so, this time, I assume that she is nothing to do with Tom.

Mr Moran stands, adjusts his robe, faces her. The house sits on a table between them, and neither of them look at it.

'Your name is Rose Ada Bingham?'

Her lips move but no sound comes out.

Without raising his head, the judge says, 'A little louder, please, Miss Bingham.'

She starts and flushes red all down that exposed throat. 'Yes, sir. I'm sorry. Yes' – turning to Moran – 'that is my name.'

'Thank you, Miss Bingham. And you live at Worple Avenue, in Isleworth?'

'Yes, sir.'

She has recovered herself a little, but when Moran asks her, 'Do you know the prisoner?' her head falls back and she gives a little moan.

'Oh, please. Please don't ask me . . .'

But this woman has *nothing*: no physical attraction, nor

youth, nor any kind of energy or charm. How can she possibly be part of Tom's story?

A man's voice rises behind me, muttering, 'Ah-*ha*,' ending on a satisfied sigh. I can almost hear him rubbing his hands together. I look over at the reporters and they are all writing quickly, glancing up at her to make sure they have every detail, then bending over their shorthand again.

Mr Moran frowns. 'Come now, Miss Bingham, you must answer the court's questions. I will ask you again: do you know this man, Thomas Ryan?'

She looks down. Nods. 'Yes.'

'And when did you first meet him?'

'On the . . . on the tenth of April of this year.'

Again, I think back to Kennington police station. The hand-drawn calendar; the finger jabbing at the numbered squares.

'Good. You're doing splendidly, Miss Bingham. Do you remember where you first met Mr Ryan?'

'We met just outside Richmond station. It was raining.'

'Did you meet by arrangement?'

'Oh no, quite by chance. I had never seen him before – I was sheltering from the rain and we . . . we just fell into conversation.'

'*Ha!*' – loudly, from behind me, and she twitches at it.

'Do you remember what time of day it was when you met?'

'It was late – nearly ten o'clock in the evening.'

'And did he walk with you from the station to your house in Isleworth?'

'Yes, almost all the way home.'

The woman in the red hat in front tuts and shakes her head so that the feather quivers, disapproving.

'On that occasion, did he tell you his name?'

'Only that it was Tom.'

Now her gaze darts to my husband, leaning forward in the

dock, watching her. When she says his name, there is a tic at
the corner of his eye, scarcely noticeable.

So he *has* known her. There is another woman involved in
all this. Not only Miss Cade and I, but this Miss Bingham too.

'Did you know where he lived?'

'He said in Richmond, but not where. I think he may have
pointed in the direction of Kew.'

'Did you know whether he was married or not?'

'Yes, he . . . he told me he was married.'

I cannot help myself – I look over at Tom again. And for
the first time in this courtroom, our eyes meet. His expression
does not change, but I think I see his face soften.

'Did he say anything about his married life?'

'Yes. He said . . .' Her voice drops again and the judge sighs.
'A little louder, *please*, Miss Bingham.'

'Thank you, my Lord. Miss Bingham?'

'He said his married life was . . . he said it was a tragedy.'

One little word, in her low trembling voice, but it is like a
slap.

My eyes fill with tears. I think of Judith. Of Billy.

And I feel the pull of my husband across the room – but I
will not look at him again. I keep my gaze fixed on the woman
in the witness box.

'And the man you met in Richmond: he is the prisoner in
the dock?'

'I don't . . .'

Without turning, Moran waves a hand.

'Let him stand up.'

'Oh, please. Don't. *Please.*' Now she is shaking, red-faced,
clutching the rail in front of her.

The judge motions for Tom to get to his feet. I still do not
look at him.

'Is the prisoner in the dock the man you met in Richmond,
and later in London and then in Sussex?'

She raises her head and looks about her with a kind of desperation: at Moran, then at Tate and finally the briefest glance at Tom before her hands come up and cover her eyes.

Barely concealed impatience flickers across Moran's face. He rocks back on his heels, seemingly at a loss, and then he says loudly, 'Would you like a glass of water?'

Nothing. Only the slumped figure, and the wet noise of her sobs echoing around the courtroom, across that vast expanse of silence.

'Miss Bingham?'

She shakes her head, drops her hands, takes a handkerchief from her sleeve and dabs at her eyes.

'I'm sorry. I . . . I'm sorry.'

'Is the prisoner in the dock the same man you met in Richmond on the tenth of April?'

'Yes.' She dabs her nose. 'Yes. It is the same man.'

'Did he say anything to you about meeting him again?'

'He asked would I meet him the following week.'

And it goes on: dates, times, telegrams, meetings – all come pouring out of her, slowly at first and then faster and faster, as if she cannot bear to hold it in.

Then Moran says, 'Did you go to Charing Cross station on the sixteenth of April to meet the prisoner?'

The sixteenth? But surely . . . surely this was the day after Miss Cade died?

'Yes. We had arranged to meet in a restaurant near the station.'

'At what time?'

'At seven o'clock.'

'And what time did he arrive?'

'I think about quarter to eight. Perhaps a little after.'

Her voice is quite casual, almost as though she doesn't remember. But she sat there for almost an hour – more, for she would have arrived early. Her best dress, washed and pressed;

clean nails; a string of cheap beads; those sallow cheeks pinched in front of a mirror. Checking her watch, blushing under the sneers of the waiters.

How many times have I waited for him like this – wondering where he might be, if he could have forgotten?

'Did the prisoner tell you where he had come from that day?'

'From Eastbourne.'

'Did he say anything to you regarding your going down to Eastbourne?'

'He asked if I would go down and stay there.'

'Stay with him? In the same house?'

She drops her head. 'Yes.'

The woman to my right leans forward. Tuts loudly. I watch her mouth pucker and the lines around it deepen. Her face is damp and fascinated.

I think of Tom facing me in that little cell on Monday afternoon. I think of how I wept as I told him that the shame of what he had done with Miss Cade was killing me.

He watched me weep and he said nothing at all about Miss Bingham.

Moran continues, 'Did you make any definite arrangement with him about Eastbourne?'

'We talked about train times. He said I should catch the 11.15 on the eighteenth. That is, the Friday.'

Good Friday. Judith was not at school. I was not at work.

But in his statement, Tom said he had been . . . had been with Miss Cade's body on that day. My head aches, trying to make sense of it all.

'Did you go to Eastbourne on the eighteenth by the train you had arranged?'

'Yes. Mr . . . he met me off the train. At about one o'clock.'

The courtroom is stifling. I glance over and see that all the windows are closed. A fat bluebottle hurls itself at one of the dusty panes, buzzing furiously.

'And during that afternoon, the Friday afternoon, before you drove out to the cottage, did the prisoner tell you anything that he was going to do in the cottage?'

'Do you mean about the lock? That he was going to put a lock on one of the bedroom doors?'

'What did he say exactly?'

'He said there were expensive books in one of the rooms. He said they belonged to his friend – his friend who owned the house – and he ought to put a lock on the door.'

The fly creeps down the glass, looking for air. Reaches the bottom. Circles back.

'And while you were at the cottage, did you see him doing anything to one of the doors?'

'Yes – I think it was on the Sunday.'

'What did you see him do?'

'I wasn't really watching; I only know he cut his finger.'

The buzzing grows louder.

'Which room was the door that he was working on?'

'I think it was the second bedroom. The one on the right of the passage.'

'And while the prisoner was doing something to the lock, did you see into the room at all?'

'Yes.'

'Did you notice anything in the room?'

'I saw a bed. And a . . .' She bites her lip. 'I saw a trunk.'

A rustle of whispers flares, then dies.

Moran goes on. 'And later on, did he say anything to you about the door?'

'Yes, he said, "I have locked it." '

'Did you sleep in the large bedroom; that is, the one next to the sitting room?'

The buzzing grows louder again. I itch to smack the creature into silence. I long to feel that ripe, swollen body burst under my hand.

'Miss Bingham? Did you sleep in the larger bedroom?'

'I . . . yes.'

'And Mr Ryan slept there too?'

I watch her throat ripple as she swallows. 'Yes,' she says. 'Yes.'

The reporters scribble with renewed energy. The woman beside me leans forward, her eyes bright. From behind me I hear, 'Slut.' And then, again, louder, 'Little *slut*.' It is hissed, low and thick, and spatters wetly against the railing. I flinch, and down below, Miss Bingham must catch the movement from the corner of her eye because she looks up suddenly, straight at me.

I bow my head, heart racing.

'Miss Bingham?'

'I'm sorry, I didn't . . .'

'I shall repeat the question. Did you see some ladies' articles in that room?'

'I saw a hairbrush. And a pair of shoes, I think. I don't remember anything else.'

I think of Mrs Bishop, bent over her sister's hairbrush. I realize there are tears in my eyes again.

'Did the prisoner say anything about these things?'

'I don't . . . I'm sorry, I don't remember.' I risk a glance upward. She is looking at Moran now. I am forgotten.

'No matter. When did you go back up to London?'

'On the Monday. The twenty-first.'

Easter Monday. Tom came home late that night. He climbed into bed with me and held me, his face buried hard in my neck. And as I reached to turn out the light, he said, 'Don't. Don't. Please.'

'Did you travel up with the prisoner?'

'Yes. We dined together in London then we went to the Palladium. Then we travelled to Richmond together.'

'And do you remember what time that was?'

'I think it was about midnight when we arrived at Richmond station.'

He left her and came directly to me with the taste of her still on his lips. I press the back of my hand to my mouth.

'I think it only fair to ask if you saw anything at all at the cottage which aroused any suspicion in your mind?'

'No, nothing.'

'And there was nothing odd or suspicious in the prisoner's manner?'

'No. He was the same when we first met on the tenth of April as he was the last time I saw him, on the Monday evening.'

Moran nods to the judge. 'Thank you, my Lord. No further questions.'

Mr Tate stands, adjusts his robe, then faces Miss Bingham, cocks his head, lets a moment pass. And then he says, 'I do not want to distress you, Miss Bingham. I merely wish to ask one or two questions to clear up a couple of points.'

His voice is warm. Reassuring.

'Tell me about the night you met. The tenth of April. It was a wet night, as you have said – did the prisoner offer to walk you home?'

'Yes.'

'As you were walking together, did he say that he had had a tragedy in his life?'

'He said that his married life was a tragedy.'

Tate's voice is like silk. 'I am wondering whether perhaps you mistook his observation that he had had a tragedy in his life, and that you have taken this as being a tragedy in his married life?'

'No, he said he was married. I said . . .' She swallows. 'I said, I am sorry, because I don't do things like this.' There are tears in her voice as she says this.

I hear a grunt from behind me, and the woman in front of me is shaking her head.

But I can't help thinking of Tom as he was when I met him.

Mam and Dad sometimes left us alone together in the front parlour. Tom would press his leg against mine and take my hand and whisper in my ear that he wanted to kiss me, and the daring of it would take my breath away.

And when he asked them if we might walk up to the fields together, just the two of us — asked them lightly, as if it was of no consequence at all — Dad said yes without blinking.

We went slowly up the lane that afternoon, our hands brushing together as if by accident, my heart racing. And then suddenly he turned to me and held my shoulders and he kissed me. I said no — damp, breathless — because I knew that's what I ought to say. He just smiled.

But by the third or fourth time, I couldn't help it — I was pressing back against him and our lips were open together and he touched my tongue with his. There was a moment before he pulled back where I forgot myself, forgot everything except how he felt, and I let the moment grow and swell between us, and breathed it out in a long soft moan.

Then there was a week when we didn't go to the fields. He didn't seem to understand the looks I gave him or the hints I dropped in conversation. I wondered what I had done wrong.

And one day, as I waited to stop hoping, he asked me to go for a walk again. Then he kissed me again the way I had longed for — and I felt myself melt and my thoughts grow lighter until they floated up and up and were quite lost to me. There was only his mouth, his hot breath, the smell of him — smoky and foreign and male — and there was the sound of my own breath, harsh and fast like an animal. And then there was his warm hand inside my dress, stroking my damp skin, stroking me, and the flame that flared and

blazed until my thoughts came rushing in all at once and I made
myself step back, made myself say No.

'No, Tom. Don't.'

'Tom, we can't.'

I don't do things like this.

He only kissed me harder. His hands clutched at me. I felt his
nails on my skin, felt his long fingers circling my wrists, my throat.
And the lack of care and caution made me shameless.

He petted and soothed me, called me his Kitty, his Katie-cat.
He stroked me and stoked the flame, higher and higher, until there
was no putting it out. And only then, as the world burned around
us, was he satisfied.

I cannot take my eyes off Miss Bingham's face. Even if she
were to look up at me again now, I do not think I could look
away.

'So you knew he was married.' Tate is not asking a question,
and she does not answer.

He pauses, to let this fact settle, and the reporters write it
down.

They have her name and her address. They have the sleeping
arrangements at the cottage, and now they have this.

I look at Miss Bingham's bowed head. At her poor clothes,
her shaking hands. They will describe her as a fallen woman.
A seductress. But she did not seduce Tom, any more than I
seduced him when I was fifteen and as green as grass. She is
not capable of seducing anyone – but this is all anyone will
know about her.

They will ruin her.

I see one of the reporters whisper something to the man next
to him, and they both smile widely. They are like thorns, those
smiles. Pricking my skin. Letting pity flood in.

Tom can be very persuasive. He persuaded me – and I think he persuaded Miss Bingham too.

If she was able, would Miss Cade tell us he persuaded her as well?

Tate says, 'On Friday the eighteenth of April, you spent the night alone with the prisoner at the cottage? You slept in the same bedroom?'

His questions come hard on the heels of one another, as harsh and definite as fists on a door.

'And you spent the following night alone with him at the cottage; that is, the Saturday?'

'And the Sunday, that is Easter Sunday? You slept in the same bed as the prisoner for three consecutive nights?'

Her voice when she answers is merely a whisper, but her eyes are wet and her shame is painted red on her face.

'And did intimacy take place on those nights?'

A pause.

'No matter, Miss Bingham, no matter. I don't want to distress you.'

He pauses again. Lets her catch her breath and compose herself.

And then he says, 'There is one matter on which the court requires clarification. Do you remember seeing any bruises or any signs of bruising on the prisoner?'

'Yes.' Her voice is low. I think she is trembling.

'Would you tell the court what you saw?'

'I saw bruises on one shoulder, but I am not certain which shoulder.'

It goes on and on, this interrogation of marks and bruises.

'What sort of mark or marks were they?'

'You say there were four marks: were they all together?'

'Were these marks more or less in the same place? Were they four distinct marks?'

'Might they have been caused by four fingers pressing into the prisoner's arm?'

Moran leaps to his feet at that. 'Objection, my Lord. This witness is not a medical expert and cannot speculate about what may have caused these marks. The court has no record of them and we have had no opportunity to view them.'

Tate bows to the judge. 'Withdrawn, my Lord. Miss Bingham, as far as you can recollect, when did you notice the marks on the prisoner's arm?'

'I cannot be certain, but I think it was on the Sunday morning.'

'Did you notice these marks on only one occasion?'

Her chin drops, and again, red floods that sallow skin.

'I had only one opportunity of . . . of seeing . . .' I hear a man laugh, somewhere in the room, and she flinches again.

And from behind me, a woman's voice. 'Dear Christ, she has no shame!' They no longer bother to whisper, and several of the reporters glance up. One or two make a careful note.

The judge frowns in our direction but says nothing.

'Where were they, these marks? Were they on his arm or his shoulder?'

'I think . . . somewhere here' – and her own arm reaches up and across so that her left hand clasps the top of her right arm. She is embracing herself tightly.

'On the back?'

'On the thick part, at the top of his arm.'

'Just point again to where they were?'

'I am not certain on which shoulder they were.'

'Never mind, Miss Bingham, we are—'

'I think they were on the thick part, at the top. I do not know what you call it, somewhere just here.' Her fingers stretch and press.

I stare at them, imagine those fingers pressing Tom's skin. Clutching at him.

'Where your fingers are?'

'Just about *there*. I may be wrong but I think that is where the marks were.'

Her fingers grip her arm tightly. She clutches her body, trying to protect herself from the stares and from the awful truth, the shameful truth, of what she did with my husband.

When the court adjourns for the day, the babble of voices breaks out louder than ever.

'How could she admit to all of that in a public court?'

'Absolutely shameless, that one.'

'I'm surprised they called her to give evidence. She's hardly a reliable witness.'

'Well, exactly. She seemed rather desperate.'

A little bark of laughter. 'Quite. Just a desperate, lonely woman.'

I look at the man who has said this. I watch him clap his hat on and fasten his jacket. He walks briskly to the door, glad to leave behind him the messy business of desperate women.

Miss Bingham is a desperate, lonely woman. Just like Miss Cade.

And then quickly, before I can catch it: *I have been lonely. I have been desperate too.*

LONDON CHRONICLE, 9 JULY 1924

What Miss Bingham Saw In The Bedroom

Miss Rose Bingham of Worple Avenue, Isleworth, Middlesex, was the chief witness at Lewes Court yesterday, when Thomas Ryan appeared in the dock for the third day accused of murdering Beatrice Cade.

Miss Bingham, who gave her age as 32, is of medium height, with a sallow complexion. She entered the witness box wearing a veil and had to be ordered by the judge to turn it back. She then held a pocket-handkerchief to her face and kept a bottle of smelling salts in one hand.

Answering Mr Roderick Moran (for the prosecution), Miss Bingham said that she first met Ryan near Richmond station on 10 April, late in the evening.

Miss Bingham admitted that she knew he was married. When pressed, she said she did not often make the acquaintance of married men – however, she then stated that she went on to meet Ryan on several other occasions.

On 15 April she received a telegram from him, asking her to meet him at Charing Cross Station the following day, where they dined together.

Miss Bingham added: 'He said he was staying at a friend's bungalow at Eastbourne. He asked me if I would go down and spend the Easter weekend there.'

Answering further questions, Miss Bingham said she went to Eastbourne on Good Friday, 18 April, and was met by Ryan at the station. She stayed at the bungalow alone with Ryan for three days and nights, until Easter Monday, 21 April. She agreed that most of the bedrooms, save one, were shut up and unused.

She provided intimate details about Ryan which we

are unable to print, due to their sensitive nature. These details were entered into evidence.

Before leaving the courtroom, Miss Bingham turned down her veil again and walked out with her hand to her face.

28

Bea, April 1924

The next morning was clear and warm. Bea woke in an unfamiliar bed and felt the unaccustomed bulk of him against her. She smelled sweat, hair oil, her new perfume.

Then she opened her eyes and turned her head, and he was there: when she reached out a hand, her fingers touched the smoothness of his hip. She stroked him like a cat as he slept on without her.

Carefully she slid out from beneath the blankets and began to dress. In this bright morning light, she noticed thin silvery lines on her stomach and thighs, and covered them quickly.

In the kitchen, the sunlight was almost white. She opened the back door wide and let the morning warm the room. The air was softer here than London air; it felt gentle against her skin. She boiled the kettle, cut some bread and made toast. She walked into the garden and picked primroses and stems of cow parsley, filled a jug and placed it on the table.

She sat, cradling the slight swell of her stomach. Now that she was safe, she could let herself think about it properly. For the first time, she wondered if the baby could feel touch, if it comforted her.

She was startled to realize that she was thinking of a *her*. She stroked her stomach and imagined a tiny hand stroking the other side in response. She imagined dark eyelashes, translucent skin. The neatness of small fingernails.

She thought of her own mother, and of the day when George was born.

She was seven and sitting on the bottom step while their mother bellowed and laboured behind the bedroom door. Their father was at work and when she'd bent double for the third time that morning and stared at nothing and groaned, Bea had asked if she should run to the pit and get a message to him.

Her mother shook her head. Panted. Breathed. Straightened. 'What for? He'd be neither use nor ornament here today.'

Then the panting began again and her face went red. She closed her eyes and spoke through her teeth.

'Fetch Mrs Young. *Now.*'

So Bea ran for Mrs Young, who came with her hands still floury and her apron stained, and led her mother upstairs. They paused halfway and her mother leaned on her and made the low bellowing noise again. Mrs Young held her waist and they bent forward together, and for a moment all Bea could see were two pairs of wide hips, a line of brown hanging skirts in the narrow staircase, shoulders that went up and down as Mrs Young patted and her mother panted.

Bea wanted nothing to do with it. She stamped into the kitchen where Jane was sitting, her dress hiked up, examining a hole in her stockings. Her knee poked through, shockingly pink. The vulnerability of it made Bea love her.

She thought of her mother and Mrs Young on the staircase. Their rough red hands. Their tired faces. She couldn't imagine their knees at all.

She watched Jane scoop jam out of the pot with her finger and said, 'I'm never having a baby.'

Jane looked at her and sucked her finger with a mouth that was sticky and purple.

'You have to,' she said, with all the wisdom of a twelve-year-old. 'Everyone does.'

Bea shook her head. 'Not me' – but then George was born

and their mother was ill for a long time, and so she did have a baby in a way.

The first time she saw him he was wrinkled like he'd been soaked in lye for too long. He was asleep but his eyelids moved with his dreams, and his rosy lips sucked and pouted.

Later he grew plump and pink and the wrinkles smoothed themselves out into soft skin, into ears like seashells, and into dimples where his knuckles ought to be.

Her whole childhood, she had felt like she was waiting for someone to tell her a secret. A truth that would make the rough clumsy fragments of her form an elegant gleaming whole.

When George arrived, their two halves slotted together like curved red apple peel and the sweet white core.

And when I lost George, I lost half of myself.

She stroked her stomach again.

When she had held George for the first time, he was dense and loose, but his head was as small and fragile as a fist. She remembered lifting him and breathing him in, and how he had smelled of milk and soap: things that are white with the faintest tinge of warmth, things that are as soft as clouds and as yielding as blown sheets on a washing line.

She had pressed her lips to his head and licked them, and he tasted sweet in the way the scent of roses is sweet, with an iron earthy tang beneath.

When this child was born, she would hold her in the same way. She would tell her every day that she was loved.

When Tom came in, she was still cradling her stomach, sitting in a spill of sunlight, drinking her second cup of tea.

She watched his eyes go to her hand on her belly. She stood and kissed his cheek.

'Morning, darling. How did you sleep?'

'Like a log.' He stretched his arms out above his head and yawned. 'Must be the sea air.'

She poured out his tea. 'Would you like an egg?'

'No, toast will do for me. Is there any marmalade?'

'Only the jam we had yesterday.'

He opened the jar and peered at the contents as though he had no memory of yesterday, then put it aside, began to spread butter on toast.

She watched him eat breakfast and thought of how she had imagined him for all those long weeks and months: breakfasting on bacon and eggs, folding down his newspaper and taking up his hat and walking to catch his train – and how strange it was that he should be beside her now, drinking his tea with the door open behind him and the golden morning pouring in and bathing him in light.

But even now, like this, there was the knowledge that she was not the first one to make him breakfast in the morning. She was not the first to notice the smooth pink place behind his ear, nor the helpless beauty of his hair growing down his neck above his collar. Someone else had been there before her, and had left behind an imprint – of her hand on his arm, of her lips on his.

She cleared her throat. 'I wonder where the nearest shop is. We might get some marmalade. And bacon. And we need fresh milk.'

'The milkman will probably call tomorrow.'

'He won't know there's anyone staying here, surely?'

'Hmm?' He had taken his tea to the window, was looking out over the garden. 'Think I'll take my paper out there. Sit in the sun for a while. What will you do?'

He turned to look at her but the light was so bright behind him that she couldn't make out his expression.

'I think I'll join you.'

She tried, but he was absorbed in the racing pages, so she decided to see what she could do to smarten the place up a little. She wanted to air out the rooms and get rid of the damp smell.

And so, while Tom lay out in the sun, she opened all of the windows and shook out the bedding. She found polish and rags, a bottle of vinegar and a carpet sweeper in a cupboard in the passage. For two years she had had only one room to clean, and at first the work was a novelty. She enjoyed transforming the dull wood, the dusty ornaments, the neglected rooms. She wanted him to see that she could make a home for him. As soon as she finished a room, leaving it neat and bright, she closed the door and moved on to the next, imagining Tom's pleasure in finding each one shining and new.

By midday she was tired and nauseous, and rather dirty. She decided that she needed a bath, and went into the kitchen to light the copper. Tom was no longer in the garden. She went into the living room to select a book, and found him sitting at the bureau with a pile of telegram forms in front of him. He didn't look up when she came in, so she picked up the first book she saw, and closed the door quietly behind her.

After her bath, she made tea, buttered bread, opened a tin of pilchards. When Tom came in, she said, 'We'll have to go out for dinner. What about going into Eastbourne?'

'Must we? I can't be bothered with other people. It's so lovely and restful here.'

'Well, we can't eat bread and jam again.'

He sat and stretched his arms above his head. Yawned loudly. 'Let's just see how we feel later, shall we?'

And then, quite unexpectedly, he said, 'We . . . in Richmond, we talked about going abroad. To South Africa. Starting again.'

She put down the teapot.

He nodded. 'I really think it's the most sensible thing to do. We ought to put some distance behind us. It'll be less painful for everyone.'

'Really? Oh, Tom, that's wonderful.'

He was smiling. 'That's settled then. We'll get it all fixed up. Is there anyone you want to say goodbye to?'

She thought for a moment of Ellen and Alice. Swallowed. She said, 'I'd like to see my sister before we leave. Maybe go and stay with her and her family for a few days.'

'I don't think there'll be time, darling.'

She looked at him and he went on, 'I mean, what's keeping us here? Why shouldn't we just *go*, as soon as we can?'

She smiled at his eager, open face. 'I'll write to her then. Tell her our plans.'

'Yes, do. Let her know we're going away.'

'We'll need passports, won't we? Or you will – I think I can travel on yours.'

'I suppose we will. I hadn't thought.'

'We could go up to London tomorrow to get one.'

He looked at her over the rim of his cup. Smiled again. 'Why not? It's one less thing to do later.'

He finished his tea, then went out to the lavatory.

When he came back in, she said, 'Shall we go into Eastbourne then, darling? We could have a walk on the seafront. Find somewhere to eat dinner.'

She smiled up at him. 'It will be lovely just to be out with you.'

For all that she'd been the one to suggest it, Tom seemed impatient to explore. They walked along the seafront for a while, but despite the fast pace he set, she was shivering under the onslaught of cold wind blowing in from the water. She was relieved when he mentioned finding somewhere to have a drink.

The pub he chose was crowded, but he found a table in the snug and settled her there, then went to the bar. While she waited for him, another couple arrived and she moved up a little to give them room. The woman thanked her and they fell into conversation. They were on their honeymoon, Bea discovered – all shy glances at one another, his exaggerated care of her evident in the way he placed her chair and hung up her coat, and in the way he was unable to take his eyes off her. Bea watched them and felt a thickness in her throat. They were so young, both of them.

Tom came back just as Mrs Stevens – and how proud she was of that title! – asked her if she was on holiday in Eastbourne? He placed their drinks on the table and glanced over at the couple, and she saw there was a little hectic dot of red high up on each cheek.

'Darling, there you are. This is Mr and Mrs Stevens, they—'

He barely nodded at them, but moved his chair nearer to hers and leaned in to speak to her, so close she felt his breath on her skin.

'We really ought to talk about South Africa. Make plans.'

He began a rambling story about a pal of his who had gone out there and invested in a gold mine and made a fortune.

At one point, she looked over and saw that the honeymooning couple had left. He followed her glance and said nothing – but something made her say, 'You were a little rude to them, darling.'

'Who?'

She thought he must know perfectly well, but merely said, 'Mr and Mrs Stevens. They were very kind when they noticed I was alone, she—'

'But you aren't alone, are you, Beatrice? You don't need them now that I'm here.'

She looked into his face and he took her hand and held the palm against his cheek, then turned it and kissed it. The kiss sat like an ember on her skin.

He said, 'We don't need anyone else.' He smiled at her, and the other couple were entirely forgotten.

They had another drink, and then another, Tom growing a little more blurred and a little more rambling with each one. She was surprised when she looked at the clock and realized it was almost half-past seven.

'We ought to have dinner. It's getting late.'

He nodded and stood, stumbling, so that she had to support him as they walked to the door. Outside the air was cold, and it seemed to revive him a little.

'Where shall we eat?'

'Eat?' He seemed puzzled. Then – 'Ah. Let's go somewhere nice. To . . . to celebrate.'

'Celebrate?'

'We're celebrating, aren't we? South Africa. All that. Let's go to . . .' He kissed her on the cheek – a great smacking whisky-filled kiss, then he raised his head and let his gaze wander along the seafront. 'Let's go to the Grand.'

He pointed at the largest and most ornate of the buildings on the promenade, and they hurried towards it, Bea pulling her coat around herself against the wind.

The inside matched the splendid exterior: a beautiful wooden floor polished to a golden shine; palm trees and oil portraits; sugar-white columns and cornices.

They began to cross the lobby towards the dining room but out of nowhere, a man was blocking their way. He wore the uniform of a commissionaire and a thick black moustache.

'Can I help you, sir?'

'Yes. You can. We would like a table for dinner. For two. A table for two.' Tom was speaking rather slowly. Articulating his words carefully.

'I'm afraid we are fully booked this evening. Can I suggest you try—'

'I don't think so.' A change had come over Tom now. All

that tipsy softness had gone: his jaw was clenched and his voice was hard and crackled white-hot.

'I'm sorry, sir?'

Tom stepped to the side, craned his neck to see into the dining room, and then looked back at the commissionaire. 'I can see three – no, four – empty tables in there now.'

'Unfortunately we are unable to serve non-residents tonight.'

'Nonsense. I've dined here several . . . several times.'

He made to walk towards the dining room again, but again the commissionaire was there, his hand raised.

'It is our policy not to serve any non-resident who appears to be intoxicated.'

Tom's face darkened. '*What the hell did you say?*'

Bea tugged at his arm. 'Please, Tom. Let's just go.'

'I'm sorry, sir, it's hotel policy.'

'How dare you.' Tom's speech had thickened. 'I want to speak to the manager.'

'The manager is unavailable, sir.'

'I want to speak to the manager immediately.'

Bea tugged again. 'Tom. Please.'

'I suggest you leave before you cause a scene.'

'How dare you speak to me like that! How *dare* you. The manager is a personal . . . is a personal friend of mine and I demand . . .'

Suddenly the commissionaire moved, and somehow they were at the door, and then out on the steps. The commissionaire stepped back, dusted down his coat, and glared at Tom. 'Now, 'op it. Go on, get out of it.'

Tom muttered something, then turned and walked away, not waiting to see if she was following.

She took a breath and pulled her coat around her tighter. Blinked. Then she ran to catch him up.

'Tom! Wait! Do wait.'

He turned and looked past her to where the commissionaire was standing on the steps, looking after them.

'Bastard. Jumped-up little bastard.'

'Tom!'

'I can't believe his bloody attitude. He's . . .'

He took a step back towards the hotel and raised his fist, and she reached for his arm. '*Tom!*'

That seemed to get through to him, and he stopped, looked at her. Then he rubbed his face.

'Sorry. I'm sorry, Beatrice.' He took her hand. 'I just can't bear that you should be so . . . *insulted* like that. By a person like that.'

'Darling, it doesn't matter. Really. Let's find somewhere else to eat.'

'I don't want to now. It's all spoiled.'

For a moment he looked like a small boy, sulking.

'That bastard has spoiled everything.'

29

Kate, July 1924

It is the fourth day of the trial, and I am paralysed.

I lay awake for most of the night, thinking about Miss Bingham and then about Miss Cade. About Tom, and about the other women who have haunted me all through my marriage: Ethel Cox, who he took to the Isle of Wight when we were first married, and Mrs Angell, our first landlady in Wiltshire, who was recently widowed, still young, all creamy skin and shining hair and plump pink lips.

I thought of the women I knew about and those I did not – for surely there were more.

And all through the long night, I kept wondering about Tom. About what he told them, what he promised them, what he made them believe. My whole world is tilting on its axis and I no longer know which way is up.

I fell into an uneasy doze towards dawn, and woke at five to my alarm clock telling me it was time to get up, time to begin the long business of washing and dressing and walking to the station and catching trains and putting on a bland and impassive face so that no one may know who I am or guess who my husband is.

But today I could not make myself do it. I tried to imagine swinging my legs around and putting them on the floor, tried to imagine lifting my nightgown over my head, and how my underclothes would feel against my skin. But it took a long time for my body to obey me, and in the end I am almost late.

I slide into the last row in the public gallery a moment before the court is brought to order and the first witness is called.

There is a murmur and a shifting in the courtroom as he enters and walks briskly to the witness box, as he is sworn in.

'Your name is Richard Montague Fawcett?'

'You are lecturer on special pathology at St Bartholomew's Hospital, London?'

'And you are now Honorary Pathologist to the Home Office?'

Even I, who never read accounts of criminal cases in the newspapers, knew who he was before today. I could have identified that handsome countenance from a photograph. And I might have guessed that his voice would be this calm, this measured.

He is pale: his lips almost colourless, his shirt white, his suit a light shade of grey. He might almost be a photograph, were it not for the red carnation in his buttonhole. It is like a splash of blood where his heart ought to be.

The newspapers describe him as unfailing. There is none of the usual shuffling and whispering in the public gallery today. We are all absolutely silent under this quiet authority.

'On the second of May, you visited the cottage at Langney in company with Chief Inspector Wild and other officers. Perhaps you would tell us in your own language what you found.'

And now he begins his evidence proper. He straightens, pushes back his shoulders, raises his chin, and he begins to speak.

'We arrived there at five past eight in the morning.' I imagine weak sunshine. Silver dawn light. The call of birds.

Then he descends into darkness. 'In the first bedroom, I found a tenon saw.'

He goes on to list the other items they found in the cottage. Domestic items: a large saucepan, a trunk, a linen cloth, a hat box, a coal scuttle. They are familiar and harmless and kind, and they are twisted and bloody and wrong.

He does not adjust his tie or his waistcoat, or smooth his hair, does not drink from the glass of water in front of him. All his focus is on the evidence. On the facts.

I hold my hands together tight. I imagine that it must be very cool and very quiet inside his head, where everything is neatly labelled and catalogued and contained: on paper, behind glass, in bottles and boxes and drawers.

All the time he is talking, I look at the exhibits that are laid out on the table at the centre of the courtroom: the trunk, the hat box, saucepans, a saw, a knife.

It is the hat box in particular that draws my attention. It is such an ordinary thing: a little dusty, as though it has scarcely been used. I stare at the gleaming leather exterior. I stare hard enough to imagine I can see what Dr Fawcett says it contained. I imagine I can see the marks and stains that must be scored on the lining.

When did she buy it? How did she imagine herself with it: calling to a porter on a railway platform? Walking up the gangway of a steamer with salt wind harsh on her skin?

Moran's voice breaks into my thoughts. 'What did you find in the trunk – that is, exhibit 8?'

'I found four large pieces of a human body.'

I swallow. It is one thing hearing a plain account of how a woman fell and hit her head, and how Tom had to . . . deal with what came afterwards. It is quite another to hear the detail of what he actually did.

But I must face it.

He did this.

He reduced her to a body. To pieces of a body.

Moran passes a photograph to Fawcett; he nods and points. I glimpse something white and marbled. Something bulky and parcelled and tied with cord.

For a moment I think I will vomit. I close my eyes. I see

her as she was outside my house that evening – white-faced, frightened, determined.

'Was the head present?'

'The head was missing.'

No longer *her* head, but the court's. No longer her body, but an object.

It goes on: fragments, portions, skin, muscle. To these men, these are merely points of evidence. Scientific curiosities.

I make myself turn and look at Mrs Bishop, over at the other end of the public gallery. She is staring at Fawcett, her lips parted and tears running unchecked down her cheeks.

I swallow again. I taste bile.

Fawcett says, 'All the material which I examined – portions of the trunk, the organs, pieces of flesh, and those fragments of bone which I was able to identify – are all of them human, and correspond with parts of a single body. There are no duplicates at all.' For the first time, there is emotion in his voice and colour in his face, and I realize: he is *proud* of how he met the challenge he faced in the cottage.

'And what were the conclusions you drew from all of this?'

'The body was that of a healthy adult female of large build, with fair hair.'

Then he raises his voice, very slightly. 'And the deceased was an expectant mother at the time of her death.'

Dear Christ, no.

There is a low rushing noise inside my head.

I hear: 'Around nine or ten weeks.'

I look up at Tom. He is staring at Fawcett: his eyes are narrowed, his jaw clenched. His fists rest on the rail.

I cannot get any air
everything is very cold
and very still

I hear beside me, 'Oh, she had him trapped, right enough.' A little, mean, satisfied voice.

I am burning up

Fawcett takes not the slightest notice of anyone other than his questioner. His gaze remains steady and he continues in that low, even voice. 'I found no disease to account for natural death, and no condition which would account for unnatural death.'

The judge says, 'I don't follow what that means.'

Fawcett turns his shoulders a little, half facing him. 'There were no injuries on the parts of the body that I examined. The head and neck were missing, but there was no evidence of the cause of death being an unnatural one.'

It is like being at the bottom of a deep dark well

everything – their voices, shuffling, a woman's cough – everything is echoing from a long way away

Moran again: 'There was no cause of death in any of the parts that you examined?'

'That is correct.'

'What does that indicate to you, doctor?'

'That the cause of death—'

The judge leans in. 'One moment. That is rather a question for the jury. I think that is an inference for them to draw from the facts.'

Moran bows to the judge. A hum of conversation breaks out as he takes his seat.

I close my eyes.

I hear, 'Nowt new there. Ryan's statement told us all that right at the start. He said she fell and hit her head.'

'Aye, true enough. All this medical mumbo-jumbo just backs up his story.'

There are murmurs of agreement from behind me, and then one man says, 'Well, other than the fact she were expecting. He never said nowt about *that*.'

Behind my eyelids, I see the face of a sleeping baby

It is Billy's face

Someone is calling for order, but they are ignoring it.

'Happen he didn't know!'

'Aye – she weren't even three months gone. I mind when the wife were . . .'

'Hush – it's starting again now.'

Silence falls but the words are still there, weaving and entwining themselves around me. Choking me.

They have taken the body of a woman and broken it to pieces in this courtroom.

And in the darkness behind my eyes I see two pale circles: the faces of the men who touched that body – *her* body – for the last time. Fawcett, and my husband.

I think of what she became under their hands.

I think of what they did to her body.

Of what my husband did to her body.

When I open my eyes, Tate is on his feet, facing Fawcett. He straightens his robe and he begins.

'You have had the opportunity to read the statements of the prisoner?'

'I have.'

'You said that you could find no injury on the body?'

'Yes.'

'And you said that as the head is missing, there is no evidence of the cause of death?'

'That is correct.'

'Ought we therefore to conclude' – one eye on the jury – 'that the cause of death was a head injury?'

For the first time, a frown mars that perfect pale countenance. 'I should not like to commit myself when I have had no opportunity to examine the head.'

'Surely, Dr Fawcett, it is possible—'

Moran is on his feet. 'Objection, my Lord.'

'Quite so – we have covered this already, Mr Tate. We have no physical evidence of the cause of death – we have established that.'

Tate bows. 'Thank you, my Lord.' Turning back to Fawcett, 'We have no evidence for the cause of death. But is it not possible, in the absence of evidence to the contrary – and I say is it not merely *possible* – that the prisoner is telling the truth about how Beatrice Cade met her death?'

'I really do not see—'

'I am asking your professional *opinion*, Dr Fawcett. Is it *possible* that Miss Cade met her death in such a way as described by the prisoner in his statement?'

I look over at Tom and I see, just for a second, that tell-tale pulse at his temple.

The room is absolutely silent. And then those pale lips part, and Fawcett says, 'Yes. It is possible. Yes.'

'Thank you.'

'However, I should like—'

'Thank you.' Tate bows to the judge. 'No further questions.'

Another rush of voices. The man beside me spreads out his hands. 'See? Just as Ryan said from the start.' He nods. 'Did I not say all this would back him up? Did I not say so?'

The man on his other side leans forward. 'It was an accident, just as he said.'

They look at one another, faces flushed. 'It wasn't murder at all.'

I do not remember the train journey home, nor alighting at Richmond, nor the walk from the station. I remember reaching the gate of the house and thinking that nothing seemed quite real. Not my hand on the latch, nor the ring on my finger, nor the pounding of my heart.

Only the terrible words I heard in the courtroom are clear. Only the pictures in my head.

I cannot take those words, those pictures, into the house where Judith might see them.

So I turn away from the gate and walk back towards the station and into the park. I walk until I cannot see another human soul, until dusk is falling and I am quite alone, and then I sink down onto the dew-damp grass and I put my face in my hands.

And at last I let myself weep.

I think of myself at eighteen, knowing nothing about motherhood. I think about the remembered pull as the baby suckled. The swelling. The heat.

She was almost a mother. That was almost a child.

And then I am on my hands and knees, vomiting and sobbing.

I think of Mrs Bishop saying, *Beatrice Cade is . . . she was my sister.*

I think of Tom, of the way he was when Judith was born. The way he kissed her fingers, the dark crown of her head, the new soles of her feet. The way he wept the first time he held her.

I think of Billy. I think of his cold legs and his terrible still face and the dense unmoving whiteness of his narrow chest in the moment when I knew I'd lost him for ever.

My face is wet and my knees are damp and squeaking in the grass. And I retch again and again and again, until all that comes up is bile and tears, until I am howling in the darkness like an animal.

The man who did this is not my husband. He is not.

He cannot be human.

He is a monster.

30

Bea, April 1924

Tuesday was grey and cold. Tom was quiet at breakfast, and when Bea said, 'Shall we go up to London today? You could fetch the rest of your things from your . . . from Richmond. And arrange the passport,' he merely nodded.

They took the 10.03 to Waterloo. Bea found herself excited and nervous at the same time – unable to sit still or be silent. This would be her last day in London, perhaps for ever. What an extraordinary idea.

She must do some shopping, of course – although she could surely do most of it in France. She could hardly believe that she might be buying her trousseau in Paris.

And a haircut. She must have a haircut before the ship to South Africa sailed, and it would surely be easier to manage in London than in Paris. Her French was adequate, but a hair salon was a different matter entirely. Although perhaps there would be a hairdresser on the ship? It was likely to be expensive, though. She ought to call in at the bank today. She would need to close her English accounts.

'How much money do you think we'll need in France, darling? Should we take it all in francs and then change it again to . . . goodness, I don't even know what kind of money they use in South Africa.'

'Pounds, shillings and pence.' Tom spoke absently, gazing out of the window. 'They use the same currency there as we do.'

She laughed. 'How funny! I expected something far more exotic.'

Then she said, 'Do you mind going to the passport office without me? I have rather a lot to do.'

He shook his head. 'I'll be quicker on my own. They're always busy, these places. Forms and queues and all that.'

'That's true. Never mind, we can meet for tea afterwards. Make an occasion of it.'

'I don't know how long I'll be. I'd hate to leave you waiting around. Better just to meet at Waterloo, I think.' He took the timetable out of his pocket. 'The last train back is at half-past eight. Let's meet in the station bar and have a drink, then catch that one.'

The train was slowing as it pulled in to Waterloo and she raised her voice over the squeal of brakes, over Tom reaching for their coats and busying himself with his hat.

'So about eight then? Or earlier?'

'Yes.' He was peering out of the window at the crowded platform. 'I'll see you then.'

He helped her down from the train, her lips touched his cheek, and then he was gone.

In London – unobserved, unselfconscious – she could be herself again.

She walked over the river to Charing Cross, then through Trafalgar Square and up the Haymarket to Piccadilly, buffeted by the crowds. Two days away and she was already used to silence and to space.

She reached Liberty's and took the lift to the ladieswear department, where the shining mahogany, the thick carpet, the gleaming brass seemed like half-forgotten luxuries.

Ladieswear was quiet. There were two or three women of the kind she used to despise: rich pampered wives with a dress allowance, elegant and brittle, women who had never had to support themselves. Bea wandered between rails of clothing, running her fingers over material she could not afford, relishing the softness.

Her hand trailed behind her to the lingerie department, where she rubbed silk and satin between her fingers, where she murmured the names of the colours like an incantation.

Champagne. Oyster. Blush. Porcelain. Smoke. Bone.

She could not really afford to buy anything there either, but she could not resist the seductive smoothness, and when the salesgirl asked if she needed help, she heaped a slithering rainbow of cream and eggshell shades into the girl's arms.

At the counter, sense prevailed, and she picked out only four items: bandeau, French knickers, slip, chemise, all in the palest blue with coffee-coloured lace edging. She paid and took her change, and the girl began to wrap them in tissue.

Bea stopped her. 'I'd like to wear them.'

The girl looked startled, but then the professional mask slid back and smoothed out her face. She nodded and showed her the way to the changing room.

Alone, Bea removed her suit and blouse, and then slipped out of her own underthings. For a moment she stood naked in the little windowless room at the heart of London. She could smell her sweat, mingled thickly with the sweetish scent of talcum powder.

She turned to the full-length mirror and looked at herself: at the red marks where seams had dug in, at the dimplings and the swellings, at the goosepimples on her arms. Then she took up the items she had bought and began to wrap herself in silk, the newness of the drawers stiff against her skin. As she put her head into the chemise, the stale shop smell filled her nostrils and caught in her throat.

She looked at herself in the mirror again and thought of Tom unwrapping her and laying her bare to his gaze, and a blush licked her skin. When she eventually left the shop, it was with a hot thrill of wanton delight rippling in her stomach.

She found a tearoom on Maddox Street, and ordered tea and a scone, which arrived warm and seeping golden butter. She ate it slowly, letting it sink onto her tongue. It was the most English thing she could think of to eat, and she wanted to savour it as she said goodbye to her life in England: to solitary meals in half-empty cafes, to grey pavements on damp afternoons, to chilly sheets in single beds; to all the things that had spelled loneliness and spinsterhood and those pinching, itchy feelings of inadequacy that were over now, for ever.

She paid for her tea; she left a large tip to celebrate her last meal in London; she took up her bags and she began to walk. She crossed Regent Street again and wove through a crowd of women peering at the mannequins in the windows of Dickins & Jones. She navigated round-toed patent-leather shoes, stuffed with stockings like shiny preserved beetles. She dodged large hats, umbrellas, shopping baskets; two curly-headed children pleading with their tired nanny for lemonade; a Highland terrier with a fierce frown. It was all so normal, so English – and she was strangely glad of this, for these were surely some of the last English people she would see. The wrinkled stockings, the nanny, the dog, even the lowering clouds – all of it was suddenly, inexpressibly dear.

She reached the relative quiet of Great Marlborough Street, then ducked through the maze of narrow streets that clustered like tarnished beads at the neck of Soho proper, until she emerged onto Soho Square. The square was largely empty of loiterers, save for one stout old man on a bench, wrapped in a shabby overcoat and muffler, his head bowed so that his nose almost met his chin.

She crossed Tottenham Court Road – and crossing that border felt, as it always had, like coming home – and then walked along Great Russell Street, looking for the hot-chestnut

seller who had his stall outside the museum, surrounded by
street boys and pigeons. And just as she saw him in his shabby
coat and the cap he always wore, she thought, *This is the last
time.*

Up Montague Street and right into the wide expanse of
Russell Square for the last time. For the last time, she walked
past the great bulk of the cherry tree in the square, like a pale
gable end; past all those dozens of high-ceilinged elegant rooms
that she had never dared to dream of entering. She rounded the
skirt of Southampton Row, turned right at the great Gothic
majesty of the Russell Hotel, and looked up at the Italianate
balconies and the pale octagonal turret, so tall that one couldn't
see the top, that had always put her in mind of fairy tales and
princesses in high towers. And so into Guilford Street for the
last time: seven doors along and past two plane trees – and then
she was outside number sixty-eight. She had been away for two
days, but it felt like weeks.

It was twenty-past three on a Tuesday afternoon: most of
the occupants would be at work. And yet she had the strangest
sensation that she might walk inside and find it exactly as it
had been when she first arrived in London: the dingy hallway,
the restless chattering groups of women, Mrs McIvor waiting
behind her high counter. Even Hetty would be there, ready to
take her upstairs: Hetty who had left them in the new year to
marry a publican named Barraclough. Bea felt as if they were
all in there, merely waiting for her to step inside and join them.

She imagined coming inside from that grey afternoon, from
that vast city, the door closing, the huge and gloomy entrance
hall tapering to the staircase, the stairs themselves twisting and
dwindling to steps the width of hips, and then the long narrow
corridor, lined with closed doors, and the little rooms behind,
each like a honeycomb cell. She thought of the cracked paint,
the dust of years, and each with a window to the world beyond.
And she felt that if she were to step inside, she could step

back into her old life: a narrow single bed and one bath a week, darning stockings and playing backgammon by the drawing-room fire, quite as if she had never met Tom and never fallen in love.

As if she had never fallen at all.

She shivered, and turned, and walked away.

She was in the station bar before eight, but there was no sign of Tom, so she came outside again, preferring the draughty concourse to being alone in a public house. She paced impatiently, pulling her coat around her, patting her neck beneath her new haircut, adjusting her new hat.

Her feet ached and her skin was chilled. She would have a hot bath when they got back: would soak for as long as she liked. There was no reason to get up early tomorrow, and she had had her fill of early mornings and shared bathrooms. Tonight she would wallow in the steam until her skin was rosy and soft and gleaming. She could almost feel the heat of it, could imagine the relief of letting her limbs relax, and then the comfort and the pleasure of getting into bed beside Tom, of feeling the warm sheets against her clean body.

She looked at the clock. Almost quarter-past eight. Where was he? She watched the minute hand tick round – once, twice. Had she missed him somehow?

What would she do if he did not come?

Then she saw him, sauntering past the left-luggage office towards the bar. She called his name, but he slipped inside without seeing her, and she had to trail after him until she could draw his attention.

At once she saw he had been drinking. His face was red, his hair untidy. She could smell whisky on his breath.

'Darling! Where have you been?' His speech was slurred and he was unable to focus on her face.

She took his arm, told him, 'Tom – we must go.'

He twisted back towards the bar, gesturing vaguely. 'Go? But I've just arrived. I need a drink. Whisky. Hey!' – this last to the barman – 'Hey! A whisky for me and a sherry for . . . for the lady.'

Bea pulled him towards the door, her face burning. 'Tom. The train is about to leave.'

He stared at her as though he did not understand what she was saying, but when she tugged his arm again, he came with her, suddenly docile.

By some miracle, they found the platform in time. She helped Tom into an empty third-class compartment, climbed in herself and closed the door just as the train began to move.

She let out a long breath. It was done. London was behind them and they were together, and that was all that mattered.

She turned to find that he had fallen asleep on the opposite seat, and leaned back, watching him. His mouth had dropped open and he gave little snuffling snores that half woke him each time.

Eventually he woke properly. Blinked at her. Sat up and rubbed his hair.

'Where are we?' His voice was still slurred.

'I don't know.' She rubbed the window with her gloved hand to clear it of condensation, but the night outside was black and empty. 'I haven't been counting the stations.'

He was squinting at his watch. 'I think we have 'bout . . . half an hour to go. Maybe a bit . . . bit less.'

'Not too long then.'

'No. 'S good. I'm tired.'

'Have you eaten?'

He yawned. 'Had lunch. I'm not . . . not hungry.'

She hesitated, not really knowing why. And then she asked, 'Did you get the passport, darling?'

He turned to her. He no longer looked tired and his face was very still.

'No.'

She tried to smile. 'But . . . why not?'

He said nothing.

'I don't understand. Why not, Tom?'

Nothing.

'Tom? You said you'd arrange it.'

At this, he shook his head. 'No. I didn't say I would.'

And then, like a slap: 'I only agreed when *you* said I would.'

'Tom, I . . .'

His voice rose. 'I always have to agree with you.'

She felt tears fill her eyes. 'Why are you being like this?'

'You're always telling me what to do. You're always nagging.'

'Don't. Please, Tom. Don't be hateful.'

'*Don't, Tom.* Tom, do this. Tom, do that.' His voice was pitched high, sing-song, presumably in imitation of her own.

'Tom. Please don't be like this. You're drunk.'

He shook his head, hard. 'I'm not drunk.'

And suddenly he *was* no longer drunk. He sat up straight and looked at her and somehow she could no longer look him in the eye.

She stared at a point below his left eyebrow, just where the hair softened and began to fan out. She swallowed. 'Why didn't you get a passport?'

He leaned forward then and she smelled sour beer and tobacco. 'Why would I need a passport?'

And she was staring – gawping. Stupid. 'Why, because . . . because we're . . .'

He laughed then, a harsh mocking laugh that felt rough on her skin. He was laughing at her and he had to stop, and there was only one thing she could think to say to make it stop.

'I love you.' Her words dropped into the space between them and hung there.

'I love you, Tom.'

He sat back and sighed heavily and his voice was suddenly weary.

'I know you do. I know.' He ran a hand through his hair.

'Tom?'

'Look, I . . .' He bit his lip. Looked away. 'I don't know what to say to you when you're . . . I don't know what you expect me to say.'

'I expect you to tell me that you love me too. I want you to tell me that you feel the same way.'

'You know I do.'

'Then say it!' Her voice was too loud in the little compartment and she took a breath. 'I've left everything for you. My friends, my job, my room at the club.'

He said nothing and now her voice trembled as she said, 'You're all I have left.'

He still would not look at her, but his face twitched.

'I've given up everything for you, Tom. I need to feel . . .'

Now he glanced at her, and that gave her courage. 'I need to feel that this is real. That you meant everything you said.'

Still nothing.

'Tom – I need to know that everything you promised me is . . . is still there.'

There was a pause and finally, *finally*, he spoke, but in a different tone this time.

'What do you mean?'

'You told me we'd go away together. You said we'd go abroad.'

He said nothing.

'You said that we would have a life together, away from everyone.'

Still nothing.

'You said that we would go away. Just the two of us. You *said*.'

And now she heard her voice becoming shrill, heard the note of pleading creep in that she'd noticed and despised in other women. She couldn't help herself. Her voice rose and she listened to it with horror.

This was not the kind of woman she was. That she wanted to be.

This was not the kind of woman that he could continue to love.

'Beatrice, please. You're becoming hysterical. We're both tired. Let's go to the cottage, get some sleep and talk about this tomorrow. We'll both be calmer after—'

'No. *No.*'

'Beatrice, you—'

'Stop it! Just stop . . . pretending. You know what you promised. We talked about it all. About Paris. About South Africa. We talked about the journey and how big the liner might be, and about the types of people we might meet on the ship. We laughed about it, for God's sake, Tom – you know we did!'

He said nothing, merely looked at her. She took a breath and tried to speak rationally. Tried to ignore the tremor in her voice.

'We'll go back to London tomorrow. Get the passport then. We can be in Calais by Thursday night and then—'

'No.'

That was all he said – just that one heavy syllable.

She chose to push against the smallest part of his refusal. 'But you must, Tom. You must have a passport if we are to travel abroad.'

Is must *a word to be addressed to princes?*

He said nothing.

'Where did you go, if not to the passport office?'

He said nothing.

Now he was slumped in the corner of the seat and his face was in shadow. She could only make out the glint of his eyes.

She asked, 'Did you go . . . did you go to Richmond?'

And then she realized. 'Your . . . where is your luggage?

Where are your things? Your clothes, your books? Are you having them sent on?'

He said nothing.

'Did you go to Richmond?' Her voice was stronger.

When he spoke, he sounded almost sad. 'No.'

'Did you write to them?'

'No.' It came out as a sigh.

'Have you told them?' She leaned forward. 'You said you would tell them.' He said nothing. 'Tom, you must. You must write to your wife. And to . . .'

Suddenly he sat up straighter, and something in his face made her stutter to a halt before his daughter's name could spill out into the space between them.

She took a breath and began again, but her voice was high and unsteady.

'You must write.' And then, somehow gaining strength, 'You must tell them we are going away. You *must*.'

He straightened his back. Lifted his head and looked at her, and said, in a voice that was empty of all expression, 'But we are not going away.'

He sighed softly, and his voice sounded as though it came from a long way away. 'It's over, Beatrice.'

His voice was so quiet and so calm that at first she thought she had misheard. But in the silence that followed, she became aware that the train was slowing, that they had come to a halt. She heard the guard calling, 'Eastbourne! Alight here for Eastbourne!' and she saw Tom pull his coat around him, open the door and step out – and the precise detail of it all and the careful way he avoided looking at her told her that she had not imagined it. That the horror of this was real.

And that she was quite lost.

31

Kate, July 1924

On the fifth day, it is the turn of the defence to question Tom. He is taken out of the dock; he crosses the floor; he is placed into the witness box.

All through the swearing-in, I stare at him – this stranger I have been married to for thirteen years. I cannot stop looking at his hands – the slim, well-kept hands that have held mine, that have cradled our daughter. I have seen those hands holding books, cups, forks; opening doors; fastening buttons.

How can these be the hands that disposed of a woman's body and the body of an unborn child? This is *Tom*.

Mr Tate begins with things we already know, but now I must hear them in Tom's own voice for the first time, in front of all these people. It is strange to hear his voice in this place, after all these other voices.

'I met Miss Cade last summer, at the office.'

'When we first met, she called me Mr Ryan – then later she called me Tom.'

He does not shift his gaze from Mr Tate as he speaks.

'I am a married man.'

'Oh yes, I often mentioned my wife to Miss Cade. She knew perfectly well that I was married.'

When he says this, his gaze is open and direct. There is a softness at the corners of his mouth and his shoulders turn a little towards the newspapermen and then towards the jury.

'I never kept any letters from Miss Cade because of the danger of my wife finding them.'

His tiny almost-smile invites those twelve men to join him: *We are all men of the world, are we not? We understand the difference between wives and women like Miss Cade.*

I glance over at the jury. Two or three are smiling. One – the well-built man with the thinning hair that I noticed on the first day – looks shocked. The others – I cannot tell what they are thinking. For all the way they look, Tom might be telling them it will rain tomorrow.

Then Tate comes to the ring.

Tom says, 'I had nothing to do with buying that ring. The first I knew of it was when I saw Miss Cade wearing it at the cottage.'

'So it wasn't a present from you? It wasn't an engagement ring?'

'Oh, *no.*' He is very casual, smiling broadly – and now there is a swell of laughter: a little too loud, relieved at this easing of tension.

Then Tom says, 'She told me she had bought it for appearances' sake. That was all' – and Tate moves on.

But I linger on it a little while. Despite everything that Tom has lied about, I believe this. And I imagine having to buy my own ring; wearing it only so that it could be seen; needing to lie about it. I think of Mrs Bishop saying, *She was very proud of it* – and I am surprised at how much this moves me.

Tate says, 'I should like to go back a little, to the early part of April. What kind of things did you talk about with Miss Cade at this time? What did she want you to do?'

Tom drops his shoulders and stands very straight. He raises his chin and says, 'She had plainly told me, plainly shown me on several occasions that she was fond of me.' His voice is low and intense as he says, 'She was in love with me.'

The woman in the red hat and the woman in the blue – the

women who always arrive first so as to sit in the centre of the front row – shift in their seats. A girl I have never seen in the courtroom before, a little in front of me and to the right, blinks and then sighs, so softly I can scarcely hear her. She is very handsome – pale, with a clean profile and bobbed golden hair, and she does not take her eyes off Tom.

The judge says, frowning, 'You were asked what Miss Cade wanted you to *do*, not how she felt.'

Tom flushes. He turns away from the judge a little and towards Tate, and goes on: 'She wanted me to go abroad with her. Of course I refused, but she kept saying that I must get a passport. She said we should take a holiday together, where she could convince me that she loved me.' He sighs. 'She suggested we should take a house where we could be alone together – *tout seuls*, as she put it.'

'Was that her expression, *tout seuls*?'

'Yes. We often used to speak together in French – Miss Cade was quite fluent.'

He smiles, and I think of the time he tried to learn French using a grammar book and dictionary he found in a second-hand shop. I asked him why he was doing it, and he said, 'Do you never want to better yourself, Katie? Do you never want to be *more*?'

He goes on, 'Miss Cade's idea was that if we were alone together, she would convince me that I could be entirely happy with her.'

'Did you ever consider going abroad with Miss Cade?'

'Of course not – my life is here in England.'

'Was it around this time that Miss Cade told you she had given in her notice at the club in Guilford Street where she lived?'

'Yes, and at the office.'

'What did you say when she told you that she had given up her job and her room?'

He sighs and spreads his fingers wide. 'Naturally, I was very surprised. I asked her why she had done it. She said she had told people at the club that she was engaged to a man named Tom.'

Again, I wonder: why would she say these things? Why would she tell people that she was engaged, that she was going to move away, when this wasn't true?

And then, for the first time, a little sly thought: *What did Tom promise her?*

What did he promise those other women? I have never heard any version of the truth but Tom's.

'Did Miss Cade tell you anything at all about this man she was apparently engaged to?'

Tom is shaking his head before Tate has finished speaking. 'I asked her. I said, "Who is this man?" and she said nothing.'

'She didn't reply?'

'She may have smiled.' He shrugs and lowers his eyes, and the man behind me exhales sharply and mutters, 'Oh, she laid her trap right carefully,' and the man beside me grunts in agreement.

'Do you think that you were supposed to be this "Tom"?'

'I took it to mean that she meant me – and I said so.'

'What did she say to that?'

Another little shrug. 'She simply told me that she was determined to gain and keep my love.'

'Quite.' Tate looks down at his notes. 'You said in your statement that this had become "an obsession" for Miss Cade?'

'An absolute obsession. She was determined that I would leave my wife and go abroad with her.'

'I will ask you again – you never had any intention of doing either of these things?'

'Never. Not at any time.'

'Let's move on to the cottage now. You arranged to go down to Eastbourne on the thirteenth of April?'

'Yes, from the Sunday until the Tuesday.'

'You took the cottage in a false name – the name of . . .' – he glances at his notes again – 'in the name of Waller. Who suggested that?'

'When Miss Cade and I first talked about the cottage, she said, "Take it in your own name"; I said, "But what about my wife?"'

This brings me up short.

Yes, what about your wife, Tom? You didn't really think that I would find out about this cottage you had rented, did you? It was miles from our own home, miles from anyone who might recognize you.

I stare at him, hard, my hands clenched in hot fists. Whatever the reason for his lie, it was nothing to do with me. I was merely a convenient excuse. As I have doubtless been many times before.

I wonder if he will feel the heat and the fury of my gaze, but he merely goes on, 'Miss Cade said, "Well, take it in another name then. Any old name will do," and she fixed on the name Waller.' And smiling slightly, 'I think she chose it quite at random.'

'So you met Miss Cade at Waterloo station on Sunday the thirteenth, and you caught the train together to Eastbourne?'

'Yes.'

'What did you do that evening?'

'We took a taxi-cab to the cottage, had supper, and we went to bed early.'

'And on the following day, that is, Monday the fourteenth, what did you do? Just tell us briefly.'

'In the morning Miss Cade did some housework and prepared lunch. I wrote out two telegrams at the cottage on forms I found in the bureau – one was to my wife and one was to Miss Bingham. I had told Miss Bingham I would write to her, and I wanted to keep my word. And then in the afternoon Miss Cade and I went into Eastbourne and later dined there.'

'And now we come to Tuesday. The fifteenth. Tell us in your own words what happened that day.'

'We had agreed that I would return to London that day. At breakfast we decided that we would go up to town together.'

'For what purpose? Tell us what was happening between you and Miss Cade at this point.'

'Miss Cade wanted to travel to Paris. She wanted me to accompany her.'

The judge sighs, removes his spectacles, rubs his nose. 'This is all so vague. "She wanted", "she thought" and so on. We want to know what took place. What did she *say* to you? What did you say to her?'

As the judge speaks, Tom's lips become very thin and a red flush spreads high on each cheekbone. He has always hated to be interrupted.

He breathes through his nose for a moment and then he says, 'She told me that I must go up to town and arrange for a passport. She was very insistent about this.'

'Where was the passport to be for?'

'For France.'

'And it was a passport for how many?'

'For the two of us – myself and Miss Cade.'

'Go on. What happened after breakfast on the fifteenth?'

'We took a train to Waterloo, and then we separated. Miss Cade went off to do some shopping, and I was to go to the passport office. Then we met again in the evening to catch the last train.'

'And what happened on the train back to Eastbourne?'

'Miss Cade said, "Have you been about the passport?" And I said no.'

'How did she react to this?'

'She was furious with me at first, then she begged me to agree to go back. She said I must get a passport as soon as possible. When I said no again, she became very angry.'

'What happened then? What time did you arrive back at the cottage?'

'The train came in to Eastbourne shortly after ten o'clock, and we took a taxi-cab to the cottage. I think it was about half-past ten when we arrived. Perhaps a little earlier.' He runs his hand over his hair. His eyes are unfocused, as though he is remembering.

'It was cold that night. I lit the fire in the sitting room and she boiled some milk. We both had headaches.'

I look over at the model of the house again: at the tiny fireplace, the floral settee. I imagine a chill in the air. Mist rolling in from the sea and up to lick at the windows. A faint damp smell.

'I went to get more coal from the scullery and I carried it in in the coal scuttle. There were several pieces of coal, I remember, all fairly large, so I broke them into smaller pieces with the coal hammer, then I laid the hammer down on one of the tables in the sitting room.

'As the room warmed up, Miss Cade took her coat and hat off and sat on the settee. She drank her milk. I didn't want mine.'

Her legs stretched out to the flames, her feet aching from a day walking around London. The easing of muscles as the heat reaches them.

I can almost hear the crackle of the fire. Can taste the sweetness of the milk.

'Then out of nowhere, she said, "Tom, I am determined to settle this matter tonight. I have burned my boats and for me there is no turning back."'

He pushes back his shoulders and raises his head, and his voice rings out clearly across the courtroom. 'She said, "Can you not realize, Tom, how much I love you? You are everything to me, and I will not share you with another."'

The girl with the golden hair leans forward. Her lips are parted.

'I said, "Darling, I cannot give you what you want – you know that!"

'I asked her, "Why can we not be friends?"' His hands are spread wide: *Was I not reasonable?* – and the women in the front row sit rapt and upright beneath their new hats.

'She said, "What use is friendship to one of my nature?" I said, "Well, that is all I can offer."' He sighs. 'When I said that, she became very upset and agitated.'

He shakes his head. 'I asked how she could possibly expect me to give everything up and do as she suggested. I said I would tell my wife the whole sorry tale. I didn't want Miss Cade to have any hold over me at all.

'She begged me to change my mind, but I refused.' He shakes his head again. 'She was very angry, and I realized that she was becoming . . .' He swallows. 'She was hysterical.'

The judge leans forward again and says irritably: 'This is all description, a sort of narrative. We want to know what happened, not what you thought and what you imagined, but what *happened*.'

There is a general muttering and shaking of heads at this interruption. Tom blinks and those two red spots glow brightly, high on his cheekbones. He grips the railing in front of him and takes a deep breath.

'I told Miss Cade I was going to bed. She said something I didn't catch, but as I went towards the door, she picked up the coal hammer from the table and threw it at me. It hit me – just *here*.' He reaches round to touch his shoulder and I think of Miss Bingham, of her arms wrapped around her thin body. 'It glanced off my shoulder and hit the door.' He points to show where the door was, and every head turns to follow his movement.

'It was . . . I was shocked. Before I could react, she leapt across the room and she . . . Oh God' – he covers his eyes with his hand for a moment – 'she clutched at my face, and . . .'

The women in front, the golden-haired girl, every woman in the public gallery is leaning forward, their faces stretched in sympathy.

I lean forward too – for at last we have come to it. This is Tom's chance to convince the judge and the jury of what really happened.

To my astonishment, he starts to weep – noisy and uncontrolled. Eventually he takes out a large handkerchief and wipes his face.

Tate says gently, 'Do you feel able to continue?'

'Yes.' His voice is thick. 'Yes, thank you.'

The judge sighs. 'Go on. We have got as far as she was clutching at your face.'

'She was clutching at my face, and I did my best to push her away. But I realized I was dealing with someone who was . . . she was quite mad with anger. I did my best to loosen her hold, but she was getting the better of me. I was terrified.' He shakes his head. 'At last I pushed her off me' – he thrusts with both arms – 'and we both fell over the chair next to the fireplace.'

A low sigh from someone towards the end of the row, almost a groan.

'Miss Cade hit her head on the coal scuttle and I fell with her. You must understand it was an accident.' His eyes go from Mr Tate to the jury. 'It was a terrible, tragic accident.'

He swallows and goes on, 'And then I think I must have fainted. With the fear and the shock, you know. And when I came round, Miss Cade was lying by the coal scuttle and' – he is weeping again – 'and blood was flowing from her head where she was lying on the floor.'

He gathers himself. Raises his voice. 'I tried to rouse her. I *tried* . . . oh, God, I . . . I pinched her and slapped her and spoke to her, and did what I could to rouse her – over and over – but she never moved or answered.'

I never knew Tom as a child, but it is not difficult to imagine him – young, bright-eyed, his soft lower lip pushed out in an angry kiss when he didn't get his own way. I imagine him running – head up, neck long, arms spread and stretched back like the wings of a bird, running wild and hard and care-less. And I imagine him hitting an object with his hand – a cup, perhaps, or an ornament – so that it floats through the air, then watching it fall and shatter, and looking away. Putting it entirely out of his mind, running on and leaving the mess behind – and when called to account, protesting his innocence.

I don't know what happened. I didn't do it.

And I see him with her newly dead body. Crouching over her, fingers searching for a pulse, a sign: anything. Hands slap-ping her, pressing her heart, willing it to start again. Willing her to gasp and breathe and stop it *stop it* stop fooling!

I see him slapping her again and again because she will not wake up – and then looking at the mess of spilled blood and the still white face, and backing away.

I don't know what happened.

I didn't do it.

He is still talking, and his voice is faster now. 'I got up and splashed water onto her face.' He sounds almost breathless. 'I called her by name, and she did not answer.'

He shakes his head and says again, very quietly, looking over at the jury, 'I hoped so much she would wake up – but she didn't answer.'

I look with him – I am desperate to see what they are think-ing, but my eyes are full of tears and all I can see are twelve still figures, and twelve pale blurred faces.

Tate: 'What did you do then?'

'I went into the garden. I think I was half mad with fear and panic. When I went back into the cottage, Miss Cade was still lying there. I think that was towards daybreak.

'She was just lying there. Dead.' His hands are at his face, just for a moment, and then, 'It struck me what a horrible thing it was, that she was lying there and just . . . just dead.'

The judge flings down his pen. 'Ryan, you were asked what you did, not all this imagination. You were asked what you actually *did*.'

Tom's head jerks up and when he speaks, it is almost a snarl. '*I am trying to remember!*'

He stares at the judge – a long wild-eyed stare, and then looks away, collects himself. 'It is not easy. It is not an easy thing to go over.' He swallows. 'I pulled Miss Cade's body into the second bedroom and laid it on the floor. I put some clothes under her head, and I covered her face and body with her coat. Then I went out of the house and into Eastbourne.'

The mention of Eastbourne – of something ordinary and real – brings us back to the present. I let out a long breath. The women sit back, and one or two fan their faces with gloves, with papers.

'It was about breakfast time. I had a wash and shave and a cup of coffee. I . . . I was in a kind of agony of fear and apprehension – I didn't know what to do.' He swallows. 'Then I remembered that I had wired Miss Bingham that I would meet her for dinner that evening. So I decided to go up to London and keep that appointment. It seemed to be a . . . a sort of definite thing to do.'

'So you went into Eastbourne, and then you went up to London?'

'Yes. The train arrived late. I was late meeting Miss Bingham in the restaurant.'

'I should like to go back a little in the story because with Miss Bingham we introduce a significant figure in this case. What were your impressions of her on the night you met her?'

The judge leans towards Tate. 'Is there anything in Miss Bingham's evidence which this witness wishes to contradict or question? It is surely not necessary to go through the whole of it again.'

'I am not going to go through it all, my Lord, but I do want to give the prisoner a chance of explaining anything he feels is important.' He turns back to Tom. 'Tell us about Miss Bingham.'

Tom shrugs. 'She was a woman down on her luck, nothing more. She was quite respectable: she wasn't a woman of the streets.'

The man next to me grunts. He leans back, folds his arms.

'Miss Bingham has said that you told her your married life was a tragedy. What do you say about that part of the conversation between you?'

'I think Miss Bingham has made a mistake.' He sounds almost kind as he says this. 'I did not say my married life was a tragedy. I said there had been tragedy in my life.' He looks over at the jury. 'We lost a child, you see.'

It comes out of nowhere, this mention of Billy, and I put my hand against my mouth to silence the gasp.

Not here. Don't you dare bring him in here.

But the women around me – and one or two of the men – have tears in their eyes as he says, 'My son died when he was just a baby. He was only a year old.'

He goes on talking, but all I can hear is the pounding of my heart, and all I can see is Judith's frightened face on that long-ago morning when I woke up to her tugging at my arm and crying, 'Mummy! Mummy, wake up! There's something wrong with Billy!'

Then I see Billy as he was when I went to his cradle: sleeping peacefully, pale and perfect, one fat fist pressed against his mouth.

I said, 'There's nothing wrong with him, love,' but as I bent to pick him up, Judith was backing away and sucking on a strand of her hair. And then I touched him and his skin was ice-cold.

I grabbed him. Put him on the bed. I pressed down on his chest. I shook him, slapped him, waiting to see his skin flush red, waiting for his indignant howl.

There was nothing.

Billy was gone. The baby I hadn't even wanted was gone, and I have lived with the guilt every moment since.

I wrote to Tom and I told him I was sorry, that I'd done my best and that I didn't understand it. I said I was sorry I was SORRY God knows I would kill myself if it would bring him back.

He wrote back and said only, *We won't speak of it again.*

He didn't need to tell me it was my fault.

But now he has spoken of him as though it was yesterday.

He has made Billy's death into his tragedy.

And no matter what happens to him – to us – I will never forgive him for this. *Never.*

Tate asks, 'Why did you invite Miss Bingham to the cottage?'

Tom looks down. 'I just wanted . . . I wanted human companionship. I was afraid to go back to the cottage alone. I couldn't bear it' – he looks up through his eyelashes and shakes his head – 'I couldn't bear to go back. I just couldn't stay there alone.'

'You couldn't stay there alone?'

He lifts his head. 'After the accident happened, as the realization of the whole thing dawned on me, it struck me – the damn place struck me – it was haunted. I couldn't bear to be there alone.'

He puts a hand to his eyes for a moment. 'I thought: I can't get my wife to come down. I can't . . . So I asked this girl. She seemed a decent sort. I thought I was doing her a good turn, I thought perhaps she needed a holiday.'

It sounds as though it is an effort for him to say what comes next. 'I think I should have gone quite mad if she hadn't been there with me.'

'So you asked her to come down by a certain train on the Friday. And you went to the cottage the night before, that is, the Thursday night?'

'Yes. I had been wondering what to do about . . . about what had happened. I knew that it was too late to come clean about what had happened, so I decided I would have to conceal it. The trunk was there – Miss Cade's trunk – so I thought I would put the body in there.'

It is one thing to read about it in the newspaper or to hear his statement read by the clerk; quite another to hear Tom speaking of it. He is talking as though this was a practical problem, an inconvenience, nothing more.

'I hid the . . . the body, then I washed the bloodstains on the floor, and locked the bedroom door. I closed the cottage up and went into Eastbourne where I met Miss Bingham off the train.'

'And you stayed with Miss Bingham at the cottage that night – that is the Friday – and the Saturday and Sunday nights, until Easter Monday?'

'Yes.'

'During the whole of that time, did you ever touch the body?'

'No.'

'When did you go back to your home in Richmond?'

'I left the cottage on the Easter Monday and went back to London. I arrived home somewhere around midnight.'

Easter Monday. I imagine the train up to London: crowds of holidaymakers, bright faces, sunshine.

And Tom, with circles under his eyes and blood on his hands.

Tom coming back to us with smiles and kisses and secrets.

Tom holding me tight and begging me not to turn out the light.

Don't. Don't. Please.

He lay close and hot against me, his breathing ragged and wet.

'I slept at home that night, and the following day, I came back down to Eastbourne.'

'What did you do on that day – that is, the Tuesday?'

'I unlocked the bedroom and opened the trunk and I . . . I made myself deal with the body. I burned the head in the sitting-room fireplace. I knew . . . I didn't know what to do. I knew I would have to dispose of it somehow.'

'What did you do on the Tuesday night?'

'I went home again – to Richmond.'

I half heard him come in, and thought I was dreaming, but in the morning he was there.

Dead to the world.

Laughter rises in me, shocking, hysterical, and I push my hand against my mouth to contain it.

'I didn't go back to the cottage again until the Saturday. I stayed there on the Saturday night, then the next day I went back to London and left my bag in the cloakroom at Waterloo station. I called for it on the Thursday.'

'And it was on the Thursday that you were arrested?'

'Yes.'

'I think the rest of the story has been covered in sufficient detail. I want to ask you just one last question, Mr Ryan: did you at any time desire the death of Miss Cade?'

He leans forward. '*Never.* Never at any time. The fact that I invited another woman to the cottage shows that it was not murder. I invited Miss Bingham to help me get through the . . . the *monstrous* task I had to undertake.'

He takes a long shuddering breath. 'I just needed another human being with me.'

He looks over at the jury and says, 'I am not a man of bloodshed or violence. I just needed . . . I needed human company.'

I study the jury. Each man is looking at Tom. Two of them – the tall man I noticed on the first day and an older man with a neat beard – are nodding. Four or five others begin to nod too.

For a single, dizzying moment, I think: *He's going to get off. We'll go home – and everything will go on just as before.*

I think: *He's going to get away with it.*

And then I realize what I have thought.

32

Kate, July 1924

Outside the courtroom, the hallway is emptying rapidly. It's Friday afternoon: everyone wants to go home.

I find an empty bench and sink down onto it. A young man passes me at a brisk, energetic pace. He hails someone coming the opposite way, and they begin talking about a cricket match they are to play in the following afternoon. It is extraordinary to think of *cricket*, of life going on outside.

I lean back against the cool stone wall and close my eyes.

They all say it was an accident. Even Dr Fawcett admits it could have been an accident.

He *cannot* be a murderer. Not Tom. He is just the victim of a terrible set of circumstances.

I know him. I know what he is capable of.

You didn't know he was capable of the things he did to the bodies – to Miss Cade and to her poor baby.

I realize my face is wet, and I put my hands up to hide it.

Admit it now, Katie. You do not know what your husband is capable of.

You do not know what to believe at all.

At that, I think something breaks inside me – something precious and irreplaceable, something that was keeping me upright. I bend over, and I open my mouth and I push the heel of my hand into my mouth, push my teeth into my skin and I scream silently into my skin because there is no one who may hear this, no one who can know.

And this is how Wild finds me.

He takes me to a cafe away from the main road. There are only two tables occupied: there are no reporters, no one gossiping about my husband. He guides me to a chair by the window. I pick up the chipped blue sugar bowl and turn it in my fingers while he orders a pot of tea for two. We are both silent until the waitress has set down the cups and saucers and left us alone again. It is a strange, almost companionable silence. For the first time in days I am with someone who knows who I am and what Tom is accused of. There is nothing to hide.

And so I simply sit and let him pour the tea. His hands are deft, his movements neat. It is an oddly domestic scene, and, without thinking, I ask him, 'What's your wife like? What does she think about your job?'

He doesn't look up, but the lines around his eyes deepen. 'She's used to it now. When we first married, when I was on the beat, she hated it. She used to worry every day that I'd get into a fight – or worse.'

'And your children?'

He adds a little milk to my tea, slides the cup over to me. 'My eldest is a copper himself now. He was always the one who wanted to try my helmet on or to come into the station on Saturdays.'

'Your wife doesn't worry about you now?'

His eyes are on his own cup as he stirs in milk and sugar. 'Well, my job now means I'm not called in until the danger's passed. Until the crime's done and dusted.'

I wonder how many murders he's worked on, and then how many men he's brought to the rope. And I say suddenly, not knowing what I will say until the words are in my mouth,

'I don't know what will happen after the trial. If he is found guilty, will he . . . will they hang him right away?'

I am staring down at the blue checked tablecloth as I say it, but I hear the chink of china and a little indrawn breath.

'I don't know who else to ask. I think you at least will be honest with me, Mr Wild.'

And now I look at him. At where he is staring at me.

'Mrs Ryan, I don't think this is—'

'Please.'

He takes a long breath. 'If he's found guilty of murder, then yes, he'll hang.' A pause, and then, 'It's usually a month or two. The law says there has to be three Sundays between the sentence and the execution. But it's usually longer.'

'I see. Thank you. Thank you for telling me. No one else would . . . Mr Edgerton just says that things are going well and that I mustn't worry.' My hand is shaking as I pick up my cup.

Wild says nothing, and I am oddly grateful that he doesn't try to comfort me.

I press the rim of the teacup against my chin until the heat of it burns me. It is only when I think I have my voice under control that I say, 'Are those the only possibilities? That he'll go free or that he'll . . . that . . .' I can't say it again.

But Wild's voice is low and steady and I can hear now that he is trying to reassure me. 'If we can't prove premeditation – if we can't prove he planned it – he may get away with manslaughter.' His face softens, just a little. 'That doesn't carry a sentence of death. A period of imprisonment, that's all.'

I nod. And then I say, 'I don't want to talk to you about what Tom . . . I don't want to talk to you about Tom. You can't make me answer questions, can you?'

He shakes his head and says, 'Well, no. Not here. Not like this, with no witnesses. It wouldn't be . . . we couldn't use anything you might say here. Legally we couldn't use it.'

'You told me once that Tom was guilty. Why do you think so?'

He puts his cup down carefully. 'Well, we caught him, Mrs Ryan. We caught him with the bag.'

'That only proves that he . . . well, that he got rid of her body. Doesn't it? He admitted to that.'

He watches me, waits for me to go on.

'I'm not a policeman, but I can see that. You've got no proof that he planned it, or that he killed her deliberately. Isn't the most likely verdict the one you just mentioned? Manslaughter. You can't prove it happened other than how Tom said.'

For a moment he says nothing. His eyes rest on my face – calm, steady. Then he says, 'My job is done now, Mrs Ryan. Now it's down to the prosecution – whether they can make the case in court. Or trip him up.'

He leans back a little in his chair. 'And it's down to the jury, of course. Juries are funny things. Unpredictable.'

From what I can tell, this jury is on Tom's side – most of them seem to sympathize with him. If I were a gambler, I would bet they will find him not guilty of murder.

I still do not know what to believe. I do not know what would be just and right.

And even if I knew, that is quite a different thing to the jury knowing and passing a verdict in court.

'Why do you think he did it, Mr Wild?'

He puts his hands together on the table: fingers straight, fingertips touching.

'I've been a copper for over thirty years, Mrs Ryan. And I've been in CID, been working murder cases, for nearly twenty. There have been a lot of times I've not had proof of a man's guilt, but you come to know.'

'How? How do you know?'

The lines around his eyes deepen again, and the tension seems to lift. 'Well, take your daughter. I bet, if she comes to you and says, "Mother, I never broke that cup" or "I never ate the last bit of cake" – you always know if she's fibbing or not. That's because you know her.'

He takes out his cigarettes, offers me one. I shake my head, and he lights one for himself. 'I know criminals. And I know guilt. You can't do this job for as long as I have and not see it.'

He sips his tea and smokes his cigarette and gazes out of the window. He looks like a man who is completely comfortable with himself and his thoughts.

I follow his gaze and look at the lowering evening sky. Wild's voice, when he speaks, seems to come from a long way away. 'How is your daughter?'

'She's not . . . she's finding it hard. Her father being away. There's been talk – you know, at school. The newspapers.'

He nods. 'You might think of taking her away if you can. Might be good for both of you.'

The answer comes fast, automatic, without thinking. 'I can't leave Tom.'

Wild looks at me. His eyes are not unkind. He says, 'Do you have somewhere you could go? If you needed to.'

'I can't leave him. He's Judith's father. She needs him.' There is a long pause and Wild does not fill it. I clear my throat. 'Maybe we'll go away afterwards.'

Wild doesn't say anything. He finishes his tea – quietly, calmly – and then he reaches into his breast pocket and takes out a card. Slides it over the table towards me.

'If you've got any more questions – or if you just want to have a chat – you telephone me on that number. Or come into the station. Any time you like.'

Then he stands, nods to me and says, 'You mind how you go now.'

33

Kate, July 1924

LONDON CHRONICLE, 11 JULY 1924

Ryan Trial: Latest
Bungalow Crime At Final Stage

No crime has ever moved the nation like the death of Miss Beatrice Cade on the lonely stretch of shore near Eastbourne.

The opening of the trial was marked by the most astonishing scenes. People travelled for miles, hoping to see the face of a monster who had killed without remorse.

They were to be disappointed. Thomas Ryan is a respectable family man, well educated and cultured, with a charming manner and appearance. He is undoubtedly the most immaculate prisoner in a trial of this magnitude for some time. He is well read – indeed, his chief pleasure is to read novels – and he quotes the classics freely and speaks French fluently.

Both victim and accused were accepted members of that section of society known as the middle class, she a capable woman of business and he a suburban man of commerce with a magnetic and fascinating personality, widely known for his prowess in games and outdoor pastimes.

Indeed, on the very day on which the bag of

bloodstained clothing is supposed to have been deposited at the Waterloo station cloakroom, he attended, in his capacity as secretary, a committee meeting of the new bowling club at Richmond. He was in good spirits and appeared just as usual. A woman acquaintance told this reporter that he 'was his normal amusing and generous self' that evening, and that he 'stood us a round of drinks and entertained us with stories until the clubhouse closed.'

This cannot be the behaviour of a man who bore the guilty weight of such a dreadful crime.

Thomas Ryan made only two mistakes in an otherwise unblemished life – he had an ill-advised affair with Miss Cade, and when, during the course of a quarrel, she fell and hit her head, he attempted to dispose of her body in secret.

Ryan's counsel, Mr Christopher Tate, is confident that Ryan will be acquitted. 'If he had only called for help when the accident occurred, he would never have been arrested. I am quite certain that the jury will acquit on the evidence presented, and that my client will be at home with his wife and his little daughter before long.'

~

All the way home, on an omnibus and two trains, I look at the other passengers, staring vacantly out of the window or with their faces buried in their own newspapers, and I wonder: can they tell?

Can they see how bruised I am by what I have heard, how *polluted* I am by my association with Tom?

I look at the fat, satisfied face of the woman opposite me, and the untroubled countenance of the man across the aisle, and I am overcome by a terrible urge to confess.

The man you have read about in the newspapers – that man is my husband.

It is my husband whose photograph you have gaped at and pointed to and passed around. It is my husband you have talked about and wondered at. And it is my husband who took the body of a woman who loved him, and destroyed everything that made her human.

I sit by the window and look out at the placid green countryside, and I want to shake these people until their teeth rattle and their world is as broken and troubled as mine.

When I arrive home, there is nothing to eat. The mutton stew I made last weekend is finished, and there is nothing else. I sit down at the table exhausted and spent. How strange that after all the horrors I have heard described in the last few days, this should bring me to tears.

At six, Judith opens her bedroom door and comes into the kitchen. We have barely seen one another all week.

I am still in my hat and coat. The stove is cold. The table is not set. Judith sees all of this and ignores it. She sits in her usual place and waits expectantly for me to do what I always do: feed her, care for her, make life go on, despite everything.

I pick up the milk jug, left on the table since breakfast, and I hurl it at the wall.

She flinches, pushes herself to her feet, runs out of the room.

'Oh God, I'm sorry. I'm so sorry, Judith, I . . .'

Her bedroom door slams. I stare at the warm sour milk on the wall, dripping and running down to the floor.

I should fetch a cloth. I should go down and tell Mrs Irvine that I'm sorry, I dropped something. That everything is quite all right, and I am managing I am managing I am quite all right.

But I am not sorry. And this is not all right.

I have always been able to turn away from Tom's lies – from the effect they had and from the reasons he told them. I have buried his past and the truth of him over and over and over.

But I cannot look away from this. His lies are everywhere and I cannot avoid them any longer.

They are under this table where we ate dinner together, where he told me about the meetings he had been to, about the trains he had taken to Carlisle, to Nottingham, to Peterborough – and the cheap boarding houses he had stayed in alone.

They are under the bed where we slept together. Where he undressed me and kissed me and lay with me and loved me.

His lies have seeped through the whole house, creeping between the bricks, tugging at them, loosening them, up around the windows and onto the roof where they squat ripe and filthy among the chimney stacks and peer down into the rooms where we have lived. Waiting for me to look up. Laughing at me.

I think of the model of the house in the courtroom. I remember how I looked down into those rooms, how I imagined her last days. Now I realize that her last days were entirely different to what I pictured. The baby inside her would have changed everything.

I am standing by the dresser and there is a cup and saucer in my hand. My hand is up at my shoulder and there is a satisfying crash and a mess of shattered china at my feet. I raise my hand again and again and again until I am spent. I slide down to the floor.

I hear footsteps.

I hear, 'Mummy?'

I pick up one of the pieces of china. It is blue and gold – part of our wedding set. I run my finger along the edge.

'Mummy?'

Back and forward, back and forward, making a red mark on my skin. It is not sharp enough to draw blood, no matter how hard I press.

'Mummy.' Judith crouches beside me. She puts her hand on

my arm and we both look at it for a moment. 'Are you . . .' She
takes a long, shaky breath. 'I'll make a cup of tea.'

She fills the kettle and lights the stove and I say none of the
usual things about fire and danger and care. I watch her sweep
the broken crockery into a corner, watch her make the tea and
spoon sugar in and hand me a cup. She presses my fingers
around it then sits beside me with her own cup. We drink our
tea together on the kitchen floor while the sun blazes and dies
beyond the window.

I finish my tea and clear my throat until my voice comes. I
tell Judith to take some money from my purse and go and buy
some bread.

'Can I have bread and jam for supper?'

I make myself smile at her. 'Or sugar sandwiches, if you
like.'

She smiles back. It is the first smile she has given me in
weeks. I kiss my fingers and touch them to the freckles on her
nose – one, two, three – the way I used to when she was very
young, and then I take myself off to bed, and I sleep and I do
not dream.

When I wake up, the house is dark. I reach for my watch
and see that it is after one. My clothes are creased and tight
around me, so I take them off and open the dresser drawer,
looking for a clean nightgown. Then I see, folded on the top,
the fine lawn nightdress that Tom bought me for my birthday.

Intimacy took place on that occasion.

I reach in and take the nightdress in my fist and I squeeze
it tight. And then I pull it between my fists; I use my nails and
teeth; I rip and tear.

It is not enough.

I leave the nightgown on my bed and I find my scissors. I
am panting and my teeth are grinding and grinding, pressed
so tight that I think they must crack. Back to the bed, to the

crumpled skin of the nightgown, and I push the scissors in, again and again.

Intimacy took place.

The blades go through the nightgown to the sheets below, sheets I once slept on with my husband.

Intimacy took place on several occasions. At various locations.

I take the scissors in my fist and raise my arm and I stab and rip and rip until the sheets are scored with lines like the claw marks of an animal.

It is not enough.

I spin around and I see, on the dressing table: rouge, powder, perfume – all the things I bought to look younger, prettier, *better* – and I am filled with a rage so hot and red I have to stuff my hand in my mouth to stop myself from screaming. Then I stretch out my arm and I sweep it across the surface – once, twice – until everything is gone, until the polished dark wood is empty and clean. The powder is broken into little pieces on the carpet and the mirror of my compact is cracked and my jewellery box is upended – and there are all the glittering beads and bangles I bought to make him love me more.

It is not enough.

I go to the wardrobe, drop the scissors and pull out his clothes. I reach for all the shirts and suits he was so proud of, the pullovers and the vests, the collars and socks, the under-wear, the ties, the hats. I grab at each one until it is all in a heap on the floor, and I take up the scissors again and I stab and score until every piece of cloth that once touched his skin is cut.

And then it is enough.

I sit on the floor and my skin is hot and wet. I smell of sweat and I am breathing fast. My jaw aches. I look at what I have done.

I crawl across the room and into bed.

I place the scissors under my pillow, and I sleep like a baby.

*

When I wake again, the first thing I feel is that I am naked and the sheets are bunched and creased beneath me. I run my hand across the cotton and my fingers slide inside the cuts I made.

I open my eyes and look at the destruction I have wreaked, and I find that I do not care.

I stand and stretch and my body is warm and limber. I slip an old nightgown over my head – thick soft cotton that smells of soap – and tie my dressing gown tight. In the kitchen, everything is as usual: Judith is eating bread and butter, the teapot is on the table, the sun is showing up the smears on the window pane.

But there are spaces on the dresser where the broken china used to sit, and the milk bottle is on the table instead of the jug. And there is a new wariness in Judith's eyes.

I go to her, crouch by her chair and place my hands either side of her face. She is absolutely still, watching me.

'I'm sorry about what happened yesterday. I'm sorry that I frightened you. I . . . well, there were reasons for it. I won't let it happen again.'

Tears swim in her eyes.

'All right?'

She nods and her lip trembles and I reach for her and hold on to her. I kiss her neck, her damp cheeks, her rough unbrushed hair.

Then I push her away gently and hold her face in my hands again. She sniffs but the frightened look has gone.

'The past few weeks have been very difficult. For both of us.' She blinks. 'And I've been . . . well, I don't know what to call it. Unhappy. Afraid. I know mothers aren't supposed to be any of those things, but you're old enough to hear this.'

I smile at her and she looks back at me. 'But I'm better now. Things will be better. So I . . .'

'Does that mean Daddy's coming home? Is it all over?'

I bite my lip to stop the automatic reassurances from spilling out. Empty words – more lies – won't help her.

'No. It's not over yet. And I . . . I don't know if he's coming home.'

'But he—'

'Judith, you're old enough to understand that it's not up to me or you.' My voice is harsh but I do not bend or soften. 'I know it's difficult. I know you want me to make everything all right, but there are some things I can't mend. We just have to wait.'

She swallows, then nods again and sits back in her seat.

'I'm going to give the house a good clean today. Then we'll go out. We can have lunch in Richmond if you like.'

She takes another piece of bread. Starts to spread honey on it. 'I can help. With the cleaning. Then it'll be done faster.'

So we cover our hair with scarves and I give her the polish and a rag and show her how to work the wax into the wood of the table and the sideboard. Then I take some old sacks into the bedroom and begin to sort through the wreckage. All of Tom's clothes go into the bags. I do not let myself think about what I am doing or about what this means. I do not let myself say *If* or *When*.

I fold shirts and vests into sacks; I tie them tight; I place them on the landing, ready to go outside for the rag-and-bone man. I go through my own wardrobe and take out all the clothes that are too small or too worn, and then all the clothes that I bought only because I thought Tom would like them.

Then I cannot help it: I think of Miss Cade buying her lace-trimmed underwear for Tom. I think of the photograph that Mrs Bishop identified: of Miss Cade's careful pose and her hopeful smile – and I realize I am crying.

I throw away the spilled powder, the rouge, the scattered beads. I keep one necklace that Judith has always liked, a cheap thing made of cloudy green glass, and a little gold ring that I

saved up to buy when I got my first job in Cartwright's shop.
Everything else that is salvageable goes into a separate box. We
will need money. Whatever happens, we will need money.

With every sack I fill, I feel cleaner and lighter, as though I
am scrubbing away a layer of dirt. I strip the torn sheets from
the bed and replace them with clean ones. And now the bedroom is empty. The top of the dressing table holds my hairbrush and my almost-empty jewellery box and nothing else.
Tom's side of the wardrobe is completely bare, as though he
has never lived here at all. I shut the wardrobe doors and go to
fetch the carpet sweeper from the cupboard. Judith is singing
quietly to herself in the front room, the song Tom used to sing
to her to send her off to sleep.

Only a violet I plucked when but a boy,
And oft' times when I'm sad at heart, this flower has given me joy

When I come back into the bedroom, I bend down to check
that nothing has fallen under the bed – and I find a button, a
jet bead, and several scraps of paper. I pick them up and sit on
the bed to smooth them out, and I realize they are the pieces
of paper I found in Tom's pockets all those weeks ago, at the
same time I found the cloakroom ticket. I had forgotten that I
put them at the bottom of my jewellery box.

There are some handwritten names and addresses, and three
receipts. A menswear shop, an ironmonger's shop, a restaurant
on Aldersgate Street.

Judith's singing grows louder – '*always knitting in the old arm
chair*' – then fades again.

Two shirts, two collars, a box of handkerchiefs. A knife and
saw. Lunch for two: lamb cutlets, apple tart, coffee.

I imagine them together in that restaurant. Their hands
touching. I think of her tired pale face as I saw it that day; I
find that I cannot imagine her flushed and animated.

I am about to crumple up the receipts when I notice the

dates. They are all from March and April: the shirts and collars, 7 April; lunch, 21 March; the ironmonger's shop, 3 April.

Shirts and collars and lunch for two tell me nothing about Tom I didn't already know.

But the ironmonger's.

Tom is not a practical man – and yet he bought a knife and saw on 3 April.

I think of Dr Fawcett saying, *In the first bedroom, I found a tenon saw.*

Twelve days before Miss Cade died, Tom bought a knife and saw.

Twelve days before.

For a moment the world goes black and there is a terrible pain behind my eyes.

Bile rises in my throat; my stomach turns over; I reach the chamber pot just in time. When there is nothing left in my body, I slide down the wall and put my head between my knees. There is sweat on my face and a foul taste in my mouth.

'Mummy?'

Judith is in the doorway.

I lift my head, rub my hand over my mouth, try to smile. 'I'm just queasy. Could you fetch me a glass of water?'

She disappears and I am left alone with this new and terrible knowledge. With his worst and final lie.

He planned this.

The murder, the disposal of her body. All planned.

And I am the only one who knows.

I hear Judith coming back. I make myself stand, take the glass from her with shaking hands, and drink.

I am the only one who knows what he did.

Judith is watching me.

'Have you finished the dusting, love?'

Her mouth moves as she replies, and her eyes search my face.

I am the only one who knows him.

I take another sip of water. A deep breath. 'Shall we go out? Have lunch?'

She leaves to fetch her shoes and comb her hair, and I go over to the dressing table to wipe my mouth.

I look at my face in the mirror. My skin is grey, my lips dry.

I didn't know, I whisper to the woman in the mirror.

I didn't know.

Oh God, I didn't know!

And the woman in the mirror whispers back, *But now you do.*

34

Kate, July 1924

The rest of the day has a queer, too-bright quality. I try to listen when Judith tells me about the story she is writing and the hedgehog she fed in the garden this morning, but when she pauses for my reply, I realize I have no idea what she has asked me.

After lunch we go shopping, then for a walk in the park. We walk in silence for a while, and then I feel her little hand steal into mine. I look down at her and squeeze her fingers and she looks back at me.

She says, 'If Daddy . . .' There is a pause and she squeezes tighter. 'If Daddy doesn't come home . . .'

She falls silent and we walk on, slower. I make myself wait.

'If he doesn't come home, we will be all right, won't we? Me and you?'

I stop and bend to take her in my arms. I hold her close and stroke her hair and I tell her, 'Yes, love. We will. We'll be perfectly all right.'

She pulls away and looks at me again, and for the first time I see in her the woman she might become. She nods, her face serious, and then she turns away – and she is a child again, scampering ahead of me.

I watch her run along the path and all I can think is that I must keep her safe.

A mother ought to be willing to sacrifice anything for her child.

Oddly it is Moran's voice I hear forming that thought: flat, factual, definite.

I would sacrifice my husband for my daughter. Without question, without hesitation. If I could save one of them, I would save her. That is a simple and clear choice – but that is not the choice I must make.

My choice is between letting Tom be convicted of manslaughter, letting him get away with murder – or taking the receipt to the police and sending my daughter's father to the gallows.

The choice is between letting her believe in a father who made a terrible mistake, and merely tried to cover it up – or peeling back the mask and showing her the monster underneath.

My thoughts swing back and forward. I am like the pendulum on a clock.

The choice is between letting her live with a lie and a father in prison, or forcing her to live with the legacy of a murderer.

Tick tock.

I tell myself that I will think about it properly when I am alone – but when I get into bed that night and turn down the lamp, it is not Tom or Judith that I think about, but Miss Cade. Every detail of our meeting is as clear as if it happened yesterday.

It was a grey afternoon near the beginning of April. When I came home from work, Tom was in his usual chair in the front room, the newspaper open on his knee.

'It's cold out there.' I went past him, closed the curtains. 'Want a cup of tea, love?'

He didn't reply and when I asked him again, he just shook his head.

'Are you all right, Tom?'

'Quite all right.' He still didn't look up. His mouth opened to let the words out, and snapped shut behind them like a trap.

I looked at him for a moment then went through into the kitchen, washed my hands and started supper. I lit the gas, boiled a pan of water, and stood by the stove, waiting for the potatoes to be done. I stuck a fork in one and then another, and all the time I was thinking of Tom in the other room, staring at a newspaper he wasn't reading.

I pricked another potato. Still too hard. Then out of nowhere there was a knock at the front door, making me jump.

It was Wednesday: Mrs Irvine would be at her sister's. I called through to Tom, 'Are you expecting someone?'

Nothing.

The knock came again.

'Tom! Are you going to answer the door?'

The knocking came again and again, as though the person outside was desperate to enter. I turned the gas down, wiped my hands and took my apron off. Hurried down the stairs and into the hallway, smoothing my hair.

There was a woman on the doorstep. A woman I had never seen before.

At first I thought she must be collecting for something, but when she saw me, she took a step back. Blinked.

Colour rushed into her face and she opened her mouth, and nothing came out.

I think I knew then. I folded my arms.

Her colour deepened and she said, 'I . . . I'm . . . I'm looking for Mr Ryan.'

A phrase of my mother's slid into my mind. *He's brought trouble to the door.*

And I thought: How *dare* you? How dare you come here, to *my* home, how dare you ask for *my* husband?

I looked right at her and I felt rage building and building. Because of her presumption. Because of her smart city shoes.

Because of the way she stood with one ankle tilted and her expensive coat brushing against the wall and not seeming to care about her bitten nails.

I called to him over my shoulder and there was no reply and I called him again, and all the time we looked at one another across that little distance and the air felt damp and smelled like a dying October although it was spring.

After a moment it seemed that it was too much for her because she dropped her gaze and bowed her head and I saw the sweat on her skin, the lines on her forehead and the dip of her eyelashes.

These were tender details – intimate, even – but I felt no tenderness for her, none at all.

I stood tall on the threshold of my house, raised my chin, thought of my husband in the living room. I thought of all the other women, of the other knocks on my door over the years, the policemen who had stood where she was standing now, and the news they had brought me.

I had come through all of that, and she was nothing.

All of those other women were nothing.

He was my husband. The father of my children. He was *mine*.

The night she came to the house was a Wednesday. For no reason other than curiosity, I get up now and take my diary out of my handbag. I leaf back through the pages, looking for the first Wednesday of the month.

It was the second. She came to see us on the second of April. The day before Tom bought the knife and saw.

Whatever she said to him – that's what made him decide. That's when he planned her death.

This was not my fault.

I owe her nothing.

I let that thought take hold.

I could throw the receipt away. The trial would end, and eventually everyone would forget about her.

Tom would come home in time, and we would be a family again.

She had wanted him to leave me – presumably she would have forgotten me easily enough. I could forget about her in turn. We could move away, the three of us, make a new start together.

She is nothing to me. I could let her stay dead and buried.

When I left her on the doorstep that night and walked back inside and told Tom there was someone to see him, I made my voice level. No hint of emotion, even when I saw the fear in his face, just like hers. I gave nothing away, even when he came back for his coat and told me he was going out. Even when Judith asked where he was.

And when his dinner went cold and I sat at the window watching the sky grow dark, I kept everything smooth and neat and buttoned down tight.

I lie in bed now, and realize that if I throw away the receipt, if I forget what I know, this is how I will have to live. I will have to keep everything buttoned tight for ever.

And once Tom has gone to prison for manslaughter, once Judith has grown used to the new reality and begun to count down the years and then the months until his release, I will never be able to go back and take a different course.

Like the jury, I have one chance to get this right.

Remember what happened last time, Katie. When you found that cloakroom ticket, you didn't keep it to yourself. You've had to sit in court and regret that every single day. Once this is done, you can't go back.

This is different, though. This is another voice. This is the voice that got me through the years when Tom was away. It got me through the months after Billy's death.

This is different. When you gave that ticket to Arthur Dean, you had no idea what would happen.

But you know precisely what this receipt is. And what it means.

I stare into the darkness and I think about Tom as he was when I met him. About what he was like, about what I thought marriage would be like, about what kind of man he is now.

I think about Judith and my chest aches. I wonder what I would advise her to do if she was grown and married and in my position.

Tick tock.

I think about how simple right and wrong were when I was a child. About how I used to know what to do, easily and instinctively.

Being with Tom like he wanted before we were married was wrong: I knew that, and I let him do it anyway. I loved him. I wanted him to love me.

Lying to Mr Morley about Tom, telling him Tom was in the army when in fact he was in prison – that was wrong.

Everything Tom has done is wrong.

But betraying him again – knowingly, this time – would be wrong.

Making Judith grow up without a father would be wrong. Making her live with the stigma of a murderer for a father would be wrong.

And what about me – do I deserve to lose my husband because of another woman?

Tick tock.

Tick tock.

I could have burned that cloakroom ticket. I could have thrown it on the fire as soon as I found it – and done so quite innocently. I need never have known.

And I could burn this receipt. No one else knows about it. It would be another form of innocence, in a way.

Letting Miss Cade lie in her grave, letting the truth of what he did lie buried with her – would it be so wrong?

35

Kate, July 1924

At five I get up and dress, drink three cups of tea and wait at the kitchen table. When Judith comes yawning into the kitchen, her hair a halo of tangles and her eyes sticky with sleep, I tell her that I have to go out.

'I'll be back by teatime. There's tongue and tomatoes in the larder and Mrs Irvine is downstairs if you need anything. Finish writing that story you told me about.'

I take the train to Clapham and find a hotel near the station with a public telephone in the lobby. I ask the operator to put me through to the number on the card that Wild gave me. They keep me waiting while they fetch him, and I am on the point of giving up when I hear that quiet steady voice.

'Mrs Ryan?'

'Good morning, Mr Wild. I'm sorry to disturb you.'

'Not at all. Can I help you with something?'

'I need to see my husband. Today.'

'Mrs Ryan, I'm afraid it's not—'

'I know it's not usual. I know it's Sunday. I wouldn't ask if it wasn't important.' I run my fingers over the flocked yellow wallpaper in the telephone booth.

I hear a quiet sigh. 'I'll do what I can. How can I reach you?'

'You can't. I'm on my way to Lewes now.'

'I see.' I can hear what in anyone else's voice would sound like a smile – but I've never seen Wild smile. 'You're a very determined woman, Mrs Ryan.'

I say nothing.

Another sigh. 'All right. Give me a couple of hours and I'll get the order telegraphed over.'

The train to Sussex takes even longer than usual, it being Sunday, but by half-past one I am outside the prison. They ask for my visiting order.

'I don't have one, I—'

'If you don't have one, you can't come in.' The guard is a little man with sandy hair and a white scar on his upper lip. He folds his arms and looks at me.

'It's been telephoned through.'

He shakes his head. 'No visiting order; no visit.'

'It's been telephoned through,' I repeat. 'Today.'

He doesn't move – and suddenly I am very tired of this. 'Go and check, please.'

He still doesn't move and I fold my own arms. 'I can wait.'

Without taking his eyes off me, he calls over his shoulder. 'Bill? Got someone here who says we ought to have had a VO through for her today.'

Another man – dark, with a neat clipped moustache, comes forward, nodding. 'That's right. What name is it again?'

'Ryan.'

'Ryan. That's it.' He moves aside to let me enter. 'Message come through about you just afore lunchtime. Someone must think a lot of you – I've never known any prisoner have an urgent visiting order for a Sunday before.'

There is a question in his voice, but I say nothing.

He clears his throat. 'All right then. This way' – and he leads me along a series of corridors and down a flight of stairs.

And all the time that I am following him, I am more afraid than I have ever been in my life.

He leads me, not to the large visiting hall that I went to

before, but to a little room with a table and two chairs. It's empty. He nods at me to sit and says, 'Might be a little while.'

The door slams behind him and I am left alone to think about what I am doing. All the way here, I was concentrating on one thing: I must see Tom before I decide. I must speak to him. And now that I am here, I have no idea what to say.

I feel like I have been waiting for hours when I hear footsteps outside. I get to my feet, my heart racing. I keep my eyes lowered as the door opens. I see the darkness of the guards' uniforms, the grey flannel of Tom's suit, a fumbling of keys and handcuffs, and then the drop of his body as he sits. Only then do I lift my head and look straight at him.

His eyes are bright and curious. 'I wasn't expecting you today.'

'No. I . . . I just wanted to see you.'

This is so difficult, with the guards in the room, and the fact of Tom in front of me, very different to the silent figure of my imagination.

'Is it Judith? Is she all right?'

'No, no – she's quite well. I just . . . I wanted to talk to you away from the court. Just us.'

He leans back in his chair and crosses his legs. He looks puzzled. 'Well, that's—'

'I wanted to ask—'

We speak at the same time and he smiles a little and goes on with what he was saying. But I am louder and I keep talking until he falls silent and then I say it again.

'I want you to tell me what happened.'

'What do you mean, what happened?' His gaze flickers to one of the guards, leaning against the wall, scratching his scalp.

'I want you to tell me what happened on the day – the evening – that Miss Cade died. And on the days following. I want to hear it in your words. Without all the questions. Without the jury and the judge.'

He opens his mouth. Closes it again.

I lower my voice. 'I want to hear the truth, Tom. Just between us.' I try to sound inviting. Intimate. 'Tell me the truth.'

'You know the truth. We went to London. We took the train back to the cottage. We quarrelled. She fell and hit her head and I realized she was dead.'

'And then?'

'And then I tried to wake her, and I found I couldn't. You've heard all this.'

'And then?'

'And then I covered up her body and left it in the bedroom. You *know* this. What's going on, Katie?'

'And then?'

'And then I went and bought a knife and saw and I put . . . I put some of her in the trunk. I took some . . . some pieces back to London, and left the bag in the cloakroom.' He folds his arms. 'The rest of it, I think you know.'

I swallow. 'And did you know that . . . that she was expecting a child?'

'Oh God, no. Not until . . . not until the police told me.' Tears tremble on his lashes as he says, 'I am a *father*, Katie. You know how much I love Judith.'

He leans towards me and turns his hands over, showing the pale vulnerable palms. His fingers spread, pleading with me to understand. 'If I had known, I would have found a way to look after . . . to look after them.'

He is talking faster now. 'I thought she knew what she was doing.' His eyes are wide and appealing. 'She was old – almost forty! I didn't expect . . . I didn't know this could happen with a woman her age.' He runs his hands over his hair. 'She tricked me.'

'Is that the truth? Do you swear, Tom?'

'Of course it is.'

'*Do you swear?*'

He leans back again. Looks at me and says, 'On Judith's life. You do believe me?'

I watch his face and I imagine how it must have been for Miss Cade. I imagine her terror – at the fact of the baby; at the possibility that Tom would leave her, that Tom would not be faithful, that Tom would no longer love her.

Miss Cade was the first problem he was unable to put behind him. This was the first time someone had refused to let him walk away from his duty.

For a moment I admire her, this woman I met once.

I remember myself – eighteen and expecting a child: lost, ignorant, frightened about the future and about the man I had chosen.

Then I think of her again, and I find that very little imagination is required at all.

'You do believe me, Kitty?'

I make myself smile at him. 'Of course. Of course I do, darling.'

He smiles back, and then he says, 'Listen, we don't have long – and there's something I want to say to you.'

I look at him. I wait.

'I know how this started. I worked it out. They picked me up at Waterloo, and so I know you must have found the cloakroom ticket. That you must have given it to the police.'

It seems like so long ago now. I think of Arthur Dean on the doorstep: his shocked face; the way he told me to wait for him to come back.

A lifetime ago.

Tom looks into my eyes. 'I know it all began with the ticket, Kitty. I know that without the ticket, I would not be here.'

I cannot look away from him.

'It all began with the ticket – and with you. I know you started all of this.'

Another small, brave smile. 'And I want you to know that I forgive you. You had no idea what you were doing. I know you didn't mean it. And so I forgive you.'

I look at him, at his clear eyes and his smile, and the thought comes to me out of nowhere: *But there is nothing to forgive.*

When I say goodbye and walk away, back along the corridors, out into the warm afternoon, it seems that I have been there for hours. But it is not quite quarter to three when the door slams closed behind me.

I walk back to the road and lean against the wall for a moment. Close my eyes and lift my face to the sun. I'm so tired I could almost fall asleep right here.

Tom has lied to me before, of course: by refusing to answer, by leaving out certain facts. He has kept me in the dark about certain things he hoped I would never discover.

But he has never, to my knowledge, looked me in the eye, listened to me ask him for the truth, and lied.

Judith has a liar for a father. If he goes to prison for manslaughter, the rest of her life will be based on a lie.

And I will have to share in that lie. I will have to lie to my daughter for the rest of my life.

I will never be able to cook his dinner again, or starch his collars or listen to his sleeping breath, without hearing the words that have been spoken in that courtroom about what he did.

I cannot live like that. I will not let Judith live like that.

When I get to Clapham Junction, I do not get on the Richmond train. I find a tearoom and I sit for a little while, thinking again of Miss Cade.

And when my tea has grown cold, I stand and gather my things, with no clear idea of what I'm doing.

In the end I am surprised at what I do. I take a train to Victoria, and then I leave the station and board a bus going north. We roll through Mayfair and along Piccadilly, round the curve of Soho, and up to Tottenham Court Road. The gentle motion and the sun on the glass are almost lulling me to sleep, when I hear the conductor calling out, 'Bloomsbury, ladies and gents! Alight here for the British Museum, for the Hospital for Sick Children, for Southampton Row' – and I am startled into wakefulness.

It was *here* . . . was it not? Yes – when I find my way to Guilford Street, I know I am in the right place. Even now, when most of the attention is on my husband in Sussex, there are still two or three newspaper reporters outside the club where Miss Cade lived.

I watch them watching the door; coming together to smoke a cigarette; moving apart to ask questions of the girls who trip up and down the worn steps. I stand on the opposite side of the road and look up at the building. There are three floors, the windows becoming smaller the higher they go.

I wonder which floor she lived on. Which window was hers.

Without thinking about why I am doing it, I cross the road. I stand at the bottom of the steps and put my hand on the cold iron railing that divides the pavement from the basement area.

She saw this railing every day. She may have touched this chip in the paint. She walked up those steps and through that door every evening.

I wonder if she ever noticed the crack on this step or the stain on that brick. If she knew that girl with the curling dark hair, or this one, in the violet dress. And I wonder how she felt when she walked out of that door for the last time.

Again, I wonder what it was like to be her. But unlike the

other day when I looked at the model of the cottage, this time I make myself stand and face her.

And for the first time, I think – *what would I say to her now?*

If I could go back to that moment on the doorstep, knowing what I do now, what would I say?

I think again of her frightened face as she stood outside my house. And I know what is the right thing to do.

I think I have always known.

36

Kate, July 1924

Monday is airless and sultry. Yellow clouds press down on the rooftops as I walk along the queue outside the court. I ignore the murmurs and turned heads as I pass, and I bang on the door again and again until a porter appears, something half eaten in his hand and grease on his chin.

'No admittance before nine o'clock.' He goes to close the door and I put my hand out to stop him.

'I need to speak to Mr Wild. To Chief Inspector Wild.'

'There's no admittance before—'

'Did you hear what I said? I need to speak to Chief Inspector Wild. Or to Mr Moran.'

He looks at me properly, and I meet his gaze. I feel the stares of the women behind me, and I think back to that first day, when I was afraid to tell the policeman there was a reserved seat for me inside, because I was his wife. I am no longer afraid.

Eventually he stands back and lets me enter. The murmurs swell, the stares press into me. And then the door is closed and it is cool: all shadows and silence.

'Wait here,' he says, licking crumbs from his fingers, and I sit on a bench in a little recess in the hallway, beneath a stained-glass window I have never noticed before. I sit with my hips and my head turned sideways, and I trace the lead patterns with my fingers, stroke the smooth jewel colours filling the spaces between. Above me is the white oval face of a woman who is weeping.

Then I hear a lopsided tread and I know it is about to begin.

My hands are damp, and when I stand up I fold my arms so that I may wipe my palms on my coat sleeves.

'Good morning, Mrs Ryan.'

'Thank you for seeing me, Mr Wild.'

I look at his face and he is exactly the same: calm, quiet, watchful. And I know that I can do this.

I put my hand into my pocket and take out the little piece of paper. I hold on to it for one moment more, and then I hand it over.

He looks at it, and then at me. 'This is . . . it's . . .'

'I know what it is, Mr Wild. I found it in his pocket.'

He tries to say something else, but I shake my head and walk to the door leading to the public gallery. The door is ajar, but as I enter, an usher stands and comes towards me.

'I'm sorry, madam, but no one is—'

'Let her in.' Wild is behind me. He shows the usher his identification card, then takes my arm and leads me to the public benches. He waits until I am seated, huddled in the front row, in the farthest corner from the dock. Then he says, 'I need to go and show this to Moran. Set things in motion.'

He puts his hand on my shoulder. 'Will you be all right, Mrs Ryan?'

I look at him and I say nothing. What can I say?

He pats my arm and leaves through the little door at the back by which the main actors enter when the court is in session. I wait for them to come now. There is nothing more to do except wait.

I only realize I am biting the skin around my nails when it begins to sting. I look down at my hands and there is blood on my fingers, and so I slide them under my legs and stare at the floor. The courtroom gradually fills around me until I am trapped by the women; by their elbows and their bulk, and by the sweet and eager stink of their curiosity.

I expect they are staring at me, but I do not look up until I hear the little door open, and then I raise my head and see the men come in: Tate, Moran – and then Wild. I look a question at him and he nods, quite calmly.

The jury file in. And then Tom, between his guards, his head up, his hands clasped before him. He looks at Tate, then at the jury.

And then he looks at me. He looks at me and smiles, and it is the same confident open smile he gave me the first time we met.

I could leave, I think now. I could simply stand and squeeze along the line to the door; I could feign illness, tears. I could faint. All of these things are possible.

But of course I cannot leave. I have to see this through. I have to find the courage to face Tom, at the end.

Because I have had a part in all of this.

Hadn't I known – hadn't I always known – that he had something terrible inside him, something that lay rotting under the smooth surface of our normal life?

I saw glimpses of it sometimes. I thought of his face as he persuaded me, sweet-talked me, into doing things I did not want to do. I thought of how dirty, how *shamed*, I felt afterwards.

I thought of the first time he had hit me: the throb and the shock of it. The bruise that had lasted for days.

'You're always nagging, Kitty. I didn't marry a nag.' He sighed, and then reached out and stroked my cheek with a soft finger. Down and under and lifting my chin until I had to look up and into his face. 'What's happened to the pretty girl I married, eh?'

Each time, he would kiss me, and then he would leave again, and I would concentrate on scrubbing the floor, on drying the dishes, on kneading the dough. On letting the air in, on rolling it out. On the heavy damp feel of it under my hand. On the dusting of flour on the table. On the itch at the end of my nose and the potato in my stocking. On the pain in my back and the cries of the baby next door.

Anything. Anything other than why he wasn't at home and where he might be and the girl that Edie Bainbridge from number eight had seen him walking with in the park.

I knew about this part of him, and I said nothing – only forgave him and forgave him and forgot the things that he had done. Because I loved him, and because of my own guilt.

I believed that Billy's death was my fault. That if I'd been a different kind of mother – more watchful, more loving, kinder, better – he would still be alive.

I let myself believe that I was guilty.

I let Tom refuse to tell me any different.

For six years, ever since Billy died, I have thought I needed you to forgive me.

I was so full of my own guilt – choked with it, drowning in it – that I paid too little attention to his.

The judge enters and the court comes to order.

Moran stands. 'My Lord, the Crown wishes to submit new evidence.'

The judge frowns. Removes his spectacles. 'At this late stage? This is most irregular.'

I feel my heart thudding. My hands are clasped together in my lap.

The judge sighs. 'Very well. Very well – counsel, approach the bench.'

Moran and Tate come out from behind their tables. They step forward together, robes lifting, billowing, and stand in front of the judge, heads bowed. The judge leans forward and the three murmur together. They are great black birds, pecking, pecking.

Tom leans forward too, as though somehow he might hear what they are saying. His eyes flicker between them. One-two-three-two-one.

The judge is nodding his head. He looks up at the clock, says something in a low voice. Nods his head again.

Tate glances over at Tom, then walks away, looking down, his brows knitted together. He reaches his seat, says a few words to his junior.

The clouds outside the windows have grown heavier and the room is almost dark now. The judge orders the electric lights to be switched on, and Tom is called to the witness box again. As he takes his position, the court shuffles, settles.

And I am not safe.

I can feel it, urgently – I have let the truth out, and I am not safe.

Moran rises and walks the few steps to the jury box where he stops and turns to Tom. His arm rests lightly on the wooden rail that surrounds the box, inviting the confidence of the twelve men within it.

He begins by asking Tom about the details of what he did with Miss Cade.

When they met. When they became intimate.

Where. How often.

And then?

And then. And *then*.

It goes on and on until I am bruised with it.

Then his tone changes. 'I would like to move to a different line of questioning now.' He looks at Tom and clears his throat. 'We heard from Sir Richard Fawcett last week that Miss Cade was expecting a child. Did you know about that?'

'I did not.'

'I shall put this to you again so that there can be no mistake about it. I am going to ask you some further questions about this, so we must be very clear. You say that you had no idea that Miss Cade was expecting a child?'

'No idea at all.'

'You had been intimate with her since the beginning of the year – that is, around three or four months before her death?'

'I have said so.'

'And you didn't know during March or April that she was expecting a baby?'

'I never knew she was expecting a child.' His voice is very strong, very definite.

Moran pauses and then says, looking at the jury, 'I suggest that it was *because* you knew she was going to have a child that you proposed to take her away – to Paris and then on to South Africa.'

'That is entirely – *entirely* – false.' Tom is shaking his head. Half smiling.

I look over at the jury – two or three men in the front row are also shaking their heads, arms folded. One man in the second row – an older man with deep lines etched between his nose and mouth – is frowning at Moran.

'I suggest you did know she was going to have a child, and that – combined with her beginning to tell her friends she was engaged to be married – made you panic and then plan her death.'

'You are wrong. Your *suggestion*' – and the sneer in his tone is very apparent – 'is wrong. Her death was an accident.'

'According to your story, when did Miss Cade first bring up the idea that you should take a house together?'

'She first mentioned it at the beginning of April.'

'Were you still fond of Miss Cade at this point?'

'I liked Miss Cade.'

'Is that all you can say in answer to that question?'

'I liked her.'

'At any rate, you liked her enough to go on having intimate connection with her?'

Tom does not bother to answer this, just stares at Moran and raises an eyebrow.

Moran looks back at him for a long moment and then: 'Why do you say she asked you to take a house together? What was the reason she gave you?'

'She said that, as things were, she had limited opportunities to show her affection for me. Her love.' He cannot help it, the little smile that lifts the corner of his mouth as he says this. 'She said that she wanted to act as a wife to me in every sense of the word.'

I almost laugh aloud at this. She could never have imagined what being a wife to Tom would mean.

Tom goes on, 'Her idea was that by having a holiday alone together, she could persuade me that I might be happy with her.'

'And what was your intention?'

'I thought that, if we had this week or fortnight together, or whatever time we agreed, I should convince her that she could not possibly keep or expect to keep my affection. I planned to tell her that I did not love her.'

'Let us be very clear about this' – Moran glances at the jury and raises his eyebrows – 'you agreed to her suggestion that you should take a house together so that you could convince her that you did *not* love her?'

'That I did not love her enough to go away with her.'

'Did you love her enough to go on having connection with her?'

'I liked her enough for that – but you must understand, if she had been content to remain intellectual and cultural companions, I should have been satisfied.'

'But you were not merely companions, were you? You had been intimate with her for several months.'

Tom raises his chin and tilts his head. He looks almost bored as he says, 'I have said so already. I have never denied that.'

'Are you really saying that if you could have remained *intellectual* friends, you would have been satisfied with that?'

'I would have been content with that.'

Moran turns to look at the jury. He waits, and then he says, 'You have said previously that it was Miss Cade's suggestion that you should take the house in Eastbourne in a false name?'

'Yes.'

'And having suggested you should take it in a false name, it was also Miss Cade who suggested the name Waller?'

'Yes.'

'So Miss Cade referred to you only as "Tom" at the club where she lived, and she also invented a new name for you to take the cottage in?'

'Yes.'

Moran shakes his head. 'I suggest that it was *your* idea to use false names, and that you were using false names so that any link between you and Miss Cade could not be traced.'

'That is quite wrong.'

'Then why use a false name?'

'I have already said that I was worried my wife would find out about the cottage, so Miss Cade suggested that I take it in another name.'

'You were quite the victim of Miss Cade's suggestion.'

This is not a question, but Tom seizes upon it. 'Exactly.'

Moran looks at the jury again. Shakes his head, and gives a little half-smile. 'And you had no idea that Miss Cade was expecting a child?'

'I had no idea.'

'Do you mean you never talked about it?'

'Miss Cade never told me she was going to have a child.'

'In these intimate relations between you, you never talked about her becoming pregnant or being pregnant?'

'I assumed she was taking precautions to prevent pregnancy. But she never told me that she was expecting a child.'

Moran looks at him for a moment. It seems that there is no expression on his face.

Then he walks to the table where his junior sits, and picks up a piece of paper. He holds it up for us all to see. 'The prosecution submits new evidence for the consideration of the court.'

It's such a little scrap of paper: perhaps three inches by two. The kind of thing one might find at the bottom of a bag or in a pocket. Easy to overlook.

'Let the record show that I am now handing the witness a receipt. A receipt that was found among the prisoner's effects.' To the typist: 'Exhibit 194.'

Tom looks down at it almost casually.

Then he looks again.

And when he raises his head, his face is white and his eyes frantic, like those of an animal caught in a trap.

Moran faces the jury and says, 'Please read aloud what is written on the receipt.'

Tom opens his mouth. Closes it again.

Moran turns, considers him, says, 'Perhaps I can help.' He is as smooth as glass. To the jury: 'It is a receipt from an ironmonger's shop in Victoria Street, London. It shows the purchase of two items.'

He pauses. Turns to Tom again, who stares at him. Then back to the jury. 'A cook's knife. And a saw.'

Back to Tom. 'You do agree that this receipt shows the purchase of these items? Of a knife and a saw?'

Tom swallows. 'Yes. Yes, but I—'

'Thank you. And the date on the receipt?'

Tom swallows again. Looks down at the paper in front of him. The silence tastes of chalk and iron.

'The date, please.'

'The third of April.'

'Thank you.' Moran turns back to the jury. 'Gentlemen, that receipt was found among the prisoner's effects. It shows that on the third of April – that is, *a full twelve days before Beatrice Cade was unlawfully killed* – Thomas Ryan bought a cook's knife and a saw.'

A loud murmur rises up and rolls around the courtroom. I hear, 'Hold on,' quite clearly, from the man to my left. 'Hold on – what's this?'

But even above all that, the thud is so loud it makes me jump. I look over to the dock to see Tom striking his fist against the rail in front of him. He does it again, and again. His face is flushed now, his jaw clenched. He glares at Moran and then his gaze moves around the courtroom. I feel it creeping towards me like a wolf scenting blood, and I look down quickly.

He knows. He knows what I have done.

I keep my eyes on the floor. My hands are pressed together so tightly that my arms ache.

It is almost over.

At last the court settles. Moran begins again. 'You have heard me say that a receipt was found among your effects showing that you purchased a knife and saw in Victoria Street on the third of April?'

'Yes.' Tom clears his throat. 'Yes.'

'Do you now admit that you purchased these items *before* going down to Eastbourne on the thirteenth of April?'

I risk a look at Tom. He is staring at Moran. His face is absolutely white. 'I do not . . .' He clears his throat again. 'I do not think I have ever denied that.'

'That is rather a disingenuous statement, is it not?'

'I have never been directly asked about when I bought the knife and saw, or what I purchased at particular shops on certain dates.' His voice is high and thin and defiant.

Moran smiles at the jury. Turns back to Tom. 'Well, let us look at your initial statement to the police, made on the first of

May. Your statement reads: "I came into London on the evening of the sixteenth of April and went back to Eastbourne the following night, seventeenth of April, fairly late, taking with me a knife I bought in a shop in Victoria Street. I also bought at the same shop a small saw. When I got to the cottage I was still so upset and worried that I could not then carry out my intention to dispose of the body. I did so on the following day, which was Good Friday." When you told the police that, were you telling the truth?'

'I was.'

'Did you not intend that statement to read that you bought the knife and saw on the seventeenth of April? Did you not intend us to think that you bought it *after* Miss Cade's death for the purpose of dismembering and disposing of her body?'

And now the murmuring begins again, louder. The women at the front are silent, their heads bowed together beneath their blue and red hats. For the first time, they are not looking at Tom. I see one of them reach out and take the hand of the other, and hold it tightly.

'I didn't . . . I didn't *intend* anything other than to tell the truth. It's a simple statement.' Tom tries for dismissive, almost sneering, but there is a hitch in his breath.

I bite my lip so hard I taste blood.

'You didn't mean for us to believe that you bought the knife and saw on the seventeenth of April?'

'*No.*'

'I do not want there to be any question about this. Let me read it to you again and the jury can form their own opinion. "I came into London on the evening of the sixteenth of April" – that is, after Miss Cade was dead?'

'Yes.'

'"I came into London on the evening of the sixteenth of April and went back to Eastbourne the following night, seventeenth of April, fairly late, taking with me a knife I bought in a shop in Victoria Street. I also bought at the same shop a small saw. When I got to the cottage I was still so upset and worried that I could not then carry out my intention to dispose of the body. I did so on the following day, which was Good Friday." When you made that statement, did you intend that the police should understand that you came up to London after Miss Cade was dead, and *then* bought a knife and saw for the purpose of disposing of the body?'

'No, I did not.' His voice is hoarse. 'I cannot . . . I cannot determine how anyone should interpret what I have said.'

'Surely if that was not your intention, you would have been clearer in your statement?'

'I . . . I didn't . . .'

Moran goes on, 'I put it to you that you could have conveyed matters far more clearly if you had said that you had bought these items, the knife and saw, previously.'

Tom is silent. Sweat collects behind my knees, in the hollows of my collarbone, beneath my hair.

'What did you intend by your statement?'

'I intended to tell the whole truth as I remembered it. That is all I have ever done.' His voice is loud, his hands are gripping the rail tight, tight. 'You must . . . you must see that the circumstances in which I made that statement were unusual. It is a statement made by someone who was in mental agony at the time.'

Moran is quite calm, quite cold. 'I want to point it out to you again. This is a clear statement. There is no alteration; it was read over by you, was it not, and initialled?'

'Yes.'

'And signed?'

'*Yes.*'

'This is a clear statement, is it not, that you bought the knife and saw *after* the death of Miss Cade, for the purpose of disposing of her body?'

'You might read it that way. I cannot make anyone—'

'Did you buy the knife and saw on the third of April having in your mind the purpose for which they were going to be used?'

'Of course not. No.' He leans forward, over the rail, into the courtroom. '*No.*'

'Why did you buy the knife and saw?'

'I needed to buy some things for the house. Things for . . . for the house. It is always useful to have tools at home. I bought the knife as a . . . I bought it as a carving knife.'

'On the third of April?'

'Yes.'

'Before Miss Cade was dead.'

'Yes.' His voice is low and is almost drowned out by the murmur in the courtroom that grows and swells until it rings with anger and betrayal.

37

Kate, July 1924

The rest of it is done quickly, in the end. There are no more witnesses; there is no more evidence.

Tom is led back to the dock. His head is high. He looks at no one.

When he is seated, he takes up a pencil and a piece of paper, writes quickly and calls one of the ushers over. The usher takes the folded paper to Tate, who looks at the words on the outside, and jerks his head towards me. I feel heat come into my face.

The usher approaches, his face even and expressionless. He leans over the low wooden screen that separates the public gallery from the rest of the court and hands it to me with a little bow. I curl my fingers around it and see, written on the outside in shaky capitals: GIVE THIS TO MY WIFE.

I fold it so the writing is not visible – then I fold it again and again. I close my hand over it. I pretend it is gone.

Moran's final statement is brief. He speaks to the jury like a man who knows he has already won.

'The case for the Crown is that on the night of the fifteenth of April 1924, Miss Cade was murdered by the prisoner. He has tried to persuade you that he was under the influence of this lady, that she was trying to seduce him and separate him from his wife, and that he was under pressure to carry out anything she suggested. But you have heard from her sister that she was always a good-tempered, quiet girl.'

He talks on, his voice ringing out clear and certain.

'Miss Cade was an expectant mother. She was pressing Ryan to go abroad. Something had to be done – and quickly.'

It is almost over. I must hold on to this: it is almost over.

'And so, on the thirteenth of April, he took her down to the lonely cottage, with the knife and saw he had bought for the express purpose for which he later used them. Miss Cade died on the fifteenth of April, at the hand of the prisoner. He has admitted that before her death he sent a telegram making an appointment to meet another woman: Miss Bingham.' He pauses, lets his gaze sweep the courtroom.

'How could he know that he would be free to meet that appointment, unless he knew that Miss Cade would be dead? I think we must assume he had murder in his heart well before the date of the crime itself.'

The women at the front are leaning in to one another, their hats touching – the red and the blue – and their four hands are clasped tightly.

'You have heard from Sir Richard Fawcett that he could find no marks on the body to indicate the cause of death. We must assume that signs of the cause of death were present on the head and neck, and we must infer that this is why those parts are missing.' He pauses again, and looks along the jury box, at each man in turn. 'I suggest those signs would not match the prisoner's account of what happened to Miss Cade.

'It is for the jury to say whether, but for Chief Inspector Wild's careful watch upon the cloakroom at Waterloo station, the prisoner would have effectively disposed of the body. Miss Cade would have entirely disappeared. Her friends and her sister would have believed her to be in South Africa, and no hue and cry would have been raised about her. It is also for the jury to consider whether, but for the discovery of the cloakroom ticket, the disappearance of Miss Cade would have been noticed at all.'

My heart is thudding so loudly I am trembling with the force of it.

'Finally, I would draw your attention to the prisoner's behaviour. The day after Miss Cade met her death at his hands, he had dinner with Miss Bingham.'

Moran is speaking quickly, fluently, now. He is like a runner who has glimpsed the finish line at the end of a race.

'He later stayed with Miss Bingham in the room that had been used by Miss Cade and himself, while that lady lay dead in the room next door. He did all of these things – and nobody noticed anything untoward about him at all. Mr Tate will tell you that this proves he had a clear conscience' – he nods towards Tate but keeps his eyes on the jury – 'but I suggest this proves only one thing.'

He looks towards Tom and then back to the jury. He makes his final statement slowly. Deliberately. 'It proves only that the prisoner lacks the feeling and the warmth that make up our essential humanity.'

When Tate gets to his feet, he looks exhausted. 'Although we are in this court dealing with the death of one person, we must remember that we are also dealing with the life of another. Is it to be put against this man' – he gestures towards Tom – 'that because, when we come to probe deeply into the history of the illicit relationship between Thomas Ryan and Beatrice Cade, it is possible to find *something* which is untrue, that we should therefore come to the conclusion that here is a man who would commit murder?

'It might be said that the prisoner is an immoral man. It might be said that he is dishonest, that he is a liar, that he is a coward. Gentlemen, he is on trial for none of these things.

'The question here is whether you can find in the case for the prosecution any motive for murder. Is the prisoner's story that he told Miss Cade he would *not* go away with her, that he would not give up his wife, his daughter, his job and his home – is this beyond belief?

'On the one hand you have the case for the prosecution that Miss Cade died from a blow by the prisoner to the head or the neck; on the other, we say that death arose through a fall after a struggle. Gentlemen of the jury, it is your duty to consider this: is the man before you an inhuman monster, or the victim of a most unfortunate set of circumstances?'

All this time, Tom's note has been folded in my hand, my fingers curled over it, the fingers of my other hand laid over that. I am like an orange with a secret at the centre.

The judge begins to speak. I had not realized he would address the jury like this.

As he sums up the evidence from both sides, when I am sure that those around me have focused their attention on him, I uncurl my hands and look at the note.

I hear: '. . . if there is anything in his story, even if you were to accept it in every particular, which would justify . . .'

I straighten out my palm and the note unfolds slowly of its own accord.

I take the paper between the thumb and forefinger of each hand, and I unfold it again. Then again, until I can see once more what he has written on the outside.

GIVE THIS TO MY WIFE

There is now only one fold remaining between me and his message to me.

I feel my husband's eyes on me now. I feel the weight of his need for me.

I hear: 'The prisoner has stated: "I said that rather than do what she wanted, I would tell my wife the whole thing."'

I stare down at the note and I hear, 'You must consider, gentlemen, whether it is possible that what really took place was that *she* said, "If you do not do what you promised, *I* shall tell your wife the whole thing."'

I lift my head at that.

I think it is more than possible.

I think that when he saw she was trying to control him – he who would not be questioned or controlled – that's when he lost his temper. That when he was cornered, he wanted to hit back.

And I can imagine that, after hitting her once, he knew the satisfaction of hurting her. I have seen that satisfaction, that pleasure in him.

And so he did it again. And again and again and again, until she was quite dead – and then he carried out his plan to destroy her. Until everything that made her human was bloody and broken.

I take a deep breath and I open the note. The pencil has scored the paper deeply. It is almost torn in places.

There are only two words, run together and repeated over and over.

JUDAS BITCH JUDAS JUDASBITCHJUDASJUDAS

When the judge has sent the jury out to retire, when Tom has once again been taken below, the tension in the courtroom lessens. The others on the public benches stand, stretch. Some of them glance over at me: I stare back at them until they look away.

Gradually they begin to leave, and eventually I am almost alone. Only two others remain in the courtroom – the girl with the mass of silvery hair who I have noticed before, and her tall, stern-faced companion. Their heads are bowed as though they are weeping or praying.

I close my eyes and lean forward and put my face in my hands.

There is a creak and the bench sinks a little as someone sits beside me. I do not lift my head. I do not care what they think of me.

And then Wild says, 'I thought perhaps you might like some company while we wait.'

I lift my head to say that I do not want his company – but I see that he has not come to talk. He has simply come to sit with me through this final part.

'I can wait here then? I don't have to go outside?'

He shakes his head. 'No. You're grand as you are.' And then – almost as an afterthought – 'I don't think it will be long.'

I close my eyes again, and we wait together, Wild and I.

And as we wait, I think of the way Tom smiled at me as he entered the courtroom this morning, his freedom in sight. It is the same smile he gave me the first time I met him.

On the day of the church picnic, Mam and I skirted the crowds, looking for the vicar's wife. Laughter broke out among a group of women and as we approached, I saw that there was a single man in the middle of the crowd. He was taller than most of them and his hands spread wide as he talked, opening and closing and slicing at the air, his head turning from left to right to see how they were all taking his words.

His suit was brushed clean and there was a single yellow bud in his buttonhole. His hat looked new – the brim was a touch wider, the crown a touch higher, than the hats of the other men. But it was his face which took my attention: the skin like milk, and the high forehead with the dark hair smoothed back from it. And the clean shape of it – the sharp cheekbones and the square dimpled chin and the wide red mouth above.

Suddenly he raised his eyes – and even from that distance, I could make out the thick fringe of his eyelashes. Then his dark gaze met mine – and caught. His smile widened, showing small, even teeth, and his hand went to the wide brim of his hat.

I found that I was hot and flushed. I could not look at him again.

I whispered to Mam, 'I'm going over to help Mrs Roberts set the tea things up,' and I made myself walk away.

I stood by the vicar's wife with my back to the group and pressed my lips together. I concentrated on unwrapping sandwiches, on slicing cake and wiping plates. A wave of sound rose behind me and I heard the approach of two dozen women, their high chatter and overlapping voices, and I felt the warmth of them behind me and the light change as they passed between the sun and my skin.

Then I was conscious of the mass of bodies moving apart, making way, and a low voice murmuring thanks. There was the weight of a hand on my arm and then I was looking into the sun, and that voice was saying my name.

'Good morning. Miss Burton, isn't it?'

I could only stare at him.

'We've met before.'

I would have remembered.

'I was a friend of your brother's. We used to play football together.'

I thought of Fred and his friends: their long legs, their deep voices, their jeering laughter. And me, all thin ankles and freckles and untidy hair, always scurrying and panting to catch up, calling to them that Mam had said they were to wait for me, wait, please, and Freddie turning round and telling me to piss off and go back home, while his friends laughed at me through my snot and tears.

There was Reg Leeward, who had terrible spots; a tall boy with a lazy eye; a fellow with red hair and twin sisters; and there was –

'Tom? Tom . . . Ryan?'

He smiled at me, and when his eyes looked into mine again I saw that they were not quite dark, as I had thought, but that there

*was a circle of gold around the brown. And the black centre of each
eye was just large enough to hold me.*

*There were voices behind me and all around me. I heard my
mother calling my name somewhere far off, heard Mrs Roberts at
my shoulder – and none of it mattered.*

*Sometimes I wonder what he saw that day. What he thought
and felt as he walked through that crowd towards me. I think
of myself as I was then: barely out of the schoolroom, standing
squarely with my back to him, determined not to look. And then
my mind skips over that slight still-childish figure, and all I can
see is him: how he glowed in the light as he chose me and claimed
me. How his fingers were warm against mine and my heart was
racing, and suddenly I had a place in the world.*

I open my eyes and look over at Wild. His head is angled away
and I am opening my mouth to ask him a question when the
door opens. They are coming back.

My hands are shaking. I push them down against my knees
to steady them.

Wild takes out his watch, glances at it. 'Seventeen minutes.'

'Is that . . . what does it mean that they're back so quickly?'

Wild tells me what it usually means as the room fills. As
Tom is led back in.

The judge takes his seat, makes a gesture, and one of the
clerks rises. Faces the jury.

My heart is hammering.

'Gentlemen of the jury, are you agreed upon your verdict?'

The foreman stands. It is the well-built man with the thinning hair. Now he is red-faced, breathing hard, frowning under
the weight of it all.

'We are.'

'Do you find the prisoner at the bar, Thomas Patrick Ryan,
guilty or not guilty of wilful murder?'

There is no air in this room.

'Guilty.'

There is a ringing in my ears and the breath rushes out of me.

It is done.

'Thomas Patrick Ryan, you stand convicted of wilful murder. Have you anything to say about why judgement of death should not be pronounced upon you according to law?'

Tom turns towards the judge. He is trembling, but raises his chin and looks over the heads of those he addresses. He is quite above us all.

'I feel too conscious of the bitterness and unfairness of your summing-up to say anything except that I am not guilty of murder.'

Those are his final words. I know from the way he delivers them: this is how he intends to be remembered.

His gaze flickers to the reporters, busily scribbling in the front row. He waits until their eyes are on him; he lifts his head, proudly, he looks towards the window, letting them see his profile. But he is trembling harder now, and I wonder if he will be able to hold this pose for long enough.

The judge reaches for something. I thought it would be a black cap. I have always read it described as a black cap. But the reality is a square of black material, like a large handkerchief.

He places it on his head and turns to Tom. My husband bares his teeth like an animal. Sweat stands out on his skin and I see the little pulse in his temple, beating and beating in time with his heart.

'Thomas Patrick Ryan, the jury have arrived at the only proper conclusion on the evidence that was laid before them. They have arrived at that conclusion without knowing anything of your past life, to which you yourself made references in your statements to the police. These references have, in mercy to you, been excluded from the consideration of the jury.'

And now Tom grips the rail in front of him. His knuckles are white.

'They did not know that you had already served two prison terms for theft, and that you had served a third term for a crime of violence against a woman. There can be no question that you deliberately designed the death of Beatrice Cade.'

Tom shakes his head once, twice, then over and over. He pushes his hands into his hair so that it stands on end.

'For that crime you must suffer the penalty imposed by law.'

'I did not do this. *I did not!*' He has forgotten that he has already spoken his last words. His composure is utterly broken now: he is bent forward, his face contorted and wet.

He lifts his arm and wipes all down his face with his sleeve, dragging the skin, and then he wipes under his nose, like a small boy on a cold afternoon.

The judge goes on, his voice as low and mournful as a tolling bell. 'The sentence of the court upon you is that you be taken from this place to a lawful prison, and then to a place of execution—'

'No. *No!* This is *not* how it ends!'

'—and that you be there hanged by the neck until you be dead, and that your body be afterwards buried within the precincts of the prison . . .'

His head falls. I see his lips move, see the words form and fail to reach me: 'Oh God. *No.* Help me.'

'May the Lord have mercy upon your soul.'

Then my husband looks directly at me, and I look back at him.

Kitty. Help me.

I do not know if he says those final words aloud or merely mouths them.

I watch as he begins to struggle. As he is held by the guards. As he begins to scream.

In his terror, he becomes something that is no longer Tom. That is no longer human.

Red and wet and black and roaring.

I watch all of this. I watch as he is taken down.

And I say nothing at all.

38

Kate, September 1924

I wake early.

I lie still and straight, Judith curled beside me in the sagging double bed. I listen to the seagulls over the quay screaming for food, to the snores of Mrs Lambert through the wall – and my mind goes, as it does every morning, to my husband.

I feel the familiar ache in my chest, the familiar sickness in my stomach.

He is no longer Tom Ryan, but Prisoner AH6839. His name is cut to a line of figures, cut to the quick. All of his names are quite unlike the name that Judith and I use now.

I think of him waking in a small room with white scrubbed walls. I imagine a hard narrow bed. A thin grey blanket and a flat voice through a slot in the door.

I have imagined this so many times that the scene is quite real to me.

I imagine three congealing meals a day, perhaps glistening with spit. I have forced myself not to flinch from these clear and brutal pictures.

This is Tom, now: seven ounces of tobacco, fibrous and fragrant and shockingly familiar under his fingers. Two tin cups of lukewarm tea. No sugar. Fifteen minutes of exercise every day – one precious quarter-turn of the clock where there is air on his skin and only birdsong and blue above him. He is all of these things – and he is eleven hours in the dark with his own heartbeat and breath for company, and the smell of fear and desperation and regret pressing and pressing.

I think he will be able to admit these things, now that he is alone.

He is quite alone – and the rest of it, all that remains to him, he must go through alone.

Strange though it seems, I think he will be surprised to find himself there. Despite everything.

He was a husband who betrayed his wife. He was a liar, who loved his daughter above everything. He was a gambler who thought the risks would pay off.

And now I do not know what he is, other than a frightened man in a little room with – I take up my watch from the bedside table: the little diamond watch that he bought me for Christmas – with sixty-three minutes left to live.

My fingers shake as I look at the numbers on the watch. As the minute hand clicks over.

Sixty-two minutes.

Tom will die at eight o'clock today.

Even letting that fact form and sharpen does not make it real.

I cannot imagine death. The nothingness of it. I cannot imagine Tom as nothing.

He is still a man with wet eyes and blood pinking his skin, and fingers that move when he commands them to.

But somehow, when the clock has finished striking eight, he will no longer exist.

I will no longer be a wife.

Judith will no longer have a father.

My breath comes faster and the watch trembles in my hand. I lay it down and feel my heart thudding in my chest.

Judith mutters in her sleep. I reach out a hand and place it on her arm. My fingers are cold against the warmth of her body. My teeth are chattering. I want to embrace her, but it would be for my benefit and comfort, not hers, so I wrap my arms around myself and hold on.

I try to breathe slowly, matching Judith's breaths, counting in and out, in and out.

I pick up my watch again. Forty-nine minutes.

I no longer know what is making my heart pound and my skin sweat. It no longer seems to matter whether I name it or not.

My jaw is tight and my chest aches. I am whispering to myself in the dark. *AH6839. AH6839.*

Forty-one minutes. The ticking sound of my watch is louder.

I count, to one hundred, to two thousand. Every number is another beat of life.

Death makes one immortal. It freezes one in time – as a moment or an action or a smile or a scream.

I wonder what moment Tom has kept of *her.*

I wonder what I will keep of him.

Then, for the first time, I wonder what he will think of as they lead him into the little room without windows. Judith? Me? Or Miss Cade?

I feel, somehow, that it will be Miss Cade's face he will see as they strap his legs and arms, as they place the hood over his head. As the chaplain begins to speak.

And finally, finally, I think: it is *right* that it should be her face and her voice that will fill his last moments.

I cannot say where it began, but this is where I say it ends: with the memory of Beatrice Cade, aged thirty-seven.

I close my eyes.

I listen to my breath.

39

Bea, April 1924

'But we are not going away. It's over, Beatrice.'

His voice was so quiet and so calm that at first she thought she had misheard. But in the silence that followed, she became aware that the train was slowing, that they had come to a halt. She heard the guard calling, 'Eastbourne! Alight here for Eastbourne!' and she saw Tom pull his coat around him, open the door and step out – and the precise detail of it all and the careful way he avoided looking at her told her that she had not imagined it. That the horror of this was real.

And that she was quite lost.

All through the long taxi ride to the cottage, Bea did not speak. Rain pounded on the roof and the wind howled outside, and Tom and the driver spoke about the weather and about the winners at Plumpton and at Epsom, and she sat silently and pressed her lips together and she refused to cry.

She found that she needed to work out when this had begun.

She needed to know when she was firmly set on a path so long and twisting that there was no way to turn back.

Was it when he had first stepped into the office and she had felt that quickening in her blood, that moment of recognition? Or was it later: the moment he had first touched her, the evening he had first kissed her?

She needed to pinpoint the exact day; she kept picturing the hands of a clock spinning backwards as though, if she could see it, she might return to that moment and set another life in motion, one where she was still a contented spinster or even married to an older man for companionship.

What she would not be was a frightened woman in a ridiculous hat, travelling through the darkness with a man who no longer loved her.

When they alighted from the taxi, Tom was still solicitous, hurrying around to open the door, taking her arm and holding his coat over her head as they stumbled up the path and as she waited, numb, while he raised a hand to the driver; as he unlocked the door; as he steered her inside.

The cottage was cold, dark, damp, and she did not care. She groped her way down the passage to the bedroom. The curtains were open and the faint moonlight was enough for her to see the shape of the bed.

She sat heavily, and thought about the first time they had been intimate together. Of the house in Soho; the woman there; the dark staircase.

He had been there before, she realized now – the way the woman had spoken to him should have told her that. Had he been there more than once? Did he already know that the bed sloped and creaked, that the window was painted shut, that the cupboard in the corner of the bedroom was empty? Perhaps he knew that any sound they made would be ignored.

And perhaps he was used to women who trembled and moaned, to women who asked him with wet eyes to be kind.

She thought of how he had knelt before her naked body, and how exposed she had felt. How wanted. How loved.

And now, in this lonely cottage on a wet night in April, she thought: *Did he ever love me?*

Did he love me at all?

The room was very dark now: the clouds heavier and the moon no longer visible. She took the lamp and felt her way to the door, and heard a distant rumble of thunder, and then a second, closer.

She held the lamp high and began to walk along the dark passage, feeling somehow like a character in a child's storybook. Little Red Riding Hood.

Why was she thinking of her?

Creeping through her grandmother's house, wondering what she might find in her grandmother's bed.

No, that wasn't right. Red Riding Hood expected to find her grandmother. What she found instead was a nasty surprise.

Lord, how her head ached!

She opened the living-room door, and there was Tom, hunched in an armchair. He had built the fire up and the coal scuttle was almost empty. The flames threw grotesque shadows on the walls.

Two nights ago, we sat here and ate a picnic tea, and we were happy.

It seems like years ago.

She sat opposite Tom and looked at his dishevelled hair, his bloodshot eyes. His collar was dirty and there was a stain on his shirt.

Was this what it came down to, in the end? Dirt and stains and clothes in need of laundering? Wherever one ended up, there were clothes in need of laundering.

'Tom?'

He stared into the fire and said nothing.

She thought of the neat room she had left behind in

Guilford Street. The polished dressing table, the scratches and rings hidden by smooth circles of white lace. Her hairbrushes lined up, her shining bottles of scent, the wooden box with the inlay of Whitby jet that she had kept her mother's necklace in.

She thought of her neat and orderly life. Breakfast at a table overlooking a London street. The delicious solitude and the space to think. A choice of clean and ironed dresses. The omnibus to the City and the hours of quiet work. The feeling of being needed, of being useful.

And afterwards – tea or a walk in the park, or the cinema, a museum or a concert. Books, picture galleries, friendships.

I had no idea of the freedom I had.

She held out her hands to the fire, felt it warm her cold skin. Her fingers were trembling.

She waited for him to look at her, and when he did not, she said slowly, 'What happens now?'

He raised his eyes to hers, and they were empty. There was no love there. No warmth.

How could she ever have imagined that there was?

'Now? We go back to London. We go back to our lives. This little . . .' His gesture took in the room, the cottage, Bea herself. 'This little interlude is over.'

She almost smiled. 'And the baby? Have you forgotten about the baby, Tom?'

He swallowed. Then: 'I'm sure you can find someone to take care of it. I'll pay, of course.' A flash of that old debonair carelessness.

She looked at him. 'An agency, you mean? An adoption agency, as we discussed before?'

He shrugged. 'If you like.'

And she knew that was not what he had meant at all.

She thought suddenly of Lil Tearney, dancing in the corridor on her birthday, spinning and laughing with her hair tumbled loose like fire.

She thought of Nancy Shawcross, pointing at her stomach, whispering about Lil. And of Annie Barton saying, *That's not the worst of it.*

Those memories burned white-hot in her chest and in her throat and cut through her fear. She raised her chin and said, 'No.'

Just that one heavy syllable, but it was enough to shake that calm expression on his face.

'What do you mean?'

'I mean you can't get rid of me like that. You can't get rid of *us*. You can't throw us away like rubbish and just . . . forget about us.'

He looked at her and she could see him regaining some of his composure. For after all, what was to stop him doing just that?

She felt sickness heavy in her stomach, but she answered the unspoken question in the clearest way she could. 'Your wife.'

And that stopped him dead.

'If you try to discard us like that – if you think you can treat us like that – I will go to your wife, and I will tell her about us.'

He laughed, but it was unconvincing. 'She won't believe you. I'll simply tell her that you're lying. That you're a fantasist.'

Oh, Tom. All those fantasies we shared. All those dreams.

But she pressed on. 'I will tell her about us, and if she doesn't believe me, I will tell her about the mole on your left shoulder and about the birthmark on your back.'

The one above your hip, shaped like a star.

He stared at her and shook his head, and she saw then that the full horror of what she was saying was sinking in, the way it had for her on that earlier, endless train journey.

This was what she wanted: for him to feel the kind of fear she had felt. The kind of panic she was feeling now.

Triumphant, she pushed deeper. 'I will tell your wife. I will write to Mr Morley. Everyone will know what kind of man you are.'

His voice was shaking as he said, 'No. You don't get to do this to me, Beatrice. You will *not* spoil things for me.'

Deeper. 'Only think of the shame, Tom . . . think of *your* shame, the way you have not thought of mine.'

Then he seemed to think of something. 'Morley won't believe you.' His voice lowered. Became almost confiding. 'No one knows about us. No one at all.' He smiled at her – and it was the smile that undid her.

'I have proof! I have . . .' She cast about, desperate, and saw on the mantelpiece the telegram he'd sent her. She snatched it up.

'"Cottage booked for two weeks". It has both our names on it. Look. *Look!*'

She pressed on. 'I'll tell everyone,' she said again, 'and they *will* believe me.'

She wanted to make him hurt, the way that she was hurting. She wanted him to know the terror of losing the thing that mattered most in the world.

And so, finally, she said, 'Everyone will know. Even Judith. Judith will know.'

She said, 'Your daughter will know what you are, Tom.'

He moved so quickly she was hardly aware of it until she felt his fist thud against her cheekbone, and then she was stumbling, falling, and there was a crack and a sharp pain.

She lifted her hand and felt stickiness. A warm trickle on her skin. She tried to sit up and everything was red and black and her head was pounding.

She looked at her hand and saw blood running down her fingers: thick and rich.

And then she was even more afraid – and with her terror came an extraordinary sharpness and a clarity.

She recalled the girl she had been in a series of jerking

images, like the movements of the second hand on a clock: her hand reaching up for Father's watch-chain, the glinting and the brass links and the great ticking roundness; her mother swollen and bellowing on the stairs, and George with his dear pink face, curled and screwed like fists or a kiss; George grown, and the unaccustomed bristles of him against her cheek, brown and auburn with speckles of white so that the thought became *he's getting old* and the feeling became a panicked one: *I've missed him growing old.* And then the dead, dull realization: *he won't ever grow old* that had lasted and lasted and made an end of her youth.

And then she recalled the woman she had been in London: the dresses, the hats and shoes, the trips to the theatre; the silks, the stockings, the nightgowns; the teal-blue scarf of soft pelt-like velvet, that she had worn all through 1922, that looked like a summer evening. She thought of the friendships and confidences at the club, the intimacies of borrowed tea and tooth-powder. She thought of crushes on men glimpsed by chance across a restaurant, on a tram – once, oddly, playing the flute on a bandstand.

She thought of Walter Montgomery who might have saved her, and his proud appalled politeness when she had refused him.

And through all her fear, her thoughts narrowed to Tom. To the great glorious roar of him that lit and coloured the world – and she thought, *he noticed* me. *He saw me – all of me, and all the wild love in me. He looked at me and he called me beautiful and it was like sunlight after such a long time in the cold.*

How could I resist that?

And she thought: *If I had known, if I could have known what it would become, would it have been worth it all the same?*

And as she thought this, her head throbbed. Everything slowed. Red and purple bloomed and softened, then sharpened into the fraying edges of the faded rug.

She heard a roaring sound. It came rushing closer. Closer.

She lifted her hand in front of her face.

Why have I never understood how infinitely precious is the pumping of my heart and the pinkness of my skin? There is life everywhere, even in the flare of the gas lamps.

And how extraordinary the fact of my brain and nerves and limbs, and now the child turning and turning inside me.

Her thoughts slowed still further, then tapered to two, white-hot and devastating.

I want to live.

I want my child to live.

They gathered strength.

Even like this, even alone, even ashamed and afraid, I want to live.

Oh God – I want to live.

She laid her hand on her stomach, and she began to speak.

Afterword

Other Women is a work of fiction, inspired by the true story of Emily Beilby Kaye, who was murdered by her married lover, Herbert Patrick Mahon, on or about 15 April 1924.

The case was huge in England at the time: it was a milestone in the development of forensic science and a journalist's dream, involving a brutal murder, a clandestine love affair, an illegitimate pregnancy – and, at the heart of it, a handsome and charming family man who was leading a secret double life.

Most of the newspaper coverage focused on Mahon. *Other Women* is my attempt to give a voice to Mahon's wife, and to Emily Kaye herself.

Chief Inspector Savage of Scotland Yard – the inspiration for Detective Chief Inspector Wild – was in charge of the murder investigation. Savage, his superior Superintendent Carlin, and Edgar Wallace (who published an account of the case) all wrote that Mahon's relationship with his wife was central to understanding his character.

Because of the weight which those close to the case gave this relationship, and because it was Mrs Mahon who discovered the cloakroom ticket – the key piece of evidence that led to her husband's arrest – I felt justified in expanding her role in his conviction. By making her the means by which justice was eventually realized for her husband's victim, Kate Ryan became the unwilling heroine of *Other Women*.

The *London Post* and the *London Chronicle* are fictional

newspapers, but all the news articles in this novel are inspired by actual newspaper accounts of the trial and investigation. The cross-examination of witnesses in the trial scenes are based on the trial transcripts and on statements that Patrick Mahon made to the police at the time of his arrest. The character of Rose Bingham is based on a woman who Mahon took to the cottage shortly after the murder. He spent the night there with her while the body of Emily Kaye lay in the bedroom next door. The newspapers printed so many identifying details about this woman that she was forced to emigrate after the trial.

The scene of the murder was as I have described it, and the model of the cottage mentioned in chapter 25 was real. Made by PC Edward Shelah of Brixton police station, it was brought into the courtroom and used by both the prosecution and the defence to illustrate what happened in the cottage on the night of the murder. After the trial, it was taken to Scotland Yard's Black Museum. Unfortunately it has since been lost: photographs of the model, and the handmade miniature furniture from the room where Emily Kaye died, are all that remain of the reconstruction.

Mahon was tried at Lewes Assizes in July 1924 and found guilty. Before he was sentenced to death, he was asked by the judge if he had anything to say. I have quoted his response in chapter 37: 'I feel too conscious of the bitterness and unfairness of [your] summing-up . . . to say anything except that I am not guilty of murder.'

He took this arrogant attitude to the scaffold at Wandsworth Prison on 3 September 1924, where he believed he could cheat the hangman, Thomas Pierrepoint. Mahon had questioned the guards at length about the execution procedure and knew that he would have to set his feet between two chalk marks as the rope was put around his neck. Immediately after the hood was placed on his head, the executioner would move away to pull the lever and the platform on which he was standing would drop away beneath him.

When he sensed Pierrepoint moving to the lever, Mahon jerked his bound feet forward in an attempt to reach the stationary part of the platform. At that point, the lever was pulled and his body jolted back, the base of his spine striking the sharp edge of the platform. Half a second later, his spine was broken – this time at the neck, by the rope.

The details of these two injuries to the spine can be found in the records of the autopsy performed on Mahon by Sir Bernard Spilsbury. Spilsbury, fictionalized in *Other Women* as Sir Richard Fawcett, was the same pathologist who performed the autopsy on the dismembered body of Emily Kaye – calling it a 'challenging human jigsaw' – and who testified to her pregnancy in court.

The autopsy on Mahon was the first of several that Spilsbury performed on executed criminals. He believed that an analysis of the effects of sudden death, where the time of death was recorded to the minute, would yield useful and unique scientific data.

For those seeking more detail about Spilsbury's role in the Mahon case, I recommend Douglas G. Browne and Tom Tullett's groundbreaking biography *Bernard Spilsbury: His Life and Cases*, published in 1980, and the excellent *Murder and the Making of English CSI* by Ian Burney and Neil Pemberton, published in 2016.

There is an extraordinary postscript to this story. One week before Mahon's execution, his wife instructed her solicitor to communicate with the police regarding her husband's property. Her solicitor gave notice to the Chief Constable that after the execution, Mahon's widow intended to claim all of his possessions, including those found at the cottage and those taken from him when he was arrested.

A note in the files of the East Sussex Constabulary indicates that a number of items were subsequently given to the solicitor to be returned to Mrs Mahon after her husband's execution.

These items included a cook's knife and a saw.

Acknowledgements

With grateful thanks to Stewart McLaughlin at Wandsworth Prison, and to all the staff at the East Sussex Record Office.

Other Women wouldn't exist without the support and encouragement of an army of people at my back.

Firstly, a huge thank-you to everyone who read *Little Deaths*, who recommended it to friends, re-read it, bought it as a gift, wrote reviews and came to events where I was speaking. Your interest and appreciation means everything.

I'm grateful to all the writers around the world who have taken me under their wing since 2016 and offered blurbs, reviews, interviews, supportive messages, and words of wisdom. Without you, this job would be a hundred times harder.

To everyone at JULA, especially Jo Unwin: thank you for taking such good care of me and my work. To Deborah Schneider, for being an industry wonder. I'm lucky to have agents on both sides of the Atlantic who are fierce, formidable, legendary women, and an absolute joy to spend time with.

To everyone at Picador who has worked on this book, especially Gillian Fitzgerald-Kelly, Laura Carr, Amber Burlinson, Katie Tooke, Hope Ndaba, Alice Dewing and Emma Harrow. I know this hasn't been the easiest project, and I know how hard you've all worked to get it right. I'm eternally grateful for your patience and your dedication, and I'm hugely proud of what we've achieved.

To Candi Bloxham, Clare and Squeeks Palmer, Faye Emery,

Frankie Pagnacco, Geraldine Terry, Helen Cullen, Helen Parr, Janet Megoran, Katja Sass, Laura Fergusson, Leah Burwood, Matthew Redhead, Phoebe Harkins, Rafael Torrubia, Rebecca Le Marchand, Sarah Steele, Steve Thomas and Yvonne Rhodes-James: thank you for keeping me sane, for believing in me, for reading drafts, and for listening to me wang on about murder for all these years. You all make my life brighter.

To Ross MacFarlane: thank for taking me into the Wellcome Library, putting Spilsbury's index cards in front of me, and leaving me to inhale the smell of his tobacco. You made those cases come to life for me.

To my Pennard group: Annabel Leventon, Cole Beauchamp, Jessica Pickard, Juliette Adair, Sarah Murray, Tessa Courage, Victoria Pougatch and William Davidson – thank you for the prompts, for your endless kindness, and for inspiring me to take risks. And to Gael Gorvy-Robertson, who will always be part of us.

To Emma Dixon, Kate McQuaile, Roger Fradera and Vjera Magdalenic-Moussavi: thank you for all the words of encouragement, for the zooms, the kittens, and for being a constant force for good in my life when the world was going to hell in a handcart.

To Adi Bloom, Alix Christie, Anna Mazzola, Cathy De'Freitas, Colin Dowland, Karol Griffiths, Marianne Levy, Neil Blackmore and Rachel Paterson: thank you for the tough criticism, the kind criticism, the encouragement, the teaching, the wine and the wisdom. Please keep telling me to cut the bloody backstory.

To my teachers: Niall Williams, Susan Elderkin and Francesca Main – thank you for your inspiration and your guidance. I wouldn't be the writer I am without you.

And to my family, with love.